PENGUIN BOOKS

ACID

Sangeetha Sreenivasan is a bilingual writer and translator and the author of *Salabham, Pookkal,* and *Aeroplane,* her most recent books. She has published seven books in Malayalam and three in English. Her translation of Elena Ferrante's *Days of Abandonment* was recently awarded the Kerala Sahitya Akademi Award, and she is also the joint winner of SheThePeople's Inaugural Women Writer's Prize 2021 for the English rendition of her mother Sarah Joseph's novel *Budhini.* Her other translations include Chris Kraus's *I Love Dick* and Georges Simenon's *Maigret's Dead Man.* She lives in Thrissur and is working on her new novel now.

PRAISE FOR THE BOOK

'Sangeetha Sreenivasan's honesty, novelty and nerve are required reading for a new generation . . . our language is continuously getting freshened in her writing.'
M.T. Vasudevan Nair, Jnanpith Award winner

'What makes this book absolutely prominent is the subject it handles and the way the author leads you down the narrow lanes of the mind you didn't even know existed. Sreenivasan looks at the complexities of life with the wisdom and dexterity of a seasoned storyteller. Hers is a captivating voice and *Acid* is a compelling read.'
Anees Salim

'The lotus in the Acid Pool, the simple style, the thought-provoking narration, unethical references together with the rich content echoing the confusing scenario of the new gen, succeed in providing a sumptuous banquet to the reader.'
Dr Sr Jesme

acid

sangeetha sreenivasan

PENGUIN BOOKS

An imprint of Penguin Random House

PENGUIN BOOKS

USA | Canada | UK | Ireland | Australia
New Zealand | India | South Africa | China

Penguin Books is part of the Penguin Random House group of companies
whose addresses can be found at global.penguinrandomhouse.com

Published by Penguin Random House India Pvt. Ltd
4th Floor, Capital Tower 1, MG Road,
Gurugram 122 002, Haryana, India

Penguin
Random House
India

First published in Malayalam by DC Books, Kottayam 2016
First published in English in Hamish Hamilton by Penguin Random House India 2018
Published in paperback in Penguin Books 2022

Text and translation copyright © Sangeetha Sreenivasan 2016, 2018

ISBN 9780143457046

Typeset in Adobe Caslon Pro by Manipal Digital Systems, Manipal
Printed at Thomson Press India Ltd, New Delhi

www.penguin.co.in

MIX
Paper
FSC FSC® C010615

Everything I write is for Sarah

Dear J,

Do you remember how we laughed our heads off the night your friend rolled the joint you had given her?

'It's her first time,' you said, as you laughed the contagious hell of laughter.

I looked at you through smoke rings but the darkness of the terrace in the sparse lighting revealed only some scraps of your face and body, the tramp-like look of your hair in the night wind, the whiteness of your teeth as you went on laughing, the poppet figurine dangling from the thin metal chain on your bare chest. What really made me nervous was the resonance of your laughter, echoing in mid-air like the sickening thud of bullets, giving out emotions of struggle. I saw an imaginary handgun, not yours, not mine.

She was twenty-two. I was alarmed when she didn't move. What if that girl had really gone to sleep her last? But you said she liked to play possum. You knew better; she was your friend. And you were right. When she came back from her stillness, she was laughing too. Then she stopped and looked directly into our eyes and solemnly quoted Dali, 'I don't do drugs, I *am* drugs.' You laughed even louder at this; in fact you couldn't stop. I saw you stomping your feet on the ground, losing balance. She was hopelessly trying to make a Dalian moustache out of a streak of her hair and to roll her eyeballs this way and that to keep you amused. I wondered what made you cheer and shout for an encore. She lifted one of her eyebrows, and screwed up her eyes and started stripping. She said she would lie down naked on the terrace and wait for the bees to cover her up. You seemed to have gone insane with that slutty laughter of yours.

I was feeling edgy and was thinking about going home. I walked towards her and poured the rest of the beer that was in the bottle on her head. I knew I was rude to do so. She was eight or ten years younger than us. I saw the grin on your face freeze as the beer ran down her navel, your eyes on draught. I thought you wanted to have sex. I walked out.

The next time I saw her, she was in her early thirties. Chekka, you won't believe it, she looked like a pickled fish in saline water, a dead face with eyes open, eyelids missing. Even her black open shoes, which she always kept polished, looked battered with scratches and were caked with mud. She was wearing some very cheap imitation jewellery, which she said were real Swarovski crystals given by you. She said you had asked her to work out to keep fit and learn to drive. When I came to know that you were still seeing her, I felt a sudden fear coursing down my spine. I called you that night; I wanted to tell you that what she needed was not a gym or a drive but a rehabilitation centre and the help of a doctor. But you were busy with something else; you said you were about to go on a cruise. You were not willing to listen to me; you said you didn't wish to hear anything in connection with her. You called her an antisocial nuisance and hung up the phone. She was your close friend, wasn't she?

Yesterday, I saw her in the mall. She was walking down the aisle, talking gibberish and digging for boogers. I was shocked; I felt myself a savage and had the immediate urge to hide somewhere. You used to say that youth begins in one's forties, but I'm afraid

I don't think she is going to see them, her forties, I mean. I felt guilty—I still feel guilty, for I had joined in your shitty laughter years ago. Do you remember, last year we ran into each other in the same mall? You were busy with the medical admissions for your daughter.

Dear J, this book is my charge sheet for you.

1

She lies naked and flat on her back in a lotus pool that surpasses the stillness of Monet's beloved ponds. The water in its greenness brushes against her nipples. The woman in her greenness shoots a hurricane of madness upwards to the window that opens to the south of the winds. And her eyes say, 'I wish I could lose you.' And her eyes repeat, 'I wish I could hold you close, so close till your breath stops.'

Opening the murky wooden window of the second floor, the window that opens to the south of the winds, the other woman exclaims, 'Oh dear, what's wrong with her?'

The first woman doesn't move. She lies with her body like a stillborn, focus unmoving, fixed on the window that opens. Purple petals kiss her black thatch. The shadows of the silver fish float like babies around her belly.

The gaze from the wooden window cuts through her body. It slices the waters as if the pool is but another piece of cake. The gaze ignores the body, dives through it, as if the body that lies naked does not exist at all. It goes down, down to the bottom of the pool, through the slender green stems tangled in knots. It is in search of something. Not the naked body, but something else. Something new, something with the freshness of the morning briers! What could it be? What could possibly lie in the oblivion of the dark gloomy waters where lotus grows? Underneath the lotus buds, flowers, leaves and shoots, an upturned world shivers, foreseeing the worst.

Under the crushing weight of negligence, over the weight of the dead lake, the woman lies shattered like a snake beaten up, blind yet still alive. The darkness around her eyes intensifies as she moans, 'Please, please don't look. I have something to hide in there.' Water hugs her, mute and warm. Water drowns her prayer. The gaze continues its maddening rush and settles down at the end of a fragile stem to which Aadi clings, curled up amidst tufts of grass green lathery moss. 'Aadi'! His name means 'beginning'. In the beginning there was only water. And black was the colour of the beginning, stillness its pace.

He closes his eyes. He sees purple water lilies in bloom. He doesn't smile. An occasional streak of light tickles his yet-to-be-born senses. With a start, his skin touches another's, as vibrant as his own. In the black water of tranquillity, the rhythms of two hearts beat together. Beats give life to the water, mud, leaves and flowers.

But the gaze continues. It brazenly plucks the purple flower cutting the stem from its root. The boys see their cords confiscated, moving away from them. Losing grips, they fatigue. Aadi's heart echoes back in a lonely rhythm.

'Where, where is Shiva?'

The dream vanishes.

Aadi opened his eyes to the yellowness of the lamps and the remnants of a weary night. The lotus pool, the two women, the heaviness of the vapour, all had disappeared. Half asleep, he gingerly walked towards Shiva's room.

Upstairs, Kamala was fighting with Shaly. There was nothing new or surprising about this—they fought constantly, with a

2

minimum of two hours' and a maximum of two days' intermission in between. The house had two storeys. Kamala lived with Shaly on the upper floor and the boys, Kamala's biological children, Aadi and Shiva, lived on the lower floor. All of them, both the women and the boys, shared the sitting rooms, bookshelves and the kitchen on the lower floor. The women were free to come down whenever they wanted. But the boys were not allowed on the upper floor.

Aadi heard Kamala scream across the room and the sound of something being knocked to the wooden floor. The room shook, and somewhere at the back of the house plaster came off the walls. Weighed down with confusions, he stood for a while and listened to the voices from above: there was something out of the way and tragic about their conversations. He could hear his mother shout, scream, hurling maddening abuses at Shaly, and he felt nervous. When Shaly spoke, finally, he understood how profoundly the severity of the morning had scraped away her voice, into shreds of whispers. He looked at the plastic flowers in the Japanese vase as he heard her say: 'Kamala, please calm yourself. Let us manage this together. You could take Aadi with you. I will take care of Shiva. Please Kamala, it's already getting late. Shall I book the flight?'

Something shattered on the upper floor. Was it the glass vase or Kamala's iPhone?

Shaly almost knocked Aadi down as she climbed hurriedly down the stairway like a blind cat, shouting, 'Do what works for you guys. I am leaving once and for all.'

It must have been a hard blow, Aadi thought, as he noticed the finger marks on her left arm. He stood in the doorway, bemused and sad. As she stormed out of the house, her eyes welled up with tears and she said to him, 'Kamala's mother passed away last night, your grandmother.'

In the kitchen Aadi set some milk to boil, his heart pounding all the while and his lips trembling. He did not remember much about his grandmother, though. He was worried about his mother, now an orphan bereft of someone to guide her.

By the time Shaly came back, she had regained her composure and she cautioned Aadi in a carefree manner to watch the coffee, which was boiling over. She shut the flame off and accidentally knocked the lighter down, but let it remain there. The bright red polish still shone on her nails, especially on her toes. After Aadi had gone to Shiva's room with the tray of coffee and biscuits, she picked up the lighter and lit the stove again and prepared some tea.

She had to push the door open with her leg as she was holding a tray laden with a teapot, cups, biscuits, toast and marmalade. Kamala stood beside the table, unmindful of her shouts or reluctant to open the door. She took no notice of the tray Shaly placed on the table. Instead, she stood there listening to some lone voices from within. Shaly should have been bitter about this, but her poise betrayed only signs of suppressed anger, shrouded in grace. When Shaly noticed Kamala's eyes closed in rapture she pulled her up by the hair and hit her hard across the face, anyway. 'What the hell!' said Shaly.

Kamala stepped back and carelessly knocked the teapot over with her hand, spilling the hot tea onto the floor.

'I'm going to kill you, you bitch!' Shaly tried to thrust her fingers into Kamala's mouth, with a force sufficient to scoop out the insides—the tongue, uvula, teeth and everything—but anticipating the worst, Kamala pursed her lips disgustedly and forced them out, so that Shaly had to give up.

In consequence, acid took the reins. It designed the maps of convulsed ecstasy under Kamala's tongue. Soon it would travel, numbing whatever it touched on the way until Kamala was numb to the world outside her eyes. Red kangaroos wearing lucky horseshoes would race up to her brain, making her forget her present, past and future in the haze of dust their hooves would raise. Neurons would mount on camels obscured by clouds to take her for a short pleasure ride.

'Bastard! What do you think of yourself? You stupid slut!' Shaly shook her hard; slapped her harder still. Kamala didn't seem to be in pain. Yet she covered her face in her hands and squatted on the floor. 'Everything happens because of you, Kamala! How many times have I warned you against taking those dumb godforsaken pills? But you don't listen. You are on medication. Do you hear me?' Tea pooled in the wooden depression on the floor.

Shaly went out to fetch a mop, saw Aadi on the stairs and yelled, 'What the hell do you want? Get out of here.'

It was not easy for Shaly to compose herself this time. After a while, she tried to fake a sympathetic look and walked to the children's room, pretending everything was under control. Before she knocked on the door she said to herself, 'Kams is a horrible woman. Everything here is garbage,' and smiled.

Still smiling, she asked the boys, 'Shall I get you breakfast?'

The boys looked at each other and then at her. 'What about grandma? Are we not going to see her?' Shiva asked solemnly.

Shaly was about to say something but suddenly the sound of the saxophone shook her up and her face turned pale and bare. Music came floating down the stairway.

On the upper floor, Kamala closed the windows, drew the curtains shut and sat on the floor in the corner of her room. She thought she was safe, no harm could ever find her. She stared at the innards of her stereo and laughed thoughtfully.

'I will bring you toast, please wait,' Shaly called out from the kitchen, as if the boys were impatient and enthusiastically waiting for something to munch on.

5

The first two pieces of toast got burned on the frying pan. Shaly wondered from where Kamala had got hold of the hallucinogen again. She had taken it on an empty stomach, in addition to the sleeping pills she had had the night before. Shaly recollected the faces of each and every peddler on the road. Bastards.

Two tiny pieces of eggshell flopped on to the yolks in the pan. White pyramids on yellow balls. She removed the pieces with the edge of a spatula. 'I should not have left her,' she said to herself.

No one knew how long a bad trip would last. Kamala's mother, frozen, white and pale, waited for her daughter in uncertainty while Kamala shut herself up in a room too far away from her mother and mused on something that would never be useful in life. She moved the gears on an unbridled, hysterical ride, on a magic journey some people mistook as life.

On top of her worries, Kamala had a pet dog called Depru. Monsieur Depression. An impalpable ghost of her esteemed hypotheses. It accompanied her wherever she went. A huge bulk, a mass of comfort. A cushioned bundle of sadness. It showed no interest in playing with a ball or a toy, no interest in going out for a walk. Instead, it would mount her shoulders, its weight crushing her. They say dogs make eye contact. It looked straight into Kamala's eyes like other dogs. But in the mauve shadow of its eyes, a child drowned every second. And Kamala wept, looking at the dying child. Lifting one of its eyebrows, the dog would sigh; place its heavy paw on her forehead. 'Do you think that man has any right to stop me?' Kamala asked it. She was talking about Madhavan's father, her father-in-law. There was anger in her voice, but mostly, there was fatigue. The dog gave her a cold nod that said 'No'.

Aadi piled the pillows one on top of the other and helped Shiva sit up against the headboard. Then he sat beside him on the bed, took his hand and pressed it gently.

'Do you remember our grandmother?'

'No, I'm afraid I don't.' Shiva shook his head.

'But, why doesn't she cry? I mean our mother?'

'You will cry when our mother dies, won't you?'

2

In the graveyard, Hozier waltzed alone. His eyes revealed the happiness of her slender waist, her splendid legs. He danced in the darkness with shadows of gloom. Sometimes she felt jealous of his dancing, sometimes of the purity of his words, of his magical voice. Sometimes a dreadful longing sucked her entrails. She wanted to roll on top of him in the cemetery. In between fatigue and ecstasy, in the midst of the smoke that devoured her, she tried to concentrate on the stereo and talk to him. Her veins throbbed under the pressure of his smile. He was no longer the singer with the face of Christ but a mournful *aghori* in sexy dreadlocks. In his tragic yet magical voice, which was lustier than the three drops of acid she had taken, he sang, '*Crawl home to her . . .*'

Love is the sigh of the abandoned dogs, the opium of the depressed souls. And invariably Kamala was a victim of love.

'Come inside,' Kamala said, looking at the stereo.

Shaly pushed the door open. Inside the room, Kamala clung to the bedpost with contempt in her eyes. Shaly searched frantically in the chest of drawers and on the mantelpiece, but she couldn't find a damn thing. She noticed a small bottle, smaller than her index finger, half hidden in the bookshelf. She flushed the contents down the toilet. She heard Kamala groan. She came out of the bathroom and sat beside her. Kamala looked into Shaly's eyes. There are things you cannot look at. Sad, she looked down at the bare wooden floor and wept.

Kamala edged away from the monster sitting by her side and weeping. Fear shot forward as she saw the monster spitting fire and the flames in turn licking up the curtains of her room. She panicked, not knowing how to extinguish the blaze that was spreading fast. She had to do something before the fire devoured her children, her house. She pulled herself closer towards the bedpost. 'My house was also there in the blaze, on the street that caught fire,' said Kamala.

'Shuddup!'

Kamala rubbed her eyes and looked again. There was no song, no Hozier, no stereo. Before her eyes, the room transformed into a shoreline with sandcastles waiting to be demolished. Alarmed, Kamala looked at the monster, by then so blown up amidst the sand dunes that it looked like Gulliver in the guise of a mad slut. 'Please, please be careful. Please don't step on my castles,' Kamala touched the polished red toenail of the monster and begged.

Shaly quickly scampered out of the room and slammed the door shut. She saw Aadi on the stairs, leaning against the banister. Obviously he was trying to overhear what was going on inside the room.

'Haven't I told you not to come up?'

'Amma,' screamed Shiva, who was sitting in his wheelchair at the foot of the stairs. There was no answer, except Shaly's cold stare. He waited for a few minutes more and then said, 'Aadi, come. I want to lie down.' Indecisively, Aadi climbed down the steps. Shaly watched the boys disappear behind the closed curtains.

'This is the problem with the middle class, especially with the women. Once you leave your house, you are done forever. The next time you have to pay for the room and board just like some regular tenants,' Kamala had once said as she was climbing into bed, laughing. Shaly was lying flat on her belly on the bed.

'Some piece of ass you've got!' Kamala spanked her bottom playfully. Both of them had laughed. But that was a long, long time ago. Aadi and Shiva were kids then, going to primary school. Kamala was a young woman, dumbfounded and mystified. Shaly, on the contrary, was a dandelion puff riding on the wind. Fancy-free! Always! They lived in a nowhere house, on the banks of a nowhere river, in the midst of a nowhere forest and, happily for them, they all spoke a nowhere language.

Ogling passers-by got the shock of their lives and gossiped at length. They tried their moral policing on the women in vain, making their frustrations stand ungratified like obsolete erect dicks.

3

Kamala's mother died last night. It had been several months since she started dying. Now that she was dead, Kamala should have been beside her body for the eulogy in absolute mourning. But Kamala felt an appallingly sincere lack of feeling and a pain numbed by dullness.

She had visited her mother three months ago. Truth be told, she went there not to see her mother but to make arrangements to buy a flat in Kadavanthra. After a long and weary drive from Bangalore, she reached her mother's house at six-thirty in the evening. In the dim light of the room her mother couldn't recognize her. She couldn't recognize her mother either. That was not the mother she had been used to since her childhood. The woman in front of her was incontinent and lay crumpled up on the bed. She was wearing large and heavily soaked diapers, and farted every so often. She looked as if she was nobody's mother, a disfigured skeleton wrapped in loose skin. When Kamala touched her, her bones rattled.

Aadi stood by the headboard, looking compassionately at the figure that was once a woman. His eyes welled up. He had seen only babies in diapers before this. When he listened to her closely he heard some unconscious prayers in an unconscious tongue. He looked at the photographs of the ancestors on the wall, arranged like surgical knives in a long tray. There was his grandfather, a man who died young, in his early forties. It seemed he had lived only to be photographed and framed, a shiny scalpel with a sharp edge.

Early the next morning Kamala set out with Aadi to Kadavanthra. As they drove to the city, she talked loudly to the land broker over the phone.

'We have to go back to Bangalore tomorrow. If you can arrange it today, please do or else forget it. We are on our way already.'

'Madam, there is a huge traffic jam here. Some strike is holding up the traffic. You can't imagine what a huge mess it is.'

'You should have informed me earlier.' Kamala disconnected the call, but she continued to drive.

It was not the rush hour. But they had to wait for hours in the long queue of vehicles honking madly every now and then. When at last they managed to get out of the car, they saw the city transformed into a garden of love, emanating sulphur fantasies and blissful delights. It exhaled the fragrance of wild magnolia and dark roses. 'Is this some kind of a festival of love? Some fancy show?' They looked at each other. Both mother and son blushed alike. Embarrassment reddened their faces. On the streets, people were kissing. Kissing gently. Kissing passionately. Kissing wildly. As if their kisses answered the meaning of their existence. Kamala felt a sudden urge to kiss her son. She held his hand tighter and continued to blush at this rainbow sight of love.

Some of the kissers had zills on their fingers, which jingled as they kissed each other. The sound of the finger cymbals reminded her of the voices of bedtime stories, and the sound of the heavy tambourines brought back unwanted memories. Once upon a time, or a long time ago, or whatever the fucking phrase was, she had kissed a friend of hers passionately on the lips. She was in her white chemise and her friend had looked like a flower, a girl in her early teens. Her tongue was a petal, as rosy as could be. And Kamala couldn't help but kiss. She kissed her hard till someone's belt whipped her on her back. Before she could turn around and see who the hell it was, she was prostrated on the ground, bleeding for the first time in her life, staining her white chemise.

Everything turned pale and purple in front of Kamala. She noticed the waste piled up in the corners of the city, the dumpsters yawning in the void, the faces of the kissers (were they lovers by any chance?) getting slimy with thick saliva, which she was sure smelled of rotten semen. The kisses slithered down their faces, evoking reminiscence of a hellish fall. When she saw the policemen swinging their canes, getting ready to charge at the kissing mob, she felt relieved. Reality means a hell of a lot in life. She sighed.

Aadi was still inside the car. He didn't wish to get out. Kissing was nothing new in Bangalore. Lovers kissed in every nook and corner of the city. In Lal Bagh, kisses bloomed better than flowers. But still, this was novel because this was a strike, a protest against the moral policing of Kerala and they called it 'the kiss of love'.

Soon the canes swirled overhead, the polish on the shoes was stained by dirt and the people began to dissolve. Someone got fed up and sang *fack fack fack* in the background.

4

Predominantly, everything dwells in duality. Kamala decided she would not think of life and death and of mother and daughter as these were the creations of *maya*. But that night, during severe hallucinogenic delusions, Kamala saw funeral cortèges passing before her eyes.

There was this young mother, a beautiful woman, dead twelve hours ago. Women bathed her in turmeric water. The yellowness of the fresh turmeric water glowed on her dead face. She had on her body an exquisite red Kancheevaram sari for her winding sheet. A single diamond with the white light of the glass coffin shining through it glistened on one of her nostrils, and cast glimmers of sorrow on her dead face. Beside her, her daughter cried non-stop and her son fell unconscious. The pall-bearers waited outside under the temporary parasol while the women came with rose petals and golden chrysanthemums in open baskets. The dead woman was to mark her way to the graveyard with petals and silence. The tarred road lay bare, waiting to be shrouded by flowers. Later, an elderly woman forcefully tried to remove the diamond nose pin. She wanted it desperately for she knew it was valuable. But this was not an easy task. The body had spent almost twelve hours in a gold-rimmed glass freezer coffin. Would it bleed if it were cut open?

Kamala remembered her mother. Her mother, too, had a diamond stud on her nose. Kamala had her nose pierced when she was a very young girl. She couldn't remember the pain or the pleasure of it. Someone might have removed the stud from her mother's nostril before she was taken to the freezer. (Did her mother have a freezer coffin?) It was not mandatory to order a freezer coffin. It took a two-hour flight from Bangalore to Cochin including the check-in and waiting and then another two hours on the road to reach the dear departed. Did she really need a freezer coffin?

Her visions swung on gold-rimmed glass coffins and sparkling nose pins, until one by one her mother's ornaments started flashing in front of her. She smiled. What bliss! When she was just a little girl she used to ask her mother, 'Mother, can I have all your jewellery when you die?' Those were the days when the family cherished talk about handing down the properties, dividing and bequeathing whatever they had. Kamala was the only child of her parents. 'Kamala is lucky,' her aunt would say. 'She need not worry about divisions when she grows up.' Her cousins looked at her with jealousy, for she was immensely rich and an only child. Everything her father had would be transferred to her as a rule of thumb. And thus she inherited his melancholy heart, either sometimes sad or always depressed. And her mother said to her, 'Darling baby, why do you have to wait till I die? All that I have is yours, my love.'

Kamala reached out to touch her mother. She stretched her hand as far as it could go. Like those one sees in ghost movies, her hands and her arms grew in length inch by inch at a rate faster than one could imagine, and wriggled and writhed and moved forward. She looked dubiously at her octopus fingers and laughed. 'Go, go, fetch me what I want.'

Her hands banged on the door and opened and closed the chest of drawers. Her hands searched for something inside the drawers, something behind the bookshelf. But there was nothing.

Her hands felt depressed and heavy and wanted to help her commit suicide. Defeated and out of control, her hands banged and knocked down the sand castles. Her room was no more a shoreline, it was a desert. One by one, the processions of death marched through the desert. Kamala choked.

'I can't walk any further than this. You can abandon me here, my children,' said someone.

Frantically, Kamala looked at the nooks and corners of her desert-room. There was a group of people and this dying old woman, a mother. The people looked like poor gypsies and the woman resembled a broken and worn-out piece of furniture that once was padded and cosy. The woman said, 'Please leave me here and get moving. I can't manage any more, I am sorry.' Her children and people surrounded her and sang dirges of abandonment. When they finished singing, they gave her water from a container that looked like a blown-up bota bag. One after the other, they kissed her goodbye and walked away. They sang as they walked. They sang and they cried and they sang and they cried and they sang and laughed and laughed.

Kamala thought of people. People were covered with shrouds, not just one but many, many layers of shrouds. In every case, on every occasion it was the same. Under the scorching sun, the old hag that was once a woman lay. She had on her nothing but the last shroud of her life, her skin. Kamala felt the old woman's mouth going dry. Her tongue rested parched in her open mouth, like the broken fields of drought. Her skin waited to be blazed away. 'Devour me, O Mighty Sun,' she looked at the sun god and closed her eyes.

The sun blinked and a weighty madness consumed Kamala. She clenched her fist and dug her face in the snuff box of anatomy. She inhaled hard. 'Give me; give me your scent, the excitement in between your thighs.' Then she struck the floor with her fist.

'I wish I were young again,' she blabbered, longing for the slender happiness of youth. She remembered how happily they used to lock the room from the inside and throw the keys up on the mounted racks. Drunk, high, one would never find one's way to the keys. One would never find one's way to the other. They breathed in the ecstasy of the well-prepared Mexican leaves. 'You asked for sex, you get it. You want pleasure? Have pleasure.' They searched for the keys only in the morning when everything was back on wheels. Shaly was both a bitch and a boon companion, a bewitching bitch who spoke to Kamala's remorse-stricken spiritual sexuality, her hatred and her ecstasy. She was from the mountains, the daughter of a priest. The mountains had taught her the secrets of the unrestrained, revolting euphoria of love. Neither nights nor drugs were as compelling and as intoxicating as Shaly.

'Every wino deliberately puts on the mask of a clown. Have you ever noticed that?'

'No, I haven't. But I enjoy making others wear the mask of a clown. You may think that I am sulking here in the desert. It is not so. I am watching my friend. I am watching people. I would like to close my eyes to the absolute bliss. I would like to become the visions I see.'

'No. You are what you are. No one becomes the visions they see. You can watch, enjoy and return to yourself, sit back and relax in some dirty armchair.'

'You? ME? Come on, who is going to leave? There is no you and me. I would like to be dissolved into the ultimate darkness where there is no you and me, not even Brahma.'

'Then why the hell do you use the word *I*?'

'That's language. *I* is a word just like a name. Things need to be represented somehow. Like Nike shoes, Juki sewing machines, Johnson's diapers. I hope you know those kinds of things.'

Kamala noticed something crawling out of the half-collapsed old house that was on the other side of the desert. People stood scattered around the house, some of them peeping inside. Kamala wondered what sight lay behind that chit of a window to keep them so intrigued. Some women who managed to get a glimpse covered their faces the moment they glanced inside. They hurriedly came back and joined the rest of the crowd. Their faces turned pale and purple. Kamala was still glued to the bedpost, she couldn't move from there. She wanted to go and take a peek. She looked around. Her octopus fingers were digging into the sand—sandcastles again? But to make castles, be it brick, sand or mud, you need water. Kamala felt the warmth of lukewarm water in between her fingers, her thighs. The water had a pleasant yet pungent smell. Her mother was incontinent before she died. Half the time, she lay on her bedspread, heavy with urine and shit. Kamala had to run to the toilet twice from her mother's bedside to vomit the nauseating smell out. She made an attempt to push her out of the wetness. But, unable to move from there, she lay in the puddle soaked to her ankles.

There is no duality, no birth, no death, no rebirth, no mother, no daughter.

'Amma, I want to travel,' said the daughter, 'I want to love myself.' The mother looked at her in surprise. She couldn't make out what had come over her. 'I said I am going to travel. I have packed my food and everything that might be of use on the way,' the daughter said, and set out. The mother was shocked by this but once she recovered she started screaming and running after her daughter. Her daughter was youthful and energetic like a young pony. She ran faster than her mother and didn't look back. The mother had to give up.

Before she left, the daughter had said a lot of things of which the mother couldn't make head or tail as she was in a fit of emotions. Now that the daughter had gone the mother sat down in a sunken armchair on the veranda and remembered the conversations one by one. The daughter had said she had attended a session run by a twenty-five-year-old entrepreneur called King Siddharth, to which the mother nodded and smiled. The daughter said again, 'Never in my life had I thought I would enjoy something like this. You know very well how much I hated classes and speeches and stuff like that. I expected him to lecture on entrepreneurship and money-handling but he didn't say anything of the sort. Instead he gave us an idea of life in general.'

By this time, the mother had lost the trail of the talk and started nodding automatically in between yawns. The daughter continued.

'I want to read as many books as possible for he asked us to start with books in the journey of understanding oneself. I went to the library after his speech and took out Gustave Flaubert and now that I am reading it, I realize how imbecilic I have been all these years. But that's another story which I will tell you later. Then, he wanted us to write. Then, he wanted us to travel. Do you hear that, Amma? 'Travel'? Such a beautiful word, isn't it? He specifically mentioned solo trips. Trips! You can imagine how excited I was after that. He said the best way to learn about life is to experience it our own way. See, when I am travelling on my own I'll be conscious of the money I have in hand, what to order, what time I have to be back . . . In short, it'll make me become more responsible in life.'

At this the mother thought for a while: What should I say? She walked out of the room, and the daughter followed her down the hall, continuing, 'Look at me, Amma, you share your wisdom with me but that is your experience or what has been passed on to you. Do you know, Amma, he said one more thing. He said that mothers are always right but if we blindly follow them it will boost only *their* confidence, not ours.'

After a pause she said again, 'I have always wanted to pack my bag and travel and spend some time on my own in some faraway, secluded place, or walk on the wild side. Amma, I want to be happy in life. Look at me; I have been trying to concentrate on a mathematical problem for the past two hours. I haven't solved a single step because I am not happy. Our strength lies in our happiness. When we are happy nothing in the world seems to bother us. Do you understand what I'm saying, Amma? He told us that through meditation and silent introspection we will be in control of our brain. I am sure you can relate to this, Amma, and I really think you should try this too!'

'Do you like that young man? What is his name? King or what is it?'

'Yes, I love him,' replied the daughter. 'Such a great fellow.'

'Are you serious about this?'

'About what?'

'About this young man?'

'Are you crazy, Amma? I think it's my mistake. I think I have shocked you enough with all this. Now listen, keep this to yourself. Don't go telling people about this.'

Once upon a time there were *athani*s on the side roads and frontage roads. Large flat stones placed horizontally over two vertical stones that resembled stone benches, on which tired peddlers could sit and rest for a while before resuming their journey. Buttermilk was served to the tired people for free, a service by the community. Someone or other would always be around, telling stories, cracking jokes, munching little bits of gossip but always ready to help a person in trouble. The mother shuddered at the thought of a world bereft of athanis. The daughter was radical. She had left home for she wanted to grasp things by the roots. These things always demanded a struggle—economical or emotional. She was seeking her share of hunger and cold.

'Kamala, where did you go, dear? Please come back. Let's travel together. I'll be there for you.'

Kamala smiled. The ultimate shroud that covers man is the forest. She heard hymns recited in voices louder than whispers. She breathed in the sickening scent of incense sticks. She saw the lighted oil lamp, the split open coconut, the casket of holy basil and the tied up toes. She had never seen her mother sleep so peacefully before.

'Cheers, Amma!' she said aloud. 'This toast is to the luckiest mother in the world.'

5

A depression opened and closed in the bog with the shutter speed of a blinking eyelid. Kamala listened for another moment, and heard her husband, Madhavan, sinking into the waterlogged marsh. She saw the ripples on the thick, chocolate-coloured water. He could've chosen some fresh water pond to drown in, she thought. Her children were fatherless now—she shuddered at the idea. She decided not to drag children into her sentiments. She did not want to think any more, because thoughts were the highest limitation human beings had ever encountered.

She looked over the marsh and then to the skies. The clouds were heavy and black. It was about to pour. She looked around. Flies were fluttering near the ground as the air thickened above. She looked down to the bottom of the rocks, to the treacherous bogs. A minute ago Madhavan had stood there, getting ready to jump.

She mused on bogs, flowers, Madhavan, flies, forest, thoughts and clean ponds; folded her hands in prayer at the abundance and said, 'This is the intelligence of nature.'

Man thinks he is intelligent. Madhavan also thought the same, believed he was intelligent. The big brag! What was there to be proud of? The new robot that fucks you non-stop! Look at nature. It is calm. It is the most sublime thought or feeling or smell or touch one could ever aspire to. Only people run amok on earth; cry and fret and crack up. When they suffer they suffer like hell. They prefer it that way. For most of them suffering is like a candy or something they love to chew on—please don't get it wrong. They pretend. They act. The great bard might have called them actors keeping this in mind. Let them have their exit and their entrance.

Kamala wanted to phone Madhavan and talk about the sad demise of her mother. But on second thoughts she decided not to. She felt death was no longer death and Madhavan was no longer a reality. In the time and space of the universe, we are in no way better than grasshoppers. She put the phone in flight mode. She looked at herself in the mirror and saw two tragic hollows instead of her eyes. Then she noticed the reflection of the fresh flowers in the vase on the table. She turned back to look at the flowers. Shaly might have put them there in the morning. There was a tea tray on the table. But the tea was cold and the toast stale. She didn't feel like having anything. The smell of omelettes made her vomit. When she came out of the toilet she felt giddy; a kind of heaviness was eating her up, working its way to the bed again. But it was time she went downstairs and greeted her children and Shaly. She tried to look in the mirror and smile.

The woman in the mirror ought to change her ways for her children. She ought not be the same woman who couldn't even move the latch on her bedroom door and walk out while her mother lay dead and waiting for her in the front hall of their godforsaken house.

When she came downstairs she saw Aadi in the veranda, drawn and tired. She wanted to open up and talk somehow. 'Most probably I'll buy that flat in Kadavanthra. But before that I have some work here.' Her words sounded synthetic and heavy, and Aadi gave her a sad smile in return.

'I don't think we will return to this place again. But Aadi, you can continue your studies wherever you want. I won't stop you from anything. Do you understand? Since you have told me that you're taking a year off, it is up to you to decide what you want to continue with. You are going on seventeen.'

Aadi sat there listless, not knowing what to say. He wanted to ask her about his grandmother but he was afraid he would hurt her feelings. He looked away and his thoughts came to rest on his grandmother's windowsill.

One, two, three and plop! Shiva was throwing stones at the frogs in the well. Aadi sat cross-legged on the stone bench near the gate, counting the cars that drove by. Sometimes he lost count. The cherry red bus disappeared long before he noticed the green one passing by through the lane. There were cars of chrome yellow and yellow ochre. As he concentrated, he saw some of them transforming into butterflies in the wind. And the road in its dust-stricken yellow hue into a painting of fleeting ghosts, too hazy to handle. Beyond the yellow trees, much beyond the yellow road, down the lane, pyres burned in a blaze. Life ends there. He was about to get up and walk down the yellow lane. Someone held him from behind and said, 'Children are not allowed to go there.' He turned around. It was his grandmother.

'How long have you been sitting here? Don't you have anything else to do?'

'Amma, you should consult a doctor. You look so fatigued.'

Kamala noticed the stress on his words and said playfully, 'Don't you play Mr Grandpa, Aadi. Get up and do something. Don't you wish to say goodbye to your friends or your teachers or do anything of the sort?'

Aadi had never thought of waving goodbye to Bangalore even though the discussion had been going on for quite a while. It seemed he wouldn't even make an effort to get up from the sofa. Kamala felt annoyed at his inertia.

23

'At least just turn around and look at the boys of your age and see for yourself how they live,' Kamala went inside in a fit of anger.

What does she know about the boys of my age, thought Aadi. They stopped chewing bubblegum a long time ago. These days they chew 7 O'Clock razors and spit them out in public. Not all of them, of course. Most of them are not happy with a 100 cc bike; they dream about Harley-Davidsons and Bullets. Bangalore had excellent showrooms for the sexiest bikes in India. But Aadi knew Kamala would never let him ride a bike. She would find a hundred excuses for not buying him one. Whenever he asked she would say, 'To ride properly on a two-wheeler one needs to have a sense of destiny and balance of mind.'

'What the hell are you doing sitting here? Are we not going to see your grandma?' Aadi turned to look at Shaly, who was looking down at her cigarette. He felt War and Peace were leaning against the door, lighting a cigarette and asking him something he couldn't comprehend. But one thing he understood pretty well. She was wearing his coffee bean-coloured T-shirt.

'How many times have I asked you not to wear my tee?'

'Oh! I'm extremely sorry, baby. I couldn't find anything else in my closet this morning and your tee was lying on the sofa. Shall I take it off now?' She pretended to pull the T-shirt up, stretching it from corner to corner so that it went nowhere above her navel. He looked at her tits, standing erect in the coffee bean-coloured tightness. When she noticed that he was looking at her breasts she said, imitating Arnold, 'My nipples are very sensitive,' and sneered at his edginess. Seeing he was not laughing she asked again, 'Can't you buy a single joke this morning, love?'

'I want my tee back washed and without a single crease,' said Aadi.

Shaly folded her hands in a contrived way as if begging for his forgiveness and went inside the house singing a cheerful tune.

Kamala's children longed for Shaly's presence even though they hated her. There was something very compelling about her. Perhaps it was the fragrance or the smile or the way she talked. A whiff of Opium she wore or a glimpse of her sexy legs would turn them on, but they hated the way she talked, the way she made fun of things. They did not dare to start a conversation with her unless it was necessary. Once, Aadi saw her reading a book in the public library and he thought it would be bad form to leave without saying hi to her. Hesitantly, he went near her and asked in a hushed voice. 'Hi Shaly, what are you reading?'

'The monk who sold his flying fart!' she said real loud. So loud that all his friends started chuckling and the librarian had to shoot a severe look their way.

Kamala's children wanted her to walk out of their house, their lives. But they also wanted her very much; they wanted her to be with them always. For they knew that without her, their house would not be a home any more.

6

Packed and unpacked, wrapped and unwrapped, Kamala and her children were never home. This was the third time Kamala was taking the things out of the suitcase she had packed that morning. People from Movers and Packers would come to collect their things tomorrow. The pale blue uniform of the men employed by the company who managed their house-shift every time was a familiar and tiring sight. This was the seventh house they had shifted to in twelve years. This was the place where they had stayed the longest. She thought she would pack only those things she couldn't stand being deprived of at any cost. Then she closed her eyes for a while and pondered over her dearest things. Her mother's pyre flashed in front of her eyes. Fire shot upwards in the left side of their courtyard that faced the east. 'After collecting the ashes I will plant a mayflower tree,' she said to herself, 'Let my mother bloom in red flowers.'

'Are you afraid?' a voice asked within.

'No, I am not afraid. Why should I be? After all, fear is nothing but a very thin line inside our brain. It is fragile. It comes and goes. It is not even half as strong as a matchstick.'

'Did you not want to watch your mother being cremated?' the voice asked again.

'I'm afraid women are not allowed there,' Kamala said scornfully.

'Did you not want to kiss your mother one last time?'

'Yes, I wanted it so badly,' Kamala sobbed. 'I should've gone there,' she sobbed again.

After all, it was a matter of hours. She opened her windows wide and imagined the last visitors of the mourning days staring at Shaly with abhorrence.

Looking out of her Bangalore window, Kamala remembered the lotus pond in the backyard of her mother's house. It was so enchanting that invariably all the children of the neighbourhood wanted to play hopscotch somewhere near the pond. They wanted to pluck flowers, make garlands and play in the water. But the grown-ups did not allow them to go anywhere near it. 'Don't you dare? There is a man-eating giant down there,' they said to the children. The beauty of the flowers was so inviting that the children didn't buy such a cheap trick. Those who knew how to swim spent hours in the water until their fingertips became wrinkled and assumed the shape and colour of the fingertips of the ghosts they cherished in their nightmares. With curled-up fingers, spooky looks and raucous squawking they ran after the young girls, scaring the shit out of them.

But when Kamala was older, she realized that the grown-ups were not selling them some foolish trick—that there *was* something real and grotesque waiting underneath, ghastly and loathsome. Beneath the motionless leaves, flowers and parrot-green rings, something lay in wait with its mouth wide open. 'Don't look down there,' she warned herself. No matter how many precautions they took, the giant sometimes emerged. Raking up the muck and thrashing the lotus rings apart, it stepped out of the water, rode on a cog from the murder wheel to gnaw at the intestines of their house, and worked on it slowly until the total system that was called family vomited curses.

'Aren't you ashamed to talk to boys? Do you know you are bringing disgrace on the family?' an infuriated uncle hissed forth. The giant felt happy at this and started working on the intestines again, all doubled up. The next time, the uncle came with a different allegation. 'Aren't you ashamed to touch a girl? How could you ever think of kissing a girl? Only boys are supposed to kiss girls. Do you understand, you thoughtless, good-for-nothing girl?'

This was not a mere pastime for the giant, for he was envious of Kamala, to whom the pond would go after her father's death. The giant noticed that the uncles and aunts were equally disappointed about the will Kamala's father made. Hence, he started working on their intestines, making life in her own house miserable and unbearable for Kamala. The law of territorial greed stood erected, irrespective of the differences between men and women, gods and demons, dogs and cats.

Relatives mean happiness for the first half hour and hell for the hours that follow, a pack of maggots one cannot easily ward off. 'Let the mourning be over and I will not let anyone in again,' she said to herself, 'Kamala will die an egoist.' There was nothing wrong in being a little bit puffed up in front of those green-eyed monsters.

She was still at the window when her cell phone rang. Madhavan, she thought, it's him. She prepared to answer the call and looked at the display, which read 'Bossy Purple Ocean' and stopped buzzing just as she saw it. She called back and her boss answered.

'Kamala, I just wanted to know if we could have the party at Peacocks in the evening instead of Hotel Royal Orchid. The crew says a pub would be a better idea.'

'I am afraid I can't make it. I am going back home much earlier than I had planned. I don't think I can afford another morning with a hangover. For you guys it is the weekend, but for me the beginning.'

'Ah, don't you worry then. See you in the afternoon at the Royal Orchid.'

Back in her bed, she wondered what she was about to begin. This was an old house, just like any other house in that antiquated quarter of the street, where each plot was bordered with frangipani, those flowers with no scent even in full bloom. The street was always busy with vehicles on the tarred roads, vendors and dogs on the granite-paved sidewalks, and smoky dust greying the air. The house was cupped in an uneven garden by curtain plants lying quiet over the tiled roof and white blossoms whispering down the eaves.

Admiring the abundance of the flowery avalanche, Shaly used to say, 'This is heaven on earth.'

Kamala felt her heart racing and tears choking her throat. She sensed a tension unlike anything grasping the innards of her house. She stepped out of her bedroom, walked down to the veranda, to her garden. Aadi was still there, sitting on the chair doing nothing. When he heard her footsteps he turned to look at her and saw her walking towards the barbed wire fencing in the corner of the garden where she grew wild orchids. He watched her pluck fat green worms out of orchid blossoms. Raking up dirt, she trampled the worms under her sandals. 'What is the use of taking care of a garden we are going to leave behind?' he thought.

Kamala ran her fingers over the softness of the pale yellow colour of the orchid petals. She knew Shaly was remorse-stricken. It was Shaly who had introduced her to acid nights, to the raves, and then to the doctor who assisted the rehabilitation of junkies. All the same, she accused Kamala of spoiling her life, she used the word 'future'. It was always future—*Shaly's future* to be precise.

Kamala sat in front of the doctor with her eyes down, staring at the legs of his table. She thought patients, especially junkies, should sit like this. Shaly said a good many things to the doctor, all in one breath. She repeatedly used the words 'disastrous' and 'regrets'. The doctor was sympathetic, though severe with his tongue. Repentance is an easy thing, he said. Looking at Kamala he asked, 'How long does your trip last?' Kamala didn't lift her eyes from where she was looking, didn't answer.

'Sometimes it lasts more than eight hours. The trouble is that she is always having bad trips and the bad mood persists even after the trip,' said Shaly.

'Obviously,' said the doctor. His eyes were still on Kamala. 'Therein lies the tragedy. LSD is hell. It need not be a happy trip always. Sometimes, some people may find it exciting as the neurons in their brains become elated. But at the end of the day, be it a happy or bad trip, you are in hell. The repercussions are grave. You get unwanted flashbacks. If your trip is happy, you cannot be happy again unless and until you are on a trip. Your ability to find joy in simple happiness and the beauty of life will diminish. If you are prone to bad trips, you start getting flashbacks even when you are not on a trip. Do you understand? I am not frightening you. But this is it.'

Kamala was reluctant to raise her face, but she said 'no' when the doctor asked her whether she was a believer.

'If you don't believe in any god, then believe in yourself,' said the doctor. 'That will help you. Look at yourself in the mirror and say, "I am beautiful. I am forty. I am a badass. I have an amazing life. I am free. I can do it."'

Kamala thought he was giving a piece of chocolate to some heartbroken teenager. She wanted to walk out of his consultation room. He was jotting down something on a piece of paper. She saw him drawing diagrams and marking points.

'May I have some privacy with her? Could you please wait outside for a while?' he asked politely, looking at Shaly.

Shaly sat almost an hour outside the consultation room. Meanwhile she looked at the other patients waiting impatiently for their turn and remembered Rita Mama, her pale, paper-white face. Rita Mama would lower herself to the bare cement floor, making faces to indicate vertigo, and cry, 'I can't manage it on my own.

Shaly, take me to a doctor.' 'Drama queen!' Shaly would shush the grumble and stare coldly. At this, Rita Mama's wooziness would wear off. A faint smile would appear on her narrow lips. Petty fears choked her as she realized that she missed Rita Mama, her house surrounded by changing roses, votive candles, prayer chants; she longed to see her. Should I go back to Rita Mama or should I settle down with Kamala in her mother's house, wondered Shaly.

Bangalore always had a jumble of quirky souls who strived for a distinctive social constellation. For all the bad things one may curse about, the warmth of the city remained the same in spite of the sprouting concrete jungles and many individuals who felt fierce loneliness. People who found it difficult to put the champagne back into the bottle still slogged and waited for some faraway comfort in that never-never land. Mothers who lived a single life were many, striving hard to raise their children with love and care and at times with senseless abandonment. Some of them got married again, leaving their kids at the mercy of newcomers. Some of them lived a lonely life, with no partners to share their sexual agonies and inner pleasures.

Kamala followed Shaly like a persistent shadow. Or was it Shaly who followed Kamala?

While the two women basked in light, the boys drowned in inherited, familiar darkness. They waited for hours in a background full of shitty laughter.

7

Holy devil! What did I get myself into, Kamala wondered as she struggled to keep the steering wheel steady; it kept veering to the left side of the road, of its own accord. The harder she tried, the stronger the pull. It seemed the alignment had gone soft in the head. The man behind her in a silver Volkswagen honked several times, lowered his window and called her names. She pulled into the next lane, into the traffic. She should have knocked down the Triumph that was trying to overtake her on the left side. 'Dirty bitch!' she heard the rider shout.

She checked her speedometer and slammed the breaks, bringing the VW to a stop amidst maddening honks. She felt dizzy, she revved the engine again, manoeuvred with much difficulty into the slow lane. The man riding pillion on the Triumph was giving her the finger. She couldn't fake anger, she laughed. She slowed down, heard the sputter of the Triumph die down and saw it transform into a black ladybird with tubes and fenders, its composite body painted a sparkling orange, flying skywards. On top of everything, Shaly was shouting, 'This is a free ride, just enjoy.'

Something was just not right. She knew she was running on the remains of the previous night's party; she was hung-over. She stopped the car on a side path as she didn't want to end up against some highway trees. Like a kingfisher pecking its own reflection in the water, something tapped non-stop inside her brain. Aadi and Shiva must have panicked, not seeing their mother last night. They were children going to school, not yet on their own. The scene in front of her pulled back abruptly, pushing the vehicles, horns, roads, everything into some wayside dumpster, urging her to seek something familiar, something far away, something from the past.

'Come on, this is a ride. There is no running away,' Madhavan hollered.

Kamala looked at him uncertainly; she looked at the giant wheel. The wheel stood silhouetted against the segments of dust rising gently in the rays of the setting sunlight. Madhavan seemed cheerful and hostile as he dragged her through the festival crowd. There was something unnatural about him, about the way he jeered at her and made scenes in public. He grabbed her by the arm and pulled her closer to him. She wrestled to get free of his grip. His hands were strong, she couldn't even budge. She feared the giant wheel; she didn't want to go on it. People who went for a ride came back safe, but that didn't convince her. She had heard the story of a child who fell from a giant wheel during some festival or other years ago and was killed. She bit his wrist, hard, and fled. Madhavan stood dumbfounded, gaping at his bloody wrist.

'We are friends; all of us are your buddies, pals and what not. Look at us, feel safe.' Kamala looked up from her cigarette. In the dim light of the room she saw faces, people. She took count: not enough to be addressed as a crowd. How can they be my friends, I don't know anybody, she thought. She heard the psychedelic music from the instruments. She felt she heard colours. She tried to concentrate on the music. 'Is that Pink Floyd?' Her voice was so loud that it shattered in her ears like a piece of glass against something rocky. Shaly and her friends formed a large circle around her, and started to laugh at her, having their share of fun. In the background, the real Slim Shady accompanied them.

Kamala dragged herself to a corner of the room and settled down on the floor, leaning against the frosted glass wall of the balcony. She could feel anger under her fingertips, but she also felt her fingertips going numb and heavy. She thought she was shouting without raising her voice, she saw the fire creeping up the walls, displaying never-ending cardiac waves in bright colours.

She decided she would not look at the walls again, nor at the dark side of the junkies. She furtively listened to those people who called themselves buddies as she wanted to ward off conflicting feelings and unsettled emotions. She listened, she heard them. They were talking about entrepreneurs and Steve Jobs in particular. They said Apples were already on the way to their Indian tables. Someone said Steve Jobs used sex, drugs and rock 'n' roll as his ingredients in the making of the perfect Apple. Kamala visualized Zen, sex and music boiling over in a large cauldron and Steve Jobs stirring the bubbling froth with his long ladle like a druid hilarious over some newly discovered magic portion. The children of Mayannur, the children near her ancestral house, flocked around, they all wanted to have a taste of the portion, the sensuously seductive apple bites. 'Don't burn your tongue,' Steve Jobs shooed them away.

'Once the balls fall what you need is a handful of mushrooms,' said the middle-aged man who sat near the table smoking weed. It was a common comment among druggies and no one laughed at this. Most of them were youngsters whose balls were in good shape.

Kamala said she would pick the mushrooms herself. Her basket was full of mushrooms. But when Madhavan plucked the juiciest of the mushrooms from the dark earth, her face fell. She was the hunter who had seen it first. Children returned home, their tiny baskets heaped with snowy white treasures. Kamala's mother washed the mushrooms in turmeric water and sliced them into long strips. She sautéed the mushroom strips in coconut oil along with ginger, garlic and a paste of black pepper. The children couldn't stop drooling over the most perfect mushrooms in the world.

8

The children did what she asked, told her only what she wanted to hear. Skilled in selecting memories, they blocked out the faint scent of musk cologne and wiped away the taste of dark slabs of Swiss Thins from their taste buds. Madhavan was a memory thus blocked and forgotten. They bluffed when asked, pretended he didn't exist in the world they grew up in. They asked nothing about him even when they were busy packing their things and getting ready to leave for their grandmother's house. They knew their father was their mother's cousin. The knowledge was shame; they were guarded all the time so as not to bring it to light. They didn't want people to think they were weird.

Peace was destined to cut the roots off Madhavan, their father who was neither an intellectual nor a revolutionary, neither sad nor silent; just one of those good-for-nothing neighbours, down to earth with nothing special to brag about. He had not laughed since the day he had lost his wife and children. He missed them in every smile he faked. He was happy they were in Bangalore; he frequented grocery shops and bookstores with the distant hope of getting a glimpse of them, his beloved cousin and darling boys. Sometimes he met Aadi in coffee shops or Kamala at some traffic signal, at other times it was Shaly cautiously pushing Shiva down the sidewalk, Shiva sitting peacefully in his pram.

Once they go back to live in Kamala's mother's house, Madhavan worries the distance will stain the vacuum with an undesirable blurriness that will weigh him down badly. At first, he thought he was lonely. Then he felt he was alone and being alone is beyond loneliness. In the aloneness he knew people intervened with everything, animate and inanimate. Though man does not sprout like seeds in the rain, though he walks, jumps and runs over the earth—touching it only at intervals, has the habit of taking his feet off the earth, he is earth, not just part of it. True, he hasn't grown visible roots like plants, but he has roots everywhere, roots of air anchored on the earth through his lungs. And the air is omnipresent, making nature his labyrinth.

This was not the first time they were moving house. Kamala kept saying that each house was an excessive investment, good for nothing. As children, Aadi and Shiva had loved the humongous cardboard containers and cartons Kamala used to pack their things in. The boxes were like caves, big enough to welcome an elephant, they thought. They would hide, sleep, eat, read comics or do whatever they felt like doing inside the snugness of their cardboard world. Life was a lot more secure and happy inside the boxes, thought Aadi.

But they remembered the stained memories of a faint Friday afternoon when two women, unaware of being watched, made love on a king-size feather bed. A painting remained stamped on the white bed sheet. One of them was their mother; the other woman looked younger, much younger than their mother. At first the boys thought they were attacking each other, a strange kind of wrestling they couldn't enjoy. Hearts in their mouths, they waited behind the transparent curtains.

Later, when the women came out of the room, the children saw nothing but joy sparkling in their eyes. They felt relieved at this less disastrous disorder of emotions and somewhat happy ending; blithely they welcomed the newcomer with bashful smiles. The fragrance of love unfurled inside the rooms, in the dining hall, in the kitchen, wherever the women walked. A huge laughter was welling up somewhere inside their dark, craggy mindscapes.

'Meet Miss Shaly, our family friend,' said Kamala. Shaly smiled and shook hands with the boys. She held their hands as if she was holding something magnificent.

'Darling boys,' said she.

'Darlings indeed, as long as they don't make a mess,' said Kamala.

'Which class are you in?' asked Shaly.

'Third standard,' the three of them replied in a chorus.

The children wanted to hug her again and sit on her lap. She smelled of something they wanted to eat.

9

The party was meant for all of them. Purple Ocean had invited them all—it was Kamala's farewell party and her family was important. But as things had taken an unexpected turn, she said she would go by herself and come back quickly. She went to the party shabbily clothed, her hair undone and her emotions unsettled. She had not informed her office that they were in mourning, she didn't want to anyway.

When Shaly came downstairs to get ice cubes and green cheese from the refrigerator, she noticed Aadi sitting in Shiva's wheelchair. He looked like an alien in trouble.

'Is Shiva asleep?' she asked.

'No. Please come inside. We would like to talk with you.'

'I will come down in a couple of minutes. Give me some time. Let me take these things upstairs.'

The boys knew Shaly was not going to come down again as they had nothing to talk about. They moved and slept under the same roof but had nothing in common. They gasped when they came upon each other suddenly, as if the looks were too heavy to be seen or taken in. The house grew noiseless, making the curtains still, the walls still, the roof still, the small tensions grow intense. Shortly afterwards, they heard Eminem descending the staircase.

Shaly, they knew then, was in front of her laptop. The music would change night into day, making her work like a fanatic. They imagined her sipping whisky, nibbling on the green cheese and going through the books and papers she had arranged scrupulously on her table. She would work late into the night. Sometimes she went to bed at dawn. The music would last till the last drop of whisky, making Vivaldi, Demis Roussos and Paul Mauriat take their turns to climb down and knock on the children's door. Sitting in her room, Shaly earned more than what Kamala made in a month at Purple Ocean.

Aadi lay on his bed, his face between his arms, thinking of his father and why his father hated Shaly. His father said he couldn't bear to see his children becoming spoiled. But when he left, he left his children at her mercy. He left because of love, the surfeit or the lack of it. Had his departure been good for them, Aadi wondered. It seemed it hadn't made any difference at all. Love was no sin. As children, they had witnessed how after the first kiss their mother began to sparkle. It was no magic; love gifted a sparkle to her eyes, which in turn proclaimed the happiness of being alive. What you learned from experience was not easy to discard by notions. If Madhavan had been kind to them, kind to their laughter, things would have been different. His children would still be laughing, his wife still sparkling, his house spic and span, his bread ready, and his car shining outside in the porch. Madhavan was not intelligent enough to live a serene life. Without trying to understand why his wife had fallen in love, he hated Shaly, he hated Kamala and he hated himself for hating them. And he wanted his children to grow up to hate her. All the restless hearts of the world would have done the same.

You polish your windows till they are shining and keep them closed. You don't seem to remember the world outside your window with its pristine, unbroken invitations. Because the only things that remain shut in the world are windows and doors. You don't venture out unless and until the sky falls on your head and the wooziness of the inside world throws you out. The closed interiors make you puke. You need air. Go out, breathe and come back, let there be love in your lungs. Breathe easy.

Kamala came home only after midnight, dazed by whatever she'd drunk. Aadi was still awake but he pretended to be asleep when he heard her footsteps coming in. She didn't go upstairs as usual. Instead, she came to his room, turned off the dim light, and lay down supine on his bed, the whisky on her breath emitting frustrations. He began to feel uneasy, not knowing whether to caress her or let her sleep like that. The ceiling fan gathered speed; it blew the air around even faster, distorting the image of Kamala in the centre. The fan rocked her as if she were lying in a devil's cradle.

Love is stronger than three drops of acid. The strangling creepers of desire will burn you down. Shaly, were you right to enter our poor lives?

10

'There, there, my baby, show me your butterfly.'

Little Shaly looked around confused, showing signs of exaggerated unhappiness. She opened the hands which had been clenched tight a moment ago and said, 'It's gone, and the butterfly flew away.'

'Don't lie, darling.'

'I am not lying,' she said restlessly and opened her mouth wide like good old Johnny, the obedient sugar eater.

Andrews pointed his index finger towards her red panties and said, 'What a lovely butterfly you have over there.'

Little Shaly flinched at that and said all in one breath, 'That's not a butterfly, it is a flower.'

'The butterfly is hiding behind the flower. If you come closer I will get the butterfly for you.'

Shaly pulled her panties down and checked. When she pulled them back up she said aloud, 'Andrews Papa plays dirty games.' Where did her white chemise go? 'Rita Mama!' she called out.

It'd been five years since Andrews Papa and Rita Mama adopted Shaly. Andrews loved her like his own flesh, but he had no idea how fathers loved their daughters, what games they played with them. Rita Mama believed that Shaly was her husband's illegitimate child, that her husband was telling her lies, increasing the difficulties with the baby girl. To top it all, Rita Mama had peeling layers of worries and queries buried deep within to support her uncertainties. Why had Andrews run away to Mizoram leaving everything—the parish, his house, a steady income and name—behind?

Andrews had said he would open a school in the heart of the forest. The early schools in Mizoram were run by Christian missionaries who were always good at making a profit. Andrews believed he would find his luck there, that God would support him. But Rita didn't think the shack could be called a school. She couldn't even find decent lodgings in the forest.

'You will see for yourself how the forest is going to transform into a civilization within the next five years,' said Andrews, 'I bought the forest with a vision.'

Forest! Rita was already sick of forests because she had seen nothing but forests around her from the day she set foot in Mizoram: the dark green groves, the thick jungle of bamboos with poles no more than a foot apart, no flat roads but valleys and hillsides, grey birds with pointed red tails, cobras, kraits and vipers, surprisingly beautiful fair-skinned men and women with Oriental eyes.

Andrews was not particularly handsome. But he was born rich and was by profession a *chemmachan* in the church, one in the process of becoming a Father—like a tadpole with legs, frog-like but not a frog. When Rita's family received a proposal from Andrews they were overjoyed thinking of the position and power of a priest in society. Rita too was happy, for she had admired his two-storeyed house right from puberty, from the time her longings began. She thought something new would happen which would make her life a feel-good movie, discarding whatever was left dark and brooding in the past. After her wedding with the priest, she would become *maskiamma*—the respectable lady of society, the wife of the priest. Since the day her father had given his consent for the wedding she had spent her time acting like a real maskiamma.

She dreamed of the white organdie sari dotted with pink flowers she would wear after her marriage, the pearl brooch that went with it and the expensive jewel-studded hair clip in her black curls. She was determined to be undeniably kind to the people of her parish, even though she would feel loathsome inside, at times. Everything about her had to be just perfect, ladylike, she thought. The way she walked, prayed, talked to strangers, gave alms . . .

But look at her! She had ended up in this disgusting dungeon where she understood neither the language nor the customs of its people. She dragged her dreams through the hostile crowd and tried not to smile at anybody even by mistake. This was not her race, these were not her people. The natives, she believed, carried poisonous spears to torture her and whenever she stepped out of her house she made sure she was not being watched or followed. When Andrews had to go back to their homeland on some business she shut herself inside the house and, like a worm wriggling towards the broken earth, she twitched behind the curtains, waiting for her husband's return. Days passed by so unhurriedly that she did not know they had gone by—and then Andrews returned in the middle of a day. He came panting, his eyes downcast and his power dispersed. To add insult to injury he handed over a soft bundle to her and said, 'Consider her your child.'

'So you went home to bring this beast here? Now I see things clearly. This is what you said was urgent and for this urgency you ran away, leaving the school unattended for days.' She hit herself with a spatula and cried out loud.

'What's going on?' Apoi came hurrying, followed by Fila. 'Is everything okay?' Rita felt her nerves crashing. She hurled the spatula at the children, shouting, 'Bastards, go back to your classes!'

Andrews's hands were virtually trembling, burning in shame and remorse. The bundle he held close to his bosom started laughing, throwing out her arms and legs. Holding the baby girl in her pink, snuggly flannel with three yellow butterflies sewn in the corner, he realized that he had been experiencing the purest moments of his life.

'She is an orphan. Father Jacob has given her to me,' he said, in a humble voice choked with tears. 'Let us call her Shaly.'

11

A breeze, a wave or a tsunami sometimes brings back the sealed kiss that has been thrown into the depths of the sea. It will come back for certain, to caress your fringes, to enliven the setting rays of the sun with a smile. Sometimes it will come and sit next to you in a bus.

Though Kamala felt fettered by responsibilities thinking of her children and her office, she was determined to take a vacation which she felt she needed badly. Thus she opened up her heart to welcome the day and its splendid scents. She was on a package tour to see temples. The bus was full of pilgrims, mostly women, who had been dying to bribe the gods for aeons and who spent their time like chat rooms open 24x7. Kamala opened her book, *The Mind without Measure*, and tried to concentrate on reading. It was a difficult task as the bus was moving but she wanted to avoid the gossipmongers at any cost. Books enable a lot of things in life. She had noticed foreigners reading books in coffee shops, on beaches, on wayside park benches, like this. Whenever she looked up from the book and noticed the activities going on around her, she gave synthetic nods or yes–no answers to put an end to artificial queries.

Kamala was overwhelmed by the idea of travel through historic relics and temples. When she saw the advertisement online the first time, she shouted with excitement. History was her subject, plus she had an additional doctorate in philosophy, a combination not so rare but enough to drive one crazy. On the day she booked online for her travel, Madhavan was furious. He said he had no idea what to do with the children while she went on her tour. She said she would make ample arrangements in advance for the days she would be gone. They quarrelled all night, and she shut herself in her room for hours on the following day. She couldn't wait to take herself away from the most chaotic place on earth, which they called home. She said she was born free. The throttling bonds of love sicken you at times and you need freedom, freedom from the known.

This girl has an aura, thought Kamala, looking at the beautiful slim figure who shared the left front seat with a middle-aged man, she on the aisle seat. When she got up from her seat to take something from the rack above, Kamala observed her closely. The girl was lovelier than she had realized, with pretty curls, soft and beautifully curved lips and a splendid behind. She had smudges of lipstick on her mouth and a shade of blue on her eyelids. She had on a yellow top in a floral print and her nails were adorned with a matte coat of red nail polish. A real knockout, enough to set one's heart on fire, thought Kamala. The girl sat listening to music with her eyes closed, two thin white wires dangling from her ears and going all the way down to her lap.

As soon as the bus came to a halt in a temple town, she hurried out and walked ahead of everyone else. Kamala followed her, not knowing how to begin. She was afraid that she would be wasting her time but she wanted to compliment the girl, wanted to tell her that she looked beautiful. Beauty is a rare thing—one may come across hundreds of made-up faces, slim and happy figures on high heels every day, but this was different. Kamala felt she had no more excuses not to talk. The street was packed with flower vendors, their baskets full of purple lotuses and golden marigolds. The girl walked straight to the temple. She didn't stop to buy flowers or sweets. She didn't stop to say hello to the woman who was following her.

Kamala felt humiliated. The girl who didn't turn her head or look in Kamala's direction was visibly dancing on the road. Was she not ashamed, wondered Kamala. What would people think of her? People were already looking at her, their eyes, mouth, nose, cheekbones, everything about them giving out invisible spittle, cold and scornful. Kamala felt responsible. 'That's enough, I said that's enough,' she whispered and tried to pull the girl towards her with endless coughs, till, at a certain point, all the gaping mouths—the sickly, chronically delicate minds—turned to stare at her, not the chick who walked in front, definitely not her. For a moment, Kamala thought, her curiosity about history, her interest in the temples of India was all going to end up in the girl's splendid behind; for it was so shamelessly compelling she couldn't help but follow her, wait till she turned back, till she smiled. She had no idea what she would do if the girl turned around and smiled at her.

The streets, the white and purple flowers in the baskets of the roadside vendors, the invigorating fragrance of incense sticks, the sound of chants, and the distant rings of the temple bells. The girl, on the other hand, had her own soundtrack, like a thick white vein permanently attached to her body. Travelling from her ears it ended up somewhere deep inside the pocket of her tight jeans, or it might have travelled the other way around. It cut her short and restrained her from the world around her, the world that was in motion. Thus she walked light-heartedly, dancing to the rhythms of the travelling wires, stopped occasionally by what Kamala imagined were sopranos to raise her fingers in the air and draw some patterns there, unmindful of the anxiety stretched tight four or five feet behind her.

Something must have surprised her, for she stopped abruptly and Kamala saw her mouth opening, making the dark hole within the circle of her teeth clearly visible, and her fingers moving cautiously over her brows. Kamala looked in the same direction as the girl; she couldn't help suppress a smile, she noticed her cheeks flaring up with shame. The girl was looking at the enormous outer stone walls of the temple decorated with erotic figures carved in stone, a beauty capable of tickling the senses; it was hard to pretend not to notice. But nobody stared like the way she did, no Indian woman for sure. The figures were vulgar, obscenity veiled in aesthetic heights beyond which no mind would travel. Huge, erect penises which it seemed no vagina could ever slake or offer solace to, impudent dicks of fantasy. Some women lay supine and animals licked their cunts, some other women squeezed their nipples. Over the stone walls the scenes extended in tension; people mating with animals, gigantic breasts, orgies, elephants, chariots, horses, soldiers.

Kamala looked at her fellow pilgrims, especially the women and, as she had expected, found them walking with their eyes fixed on their feet, chanting prayers, munching an occasional joke, swallowing something they didn't wish to share; sometimes their throats choked, they felt an aching deep in their bodies, and they walked more cautiously, more dramatically. They didn't dare to look at the pornographic sculptures; they disappeared inside the temples with their heads bowed. This was not sex tourism. This was a pilgrimage; nothing rotten should enter the soul, no temptations should ever stop them; no visions should blur their eyes which were now filled with momentary tears. They folded their hands before the idol and prayed aloud, 'O Lord, please save us, please don't let us be misunderstood, please save us.'

The girl was now staring at a particular statue. Two princes were screwing a wild horse, one from the front and one from behind. Next to it, a girl was standing on her head in a yoga posture and three other girls touched her genitals and nipples, trying to dig into her flesh, their faces serene, calm, devoid of expression. They stood as if they were born to be like that, to maintain that glorious posture throughout the years and days to come, without the spiteful looks of the porn world. The walls licked and sucked, celebrated the cocks and the cunts; it seemed the world circled around in a fucking motion, invigorating the senses with the flavours of bodily juices. The girl turned around and saw Kamala and she smiled.

'Excuse me, could you please take a picture against this background,' she pointed at the sculpted walls. Kamala took her cell phone and while focusing she said apologetically, 'I am not very good with photos.'

The girl posed in front of the princes fucking the horse and in front of the four naked girls. Two candid photographs and a third one that came out blurred and was taken just for the pleasure of clicking.

'What's your name?'

'Shaly, and yours?'

'Kamala.'

'Beautiful name, it means lotus, isn't it?'

Kamala nodded and glanced at the small flower basket in a woman's hands. There was a half-blackened purple lotus ready to wither away along with the other offerings.

'My name has no special meanings,' the girl said timidly.

'Are you from Bangalore?'

'Now, yes, I am searching for a job there.'

'Your family?'

'No, no family, I am alone.'

For a moment, Kamala felt ashamed. She carried those heavy books in her backpack just to ward off inquisitive glances, and now look at her, she had ended up asking the same questions she dreaded most. She shuddered and decided not to ask anything else. There was her scent in the wind, and that was enough.

They looked at the hedonistic stone carvings in detail, took as many photographs as possible, discussed the latest bricolage trends at length, found their smiles intervening, their fingers interlacing with happiness.

'By birth I am a Christian. I hope they won't mind if I enter,' said Shaly.

'Even if there is a problem, no one is going to identify you here.'

'Do you mind if I ask you something?'

Kamala shrugged and said reassuringly, 'Please.'

'You are a Hindu, right?'

'I don't think I belong to any religion or caste, but of course, I was born into a conservative, upper-middle-class Hindu family.'

'Then you won't feel bad if I ask?'

'Ah come on, no hurt feelings,' Kamala opened her arms wide and smiled.

'This is a temple, a spiritual place—it is supposed to be holy and pure. But look at all this erotic abundance; I can't make out anything except that they are wonderful. I mean artistically carved, deprived of emotions but sexually tense and exciting. The deity must be somewhere inside the temple, but may I know why this excess of obscenity on the walls outside?'

'It is easy to define, but I don't really know how easy it is to understand.'

'I am not a girl in her teens, I can understand.'

'Have you heard of Ramana Maharshi?

Shaly said no and for a second Kamala pondered on what she was about to tell the girl. She wanted to say something with precision, something that would unveil Hindu philosophy, but it was, she was afraid, a hard nut to crack.

'Maharshi used to tell a story from our epics. The story goes thus: When we close our eyes with our little fingers, the big, vast universe disappears, even if for just a second. Likewise, the little minds are obscuring the universe, the ultimate truth, or rather, the Brahma,' Kamala said. 'We should search for what these erotic images are hiding.'

Shaly folded her hands as if to pray and said, 'I don't understand a word you say.'

'Well, look at those pictures; can the carnal desires of the body, the sensuality and sexuality of human beings, ever cross beyond the stories of these images?'

'It would be difficult,' Shaly smiled at the penetrating symbols of lust. 'I don't think people could fantasize that much.'

'They may think, they may not, but those who give undue importance to the fantasies of the flesh can only walk around the outer walls of the temple. Whether they enter the temple or not, whether they see the deity inside or not, they can never reach the deity. They will simply go over the same paths, repeatedly, through the intricate passages and labyrinths of mind. This is just an outer layer, the hollow surface where the self walks, indulging in pleasures unknown; you are grazing there, all day long, you are exerting in bed, all night, and you find yourself buried under the six feet of earth one day. The man who thus enters the sanctum will cry out, to be forgiven, to be rescued from what he knows not. Who knows who can save whom? Do you think the deity inside is capable of saving you?'

'What are you trying to convince me about? Are you implying that only celibates have the right to enter this place? Do you think that sex is a bad thing?'

'No, sex is beautiful,' Kamala said discreetly. 'This is not a question of lust and fuck. Temples are symbols, places where people can find themselves, a place that helps people pierce the surface of things, and delve deep into the heart of matter. The outer walls are lessons we learn. We learn that excessive sexual fantasies and temptations of the inner folds of flesh are no more than moments of fleeting happiness, or sometimes a permanent impression of happiness, but that they will definitely not help us find ourselves. The insides of the temple, the sanctum, represents the mind. It is maya, the hallucinogenic notion, that prevents us from stepping within. Maya is in constant motion, a game where the levels are too high to achieve lust, anger, displeasure, resentment, appetite and more. This is why people are waddling like aimless ducks in the mighty folds of duality.'

Kamala spoke under her breath and Shaly thought the conversation was delightful, she felt the unknown creeping under her sole, throbbing under her skin, pulsing through her veins.

'It is hard for a person to concentrate on thoughtlessness. When you enter, please observe, there should be mirrors on the walls—this is a moment when you should open your eyes to see yourself. There is no god, no deity ever born to save you. You are the saviour, the only one. You may be entangled in vicious circles of duality, but reality lies within all the while.'

Kamala's tone was getting even more complicated, but something compelled Shaly to follow her words. When they stepped inside, once again Kamala spoke under her breath. 'Look at the deity, look at the lamp and flame, now close your eyes, let the flame fill you and let the meaning of everything penetrate your heart.'

Shaly closed her eyes; Kamala whispered in her ears, 'That is you.'

But this was a symptom of happiness, thought Shaly. This woman, in her printed silk-cotton sari, metal necklace, silver jhumkas and embroidered cotton bag on her arm, looked like an exquisite piece of art work, but with something definitely wrong in the head. Had she just crossed her late twenties, or was she straddling her thirties?

When the passengers were on board the bus again, Shaly gently asked the man who sat next to her, 'Uncle, could you please move to the next seat, there is one vacant behind us. May I sit with this lady here?'

12

Clutching the edges of the bed, Kamala got to her feet. In the upstairs room, music stopped, the lights turned off, creepy darkness crawled down through the stairs. Kamala looked at Aadi who was sleeping with his mouth slightly open. A tender figure abandoned at a tender age, he worried her.

Madhavan, you will have to answer for this. I became a useless woman because of you, because of the pain you inflicted, the wedding bonds you forced on me, whereas you still maintain your dignity in society, the dignity of a man whose wife knows no ethics, no values. It was your fault. I was your cousin, you had a girlfriend, how many times had I begged you not to drag me into a marriage? Where were you then? You didn't listen to me; you didn't even listen to your girlfriend. What about your sister who kept teasing me for kissing a girl? She made me the laughing stock of her playtime stories; sometimes you joined in too. But what happened to you and your sister when you came to know of the large legacy I possessed? It was your father, my wicked uncle, who plotted, and you were puppets in his hands. Were you not ashamed of turning your girl down for this crap called money? That woman, my sister-in-law, was she not ashamed of coming to my house with sweets and making proposals to my mother whose only ambition was to give my hand in marriage to the first person who gave her a nod of consent? You certainly didn't want me to deliver the children of others, the flesh of someone nowhere connected to our bloodlines. Thus I found myself in front of leaping marriage flames—they seemed almost like a funeral pyre to me then—tucked into a heavy silk sari, loaded with ornaments, gold and precious stones, each necklace and garland like a chain entangling me within myself, making my movements short and clumsy. And now, you don't want my children. You abandoned them. Your family talks about them as 'Kamala's children'. Just wait and see, you will soon learn what lies in store.

She hurled the glass vase with the Chinese bamboos that was on the table—pebbles and water flew everywhere, the sound of falling pebbles making explosions in the ear, the bamboo shoots scattering on the floor. Bamboos were auspicious, they had said. Kamala had had no intention of buying the green shoots, but the vendor had insisted, he said it would bring her luck. Here was her luck, strewn on the floor.

The party at Purple Ocean was a festival of memories, a party of endless reminders; with each drink she saw the paths she had traversed so far. Kamala was a sapling uprooted from her ancestral ground and replanted amidst the steel rails of a metro life, no air, no water, no anything needed.

Wild jasmines rained non-stop over the stone pathways, it was all Kamala had dreamed of and longed for when she was a girl, but now she didn't want to step on the white petals, and so she hesitated, holding Aadi against her. They had to cross the pathway to reach the ashram. When Madhavan came after parking the car, he crushed the petals under his boots; it seemed he hadn't even noticed the white shower, but she saw him brush off some petals from his shirt sleeves. Kamala and Aadi followed him uncertainly, and all the way, Aadi kept wondering at the falling flowers and the rising butterflies.

Through the microphone connected to his white linen shirt, the Swami laughed, spoke and sang, and the room echoed with sing-song speech, and linen clothes swayed and ruffled underneath the fan. Why was he laughing, wondered Kamala, what was there to laugh at or even smile? Everything seemed serenely exaggerated, the extravaganza of a reality show. Kamala looked at Aadi: he was surveying the room, not at ease among the whirlpool of white linen, the dancing men in white with long beards. Women were also clad in white, clapping their hands and swaying their bodies in time with the rhythms.

The fragrance of incense sticks annoyed Aadi, his eyes welled up. He knew his father had decided on something, something not good. There were children, little ones, but they all looked different. A boy of ten years was banging his head on the floor while another was laughing at him uncontrollably. Some others were sitting in motionless postures like imperfect handmade wooden carvings, staring at nothingness.

The night before, Madhavan had written a letter but he hadn't shown it to her, and so Kamala drew back when he took the blue envelope from his pocket and held it out to the Swami. She had no idea what it was, she thought it contained something unpleasant, something she didn't wish to know. Somehow she shared the vague fear Aadi felt, something not good. The Swami was in no hurry, it seemed Madhavan had even paid for the appointment, thus it was his time, Madhavan's time. The Swami opened the envelope.

Swamiji,

We are grateful for the love you are showering endlessly; we have no words to thank you. But we must admit we live in constant pain. As you said once, the centre of life is love. But what if we lose our grip on love?

We live a lost life with our twin boys, Aadi and Shiva. Two years ago, Shiva was partially paralysed after long and unfortunate hours wrestling with cold water and death. After that incident, Aadi—his twin, the one who is with us now—became exceptionally slow. His slowness frightens us; he moves only inside the house or sits in some lonely corners as if wrapped up in a mysterious, tragic dream. Shiva was a very smart boy, very active and always enthusiastic and ambitious, but Aadi was not so. He was a silent observer even when he was a toddler. Please help our child. We would like to enrol him in the mind empowerment program you are conducting for children. Please bring him back to life.

With hope,

Madhavan

This was news to Kamala, strange, unexpected news, her muscles froze and vision contracted, she wanted to scream at the insensitive male psyche.

'But Madhu, those children are differently abled. I cannot let this happen.'

Madhavan paid no attention to her, but said in a fleeting way, 'Not all of them. They give special attention to children who wish to forget a bitter past, everything unpleasant that happened in their lives.'

Like a zombie summoned to life, the watchman opened the gate and out they went, leaving Aadi behind.

Blackness filled her insides, her stomach ached, and she realized her underclothes were getting soaked in blood early. The decisions were always his. He said the house was on fire, he repeated it the next day, slightly modified; he said the fire was to devour their children, and on the third day she woke up from a nightmare to see the cinders.

In the car Madhavan talked about how swamis train children in ashrams. He said India was a land of great gurus, and added that they would come in useful where parents failed pathetically. But he remained silent after that. At a certain point, she thought he was crying.

Their relationship came to an end exactly after a year. She looked blankly at the roads he left open, but didn't bother to take a ride.

Kamala and Shaly went to the ashram and brought Aadi home. Aadi now knew the art of transforming tears into crystals, making the eyes sparkle.

13

On a very fine December evening, when the sun was growing colder, the warden walked out of the hostel premises in the hope of burning a few calories. He forgot to lock the gates of misfortune behind him. Usually, the task was the gatekeeper's. Where was he on that dreadful evening? Nobody knew. Despairingly, the warden looked at his belly and sighed, the football in distress. This time he seemed determined, for he flew out of the premises like an athlete.

Children were always butterflies—well, not all, some were cats and others monkeys, though all of them were good at tossing Frisbees. Above the green meadows, bordered with white-fringed violet petunias, colourful Frisbees flew through the air, up, down. Some of the children made paper Frisbees in the shape of aeroplanes and others waited impatiently for their turn to toss them.

Shiva was really impatient, he couldn't wait any longer, he kept shouting at the elder boys, 'Next is my turn! Vroom! Vroom! My turn! Vroom!' Aadi was sitting on the lawn watching the progress of the games. Out of the blue, a pirate who had covered his left eye with his uniform tie jumped in front of him and asked him to raise his hands. Aadi did as directed and the pirate shouted, 'If you move, you will grace the obituaries on the notice board.' Aadi stood there watching the girls dance to a song.

In a land far away
A girl kissed a frog
That just made his day!

One of the girls had a doll in her hand, a lovely doll with golden hair and blue eyes; a foreign doll. As the verses progressed, as they danced and moved at random, the girl squeezed the doll hard, making it cry.

Far across the forest
It is fun to know
How Goldilocks got away!

It was only then that Aadi noticed that they had with them an elephant-shaped gun for blowing bubbles. Rainbow bubbles floated everywhere; so high, some faded in the thin air and some settled on the delicately frilled petals of the petunias. For a second Aadi forgot that he was a prisoner—he ran after the bubbles as if he were chasing dreams.

Just outside the unfortunate gates, a fabulous splash of bougainvillea intertwined with an old oak tree cast scattered shadows on the surface of the evening lake, over the subaqueous disorientation of the water hyacinths, its banks encrusted with rushes. It had been decided much earlier that a red Frisbee would fly out like an ignited aerofoil and little Shiva would follow, then Aadi in search of Shiva. Slowly, in a dark mood, the evening silhouettes reflected the song of the girls. How could Goldilocks have lost her way? Silence touched the folds of water, water lilies opened their mouths.

It was getting darker. Usually it didn't rain at evenfall in Bangalore, but that day the skies opened, emptying out chaotic pressures and cold anxieties. Madhavan and Kamala were on their way back from Murdeshwar, the place where the phallus of God once materialized out of a piece of cloth which was thrown away in a fit of anger by the demon Ravana. The sky was pouring like mad, it seemed it wanted to remain parched, devastated, without getting wet again. At a certain point, Madhavan had to stop. Kamala offered to drive, but she was equally exhausted. They wanted to clarify many things, discuss the separation, but they didn't do it. Instead, they wandered at random as if they were just strangers, bored and exhausted but forced to be on the move. Reality remained—they wanted to talk about the children. It was no good separating the twins. Both of them knew it. He was okay with her keeping the children and she was okay with him leaving them forever. Now what was there to discuss? So, he said, 'The rain is not going to stop.' She answered, 'I am afraid it is not going to.'

When they had started out in the morning there had been no sign of rain, the skies were unusually clear and blue and the wind was hot—whenever they opened their windows to throw anything away the wind slapped their faces and they had to immediately close the windows. After an hour and a half, Madhavan parked his car at the roadside pull-off opposite the sea for a quick snack just as Kamala was slowly waking up from her nap. From a paper packet he took a knife, a loaf of bread, a packet of peppered cheese and some fruit. He cautiously cut a kiwi into two, and offered her a half. She looked at the fruit and saw the splash of chlorophyll spotted with black seeds inside the hairy pelt—felt a muscle contraction; she had forgotten the date of her last period—pressed her tummy and declined.

The heat outside intensified. This serene place sandwiched between the Western Ghats and the Arabian Sea unfolded before her eyes like a far-flung, sanctified settlement. The unending turquoise water was yet to succumb to beach bums. He started the car.

'If you are willing to leave Shaly, we can bring the children home; they need not stay in a hostel,' he said, voice faltering. It seemed pointless to ignore his request. She knew how her children

61

detested hostel life. They took turns over the phone and cried, 'Amma, when are you coming? Please come soon, we don't want to stay here.' Something clogged inside her chest; she touched her breasts and shuddered at the pain and dampness around her nipples. Suddenly she saw her children in front of her; they were standing in the last row of the school assembly, their right hands placed over their hearts; they sang in unison, their voices reverberating in the nooks and corners of the building, evoking the bright goddess.

The previous night, inside one of the resort rooms booked by holiday makers from Bangalore, Madhavan had stumbled in the semi-darkness for words, for hours. He violently shook the long ash from the stub of his cigarette. He had a lot of things to sort out. Crumpled amidst the white bed sheets, Kamala looked at him for a while. It had been years since they had shared their bodies; she no longer remembered the smell of his fluids.

'Madhu, we are educated . . . do you think people marry their relatives these days? It is a modern society, we should act accordingly.'

Madhavan was not at ease. Still, somehow, he said, 'Kamala, look here, education has got nothing to do with traditions and family names. We cannot throw away the hopes of our parents.'

'Yes, but you have to make it clear whether it is the hopes of our parents or the money of our parents that you're not throwing away. You are answerable; at least answer this before we proceed with this monkey business called marriage.'

'Both.'

'Do you think you can love me? You were like my brother, Madhu. Is it possible?'

'I will try, what else can we do?'

'Why take all the pain, Madhu? If you were to insist, your father would desist.'

When did Kamala fall asleep, still crumpled in those white sheets? When did Madhavan come from the balcony and lie beside her? How many cigarettes had he smoked so far? At home they had two separate rooms.

Kamala had a nightmare, she saw Aadi falling, falling endlessly from some hanging rocks. She shrieked and opened her eyes. The bed sheets reeked of whisky and she saw her husband snoring beside her, and immediately she hated the sight. It is true that Kamala loved Aadi more, more than Shiva. He was so fragile that she was afraid of wounding him with a scornful smile or angry tone. Shiva was smart; Aadi was sensitive. She remembered the glass menageries Madhavan had bought on his way back from Rajasthan: seven camels of different sizes, the colour of a drop of pastel brown dropped in water, unreal yet tangible. When she came to know that Madhavan was not alone when he went to Rajasthan, that he had a woman with him, his lover from before their marriage, she pushed the glass camels one by one off the edge of the dining table with her little finger, making them explode on the cold floor tiles, their melancholic explosions invigorating her painful insides. How easily the heads came off, and the legs, and the hump on the back! Aadi too was a glass menagerie, very fragile—she had to pay attention, for he was her responsibility.

'I will not give my children,' she pushed him hard. He was in deep sleep; it seemed he had no idea about the tension that was brewing inside that artificially decorated room. How can I trust my children with Kuljeet Kaur, the woman who hates me?

Kuljeet Kaur!

It was on the day before her wedding that Kamala learned her name, on the back cover of a blue envelope, a quarter of it under the postal seal. She was a girl from Mumbai. The letter was written in simple English. She ran to the lotus pond and sat on the steps and read the letter twice. The letter revitalized her with hope: her condition, she thought, was still remediable. Madhavan has a girl, and she is pregnant. Madhavan is answerable. She wanted to run, holding the letter high in the air, and shout. But the sight of her uncle, Madhavan's father, drained her energy in an instant.

63

'What are you doing here?' he asked her.

She wanted to congratulate him, for he was going to be a grandfather. But she couldn't gather the strength to retort. Instead, she gave him the letter. He couldn't read English, so she explained the situation to him in one breath. She saw his face grow pallid. Happiness thundered inside, and with an air of authority she asked for the letter back. She saw him tearing up the paper and throwing it into the lotus pond, its ink forming microscopic patterns on water.

'Give me back my letter!' she cried.

'First, that is a fake letter, second, it is not yours, and third it is a bad habit reading somebody else's letters.'

'I don't believe you. I can't marry him! I will talk to my mother.'

He almost slapped her then but she lay prone on the ground and started making a scene. The house was full of guests, friends, relatives and neighbours; the tailor was waiting for her, he had her wedding blouse ready and he wanted her to try it on.

'Get up, get up, Kamala!' shouted her uncle.

'Madhavan, wake up!' I cannot leave my children at any cost, thought Kamala, who had lost her sleep, embittered by memories; she looked at him with vengeance. She rummaged through the bed sheets to find a comfortable corner; what she found instead was a heap of unusual memories. Those who came and those who left asked the same question, 'Has the other baby opened its eye?'

'Not yet,' Kamala heard her mother say in a whisper. 'Don't let my daughter hear this, poor thing, she is already very upset.'

Kamala feared that one of her twins was blind. Shiva was born just after midnight, while Kamala was still shrieking with pain in bed. She didn't open her eyes to look at the blood-smeared baby, for she was carried away by a physical pain more powerful than her maternal emotions. The warmth of blood caressed her thighs and travelled along the length of her body. The possibility of a second baby had not been mentioned during her medical exams. But there the child was, blocking the vaginal passage, ready to die. The doctors had to carve open her belly to untangle the second baby from the cord—it was that reluctant to leave the dark maternal fluid. The child was underweight, like a strip of fabric in the wind and they had to transfer him to the incubator. Meanwhile the other child, the one who descended first, opened his eyes and smiled at everyone, and his mother, who was disoriented thinking about her baby in the incubator, crushed his nose many times against her heavy nipple, making him sneeze and suffocate from time to time. It took another ten to fifteen days for the baby boy in the incubator to open his eyes, and when he did he trembled in the light. He closed his eyes faster than he had opened them, and smiled in his sleep.

The exhaustion of the weary night in the resort made her sleep in the car. Dented memories and displaced fantasies made her fidget in her sleep. Madhavan had to wake her up at one point and force her to wear the seatbelt. Again she fell asleep, again the visuals of Aadi and Shiva clogged her closed eyes, her brain. She saw the children playing hide-and-seek, not only them but almost all the kids in her ancestral home—including herself, when she was a girl of eight, her husband when he was small and good, his hair combed to the right and his shirt neatly tucked in his shorts. Some kids were playing happily around the merry-go-round and some others were on the slide. The slide had two big holes on the wall, two very big, very dark holes. Aadi was looking for a place to hide when he saw the holes. Somehow, he managed to get inside a hole and there, with his heart pounding hard, he waited for Shiva. Meanwhile someone picked up a stone from the ground and placed it near the hole. In no time the stone grew to a certain height and width, blocking the hole completely. Kamala could hear Aadi cry from far away, he was calling her name, while she was playing with her friends. Madhavan was playing too. And when the cries grew louder, and became a real annoyance she couldn't resist any longer, she came to complain to Madhavan. He was telling a story to a large group of children, and to her relief she thought she found Aadi and Shiva in the midst of the children, listening eagerly to whatever Madhavan was saying. He continued, 'And when they all looked in that direction, they saw Lord Shiva emerging out of a cow's ear! Isn't it funny? Just imagine, gods can do anything they want to do.' Kamala observed closely and when she saw Aadi clapping his hands and smiling with the other children, she felt relieved.

Kamala woke up, embarrassed, and drew away from Madhavan's shoulder. She realized that he had taken a diversion from the highway as he always did on a long journey, as if to manoeuvre his moods with the jet of air that whistled at the windshield.

He pulled off the road thinking that Kamala might be in need of a little break from the drowsy coastal drive. But she showed no interest in getting out of the car.

'Look here, Kamala, I hope you know why we are here . . . we are definitely not vacationing. We have to take decisions regarding Aadi and Shiva. We can't let them suffer the consequences of our mistakes. And I want you to speak. Today you are my wife; it may not be the same tomorrow. You are their mother.'

She didn't respond. She didn't even raise her head or comb back the lock of hair that blocked his view of her eyes. She sat with her eyes downcast. Frowning, he turned the ignition on.

'Damn it!'

He lowered the window and threw something out in anger, with force, letting the harsh air in, then set off at a speed he really didn't intend to drive at. Kamala wiped her eyes with the pallu of her sari. Relentlessly, the car sped through Shimoga, through the long and winding rows of casuarinas that lined the roads like tempting belly dancers, through the abandoned squares; they had to reach Bangalore before nightfall. The car left behind two enormous temple chariots and the sleepy old streets of the village which was formed by the ear-shaped union of two rivers. When they came across Apsara Konda Falls, the pond of the celestial nymphs, Madhavan stopped the car. He had often nonchalantly told her that a fine black tea brought freshness back to life and Kamala would need to empty gallons of tea if they were really going to resurrect her.

She looked at him now, standing against the background of the waterfall, his hair ruffled in the wind and heavy with water. He was searching in his pockets for coins for the use-and-pay toilets. When she came out of the toilet she gave a stern and severe look to the woman at the entrance, collecting money.

He headed towards the wayside teashop. She knew that for him a black tea was enough to revitalize his senses; meanwhile, even if she were to drain out this waterfall, she would remain thirsty. She leaned over the rails and watched the water bubbling up, then saw him walking towards her with two cups of tea.

'Would you like to have a samosa?' he called out. 'It is really spicy and hot.'

Nothing could spice up her life at this point, she thought and shook her head. She leaned over the rails again and he warned her to watch out. Of course she didn't want to jump; she smiled faintly, at the great attention he gave to putting on airs. Her eyes held on to something in the whirlpool of water, maybe it was garbage. Whatever it was whined like an infant, and the whimper vaguely echoed in her ears. She tried to concentrate; it was time she consulted an ophthalmologist. She narrowed her eyes further. Some sort of a bundle, she thought.

'Madhu, what's that?' She pointed at the bundle.

Now he was also leaning over the rails looking at the ripples and listening to the whining. Slowly, very slowly, their eyes got accustomed to the dark and they realized that it was a small puppy, alive and struggling. She caught a glimpse of its frightened eyes, maybe the saddest eyes she had ever seen, and thought it was looking at her, asking her to help. It panted amidst the rises and dips of the water; its heartbeats, loud and petrified, started knocking against their skins, scratching them with invisible paws.

The playground was almost deserted. Even the last bubble of the dream said goodbye and vanished. Now, with the next bell, the children could go to the toilets and wash themselves, and after that, straight to the mess hall. Those who wanted to take a shower first left the playground long before the bell rang. Two or three girls lingered for a little while, but after that they too ran off. One by one the neon lights came to life, bathing the playground and the green grass in yellow. The boy who was irritated with the bell, who didn't wish to leave the ground, threw the red Frisbee with such force that it flew out of the grounds. Shiva watched it flying, excited at the thought of getting his hands on it; he followed, in fact he ran, wanting to catch it before it fell. Aadi saw him going towards the gate, the children were not allowed to cross the boundaries, but Shiva was already out of the premises.

'Shiva, Shiva, come back!'

He might not have heard, for he flew like a Frisbee himself. The red Frisbee was there, underneath a lonely bench near the lake, lying on the lawn. It was already dark outside. A single mynah sat watchful over the bench, it was time it roosted. Shiva grabbed the Frisbee with great enthusiasm and flung it high with all his strength. Scared, the mynah shot upwards. The Frisbee cut through the air like a seabird, it even resembled the little aeroplanes that were exhibited during the Bangalore air shows, but later it surrendered to the subaqueous command, and invitingly landed on the silent rushes.

'Shiva, come back, it is late.' Now Aadi was outside the gates as well.

Somewhere in the darkness, somewhere near the lake, death warmed itself by the fire, waiting with an expression colder than that of the treacherous water. Shiva placed his left foot on the ice-cold surface of the water, balanced on the other foot, tried to stretch his arm as far as it would go. Now Aadi was running. He saw his brother kneeling; it seemed he would never reach him.

'Shiva, please.'

Voice became breath; a faint smudge in the air. Aadi realized that his voice was not forming, not taking shape or dimensions, yet Shiva heard him, and he turned his head and tried to hush him. Aadi thought his sudden appearance might frighten his brother but the composure Shiva maintained unnerved Aadi, and once again he searched for the proper words to call him back. Now Aadi reached near the concrete bench, he slowed down a bit, in fact, he was out of breath. For a while, he stayed where he was, just at the foot of the concrete bench, holding on to it, trying to raise his voice again.

The depth was widening, brushing aside the water hyacinths, its crystal eyes opened and saw the boy kneeling down. Over the flowers, the moonlight cast patterns and now it was no longer a lake but a fantasy, the Frisbee seemed so near, the one towards which Shiva walked. He floundered, the ground underneath was moving, the rhythm of the outer world was suddenly changing, and Shiva thought he couldn't hold on. Now Aadi was crying loudly, even though he didn't move an inch from where he was standing. He thought he saw his brother dissolving on the membrane of the water.

'What could I have done?' Madhavan looked at Kamala. 'You saw how strong the current was. Even if I managed to get down it would not have survived. Sometimes we call this fate.'

Leaving the puppy to its fate, Kamala rushed towards the car. Maybe to alleviate the tension, Madhavan turned on the music. Indistinguishable from the sorrows within, the voice of Narayana Swami echoed faintly.

Sokamenikkyu mathram . . . sumukhi . . . tharuvathenthe . . .
Why give the sorrows to me alone, O most beautiful woman

She thought he was reminding her of the artificiality of life, that it was a pain travelling with him. It was far better confined within the house, no questions, and hence no need for answers. They were like co-passengers, or rather strangers, in the waiting lounge of the airport.

'Your flight is in the morning, right?'

'Yes.'

'You must be planning to sleep here somewhere.'

'Yes.'

But their flight didn't arrive in the morning, or in the mornings that followed, sometimes they repeated these questions mechanically, sometimes they behaved as if they were total strangers, sometimes a little bit cordially: 'What would you like to have for breakfast?'

'Anything but bread and butter.'

Kamala removed the black sunscreens from the windows and looked outside. Laughing idols, countless effigies with their hands held up as if to bless the passers-by, lined the banks of the Cauvery and spread the toxins of their painted bodies in the water. Some of the gods were floating on the surface of the water. The car sped past. It began to rain, suddenly. The torrents cleaned the mud, thick on the still-sticky paint. By the end of next week, she thought, everything would be back to normal, the floating gods and her abandoned life. The fiery gulmohar flowers, now drenched in rain, formed liquid patterns of red on the stone pavements, like pastel colours in excess of water. The sky, which was still not clear, welcomed them to the traffic jams of Bangalore; how long, how long, each vehicle honked. Only minds were allowed to race in Bangalore on the roads, behind the wheel, in front of the signal lights and mocking queues. Wrinkled whores tapped on their thighs, bit their lower lips, and outlined the darkness irrevocably.

The windscreen wipers sharpened the vision and both of them saw the yellow lights and flashing torches from a distance. A splash of water blotted out the vision and he had to increase the speed of the wiper. Once again, they saw clearly the searchlights and torchlights and the way people moved around the lake.

They sensed trouble, a bad sign, the smell of fear mingled with the strong smell of dampness. She was frightened, she thought, she should not go there, she wanted to see her children at the earliest.

'What is happening at the lake?' she asked.

'I don't know, maybe someone is drowning,' he said.

The puppy was still there, she saw it again; she thought, it was drowning again, maybe it would be that way forever. Fear choked the insides of her throat; she said she wanted to throw up. It is the drive, he said. He parked his car between two magnolia trees. A few moments from now, the couple would lose what they had wished to hold close to their bosom throughout their joyless marital years. After long and wearisome years of abandoned disorder, they were finally going to be completely disoriented. Fear filtered down his spine when he saw Aadi sitting in the middle of the crowd, his eyes fixed on the stillness of the water. The warden, from whose face colour was leaching away, looked totally unnerved and desolate, yet he was arguing with someone, shouting at someone else. It was evident that he was gripped by anxiety, that he could not answer even a single question, instead he howled at people in an uncertain dialect, racked with guilt. Voices droned like bees on a funeral night.

'Where is Shiva?' Madhavan yelled.

Fear was frozen inside Kamala—she could neither walk nor move. She saw Aadi; she told herself that it was her son Aadi and pretended happiness at the sight of him. She realized that his twin brother Shiva was not there; he is taking a shower, she told herself.

'Where, where is Shiva?' Madhavan was now shaking Aadi. But the child did not respond. She said, 'Madhu, don't shake him so hard, he's a child.' From a distance she tried to console her son, she even tried to sing a song to him—he whose eyes were crystals by then, looking bluntly at nothing.

The lake water was half frozen, for it was a December night in Bangalore, and the water was burning with cold. From behind the magnolia trees they heard sirens and saw an ambulance approaching. Madhavan shuddered at the sight of the ambulance with its penetrating cry.

'Where is Shiva?'

'There is nothing to worry about Mr Madhavan, Shiva is safe. The doctor said he will be all right soon. But . . .'

The man pointed a finger at Aadi. 'There is no need to tell you how twins behave when one of them is hurt. All of us were busy rescuing Shiva. It was only after he had been carried away to the hospital that we noticed Aadi sitting there. We tried our best to convince him; we thought it would be dangerous to forcibly move him from here. We were waiting for the ambulance. You know twins . . .'

Twins! Aadishivam! Like a reed in the wind Madhavan stumbled towards his son, sat beside him at the foot of the empty concrete bench.

'Enough, enough, enough, my child, come, let us go to Shiva.' He lifted him in his arms and carried him towards Kamala. Fear trailed behind them, leaving them no hope. Inside the ambulance Kamala lay prostrate on the floor, unwilling to sit or lie down on the seat. Aadi's lips trembled and he asked in a soft whisper, 'Where? Where is Shiva? Where is he?'

14

Be notorious, be wanted, plunge into the darkness, the red region,
you got to go beyond, beyond you.

It'd been years on a bed, camouflaged amidst crumpled cotton
sheets, like a thick blanket of human flesh, blood, veins and every
other thing within the skin; mucus, spittle, faeces, urine and
semen at fissures. There was a remote control in his hands nearly
all the time, his fingers tight around its waist. Sometimes he spoke
the language of an automaton; sometimes he answered his own
questions.

Speed!

The uncontrollable race of vehicles, countless people crashed
on the pavements, the prairies, on every possible spot of nature's
benevolence, spurting the red fountain of human liquid. He had
killed people; he loved killing them, listening to their shrieking
moans mixed with the deafening roars of speed. Sometimes Aadi
came and sat beside him, watching his massacre rituals in the
morning; it was he who brought him his bed coffee and morning
biscuits.

He liked having Aadi near him, someone to witness his
triumphs, the unconquerable, insatiable desires of a beast, the
concentration of a champion, the magical movements of his

fingers on the controller, and above all, the kindness of a strong man who let a weakling watch him win.

This was not a room, what you saw mounted on the wall was not a 42-inch LED, the black box on the left of the table was not a PlayStation, and the one on the right was not an Xbox. To be precise, primarily, this was a kill zone where Shiva the ninja vanquished evil. At times, Aadi had proved to be a useful observer; the soundtracks and the electronic dance music are a bit strange to his tranquil ears though.

There was one particular bit of music, of rhythm, Aadi thought he liked, though he was not very sure. He had no idea that the voice was actually speaking English. His mind danced to the beats, while his brother, now a reluctant victim, battled with nature, firing at fields of grass. The fiercer the fire, the thicker the weeds, but Shiva was born to be an annihilator, the cosmic dancer.

When Aadi asked him about the music, he became outraged and said scornfully that it was humiliating to have dubstep play while he was hunting and massacring. He said such awful things happened around us because God had abandoned the human race.

But back in his room Aadi searched for more music on the Internet, and this time he understood the language. Later, while they were having tea, he reflected on the meaning of some of the lyrics. In one of those songs there was a mother who brought her son up like a crazy dog and let him wander through the streets in a mad rush. But her son went on saying how he loved this life. Aadi wanted to cry for a while after the tea.

Shiva was about to fall asleep but then he heard the click of a door shutting upstairs and the perfume touched his sinews, his joints ached. Anointed with Opium, she descended the stairs; it was a Thursday afternoon. Maybe it was the exhaustion of the hot afternoon, or maybe it was the expectation of the unknown, he was not feeling well—he tossed and turned in bed. From where he lay on the bed he could see a cluster of crystal hangings shining unsteadily against the backdrop of a painting. In the picture, Venus, the goddess of love, was seducing Cupid with a kiss; while his arms wrapped around her body in search of her creamy mountains, she was reaching to steal an arrow from his quiver. There was one more artwork on the wall, one that Shaly said was a very famous painting called *The Stolen Kiss* by a renowned artist, an exquisitely preserved moment in time. The rays reflected from the crystals fell directly on the naked breasts of Venus and on the delicate drapery of the other woman's fabric. Each time the light flickered, it seemed to him that the breasts swayed and the fabric ruffled. On each glimpse, he felt himself aroused. He had access to the Internet, he had visited porn sites, but this was something different, something permanent, like a wife one had till one died. It had been there on the walls right from the first days he remembered. Venus, with her apple-sized breasts and plump hips, and the other woman, with her elegant curves, her arms, her neck, her slightly opened mouth—these two women had been a part of his life; on the conscious level from the first day he touched his sex with purpose, on the unconscious level when the world thought he was a child.

Suddenly, Shaly came to his room. At some point, the bed sheet was tented, and he felt ashamed. She was asking him something, but he could understand neither the tone nor the voice; he looked at her blankly, he thought he smiled. She noticed the unease on his face and thought something was wrong with him. She touched his forehead, asking in a hushed voice, 'Are you all right?' He held her hands against his chest and nodded yes and she noticed the irregularity in the way his heart was beating. She sensed something forbidden; she asked herself, 'But what is forbidden?' She truly had no idea whether a bedridden infant whose flesh grew over time was forbidden or not. She embraced him, brushing the softness of her breasts against him and kissed him on the forehead, on his cheeks.

'Can I bring your wheelchair? Can we go out for a while?' she asked sweetly. But he didn't answer her. At a certain point she realized with pain that his fingers were grazing her nipples. She didn't protest. Like a suckling, he felt secure in her embrace. For some creatures on earth, touch is a fundamental necessity.

People are born selfish, thought Shaly. Me, myself and I, and everything always predominantly me, predominantly mine. All the good things have to be taught; share your food, don't speak obscenities, no fighting, no quarrelling. Bad things flow, like a natural spring or a fountain or an avalanche through the veins.

Who was it that drew this bloody fucking fine line between dos and don'ts?

Fear!

Basically, people are cowards. Their egos are rooted in duality, thus mankind created texts and subtexts.

Shaly had no pretexts, no definitive columns for dos and don'ts, no remains or corpses of additions, subtractions and multiplications, no rights, no wrong; above all, she believed, she was good. At times, she found herself confused, her senses muddled, and it was Mimi who answered her confusions, the girl from Mizoram, not more than fourteen or fifteen years old at the time. Mimi said nothing was forbidden, nothing impermissible. She said they tried to block her, that what they feared was her naked body. Nakedness was no sin, but the fear of it was the root of all evil.

Years ago, when Shaly was just a girl of eight, she used to get upset over her kinky curls; she wanted long, silky, straight hair, just like the kind she saw in films. Rita Mama reassured her, 'Such lovely hair you have, you should be thankful!'

True, very true, compared to Rita Mama's wiry unkempt hair, which was greying at places, Shaly's hair looked attractive, but that was not what she thought of. It was those girls, the very sexy girls of Mizoram who took your breath away, their long, silky hair that would never get tangled, never lose its shine. They were like dolls with delicate yet firm silk threads hanging from their scalps; silk ribbons of happiness in the wind. Shaly couldn't take her eyes off these wonderful, wonderful creatures of the forest. But things change, and one day Shaly stopped admiring their beauty. In fact, once she stopped looking at it, the feminine charm of the forest of her hair began frightening her. The chapter was both relevant and reflective in Shaly's journey as a young woman, for which, later on, she was grateful. It all started with Mimi. It all ended with Mimi. She had a jet-black, lustrous abundance behind her which could in no way be described simply as 'hair'; it seemed night itself trailed after her, sometimes darker than the darkest night, in the daylight, under the yellow sun.

It was an ordinary afternoon, simple and unsophisticated. In the kitchen Rita Mama prepared meat in ginger–garlic sauce, she said it was their Sunday special. But Andrews Papa didn't eat his lunch, he seemed excessively agitated, he said he had to do something urgent and left. They saw him walking down the hillside, they heard him curse at God knows whom. After lunch Rita Mama went to sleep as usual on the floor mat in the entrance hall and Shaly found her playthings in a corner of the same hall. A little later, Shaly heard a din outside, some sort of commotion. She wanted to go out and see what was happening. 'It's probably some vendors honking or some crazy people,' said Rita Mama, half asleep. Shaly was decisive, she was about to open the door when she heard a distinct shriek of pain. She looked at Rita Mama who was lying on the floor mat with her eyes tightly closed. She opened the door and heard a woman cry, the sound was now very clear but there was no one around. Shaly stepped out of the house and walked in the direction of the cry. She saw Mimi in the distance and was about to wave her hands and say 'hi', when she realized that Mimi was not alone, and not in good shape. She was being dragged by four or five men who were shouting obscenities and beating her hard. Shaly felt her head spin, she wanted to call Rita Mama. Just as she opened her mouth a massive hand pressed on it, stopping her words with such force that Shaly thought she was about to be strangled. Screaming with no audible sounds she turned her head and saw Rita Mama standing behind her. Rita Mama's face looked pallid as if she were watching an apparition, she asked Shaly not to raise her voice or move. Shaly had heard her express her fear about this land as foreign and its people as savages. She thought she didn't want to frighten her more.

They were dragging Mimi to Andrews Papa's school building. Something must be done. Stagnation suffocated Shaly. She picked up pebbles and took aim but Rita Mama boxed her ears so hard that she had to let them fall. This is how one becomes mute, thought Shaly, to survive was to rebel, but this was no time for a rebellion. The girl was going to get killed; Rita Mama feared that they too would be killed if they dared to open their mouths. Her dread tightened its grip over Shaly's mouth; the rough skin of her fingers abraded Shaly's delicate lips, and in turn, Shaly's teeth cut through her swollen fingers.

But the men didn't pay attention to Shaly or Rita. For a second, Shaly thought the men had seen them but they behaved as if the two of them didn't exist. They were focused on Mimi; just her. Each of them was twice her size; they tied her to a pillar, called her names and spat on her face. Shaly saw Mimi combating their moves with sudden jerks of her body, which now resembled a trunk with the movable parts all tied up. But suddenly one of them pulled a knife out of his pocket and jeered; Shaly thought that was the end.

'Whore! We will make you bald as a boiled egg,' they shouted, exhibiting their brute craving to kill. 'Whore! You dirty whore!' The youngest of the men grabbed her hair and pulled it forcefully towards his face. A pathetic and dehumanizing pain combined with revulsion tightened around the girl's face; her features twisted, her eyes bulged, the muscles of her face contorted. Rita Mama tightened her hold on Shaly, both of them petrified into stillness by then, trying hard not to breathe a word aloud. The knife whipped the air above, its gleam vivid in the afternoon light. The next second, to her disbelief, Shaly saw them cutting Mimi's hair from the roots, the long, silky threads of a European doll. Like coiled black snakes, locks of hair slid down shoulders marked with tears. Shaly looked at Rita. Perhaps, she thought, Mama was praying.

In no time, they had shaved her head, leaving ridiculous tufts here and there, making her face look grotesque and bruised, all the while repeating, 'Whore! Prostitution is a sin.' In a very feeble voice Mimi retorted, 'You are sinners, not me.'

They slapped her hard on the face; her lips split, bled. At last they set the little prostitute free, tears staining her cheeks, the fire still ablaze in her eyes. When they finally left her, she sat on the floor for a while, ran her hands over her scalp, now hairless. She cried for some time, and though tears didn't flow down, it was clear she was crying. She gathered the rolls of hair now surfing the floor and tried to put them back where they had once been. The smooth surface didn't hold. She saw the men descending the hills with their knife still whipping high in the air.

'Bastards!' she shouted.

She cut a very sorry figure, thought Shaly, her almost bald head with little bunches of hair here and there resembled the tufts of grass Shaly sketched using crayons. Mimi didn't seem to notice Shaly and Rita, though she saw them as she climbed down the hill. She muttered, 'How beautiful my hair was, long and silky.' After Mimi had left the place, Shaly, still fearful, went to check the insides of the building. She had seen Mimi carrying her strands of hair, as if cradling a baby, but there on the floor, hanging in the air, long silk threads nevertheless crawled in vain. She sat on her haunches and surveyed the place; she took a handful of hair. She hadn't seen human hair as silky as this, nor experienced a greater sorrow. Flesh is sin—Rita Mama crossed herself.

The black threads of silk served as a reminder, to remind her that the body was no sin.

15

Slightly above the floor, the bedpan suspended in the air, tied to the middle of the bed and braced by two wooden poles, inviting assistance or a word of solace. He was not completely paralysed, he could sit on the bed, or move around in the house and the garden in his wheelchair, though not on his own. At first he used to walk with the help of a wearable walking system, supporting himself against the walls. But he would collapse on the ground every now and then. Each time he staggered, he got frightened, imagining that he would stumble and fall. Once he tried to walk towards the sit-out, where he liked to sit, watching the activity outside, on the roads, on the pavements, in the garden across the road. But he had hardly reached the entrance hall when he fell down. Their maid was on leave that day, and there was no one to call for help. He tried to get up, but that proved useless. He realized he had hurt himself, for there was blood. At first he had no idea where it was coming from, and then he felt a lacerating pain near his left temple. He touched to see where it was, and shuddered when he sensed his fingers were getting soaked. Nevertheless, he ran them over the deep cut, which he realized was over the left eyebrow. Blood was oozing, faster than his heartbeats, now dousing his eyelids, now wetting his lips. He felt the bitter, unkind taste of blood in his mouth; defenceless, he spat, white bubbles on top of red liquid. He felt frozen within: his hands refused to move, even his fingers. Swallowing the lumps of distress, he lay motionless in a pool of blood. At some point, the blood clotted, making it a little better. Aadi came home in the evening, tired and worn-out.

After that incident, he stopped walking on his own. Either Aadi or Shaly had to be beside him. Shaly was a relief to Kamala, who had recently cut short her visits to the children's room. She was thankful these days, she realized, failing miserably to grasp the meaning of happiness; she wanted to show that she was light-hearted, something they called being motherly, but it was not easy to convince her children. Even if they didn't ask her questions, it was difficult to bear their looks. Sometimes she wondered whether they were her own blood, the same children she'd delivered inside the hospital room—they had looked so different then, small, bundled up in white muslin. She remembered the delicate curves of their mouths, and the way they had yawned under the fullness of her bosom. She also remembered how once, when she was a teenager, her blue skirt with bright white flowers had yawned unnoticed.

One of her sons now grew in a bed, just like a favourite plant grows in a pot. In her childhood, she remembered, her mother had told her the story of two women, Kadru and Vinata, who raised their sons in pots. The women, her mother said, had to be patient, patient enough to tolerate any kind of delays. Both the women waited steadily for their eggs to hatch, they waited almost five hundred years. The pots in which they had put their eggs remained unmoved. They watched for a cry of birth, a stir. At last Kadru's eggs came to life: a thousand serpents. Overwhelmed by victory, she challenged Vinata, who was by then burning in a potion of jealousy. She was decisive, she couldn't wait any longer. After all, the five hundred years of waiting was a game, a competition, one ought to win, not lose. Green-eyed wrath must have filled her insides for she broke one of her eggs out of desperation. She was shocked to find a half-formed son, blood, veins, sinews not yet covered by skin, half the portion of the muscles missing. The son, bursting with the fury of heaven and hell, cursed his mother.

Vinata, the mother, became a slave of the other woman. A slave of the other woman!

Shiva's room sometimes reinforced the silence of the stillborn child, but at times it filled with the roar of killer guns. Kamala saw to it that the games reached his room the day they were released in stores. She was very particular about this; the games were like the substitute powders you feed babies sometimes. She was more worried than Shiva about the next edition release of Assassin's Creed. In fact, Shiva never worried about anything. He knew his mother would call the salesman at Music Park in advance. Sometimes, overcome by a sort of strange anxiety—in Shaly's words 'undefinable' and 'unpardonable'—and irritated by the never-ending muzak, Kamala shouted at the man, 'Don't you know how easy it is to download games these days? Everything is available online. But I insist on quality. That's the only reason I call you, and remember, this is not the only shop in town.'

Both of them knew it was not that easy to download a new game for free, unless and until it was for sale. In fact, neither of them had any real idea how these modern games worked, whether a disk was needed or software. He was a salesman at a music shop; his job was to sell the games. He asked her humbly, 'Madam, would you like to buy the new edition of Gran Turismo?'

'No, we have it, thank you.'

At times, even Shiva's doctor wondered at the exceptional skill and precision with which he managed the gadgets. And at those times, Kamala exhibited all the regular behaviour of a regular mother, 'See, my son has scored an S.' She kissed her son, and said to herself, 'My son is better than a thousand normal sons. He is exceptional, he is extraordinary.'

In the dead of the night, confined within the four walls, a black Bentley raced forth in infinite anger. In the turquoise waters, a ship wrecked by fire. Bombs rained from the ceiling; there was nothing to hold on to. He knew Aadi was sleeping in the next room with the weight of his head on the spine of his book, an empty coffee cup on the night table. In the morning he would see the spine marks on his cheek, and he would cry, 'Oh god! What have I done to my book?'

Crudely delighted by his fantasies getting pulverized, Shiva would lie in bed, thinking, he was born good. But once when Aadi was washing the smells that came of those fantasies from Shiva's underclothes, he said, 'We were born sick.' So sick their bones melted.

There was a girlfriend. Her name was Rhea.

'Is she a feminist?' Shiva asked.

'No, I don't think so, she is just a girl, a student,' Aadi answered.

In the room, Shiva has a glass fishbowl. It was a gift from Shaly. Inside it are three goldfish, some pebbles and a boy who pees nonstop. Watching him, one felt like peeing, just for the pleasure of it. The fish, orange-gold with sedative movements, Shaly said, were feminists. Regardless of whether they bite their lower lip, or whether they shake their ass, pay them respect, they might turn into terrorists, any time, any day.

Rhea had visited this room, two years ago, one fine day. At first, Shiva didn't find her particularly attractive or sexy. She was a small girl, but her perfume was rather strong. She gave him a present; it was wrapped up in glittering paper with pictures of Angry Birds on it. When he stretched out his hand to receive it, she said, 'Oh my God, both of you look just the same! The same eyes, the same lips, the same nose, even the hair is same! How do people make out who is who?'

Maybe that's the reason I'm in bed, thought Shiva and said light-heartedly, 'I am fatter than him, I eat a lot of chocolates. I don't walk much, and I put on weight that way.'

He opened the present with great care. Before he could see what was inside, she said, 'Home-made chocolates,' and laughed. He tasted one and said it was wonderful. She watched with rapture as it melted in his mouth—from the way she looked, one might think she was looking at his taste buds magnified a hundred times over. His first assessment was not correct. She was beautiful and smart, and he particularly liked the way she laughed. Some school rhymes girls used to sing on that old forsaken lawn came to his mind: *Morning bells are ringing, morning bells are ringing, ding ding dong.*

When Aadi went to the kitchen to prepare coffee, Rhea sat near Shiva's bed, on his wheelchair. She noticed the small box on the night table and asked him, 'What's inside that box?'

He said it was a key chain and added that it was of no use to him, and that she could have it if she liked. He asked her to open it. She held the small case and turned it over with her fingers for a while. She knew what she would find inside; she had seen such surprise boxes before. Sometimes when you opened them, you got a punch on your nose; sometimes there would be an ugly snake or a lizard or a spider or a frog that would pop out the second you opened the box—very commonplace games of boys. But she feigned ignorance and smiled as if she was expecting something wonderful inside. For a second, she remained silent, thinking she would give out a cry of alarm, or draw back in fear, shouting loudly, or she would just cry to make him happy. In a casual way, but of course cautiously, she opened the box. Inside it lay the soft feather of an African parrot.

That night, Shiva couldn't sleep. Her perfume was still strong in the room, lingering on everything she had touched. He played with those glittering Angry Birds for a while. He wanted to cut out each bird from the paper and stick them on the walls. He wished he had a pair of scissors. Rhea had the face of a little angel.

'Copycat,' the teacher had called him. They were in junior classes then, Aadi and Shiva. Shiva hated classrooms, notebooks, paper, pens, erasers and homework. He always copied what his brother had written. Once, the teacher boxed his ear, and once she spanked his bottom. 'One more time and you will find yourself in the detention room,' she said. All the kids were afraid of being abandoned there, at the mercy of the half-obscured science charts on the cold walls that exhibited parts of the human body cut open and the shuttered windows, with no other child to talk to, right under the nose of the verdigris-covered statue of the founder principal. Frightened, his anxiety not easy to mask, Shiva repeated his little crimes, his expertise sharpened. Now, he would like to tell his teacher about the permanent detention room in which he lives. Still, unwilling to hide a puzzling confusion, he asked: 'Aadi, have you ever kissed her?'

16

The walls of this house had witnessed his first kiss. It was a kiss with the vanilla flavour of love, and she was a girl who trembled for the sake of trembling. The clock struck the hour and, like Cinderella's manifesto, she said she had to go.

'I have to go.'

She threw the joystick on the bed and stood up, her lips now visibly trembling, her breath faster. She looked at her watch, the dials of which were studded with little diamonds, with a very thin gold strap. The game had not yet reached halfway. Shiva's face fell.

'Aadi, you take the control, let's finish this. Okay, Rhea, bye,' he immediately said, straight out.

'Wait, I will walk her to the bus station, it won't take long. Please,' Aadi said apologetically. He followed her to the entrance hall where she slipped on the floor mat. Aadi saw one of her glass slippers flying high in the artificial light leaving dappled shades on the floor. She gave a short cry, as if her ankle had twisted. He tried to help her up, his breath, his infantile smell, now on her lips; her trembling grew out of control. Kisses rewrite people as dreams. The next second she ran out of the room, leaving the scattered glass pieces behind.

The fragrance of ylang-ylang invigorated the night. The flowers hung from the branches like big fat spiders. On the windowpane, Aadi saw a small lizard. Its tiny limbs resembled those of a human embryo. It was trying to crawl, but the glass seemed slippery, it couldn't hold on; losing grip, it fell down. Aadi looked at Shiva, who was sleeping peacefully. Aadi closed his eyes.

He saw the room in which his grandmother had lain dying. In that house, darkness prevailed in each room, cut out to the size of matchboxes; one might suffocate under one's own breath. He tried to conjure up a picture of his brother in his wheelchair struggling to move through the blackness of the dilapidated corridors. What could Shiva do in such a place? Where were they going to arrange his electronic gadgets?

A penis, like a wounded snake, tried to raise its head and fell. Hunger, it was the night of hunger games. Something twisted in between a half-paralysed young body and an uncontrollable young mind. White Mountains! Dark Holes! Inside the dream, under the unconceivable hunger, the body rushed, forgetting its drowsy languor. Bed sheets crumpled. In the morning, Aadi scrubbed the pallid patches off Shiva's lilac sheets.

17

It was their last day in the house, all of them were busy. Books, clothes, memories, everything had to be packed carefully. No one talked much during dinner. Kamala couldn't sleep, though she felt weak within. She was afraid of the procession of bad trips. Nowadays trips happened without invitation, without even a touch of acid; the only thing that went without saying was that it was always very bad, even ugly at times. Nothing like the pageant of sumptuous breakfast crossing the ceiling in a Mansfield story. In my visions, thought Kamala, there is nothing worth inviting. She searched for the blister pack in the drawers, and took two antidepressant tablets with a glass of water. Tranquilizers are good for the bitter coldness of the night, though they leave you more depressed the following day. She looked at the fan—she wanted to concentrate on something, clockwise, or counterclockwise. She had heard that ballerinas could do multiple pirouettes with no signs of vertigo by fixing their gaze on a single spot for as long as they wanted, falling out of step the second it faltered. Attention, she thought, is a very important word. She tried to concentrate on her eyes reflected in the centre of the shining, spinning fan, but it was not as easy as she thought.

'Aren't you feeling sleepy?'

'How on earth do you expect me to sleep in this dungeon, Amma? Look at all this waste you have hoarded on the racks. I am afraid there will be some snakes or lizards somewhere in this crap. Amma, let me make this very clear, if you are not going to make some arrangements to clean this room I will go back to Bangalore.'

'I have asked Sankaran and his woman to come tomorrow; they will take care of everything.'

'Good for you.'

'Why do you behave like this, Kamala? Can't you at least consider that I am your mother?'

Kamala saw her mother crossing the threshold with difficulty. Amma was getting old; Kamala felt a teardrop at the back of her throat. It was a rather high threshold; Kamala had noticed that Amma had taken time to enter and turn the lights on. She didn't sleep much during the nights, Kamala could see. She must have taken at least half an hour to climb the stairs, as the top of the railings was too high for her to hold on to. Kamala knew Amma depended mainly on the long rope suspended from the ceiling to the foot of the stairs, fastened to the wall at regular intervals. Kamala sat on her bed, drenched in sweat, and fixed her eyes on the loft. Amma, worried about her daughter, thought she would sleep with her in the same room, and looked at Kamala sadly, unsure of her welcome. Her eyes still fixed on the loft, Kamala asked, 'Why do you keep all these things, Amma? What pleasure is there in hoarding dust and dying of asthma?'

'Just in case, dear, who knows what'll come handy when?'

Kamala took a deep breath. She was waiting for her eyes and her ears to get accustomed to the loft crammed with whatnot, cardboard boxes and plastic wrappers her mother had kept 'just in case'. She was sure there was something crawling over there, maybe a lizard, or something harmless, like a squirrel, but whatever it was, it was a pain right in the centre of her head.

'It's probably a squirrel; there are plenty of them in the mango groves. Better you keep the windows shut and sleep,' her mother said.

'So you want me to die of suffocation? I don't understand what we need a loft for. I am going to set this on fire.'

Sankaran and his woman came early the next day. Each and every cardboard box was burnt to cinders. But even after that, that very night, something crawled and hissed in her room. Kamala gave a shriek which her mother must have heard, for after half an hour, the poor woman arrived, breathing hard.

'I asked you to keep the windows closed,' her mother said.

'And I told you that I don't want to die of suffocation,' retorted Kamala, harshly.

'Don't forget this is the same house in which you lived all your life before your marriage.'

'No windows were closed before my marriage.'

'Do you behave in the same manner with your husband?'

'My husband? Do you mean Madhu? No, I am very gentle towards him. I have always been very good to him, right from my childhood. Neither you nor my uncle ever complained, right?'

She knew any kind of fight would enrage her mother even further. Amma will never believe, Kamala thought, that there is a snake inside this room. I am sure it is a snake, could be venomous too. Whatever it was, it had been there for a long time and the loft was its abode now. It must think of her as the intruder. Venomous creature, she hissed back. No answer came from above.

Each night, she jumped up in the middle of a dream, or a late-night thought. This had almost become a habit. Each new disappointment threw her back to her convictions: the presence of a snake in the house could not be denied. Sometimes, she looked at the ceiling and said, in a casual way, 'Dear roommate, respect the privacy of other people—well, I mean other creatures'. But then she realized that her baby was due in a month and she could not drag this out any further.

She believed something cold was looking at her secretly, but what she could not tell. If a squirrel or a lizard happened to come into the room, a hushed hissing was heard from above in acknowledgment. A hundred times Kamala made her bed, turned the hamper upside down, cleaned the drawers and discarded whatever she found useless. Nevertheless, the noises from the loft continued to wriggle in and out of her ears. What she needed in life were order, cleanliness, pure air, and all these in excess.

'There is a smell of wet earth under the bed,' she said. 'Clean it properly.'

Sankaran's woman, by then, was tired of cleaning and washing Kamala's room. 'It's my poverty, my starving children,' she cursed, each time she entered the room with a rag and a bucket of water.

At times, on the verge of madness, Kamala dreamed of two little snakes moving around her oversized belly, making purple blotches on her skin, filling the room with the mild smell of amniotic fluid whenever they opened their tiny mouths. Inside her veins, she thought, she sensed clotted venom. In the morning, inside the bathroom, when she rinsed her mouth, the smell of the previous night, of the open mouths of the little snakes frightened her.

'Slide down at once, Amma cannot wait any longer,' she ordered her yet-unborn babies.

She waited for the first cry of her baby, its sweet voice, but instead, she perceived a number of other sounds: squirrels jumping through the pepper vines, rats grinding inside earthen holes, cockroaches gnawing under solid wall bins or large containers, and even the rustle of wet bamboo leaves in the wind, at a distance. Each sound seemed more animated, its bass louder. She covered her ears with both hands, as if to block out every sensory, auditory stimulus from outside, but then she realized that she heard the sounds from within. They didn't stop, they grew out of proportion:

she thought she heard trees talking, the air whipping hard against the roof tiles, and above all, crickets crying non-stop.

'I think it is tinnitus. Let us consult a doctor when I come,' Madhavan said, over the phone.

He said it was a problem with her hearing, nothing to worry about as it was not a major issue. Later in the evening, he called again to ask if she had a whistling sound in the ears or a tinkling, or a ringing sound, as if he wanted to compare her answers to the information he had collected from the doctor. She said no, in fact, she said a vehement no, and the certainty of her voice calmed her. It was not tinkling or anything musical, it was not like the endless muzak that irritated one to the point of shouting. What she thought she had in her ears was the sort of hissing sound reptiles make. That night she dreamed that she had delivered two golden snakes; a coiled pressure lifted her breasts, purple mouths opened at her nipples, tails trailing down into her navel or down to the place from where they had emerged.

In the morning she opened her eyes in fear and shame. When the lights are not favourable, one cannot trust one's eyes. A strand of her own hair frightened her while she was brushing her teeth in the bathroom and her fears, now enormously increased, made her scream, 'Amma!'

'I don't think I can live here. I want to go back, you can also come with me,' she begged her mother.

Four workers came that morning, including Sankaran and his woman. They pulled the huge antique rosewood chest of drawers forcefully out of Kamala's room, its heavily decorated corners destroyed by tangled webs and termite mounds, the knobs and drawers coming off every other second; they had to stop several times to rest their muscles. They took one of the two chairs, difficult to lift or move, to the entrance hall, then removed the old curtains from the windows and likewise the knick-knacks, the old carafe and even the bookshelf loaded with books, bags, bottles and face creams. At first the room seemed almost drained, empty. While the workers opened and cleaned the windows, changed the sheets and the pillow cases, it looked bleak, a space deprived of the ghosts of antiquities.

Soon, the loft appeared immaculately polished, breathing out pristine air. That night Kamala slept peacefully, on newly washed and starched bedclothes.

They had cleaned the entire house that day, not just Kamala's room. They dragged out each and every object that had turned yellow and looked old and piled it in the kitchen yard where they set fire to the heap, time and again: things piled up, bulbs with broken filaments, dented steel glasses and copper vases, old clothes, papers, even the wrappers and the glittering cardboard packets Kamala had received on her wedding, the remnants of her broken life. Everything was in order, not just accumulated, though dusty and graced with spiderwebs, battered and filthy. But what Kamala said was true: Even her mother couldn't believe the dust and cobwebs accumulated in the yard on top of the junk. The plastic covers they kept separately in an even bigger cover—to accumulate or to sell, who knew—burdened their hearts.

Finally, at five-thirty in the afternoon, after removing the ashes and cleaning the place once again, they all went off. Their regular time being five, her mother had to pay them extra money for the extra half an hour they had worked. Kamala thought her mother looked distressed, and so she said, 'Keep a paper bag or jute bag in the kitchen shelf for shopping, not more than two.'

The following evening, Sankaran's woman burnt camphor and neem leaves in a big earthenware wok and kept it for a while in the rooms, particularly in Kamala's; the air instantly seemed purified and refreshed with the pleasant smell of camphor. A second pleasant night at home, thought Kamala, but around midnight she woke up with a contracting pain in her stomach and a spasm in her joints. She felt warm liquid on her thighs, and she couldn't get up, all of a sudden, or manage to call her mother for help. Somehow, holding fast to the edges of the bed, she got up and

94

walked unsteadily to the bathroom. She removed her underclothes and a big lump of blood, almost jelly-like, fell on the floor, like a piece of liver.

In her sleep, she heard Madhavan talking from the veranda outside her room: 'Twins, baby boys.'

Between the trippy wakefulness and sleep, Kamala dialled, and Madhavan answered.

'Madhu, tomorrow I am going home with the children. I don't think we'll be coming back again.' She didn't wait for a reply and she switched off her phone.

Kuljeet was upset over the late-night call. She turned on the lights and grabbed the phone from his hand and checked the number. In an instant Madhavan saw his phone flying in the air, crashing against the wall and landing on the floor, luckily in one piece as it was before, but with scintillating patterns running beautifully across its glass surface.

'That iPhone was my gift! If you want to call that whore, call from some other phone. Don't make her wet with my money. Why can't that slut just sleep after midnight?'

In fact, it was Madhavan who hadn't been sleeping, going crazy with his thoughts, feeling the heaviness of molten lead upon his eyelids and sick of living awake. How would he ever sleep again? His children were leaving. Living in the same city, somewhere near them, with the possibility of accidentally running into them at coffee shops, libraries, the grocer's or at the cinema was a blessing, though he felt heavy within. He felt sad thinking about Kamala. He knew it was his mistake; he was to blame.

Madhavan had known about her mother's demise. He thought she had already gone to the house, he wished he could join her, but he couldn't make it—Kuljeet wouldn't let him go and peace had to be maintained somehow. He remembered how Kuljeet had once informed him, 'I have heard that your ex-wife is on sensual drugs these days, I met her at a rave night ticket counter. That woman was also there.'

Perhaps, Madhavan thought, Shaly would be accompanying them.

18

'What's happening here? What the fucking hell?'

Shaly rushed to the bathroom the moment she saw Madhavan entering the bedroom and closed the door.

'Madhu . . . Madhu . . . I . . . Madhu . . .' Kamala's tongue felt numb, her words faltered.

Her face pallid with fatigue, she tried to cover herself with the bedcover, which was very heavy so she couldn't manage it properly. Madhavan snatched a piece of clothing lying on the floor and with a scornful expression, threw it over her naked body.

'Bitch!'

Inside the bathroom, Shaly rubbed her face and washed it many times. She rummaged in the shelf for a pack of cigarettes but there was none. She knew she had nothing else to do but wait, so she put the toilet seat down and sat on it. She could hear him shouting obscenities and smashing things, she had no idea what. He had left the previous night, saying he had a flight to catch, a conference to attend at the JW Marriott in Delhi and that he would return only after three days. What the heck had happened to him? Was it really he, she asked herself, who had sneaked into their room? She had had just a glimpse of him—he looked very much like the drunk on the other side of the road, dishevelled and ruined. It was time husbands were prevented from entering bedrooms without knocking. She heard him shout again, this time it sounded like a command, or rather a threat.

'No one is going to leave this bloody fucking room.'

Madhavan was roaring with rage. He destroyed everything destroyable. He threw the framed wedding photograph on the floor and set fire to it with his lighter. When the fire started to blaze, resembling the painting of an English autumn on the wall, he spat on it and tried to extinguish it by stomping on it.

'Come out, you slut!' He knocked violently on the door. 'Come out or I will come in. When the children come back from school, let them see their mother dead on her bed and a dirty hyena dead in the bathroom.'

'Madhavan, please leave!' Shaly said harshly.

'Aha, that's something at last. Whom do you think this house belongs to? Whom do you think that woman on the bed, drunk and unconscious, belongs to? You want me to leave, right? I am afraid, young lady, you have to answer me.'

'Enough, leave! I don't care a straw about ownership. I want to go.'

'Is that an insult, you slut?'

'Whatever. I told you I don't care, I want to leave and I want you to go first.'

'Don't try to act too smart, Shaly. I want you to be destroyed in the same destruction you've caused. Do you understand? Come out, plague on you, slut.'

The door opened and she came out, stark naked. He found himself speechless, he shuddered. She looked at him with fiery eyes.

'Plague . . . plague . . .' she muttered as if she had gone mad.

The nudity of an extremely beautiful woman frightened Madhavan. This unexpected manifestation of such a vision weakened his senses; he felt how imbecilic men were. This was an apparition; he had heard stories about gorgeous vampires who could suck the blood out of men like him. They chewed men like betel leaves, crushed and tasted their fluids—and finally spat their pallid flesh out, totally drained of body fluids, on the pavements. This woman, he thought, is a female vampire. And like a zombie already out of blood, he stood motionless, like a stillborn child. In front of his lifeless eyes, Shaly bent over the floor and picked up her clothes. She dressed and went outside, slamming the door on his face.

If doors remain closed in front of you, if someone asks you not to open them, don't try to open them with force; at the very least, ask what is happening inside the room that you should not know. Usually, people don't care, they don't bother to ask, and they don't wait for answers. Why did Madhavan lie about his Delhi conference? Why did he come back without informing Kamala? Why didn't he ring the calling bell? He deserved it. He had asked for this shock.

19

'Oh God, Rita Mama!'

'I'm coming,' Rita yelled. She was busy in the kitchen, uneasy as always, dragging her left foot—she had developed signs of rheumatism recently—and cursing everything that got on her nerves. She turned the flame down; the last thing she wanted on a Sunday morning was for the milk to boil over, spilling everywhere to make a dirty white puddle in the kitchen.

She walked to Shaly's room, followed by Andrews who had also woken up on hearing Shaly cry. When they entered her room they saw Shaly jumping on the bed, the bed sheets rolled up in her hand.

'Get down, you will break the bed,' said Rita.

'No, Mama, I felt something crawling on my knees while I was sleeping.'

Rita, who had quarrelled with Andrews the night before, looked at him with flaring anger. He understood the meaning of her look instantly. He was about to leave the room, when Shaly said, 'I woke up and I saw a black rat on the headrest. It was staring at me. I am afraid it has already bitten me.'

'There is nothing in this room; even if there was a rat it wouldn't be sitting on the headrest to watch the princess sleep. Do you understand?' Rita walked out of the room dragging her foot.

'I don't see what there is to get so excited about a cockroach or a rat? These girls!'

'I will get you a cat, don't you worry!' Andrews laughed and bent over to inspect under the bed. He also checked for cracks in the walls and the floor. Shaly sat on her bed, her legs stretching out; she rolled up her skirt and examined herself. There was a dark purple blotch just above her right knee.

'Look, look here, now you know I'm telling the truth!' Shaly said.

'I know, I know there might be rats, so let us be more careful,' Andrews said.

Andrews turned the lights off when he went out. Shaly was not sure if she could sleep again, but it was Sunday and there was nothing else to do.

At first, a single grove of bamboos flowered; it must have done so under the cover of the night. Then like a forest fire, spreading fast and furious, it started flowering everywhere on the hills, wherever there was a grove, turning Aizawl the colour of gold, announcing its impending death. Damn! Damn! Damn! People cursed in anxiety. Damn!

Rita was reflecting over the skirmish she had had with Andrews the previous night—just another episode from the long battle. The fight was always over the house they owned in their homeland, in a beautiful neighbourhood of simple people. It had been sixteen years since they had left the place. Rita always wanted to go back, and settle down in that lovely house, and live the way civilized people lived, talking their mother tongue, eating the rice of their choice, visiting friends and family, and living the life of a priest's wife. Andrews had given the house out on rent and now he was having trouble getting his tenants to leave. His brother-in-law was fighting the case for him, and though he had had to go three or four times to make the necessary arrangements, he hadn't taken

Rita with him, not even once. She hadn't seen her family since her wedding, after they settled in Aizawl. Andrews had finally won the case and the previous night, while he was having supper he had said, 'Now we can sell the house.'

Shaly marvelled at the speed with which the spatula flew from Rita Mama's hand in the kitchen and landed with a big thud in the porridge bowl in front of Andrews Papa. Even Rita was taken aback; she couldn't believe the force with which it happened.

Maybe a desire for the ancestral roots, maybe hatred for the forest? Andrews pondered over his wife's interest in that house where she had lived not more than seven or eight months. Then he said, 'God is great, no harm done,' and left the table without finishing his supper.

But on Sunday, when Rita returned from Mass and saw the flowered bamboos in the backyard, she forgot the skirmishes and called out proudly, 'Hey look! Even our bamboos have flowered.'

Andrews, who was watering the vegetable garden, was shocked to hear this. Fear was etched on his face. Half-asleep, Shaly came out of the house to see the bamboos in bloom.

In the forest, *mautam* had started its dance of death. Mautam means death of the bamboos. Inviting the rodents, luring them with the bittersweet smell of their fruit, the bamboo groves were getting ready for their final call. This, the forest knew, would be a magnificent spectacle, splendorous golden beauty to chill the bones, a dazzling vision—one unlikely to be forgotten. But after that, what would be left in that forest? The forest, it was sure, would soon be wreathed in the burnt-out smoke rising from the pyre. What was meant to happen would happen for sure.

Shaly parked her cycle on the roadside and lifted her eyes to the splendid benevolence of the golden bamboos. It was spectacular, more glorious than what she had imagined, in fact, her imagination came nowhere near. Bamboos were swaying in the wind, but with a speed that exceeded their usual rhythm. The strange scent of flowers made her uneasy, slightly nauseated, but still she couldn't take her eyes off the sight. Suddenly, her eyes caught something funny, something incredibly out of tune with the contours of the vision. 'Not the bamboo fruit,' she said to herself. They were there on almost all the clusters. 'Oh my God!' She squinted hard to see better and saw what resembled black balls of yarn hanging on the stems, or rather, wriggling along. It was not easy to get to the bamboos on her cycle, the ground was not even, and the loose stones could be treacherous. Nor could she risk leaving the cycle unattended—it might get stolen. She decided to walk. Cautiously she walked, rolling the cycle gently beside her, watchful not to step on the dog droppings. She knew some pigs must be moving around not so far away, and decided to face it. She felt that something was holding her back, some sort of uneasiness, a hollowness, making her break out in a cold sweat. She moved forward.

Now she could see the balls of yarn clearly. For a second, the day appeared like a pitch-black night at home: rats ran all over, scurrying down the entrance hall, the corridors, and the bedrooms, making purple blotches on the skin, and sitting on bedsteads. For a second, she saw herself inside a rat hole. She looked up. Each inflorescence carried three or four rats. Gripped by fear, she looked down, 'God, help!'

In the bamboo groves, on the ground, over the faded and yellow leaves and the bamboo rice falling down from the blossoms, rats ran amok, hundreds of them, all in a wild rush. When something cold moved around her feet, or rather, started to climb up, she looked down—was it fear creeping up, or a snake crawling over her to devour the rats? The ground beneath was packed with thousands of rats. Pitch-black! She saw their white, chisel-like incisors laughing at her; she thought they would run all over her, and forgot how to ride back home.

At first she tried to run while grabbing the handlebar, but then she left her cycle behind and took to her heels. Chaotically, she thought, the rats were more frightened than her, that they would be moving faster than her. In this gregarious flowering of the botanical enigma, rats, bamboo and humans were all caught on the wheel of suffering.

Though the old generation had experienced it before, though their nerves were still not free of psychosis, though they knew their paddy and crops would be eaten after the bamboo fruit, they hoped that mautam would never return; it would never happen again, it was an adolescent nightmare, people and rats running amok, famine and death ruling over them, digging holes for both human beings and rats. But, like pestilent birds, they came in large groups and attacked the *bhupui* vegetation. They needed something to gnaw at every other second, to keep their incisors from curling up, touching their hard palates, becoming useless. Peasants, with their children crying after them, ran for help, famine chasing them. It seemed the gods were playful or sleepy, watching people run as if in a video game. The *thai* harvest of the months of September and October had already been destroyed by wild boars, pushing the farmers into pits of despair. The smell of swine then marked the death of dreams; it had been hardly a month and now like dessert after a sumptuous meal came the rats. Were there any gods in the sky? Through the newspapers and television channels, the whole of India came to know, the whole of the world came to know, how the little black rats pirouetted through the jungles of Mizoram, to the rhythms of death.

Kamala was on her way back from her office. She strained to concentrate on the radio news aired by AIR Bangalore, to deviate her attention from the rumble of the motor roars around her. She was tired, as usual, after a busy day in the office, and she couldn't concentrate. She wanted to be immersed in a bathtub that was full to the brim, or float over the ancestral pond, dead and supine—either sleep or die.

The radio announced:

'The gregarious flowering of bamboo that takes place every forty-eight years has brought famine and death yet again to Mizoram, the only place on earth where history is intertwined with such an event. The hills are witnessing the phenomenon of bamboo flowering and the subsequent increase in the rat population, which has devastated the crops, resulting in famine. This also caused an outbreak of various pests, insects and other organisms. Guarding the fields for several nights, the farmers become exhausted and suffer from irreparable health issues. There is no food to buy and the external supply is not enough. The government and NGOs have attempted many remedial measures. In 1959, when the bamboo flowered, it brought with it famine, migration and twenty years of insurgency against India, finally leading to the creation of Mizoram in 1987. Now it is 2007, and once again . . .'

Kamala parked her car in the garage. She was late. Inside, she found her children sleeping in their room, and she heard her maid snoring, Madhavan was not home yet; these days he came only once or twice a week. Bamboo and rats were not her issues. Farmers were dying all over India. The newspapers said 'suicide', 'famine', 'debts', but it was clear that they were being massacred brutally by the policies of governments in some way or other. It had become everyday news, nothing remarkable, just something readers sighed over for two seconds.

On the table, Kamala checked the growth of the lucky feng shui bamboo in the glass vase. Well, it had grown some inches, though it was hardly noticeable. The vendor had said it would bring her abundance, prosperity. Wait and see, what the bamboo brings, she thought. After a quick shower, she went to her room where the weariness and boredom of the big double bed yawned at her, making a gruelling grinder turn restlessly in her head, a grave hope in her bosom. As she sank into the soft down pillows, she said to herself, 'Wait till the bamboos bring me someone.'

In the forest, plague showed its white incisors and laughed at people. In the nights, farmers waited with rat traps. What the government had given them in plenty was poison—not for them, for the rats. To give away, experiment with and exchange, poison was the best thing on earth.

They killed the rats that got caught at the end of their long trap poles and smashed their tiny heads to death, for the farmers were not just hungry but vengeful and rat was the only meat available— at times, the only food apart from the leftovers of what the rodents had eaten. The children of the farmers watched the massacre with rapturous energy, for they were hungry and their bones had started protruding from their skins recently. The children threaded roasted or fried rats onto large skewers and waited on their doorsteps or pavements to sell them, their now prominent ribs proud under their naked skin. The prospect of commerce gleamed in their eyes, and part of their childhood games lingered in their business as they wrapped up burnt meat in *mahur* leaves with professional expertise. The rhythm of hunger, the percussions of poverty and the cabaret of death waited their turn backstage.

'The wrath of gods,' said the old men and women who didn't die. They muttered in despair, 'It is the wrath of some god that cuts the roots of man's desires, his crops and his food. His wrath is raining over us in the form of rats. Black Death.' Sometimes, to their surprise, it also rained food packets and clothes from the skies; they looked with wonder at the spaceships in which the gods flew.

Youths turned into insurgent groups, schools were closed down; no offices, no entertainment, no food. Filthy and hopeless, they looked at each other. 'Something has to be done,' they chanted like a non-stop prayer. They were worried about their dear departed. People were dying like termite flies.

Rita couldn't believe how those wonderful blossoms had paved the way for death squares. Andrews too was at a loss. At one point he thought of abandoning the place, but later, as always he decided to stay back, to face the inevitable. They didn't open their doors and windows to the streets that reeked of death, they were frightened that they would catch the same disease. A cry or a wail always lingered in the air, and even the foliage gave off the smoke of death. Even in an emergency Rita was not willing to step out of the house. Shaly, on the other hand, was not ready to step in. She wanted to spend her time with the miserable people; she was not afraid of rats or death.

'Beware! You will die of plague, you rotten, disobedient girl!' Rita, poisoned by fear, warned Shaly every so often.

Each curse weighed heavily on Andrews's mind, he grew weak. He thought Shaly had the same beautiful face of Joseph, her father. 'Through my fault, through my fault, through my most grievous fault . . .' he whispered in his mind, looking at Shaly. 'This girl, this daughter, who was fated to be raised in this forest, has taught me life,' he said to himself. 'I have sinned through my own fault. I should have taken better care of this poor child.' He imagined Shaly going to church with her true mother in their Sunday finery, and sighed in distress—the course of events cannot be altered by the fantasies of the mind.

Death hid inside the houses, under the bed sheets, over the porridge pots. No piper at the gates of dawn came that way. People in distress set the bamboo groves on fire. They had been their means of livelihood some months back. The rats that devoured fire lay dead and flat among the half-burnt stalks, and children came running to search for flesh. The smell of death suffocated the patients waiting in the primary health centres and the single local hospital; they twisted and turned in their own faeces and urine. Collecting everything they could, people migrated down the hills, leaving their houses to the rats that multiplied. Church bells rang continuously; priests were busy praying for the dead and for those who remained. They asked the stricken multitude to trust in God, but people no longer believed in Him. They shouted at the church, they rebuked and retorted with an anger that was strange. It has always been like this. Plague was a big poison that made a beast out of a man—history had witnessed this, many times. People blamed each other; Jews, missionaries, foreigners, beggars and prostitutes were stoned to death. 'It is all happening because of them!' the masses shouted. 'They are the reason . . . Eliminate the reason!' People spent whatever was left on black magic. Missionaries, standing in the middle of the rats that rained from the heavens, shouted, 'Love your neighbour, like you love yourself.'

The man who had shaved Mimi's head was dead this morning; Mimi had climbed down the hills with her family the other day.

Shaly gave the children money, not because she was hungry or she wanted to help them, nor out of hatred and fear, but because she felt she was a part of the hills, like the other Mizos, or rather, she felt the hills were in her veins, a part of her. Death squares were frozen; no one bothered to shed tears any longer. If you lose your mother, you better be the one to weep, we have something else to do. They went to the forest in search of food and returned with the bitter frown lines of self-mockery. They should have been there crying beside the corpse of the poor woman.

When Shaly reached home, she placed the packet of mahur leaves on the table. She didn't say what it was or from where she had bought it. When Rita made black coffee and they all sat down to drink it, Shaly opened the packet. The coffee cup fell out of Andrews's grip while Rita looked at Shaly as if she had seen a ghost and made the sign of the cross.

That night, Andrews said to Rita, 'Get ready; it is time to return to our land.'

Rita couldn't believe what she had heard. 'Thank God! Thank the plague!' she said thoughtlessly. In fact she expressed her gratitude to all the rats and all the bamboo of the world; she forgot the dead children on the pavement, the dead cattle in the fields. Visibly, a smile, a halo spread around her. She remembered each and every house in the street, in the neighbourhood, the cross-shaped roads of her adolescence, her dreams, her roots.

'It's a good thing that I couldn't sell the house. Collect the keys from my brother-in-law. I want both of you to live in peace, do you understand, without making any problems for each other.'

'What do you mean by that? Aren't you coming?'

'No, I can't come. I can't leave my school, my mission.'

'In that case, we will not go anywhere either. Let us all rot in here.'

'I am afraid things are getting out of hand. Didn't you see what she brought home today? This isn't safe for Shaly any more. Please go.'

On a piece of paper he laid out a detailed plan for their journey, where to get down, how to travel and about the people they should meet once they reached. He said they were lucky as the railway was going to ban the migration of people in three days' time. He was not sure of the news, but he thought the sooner, the better. Both of them had bank accounts; he handed over their passbooks and other necessary papers to her.

'There is plenty of money, you will be thankful to this forest for this at least,' he sighed.

Rita couldn't control her sobs—she couldn't understand what was happening. In the train they sat like two abandoned, broken shadows. Leaving the death squares behind, the train sped forth.

Andrews could feel the thud of his heart when he said, 'O God, please save my child. She is the spitting image of her father, blessed with her mother's benevolent curves.'

Four or five black rodents dropped to the ground from the ceiling of the school building.

20

Like Kamala and Madhavan, Shaly couldn't sleep that night. Even their mattresses had been packed and taken away by the movers and packers. The house looked bleak and desolate. The spaces had lost their meaning; the dining room, where they used to sit around the table on their respective chairs, where they always had a jar of cookies on the top of the side table, was no longer a dining room. There was nothing in the house except the floor tiles and the bare walls and the bedrooms and the bathrooms. It hurt to see a kitchen without a gas stove, utensils and jars. Now she remembered how dear that refrigerator was, how, even when it had nothing inside it, she opened it many times a day, as if the opening itself had given her the pleasure of it. Just like the body, there should be something in a house to open and close. The vacant, empty spaces upset her. Why should I accompany them, she asked herself, what will be my role in such a house? What if I say outright that I am not going? Friends, Kamala used to say, would turn down everything in the last minute. If you go seeking help, most often money, they would say, 'If only you'd come just half an hour earlier' and that settled it.

I can't abandon Kamala, she thought, particularly in this condition. I have to fix her appointment with the doctor once again and make her undergo the treatments. I have responsibilities, in a way; I have responsibilities to the children too. I cannot let her go all by herself. The fire she is devouring now is the consequence of my mistakes.

There had been a huge peepal tree in front of their house in Aizawl. Rita Mama used to say that the tree was miles away from their home, back when they started the school. The school expanded in length, width and height faster than they had imagined. It took only four or five years for the school building to grow from having six rooms to eighteen. When Mimi had been attacked there were only seven rooms, that too in pathetic shape.

In no time the school was big enough to accommodate a lot of students, and teachers came from all parts of India in search of work. Keralites were, of course, given preference. The teachers came with their families, and they enrolled their children in the same school; their children in turn learned the language and the bamboo pole dance of the Mizos. They sang English songs in church, learned to walk on high, pointed heels and wear lipstick, some of the women even cut their hair short and some men, funny though they appeared, started wearing ties—they did everything that they were ashamed of doing in their motherland. The forest made them fashionable.

Andrews's small hut also broadened in no time. 'Good earth, bamboo, and fantastic masons,' Andrews would say, with pride. At first, when he had begun his life in the forest there was only a room and a kitchen and half a mud wall in between them. Gradually he built a room for Shaly, then added a dining area the next year and a hall at the entrance after that. Three more bedrooms were added to the main structure in the following years, with bathrooms both attached and separate. Andrews was the main mason, and did half the work himself. Rita prepared tea and boiled tapioca for the workers. For Shaly, it was like festival time, with lots of people around and work in progress. As the house expanded, the tree came nearer.

One day three workers came and said they had come to cut the tree down. When Shaly found out it was Andrews who had sent for the woodcutters, her face fell. Rita asked them to cut the cotton tree as well. Such a mess, she said. That tree had been her headache for a long time, with the cotton shreds always spreading around, her broom knew no rest.

The leaves scattered. Where is the broom?

The flowers fell down. Have you seen the broom?

Who is going to clean this mess? It is spreading fast, it is spreading everywhere.

Oh, don't walk beneath that tree, the seeds are heavy, they may fall on your head.

Shaly, do you hear me?

But Shaly had a secret liking for that tree. It reminded her of the Russian stories she had read as a child; seeing the cotton fly around, she imagined the tree rained snow around her house, on top of the school building, on the ground, everywhere—white, sweet balls of snow. She wanted apple trees, snow, gingerbread and an original Christmas tree. The cotton tree that Rita Mama had decided to cut down was the one and only substitute for all these dreams put together. The soft white shreds of cotton would suffocate her in her dreams hereafter, as if the crime were hers.

The cotton tree was history by half past eleven in the morning. Rita gave the woodcutters black coffee and tapioca cutlet. Now, it was the turn of the big fat tree. Shaly started crying. She had seen a bird's nest on top of that tree. Weeping, she said to Rita Mama, 'You are destroying the birdie's house to make your own house look more beautiful. You are bad.'

In the summer she had found two eggs on the flower bed beneath the mango tree, two exquisitely beautiful blue-green eggs. She had had no idea how and when they had fallen down. She took them in her hands and patted them gently. How smooth, soft and silky the shells were. She took the eggs inside the house to show Rita Mama. But Rita Mama, her face looking as if it had been pickled in vinegar, said that the eggs would never hatch; birds wouldn't care for what human beings had touched. When Andrews came in the evening, she asked, almost in tears, 'Is it true that all the things human beings touch turn bad?'

Andrews shuddered at her question. He shook his head and gave his shoulders a shake, it could be yes, and it could be no as well. She waited for the birds to fly away, and when she saw them leave, she placed the eggs inside the nests, cautiously. She was sure the birds had not seen her touching their eggs. The next morning, she saw a rattlesnake on the tree, its belly somewhat swollen.

In the night, two hatchlings came out of the broken shells. Their heads were bluish green in colour, but they had no feathers. Only then did she notice that the hatchlings still carried the shells on them. Hurriedly, without paying much attention, she smashed the shells. The hatchlings got crippled: they could neither fly nor walk, they crawled all over her. She cried aloud in her sleep.

'Wretched girl! Won't let other people sleep,' shouted Rita Mama.

Even after that sorrowful incident, many eggs hatched in the forest, on the trees in front of her house, and even on the top of the school building. A lot of birds flew away, some died, days and years passed by.

Was it two in the morning now? There was a light inside Kamala's room. Hadn't she slept still? How would she drive in the morning if she didn't sleep? Let me try to get some sleep, somehow. Shaly tried to close her eyes, but she saw neither sleep nor darkness. She imagined growing a beak like a woodpecker, pecking through the bark, stripping it down, into the darkest forest, tap, tap, tap, into the heart of Aizawl. The forest was a place of music, and that is where Shaly always wanted to go, to fly away like a Mexican lovebird. Rita Mama's changing roses must be sleeping now, she thought, who's there to guard her parrot green house at night? A woeful cry doubled up in the back of her throat. 'Hey girl, are you responsible?' someone asked. A woodpecker pecked vigorously on the trees. Someone was playing *khuangpui*, the big drum in the forest, and some teenager sang an old English song, imitating CSNY in his melancholic voice, '*Midnight, that old clock . . .*'

The woodpecker stopped for a while and listened, and a little later repeated after the boy, '*Midnight, that old clock . . .*'

21

The little holes, the acid designs on the bleach marks in the crotch of her panties, like a beehive, sometimes reminded her of the futility of living biologically. Love has the fragrance of henna flowers, the piquant, burning sensation of pepper buds. It makes one wet with happiness and leaves the eyes sore with desperation.

Body of a woman, white hills, wrote Neruda. Her aesthetic sense and longings developed with his words, the words of the poet. Every word, every single letter was in praise of woman, her curves, her apples, her magnificent fluids. No one ever praised a dick; there was not even a mention of the word 'phallus'. Even if someone had praised the little head in the colour of a pig's bottom, showing off occasionally with a miniature clit or some suggestive small opening, such writings were not available amongst the rude provincials she had grown up with. Pubic hair, she thought, belonged to women only; it had taken years to learn that men had such undergrowth too. The phallus remained a misunderstood idea in the mind, a word never materialized; a concept to impregnate wombs. 'Impregnated female bodies' would have been a much better phrase; 'womb' was not so sexy and a reminder of responsibilities, an overrated word. Poets, writers, writers of the Yellow Pages, they were all voluble on manipulating the female body—not a word on manipulating the male sex organ, the male anus. The world, she realized, was a strange concoction of lies. Men wrote about women; women wrote about women; men admired women; some women who followed the aesthetics of words, the tragic beauty of written matter, admired women. Like Madhavan, the first time she masturbated, she had imagined the flesh around the hips of a woman. And perhaps, in her own way, the flesh of her own newly rounded, softened chest. Thanks to porn, the children could never think of half-baked, obscured sex any more. Thanks to porn—not available in her adolescence—she grew up thinking sex was beautiful, that the body of a beautiful woman should be manipulated beautifully. Kamala was raised by love, by the sweetest thoughts of love. She was like Cupid, who, while sleeping among roses, was stung by a bee. The bee was a relative, not harmful, but a sting is a sting.

Among her friends, he was a hero, who with a single glance was capable of making female spaces wet. *Passionate love, Mannered love, Physical love, Vanity love,* she read as she waited leaning against the protruded roots of an old banyan tree outside campus, cursing him for being late for she was not allowed to travel on her own. While he, after his classes, went straight to the football ground, and sometimes forgot about her, the young woman sitting on the roots eating a mango or a banana in disgust. Funnily enough, he scolded her for his delay, and unbelievably, she expressed her apologies. Maybe it made them laugh now to think how absurd they were back then. It had taken them decades to understand why they grew up like that, him arrogant, and her, submissive. 'The families,' she said. 'The families,' he said.

One of those days, he started wandering around the rustic neighbourhood like a country cousin who considered physical pleasure an added comfort of Sunday afternoons. Soon the girls started talking about him as 'handsome Madhu', and only then did Kamala notice that he had grown to become what people called 'manly': his chest fuller, his waist narrower, his biceps compact, his features sharp, his torso covered in hair and a thin line stretching down temptingly towards his navel in a whisper, the innocence missing in all these features. Who is he, she asked herself, a homespun Greek god, the prince of some children's classic tales, or the Tirthankara of the history textbooks? It seemed even the hair in the centre of his chest would have the erotic scents of dreams, of mild acid. But she couldn't hear the voice within that said: *What pleasure to kiss, to be kissed.*

And Kamala asked herself why she didn't feel anything for any man, and she wondered why the girls were so crazy after him.

He climbed like a monkey to the topmost branches of the tree, and plucked *champak* blossoms for girls, and she was always the go-between. The perfumed flowers that grew in abundance in the courtyard of Kamala's house were just a token of love he threw to the girls who praised him through the concealed gleam of their eyes and hushed smiles.

'Do you really love any of these girls, Madhu?' she asked.

He looked at her as if she were saying something incomprehensible.

'You need not come to my college any more. I can't tolerate a cousin like you.'

'Thank god, Kamala darling! That's the one task I hate. Do you know how much time I waste on this? You are a grown woman, you can come home on your own. I will talk to your mother, and remember, if this works out, I will be grateful to you.'

'So you're saying you don't enjoy the company of my friends?'

'Don't talk as if I haven't seen girls in my life, or as if you are the only person who is going to college.'

'Of course not! You are also a college student, but pathetically, a men's college, where you starve for a whiff of perfume.'

'Wait and see what I have got in store for you. Today onwards you are going to be on your own. I don't care what your mother says about it, do you understand; don't expect anything from me any more.'

And that was how it was.

22

With a thick book in his hands, Aadi opened the doors to the wild rush of wind. He had had his shower early in the morning and his things were ready. But it was still dark outside; light was on the way, riding on the ticking of some old clock. The wind was strong, and pushing him a little to the side of the door, it rushed through the narrow path he opened for it, and the book in his hand fell down on its spine. The wind rushed through the leaves of the book like a robot scanning the pages, devouring the contents. He bent and picked up the book and read a few lines from the page the wind had opened for him.

As so he grew into his larger self,
Humanity framed his movements less and less;
A greater being saw a greater world

The wind was getting stronger; it knocked down everything in its way, papers on the wall-mounted table, burnt-out candle remains, and Kamala's driving gloves. It made little bits of paper fly in the empty entrance hall in circles, and outside the house, in the garden, he saw dust rise to the sky like tiny whirlpools, curtain plants and bougainvillea swaying in a frenzy. It really means a lot to abandon a house, he thought, it takes much courage. When he contemplated the mornings that were to come, he felt pained. He said to himself, 'Tomorrow, there will be a wind, similar, or almost the same, but we will not be here. The wind, where we are going to live, will have a different scent, entirely strange to our olfactory systems.' From the innards of the empty house he heard his mother's voice echoing, 'Let the winds slow down a bit, let us wait. Aadi, have you taken everything? Is there anything else . . . have you checked? Hey, where are you?'

'I am here, on the veranda,' he said.

She came out in a hurry, her face drawn and paler than usual, she looked really sick. She tried to take the book from his hands.

'No, Amma, let me keep this with me for the journey.'

'Reading inside a moving car is not good. Give it to me, I will keep it in my bag.'

'Not for reading, it is a gift from a friend.'

She stood silent for a while and cautiously watched his gestures. She saw nothing but the morning wind caught in his eyes.

'Which book is that?' she asked.

'*Savitri*,' he replied.

She went inside. She didn't ask which friend it was—it seemed she didn't want to know. People, each minute, are forced to leave behind something dear to them, it happens everywhere, not too much to cry about. Let him carry his book. Now the wind, with the strength of a gale, knocked down the packets of snacks she had placed on the table two seconds ago. The electricity went off; the house was engulfed in darkness. He felt he was growing wings like a butterfly, he also felt his wings were too soft, too fragile to resist the maddening rush.

'I think we had better wait till dawn.'

'Are you sure nothing's left upstairs?'

'Don't you worry, I have checked it twice.'

The incandescent white tube of the emergency lamp was throwing light and shadow patterns on the walls inside, the blown-up figures of kaleidoscopic images.

'Would you like to have one more tea before we go? I am going to make a cup of coffee for Shiva.'

'I would like to have some tea,' Aadi said, and it seemed the word itself invigorated his senses. He wished the wind would not abate and that they would be stuck. He wanted to sip from his teacup for a while, and watch the gusts of wind endlessly blowing outside his lovely apartment. Kamala came outside and sat on the veranda, sill watching him silently, wondering what he was thinking. When she saw him looking at her, a sudden unease fell over her features and she forced herself to ask a question: 'How is it? I mean, have you read that book?'

'No, Amma, I got this only last week.'

'Maybe we could make a trip to Auroville sometime. I think it is an eight- or nine-hour drive from our home, you would enjoy it. It is some sort of an experimental township, or rather a lonely planet—that's what the inhabitants call it, a place dedicated to peace alone.' This offer was nothing new, but every time, at the last hour, it got cancelled; when it came to managing Shiva, they would stumble on the practical difficulties.

'Ha ha, ho ho, what wind is this? We need ballast before we fly away!' Shaly brought the tea, no tray, no biscuits. Aadi looked at the dented old steel glasses with a frown on his brow.

'No need to give me looks, dear, your mother has packed away everything that was in good shape in this house. I dug out these glasses from the abandoned heap and washed them clean so you can enjoy your tea in peace.'

'Shaly, we should take him to Auroville once. But let him finish reading *Savitri* first.'

'That's great. Auroville is a very good idea, and Puducherry is amazing. You'd love the place, even the breeze has the scent of Bacardi Breezers.'

'I am taking my children, not going for a booze party. Grow up, please!'

'Oh God, I was just kidding. Can't you take a joke? I don't think it's a picnic place, children might get bored there. Goa and Pondy and the like are meant for booze bums, not for kids, and above all it is very hot, you get the sun straight on your face.' She went on explaining for a while. She didn't ask or say what did all that matter to Kamala who had lived a life of her choice, didn't say that her son, no longer a small boy, should do whatever he likes, let him fly away.

Kamala felt unease, as if memories of her adolescence were mocking her; her mother begging her not to go, and she nevertheless going out, bringing unbearable pain to her mother's face. Words kept flowing from her mother's mouth, and she thought she saw a piece of white cloth, exactly like the ones with which her mother used to blindfold Kamala when they played together. The situation grew tense, and Shaly was tangibly disappointed with the look on Kamala's face.

Aadi felt compelled to ask something. 'Have you been to Matri Mandir?'

'Do you mean the golden egg?' said Kamala.

'How do you know all these things?' said Shaly.

'The Internet! I would love to go there. The place looks perfect, and I want to travel,' Aadi said.

Travel, a beautiful concept. All travels need not be beautiful, though it was a word capable of abolishing the ruinous energy harboured within, and refilling wonders, surprises, tastes, love and the pleasure of listening to someone speak at an evening supper. *Every man carries within himself his natural dose of opium, ceaselessly secreted and renewed, and, from birth to death, how many hours can we reckon of positive pleasure, of successful and decided action?* If possible, let your arms swing at ease—travel light, like the monks say; heavy baggage will drag you back, you will lose your interest in moving forward, you will feel each step weighing upon the earth and the earth weighing upon your shoulders. Touch the universe, be a part of it, realize the universe within. Aadi wished he could travel, but with Shiva in the background, travel seemed a distant possibility. All teenagers do not live in soothing, green shade. Aadi stood beneath a liquefied yellow sun, green shade merely a desire.

The wind abated a little. Dawn appeared among the branches.

'Aadi, finish your tea quickly and go and check once again if you've left anything,' said Kamala.

'That's right, Aadi, hurry. Why waste time chatting?' remarked Shaly.

In the bedroom, Shiva had finished his coffee. He was ready, and a bit anxious about the journey. Aadi helped him into his chair and wheeled him to the entrance.

'It is very windy outside, isn't it?' Shiva asked.

'Yes,' said Aadi.

This was an old house, the garden was older still. Once again Kamala went through abandoned rooms and voids and came out and locked the house. She straightened the flower pot the wind had knocked over and put the key inside it. Now this key, the lock, the door and what lay beyond it belonged to the owner, and he would come and collect it as directed.

Tears welled up in Shiva's eyes, and Aadi gripped his shoulders gently as if to say, 'Don't worry, baby, we will get you a new one.'

'Now, just walk, keep walking,' said Kamala.

'Do you need help?' Aadi asked Shaly, who was trying to lift a heavy black American Tourister. Aadi trailed after Kamala, wheeling Shiva's wheelchair. Shaly was the last to step out of that beloved house, for she was in charge of the baggage. She didn't let Aadi or Kamala carry the bags. She felt, once again, that she was waving goodbye to the forest in the hills. Each failure is a fall from the woods to the glade. She felt like crying aloud, as she had not cried before. How beautiful Kamala had been once—she was her own woman, like green woods and blue sea, like a clear stream of water. She lifted her face and looked upstairs, to her room, the window of which was open. She saw a woman there, the ghost of her shadows, who was spying on her, spying on each of them who was abandoning her and moving towards the car. She remembered clearly, how tense Kamala had been once.

'No, Shaly, I don't want to,' Kamala had said. 'I am not free like you, I have responsibilities, I am responsible for the two souls I brought on earth. They need me and I need them.'

'I thought this would lighten your mood swings. But if you don't feel like taking it, then it's okay, I won't force you. I thought I would give you a taste of life. There is nothing wrong in getting some happiness free of cost.'

'I understand, but I am afraid I don't need surplus happiness.'

'All right, all right, but that sentiment, that of the two souls and responsibilities, that sounds a bit outdated.'

Shaly pulled the bags and walked behind them. Mother and sons slid along like snails. Who am I to them? What do they think of me? A web of sadness linked the three of them, yet somehow she was there too, trapped, even though she was there of her own free will. But she was invisible, someone who didn't touch even a single strand of the web, not even the thinnest. She sat on their sofa, slept wrapped up in their quilts, operated their remote controls, opened their fridge, heated things in the oven and used their toilets, electric bulbs, floor mats. Even if she ran naked among them, they would not notice her presence, would not acknowledge anything that belonged to her. Happiness lay shrouded and shuttered between them, they were afraid to laugh aloud, they were not sure of anything, not even themselves. However hard they tried they couldn't lift the shroud that was heavy and brocaded in a strange fashion, they couldn't unveil the corpse of happiness—day after day, almost on an hourly basis, its heaviness increased. If only people were willing to sit around a table, face-to-face, and talk. If only they were willing to argue before taking decisions, if only people were a little less complicated.

Aadi and Shaly helped Shiva into the back seat.

'I know you are tired. Can I drive?'

'Hey, no. I am perfectly all right. I may get really tired if I just sit idly.'

When Shaly asked her again Kamala looked at her harshly. They all knew she didn't like someone else behind the wheel, even if it was Shaly.

But Aadi knew how important it was for her to get the Michelin down the road on her own.

23

Rhea had left Bangalore much before Aadi. Last year.

Aadi remembered how kisses rained down like leaves from deciduous trees, how in the heat of summer, under the blazing sun, mayflowers blossomed in a line, like a forest caught on red fire; how, windswept, he got carried away like a butterfly, leaving Shiva behind on his bed. He was just a teenager then, a tender boy. And maybe that was the reason he cried all night when she left him. Why he cut his arm—a long gash—dipped his finger in the blood and wrote love letters on sheets of handmade paper. That ink, to this date, remains and should be branded as the lovesick teenager's favourite. People should not treat it as trivial, because it is not; the butterfly has to go through many stages to reach its glory. When the ink dried on the paper, he smelled it, and the scent cut tragic paths through his olfactory senses, forcing him to write more. He thought the dried-up letters were heavier, and thus slowly, very slowly, his mind became calmer.

But he continued chiselling out love letters or her name or the age-old happiness of his name plus her name is equal to love on the bark of trees or on the river banks.

'So you are the one.'

He turned his head to see who it was. It was the senior disciple Anuraktha, the one in charge of the PUC.

'Do trees get hurt, Aadi?' he asked.

A whiff of sap from the freshly cut wound of the trunk filled his nostrils; his fingers, he realized, had the same smell. Like a child who has made a grave error, he looked uncertainly at Anuraktha.

'Our tools should be sharp, be it pen, a chisel or a scythe, or even a stone. But we should leave the decision of when and where to use them to our consciousness.' Anuraktha embraced him and asked, 'Which section were you in, in the morning?'

'I was in the perfumery,' said Aadi.

'Good. Is this your leisure time?'

'Yes, it is.'

'Do you play drums?'

'No, I don't.'

'Guitar?'

'No, I like to listen to music.'

'Music demands a lot of patience, it is work and passion on a daily basis and time plays a key role. Okay, now tell me, what are you really interested in?'

'I . . .' he hesitated for some seconds and said, 'I would like to write poems.'

'That's really great, come with me.'

Aadi followed Anuraktha, like an infant follows its mother. When he noticed that Anuraktha had no sandals on he decided to tread as softly as he could, and on reaching the building he took off his Nike shoes. He walked barefoot on the long veranda that led to a Dutch staircase. The walls on either side had photographs of the Divine Mother, adorned with red hibiscus and white plumerias. The floorboards creaked as they stepped on them. The staircase led to another long corridor that ended at a very big closed door.

Anuraktha pushed the door open. Except for the very tangible beam of light that filtered through the single glass tile on the ceiling, it was dark inside. A piece of sky was clearly visible above the glass tile. Aadi turned back to look at Anuraktha, but he was not there. He heard some pigeons cooing, the Dutch stairs creaking, someone descending—maybe it was him. Aadi searched on the walls for switches, and he opened the windows and drew the blinds to let in more light. The room was exceptionally big with high ceilings and Victorian model ceiling fans, which had wider, longer blades. He saw the stacks of bookshelves that reached up to the ceiling, the sunlit library seats and tables, the stepladder and the silence. He flipped on some of the switches and a few of the fans whirred, breaking the silence. A light came on in the corner. There was enough light so he didn't bother to search for more. He remembered that in one of Rhea's notebooks the words 'A library card is your key to the world,' were written in golden letters. He looked at the stacks and saw his passport, visa, and travel tickets and smiled; there was even an invitation to the lounge, to the sumptuous display. He walked towards one of those shelves. He had no idea what to look for—poems, fiction, history. Did he really need any books? For some time he wondered why Anuraktha had brought him into this room. Was it some sort of detention room for harming the trees in the garden? He touched some books, read their titles and that was all. Like a child who lost track while counting stars, he looked above in desperation. It was almost the end of summer; the first raindrop fell on the glass tile above, blurring his view of the sky, making the birds fly and dimming the lights inside. He closed his eyes and cautiously took a book off the shelf. Whatever book it was, he kissed it before opening it, and then, to the sound of the first drops of rain and the cooing of pigeons, he opened his eyes to look at the title.

Savitri.

It was to return the book that he had gone back, again, last week. He wanted to meet Anuraktha. This was a book from his personal library, though, and for this reason he was not sure whether to return the book or not. It could very well be a gift—but for hurting the trees?

They had started their preparations to go back to his grandmother's house two weeks before she died. His mother was busy settling the problems she had to sort out.

He really had no idea what had to be done with such a thick book, for it was neither fiction nor the poems of a teenager's choice. Sometimes he placed his head upon that tome and slept. Finally, he said to his mother, 'Amma, I have to go to the ashram to meet someone.'

Anuraktha smiled when he saw the book in Aadi's hand.

'Why do you want to return it so fast? I know you haven't read a single page from it.'

'We are going back to our mother's house. Most probably we will be settling down there. I don't think I can continue somewhere here for my higher studies.'

'In that case, you can take the book with you . . . it is yours.'

They both had tea together. 'Is it to your taste?' Anuraktha asked.

'Yes,' Aadi said.

'Do you know the name of this tea?'

Aadi thought for a while and said, 'Chamomile.'

'No, it is called "Lost Love". Pure and simple, isn't it?'

Aadi smiled bashfully, and Anuraktha joined him.

Their car had reached the first toll booth. Each line had long queues of vehicles that honked incessantly. Unmindful of the noises outside, Shiva slept peacefully. Kamala missed the hump in front of her and the car came to a sudden halt. She fired up the engine in distress and reached for the money in the dashboard; Shaly took a hundred-rupee note from her pocket and handed it to her. Meanwhile, waiting for their turn, Kamala drank from her water bottle, and inquisitively looked at the car ahead, whose driver was shouting at the girl in the booth. Aadi saw his mother's face in the rear-view mirror; he looked at it for a while. She had dark circles around her eyes and she looked very pale, like a flower about to whither. He felt sad.

Once they crossed the toll booth, she pulled the car off the road to have breakfast. They had to shake Shiva really hard to wake him up; it was obvious the boy had not slept a wink the previous night. Highways are always open spaces, vast expanses where you get the maximum sky. The children were happy and they sat near the glass walls of the restaurant and ate dosa and chutney looking at the rows of hills in the distance. Shaly ordered pongal and when it came she divided it into four equal parts.

In groups, in clusters, like little bouquets, butterflies rose from the endless rows of flowers and flew around like another set of airborne blossoms. On the divider of the huge tarred highways, flowers of every possible creamy colour, particularly the small varieties of frangipani and plumeria, bloomed in clutches, obscuring the leaves. Just above them floated thick masses of silky white clouds and in between fluttered the butterflies with their gaily coloured rice-paper wings moving up and down. You don't get to see such vast skies in the city, such immeasurable stretches of happiness. The butterflies flew from the flowers to the skies and to the windshield of the car. Each time one of them hit the windshield, Kamala sighed anxiously. The children were confused: ought they concentrate on the colourful spectacle of flowers and butterflies, creamy-white clouds, the beautifully tarred roads and the blue sky in the middle, or admire the long line of hills made up of round hanging rocks that stretched along both sides of the road against the crystal blue sky, dotted with green trees. The sun was already up; Kamala stretched her left arm and opened the case on the ceiling to take out her sunglasses. In a second she realized that she had forgotten her driving gloves on the table back at the house, but she also remembered checking the table twice. Maybe, she thought, the wind had deposited them somewhere on the floor. With her sunglasses on, Aadi felt her face looked better, the creases of stress were hardly visible and her expression appeared more serene. The car gathered speed to compete with the butterflies. Kamala swayed her head in appreciation of the music, occasionally putting a piece of Dairy Milk chocolate in her mouth to ward off sleep. Kamala had insisted on not having liquor in the car—it was not just the check posts, it was a policy—so Shaly had kept some Rémy Martin cognac chocolates to boost her own palate.

When he woke from his next stretch of sleep, Shiva said in a complaining voice, 'Could you please change the music, this is getting on my nerves.'

Someone must have pressed the remote control, for, abruptly, Kumar Gandharva stopped singing. Kamala, without realizing this, sang one more line: *Mori maa . . .*

24

By the time they reached Krishnagiri, the children were fast asleep. The car was flying. Shaly checked the speedometer. Kamala sat behind the wheel unmindful of the way the engine accelerated, from one-forty to one-sixty—the speed warning alarm sounded and the light blinked on the display. The road had sharp curves and unexpected steep dips and climbs, and the hanging rocks on either side proclaimed the danger at signals and turns. There were no cameras to check their speed and the road was rather empty, deprived of competition honking. The hills here were formed out of solid, huge—very huge—boulders, like installations, magnified white pebbles collected and put together in different patterns with the help of big machines. On the divider, Shaly saw a signboard, half of which was hidden by the flowers: 'Drive like hell, and you will soon be there.'

'Kamala, please slow down. If you are not feeling well, I will drive the car. Please listen to me.'

Shaly couldn't read the expression in her eyes through her large Prada glasses, but as unsure as she was she continued, 'You know the condition of the tyres better than me, how worn out they are. They look almost like four eggs. How many times have I warned you to change them! And look at you, at the way you are driving, at this speed, with these tyres.'

Kamala pumped the brakes and Shaly screeched, 'Listen to the noise, it sounds awful, step on the pedals more gently!'

Kamala turned her head to look at Shaly, 'Why the hell do you behave like someone with OCD? Why do you panic so much? You are going to frighten the kids.'

'They are sleeping.'

'Ah yes, then what is your problem, Shaly? Why can't you just relax, or better yet sleep, or do something better than backseat driving?'

'Yes, I was thinking of having lunch, but I guess we need to reach either Dharmapuri or Salem to find a nice restaurant.'

'So you mean to tell me that your problem is hunger?'

Shaly didn't say yes or no. She just sat there looking outside; she was relieved the speedometer showed one-ten.

'Do you remember, Shaly, how happy you were with me? You used to tell me that you felt very secure when I drove. The engine and the woman behind the wheel have not changed, but what has happened to you?'

'Yes, I don't deny it; you used to drive me around slowly, maximum a hundred, as if you were the chauffeur of the President of America. But not any more.'

'That's news, Shaly. I have never thought that the President of America would be travelling under one hundred kmph.'

'No wonder it is news for you, and that's exactly why I told you that you are out of your mind. There is a lot of difference between a high speed rating tyre and a normal one, mph and kmph, the machines and the roads. My bad, I should have said the President of India, instead.'

Both of them sat silent for a while. Eventually Kamala admitted that she was losing control. Shaly begged her to pull the car off the road, to which she said, 'I am sure nothing bad will happen in my life again.' Then she pointed towards the sign of a petrol pump and said, 'Let us stop there for a while, we can fill the tank and use the loo as well. This is a beautiful place—we used to stop here for some fresh air.'

What Kamala said is true, thought Shaly. The place was boundlessly beautiful. One could take a closer look at the huge boulder rocks, each standing atop the other in threateningly precarious positions. There were a lot of small teashops beneath the rocks, and some people were trying to climb up the rocks. Some were busy taking selfies, and others were shouting at those who were climbing. Had time permitted, they would have definitely gone up there. Shaly wanted to wake up the kids and show them, but Kamala didn't let her. She knew once they were up they would start asking for the hotel, troubling her with questions. Shaly couldn't understand why Kamala still considered her teenage children toddlers.

'There is no guarantee, no security for anything,' Kamala would say a hundred times a day. The thought troubled her to the extent of tempting her to take the most chaotic decisions, moves one might not even imagine. Her decision to leave Bangalore, her decision to avoid her mother's funeral, her decision to live a life on drugs—everything about her served as an example, revolving around her idea of securities and guarantees. What does she need the guarantee for, thought Shaly. Now if her children woke up, she would consider that a threat to her security, her safe-mode drive. She felt the speedometer exaggerated. Strange woman, why was she so afraid, so anxious, what was she worrying about so much? Wasn't it possible to live a life without encounters, aims and a future prospectus?

How peaceful it was on the hills above. In the morning, along with the smoke that rose from the chimneys, music flowed from within the houses, from the streets and forest paths. Not just birds, each mind was in tune to the rhythm of music, each body swayed in dance. There people shared 'love', something difficult to find on the plains where people were afraid of that beautiful word.

'Can we go?' asked Kamala.

'Can we go there?' Shaly pointed to an assembly of mounted boulder rocks.

'Yes, but not now.'

The bird that looked forward to flight, that got excited only by the prospect of migrating to faraway places, found itself sitting in the corner of its nest, unmindful of the restlessness of its own wings, and looking after the two hatchlings with broken wings, mending their heavy, neurotically inflexible feathers. Meanwhile, spring kept calling out to her: 'Far away a magnolia blossomed just for you.' It must be the wind that covered its naked roots, projected on the surface of the earth, with flowers. The wind said, 'Come, something lies deep down in the heart of the earth, naked for you.'

'Paru, Parukkutty, Parukkuttiyamma, do you hear? I will give you a list—make me the dishes of my choice. I would like to go for a picnic, at the very least, I would like to go and sit on the roots of that tree.'

Removing the silver wrapper of the chocolate, Shaly inhaled the aroma of Rémy Martin. The children were talking in the car. Shiva kept asking the same question, and now Shaly understood why Kamala was anxious about them waking up. This was the umpteenth time that boy had asked, 'How long will it take? When are we going to reach, Amma?' Children really are something, thought Shaly.

'Would you like some chocolate?' she asked, extending the packet towards them.

'No,' Kamala said harshly and rather loudly. Something flew off in front of the windshield and Kamala had to slam the brakes, making a screeching sound.

'I didn't mean it, Kamala. You know they are my children as well, not just yours.'

The boys had heard this many times before. Once, years ago, Aadi had got really enraged about this kind of talk in the midst of an argument with Shiva. The boys were secretly discussing Shaly's role in their house.

'I don't want to be her son, whatever happens,' said Aadi.

Just then Shaly entered the room, and heard him. The child was immediately sorry for embarrassing her; he felt he was demeaning himself. Shiva feared she would turn spiteful on them, for he always longed to please her somehow, to remain in her good books. At first, when she sensed the fear in his eyes, she wanted to harass them, defend herself, but instead she just laughed and said, 'And may I know who said I want to be your mother? The truth is I want to be your lover when you grow up, understand?'

She saw Aadi sitting, looking out of the window now, his head down.

'Kamala, we should have bought something to drink. I need to have something. I hope there are some tea shops or cool bars on the way.'

'Yes, cool bars,' echoed Shiva.

What they saw on the way was no cool bar but a roadside vendor, selling lemonade and sugar cane juice, and that too on the opposite side of the road. Luckily, Kamala spotted a U-turn near the vendor and taking it, she parked the car under an old tamarind tree. They watched the man passing the sugar cane stalks through the rotating crushers of the motorized machine, squeezing lemons and pieces of ginger into it. It was a delight watching him do that, the sight of something being crushed to death, drained of fluids. He poured the light green juice right up to the brim of the glass cups.

'Where is Shaly?' Kamala turned around to look for her.

Aadi walked a few steps in search of her, not too far in the open space, just behind a very thin, sun-scalded tamarind tree; he finally saw her peeing at ease in a squatting position, a cigarette butt burning in between her fingers.

'Shameless woman!' He walked back.

25

The entrance gates were wide open. Suddenly it seemed as though light was no longer light but a well of darkness. Death lingered under the tarpaulin awning of the funeral gathering and on the features of everything, animate, inanimate, blurring impressions. It could be the headlight of the car; Kamala saw the relatives, mostly relatives or neighbours from her native village, getting up from their seats as if to have a look. But no one stepped outside, some of them remained standing and some others went back to their seats. She imagined their conversations.

Has she reached? The one and only daughter? Why did she take so long? It is only a ten-hour drive . . . surely, she is not coming from America. Is her husband with her? Have they separated? Is he not in Bangalore any more? Why didn't they come together? At least he telephoned on the day of her death; she didn't bother to do even that. Poor Madhu, why should he have the sorrow that her own daughter doesn't have? What a shame. Our poor aunt, look at her fate, her daughter has finally arrived after her cremation.

The women from the halls were craning their necks to see what was happening in the outside world of men, some of the elderly women even ventured to come out at this late hour. No one extended a hand even though they saw how Aadi was straining to help his brother out of the car. Hatred, accusations and resentment hung in the air without a proper shape. The children looked at their mother's face. She didn't seem bothered about anything any more. No regrets, no acknowledgements, no confessions, and no anxieties on her face—nothing except a cold and empty look that proclaimed she no longer had any commitments to worry about.

There was no 'mother' inside the house. There never would be.

Before entering, she touched the steps by the doorway, and after a lapse of seconds, she bent over and kissed them. 'Amma, how are you?' she asked.

That night she slept on her mother's bed. She didn't seem concerned about those who had come with her, not even about Shiva who was sick and Shaly who was an outsider. She went to sleep with the conviction that pain and suffering lay within her, that the self itself was the cause of everything. Though she had ventured into the outer world with a vast sky above her, she realized that she was shrinking into her insides, becoming smaller and smaller, no bigger than a worm slithering and wriggling on the earth. Now she cut a figure more sorrowful than her mother on that old bed—she remembered her mother, in big diapers at the end, double the size of her buttocks, her legs folded and held together and swinging. This room, the size of the matchbox Aadi described, had more space and volume than the world she had seen outside. Its depth knew no bottom, she could dive endlessly. The plastered white walls within which she was confined had no real boundaries. She felt the walls were calling her, the depths were calling her, to a space where time or distance was no longer an issue. Here, Kamala need not panic; she had ample time at hand, no more frets and worries.

She looked calmly at the thick wooden window with the metallic latch; she even talked to the wood of the window shutters for a while before opening them. They opened with the sound of someone walking on piles of dried leaves. She looked outside and saw darkness, the darkness of the village roads at night. She remembered the tree near the river on which glow-worms blossomed in the night, a spectacle of her childhood memories, the iridescent sheen on the surface of the black water, a vision she regretted leaving behind. How many times had her mother taken her to the river banks that were often lined with wild chrysanthemums or lilies, to watch the glow-worms pirouetting down the stream? How many times had her mother made her swear on her life that she would not go there on her own? What kind of life did my mother live, Kamala wondered, in this small, very small circle of space. Is my life in any way better than the life my mother lived, she asked herself. Who lived a better life? One who knows no life knows no death as well. Even while sinking into the whirlpools of trouble, her mother had been afraid of death. Death had wiped away everything that formed her, everything she had known while alive—relations, love and accounts. I would like to experience death while I am still alive, thought Kamala, the state where everything is erased and at the same time nothing is erased—a moment without relations, bank account statements and identity cards. Life!

Amma, why didn't you teach me? I haven't learned life yet. I thought I knew myself, my likes, dislikes, travels and happiness. The more my happiness increased, the more did my pains. Amma, you should know, I never loved Madhu the way you wanted me to love him, however good he was. The letter I received the day before my wedding, the same one his father destroyed, was my last hope. I fought for my life, literally, I was fighting for my life then, but the ceremony took place all the same. Why couldn't I gather the strength, Amma? Where did I fail? Who was responsible for my failure, me or you? I saw you crying on the night of my wedding. You said you felt relieved, you said those were the tears of happiness. That same night I was crying too; crocodile tears of my complete failure. I am happy at least you were sincere in your tears. I know you are not inside this room now, you are nothing more than another soul that has become part of the universe wherein nothing is distinguishable—yet I believe I can see an infinitesimal polka dot beating under the ribcage of the universe, the same rhythm, the same irascible wrath, the same ecstasy of pleasure, the same sea. No one is around me now, no, not even me, but still I am afraid, Amma, I am sick of being worried. It seems awful to announce even now that Kamala could love no man in her life, that her orientation is different.

It is true that I was afraid of you while you were alive; it is also true that I had a strong dislike for you. Do you remember the rag doll I used to have when I was a child, maybe a child of three or four? You may not remember, those small things were not matters of importance to you then. And now that you are dead, it will be even harder for you to remember, to drag something out of the collective consciousness of the universe . . . just to remember, sounds like a task, doesn't it? Forget it, Amma, I will tell you how it went. The rag doll was nothing special, nothing of great value; it was just a handmade thing. If my memory serves me, one of my aunts made it, but somehow it was very dear to me. One day while I was playing with my cousins, I slid the doll under my chemise and covered it with a piece of cloth. It didn't hold there, slipping out every time I tried to fix it there to make myself look like a pregnant woman. It was then that I put it inside my panties; I thought it looked more realistic that way, one of the doll's feet bulging out of the crotch of my panties and the rest, the head and torso and the two arms and one foot perfect over my belly. I felt happy and proud, but I remember the fierce look on your face, the scornful laughter of the others, and the purple finger marks on my cheeks, which at first I didn't realize I bore, and then saw in the mirror very clearly, the mark of your hand smudged by my tears.

Nothing improved in my life; I grew more suspicious, and more disheartened, afraid even to embrace my cousins or share an obscene joke with my friends as a teenager. I thought it was better to be me, to be by myself, with my books and my walls, my dreams for travelling around. I was trying to run away, from the solitude that was terribly demoralizing. Mother, I was sympathetic only towards myself, my feelings, poor me. I entered any place where I thought I would find happiness, without hesitation. I should also be happy in life, I thought. I didn't stop to think whether the happiness I found satisfactory needed me in turn. Forcefully, I dragged the happiness and tethered it to my bedposts, but it was not as easy as I had imagined. I had to manoeuvre the way the people at my office do for business correspondence, I had to negotiate, make everything profitable, tug my happiness to my own shelves.

It was I who dragged her along—did you meet her?

There are lots of women who share apartments in Bangalore. I had seen such women in restaurants that were too crowded, at poker parties and in sentimental libraries, where nobody cared who was who. Different places, different people, where energy and happiness bubbled up in a jiffy. Here again, I failed. I had opportunities to correct myself, in fact I should have corrected myself, but I didn't, I didn't bother. Amma, you had accused me of ruining our lives. You said I ruined the life of my children. But now let me tell you, Amma, I think it was you who ruined it all, made things impossible for me. Amma, are you listening?

Do you remember the day Madhu came here, the day he made a big scene, the day he threatened to take Aadi and Shiva with him? He also told you that he loved me and his children. I thought he was making contrary statements on purpose, just to confuse you, confuse all of us, but I never suspected for a minute that *he* was so confused. I remember how his father turned his face against the wall and stood motionless, and how you cried, uncontrollably. I wanted to ask you why you were crying so helplessly when your daughter and her children were alive and healthy, but I couldn't ask it then, which I regret now. Madhu loved himself, only himself but he announced his love for us in public, cunning fox, and he portrayed me as a woman, a dyke, who followed her pleasures neglecting her husband and children. And you were not willing to listen to me, to hear what I was going through. I want you to know all this, even if it is too late now, and I want to ask you one question: How the hell did you manage all this, your marriage with my father, your role as a widow, your task of raising me, and above all, how did you live inside this huge house with its pocket-sized rooms, in the half-darkness? When you get time, if at all you get time, please tell me, for I think, the lives of some women are real wonders.

The woe of departure brewed in the pots on the gas stove, making the relatives feel depressed about being idle inside the kitchen. A careful voice scolded a girl who knocked down a glass jar full of pickled mangoes. Kamala didn't go into the kitchen; she was not willing to face any of her relatives. She knew that in the kitchen veranda, in the centre courtyard, inside the family bedrooms, her relatives were busy sharing their memories of her mother, sharing what they knew and what they did not know. This was customary, or rather an undocumented ritual of mourning, and they wanted the dear departed's daughter by their side, to partake in the games of the grown-ups, to join in their sighs, complaints, nonsense. They wanted Parvathi's daughter, sitting somewhere on the floor, head down, wracked with an occasional sob, for they believed that would give meaning to the funeral rites, to the relatives lingering in the house of the dead. Tomorrow, hopefully, Kamala thought, they would all go, after the morning prayers and offerings, and hopefully, the house would be peaceful soon.

26

It had been one night and a day. Was it raining outside? Shaly
tried to open the wooden shutters of the window, which she found
really heavy. It took a while, and then she sat on the dilapidated
windowsill carved out in the shape of a half circle and looked
distractedly out of the window, keeping a count of the people
exiting and entering the gatehouse some feet away from the main
building. The tarpaulin awning having been removed, she had a
clear view of the vast courtyard though it was very dark outside
except for the light and shadows formed under the solar lamp.
She had been sleeping all day, as there was nothing else to do. At
times, inanimate things share some kind of sad dimensions with
the living souls around: perhaps that was the reason she smiled at
the old, frosted glass panes and at the solitary electric bulb that
was suspended above the bed, a very old-fashioned electric bulb,
whose filaments, she checked, worked. In Bangalore, she thought,
the four of them were in four separate rooms and here they were
on four different continents. Where are the boys, she wondered,
and remarked on how they had all come together in one car and
then been sucked up individually by hostile black holes. But now
a fear much stronger and more lonesome startled her, she felt it
under her skin; she whispered that she was an outsider. This is not
mine, these are not my things, I don't belong here. She noticed

the food tray on the table, and lifted the lids to see what was inside; someone might have brought it there while she was asleep. Not very long ago, she could tell, from the warmth and smell of the dishes. Could it be Kamala? She wondered why Kamala was behaving like a total stranger. What had happened to her? The previous night, she had called her before going to bed and Shaly had to strain to understand her as the reception was very poor here. What she understood was this: 'The relatives will be leaving by tomorrow evening after the rituals, so till then you take rest. I will join you later.' How very official! Couldn't she just come up a few stairs? Am I supposed to go down . . . do I have the freedom to do that? They hadn't discussed anything like that so far. What does she think of me? I didn't even drive the car, why on earth does she want me to rest for two long days? I am tired of sleeping; I can't afford any more sleep. No WiFi, no proper cell phone reception, no sense of time—this was torture. In Bangalore, people worked like machines, no time for a good night's sleep, and no time for sex. There people saw each other without really seeing, and did things without doing; there was always a veil in between them, some sort of an excuse like the one among the many you make when you don't want to kiss a certain someone. There, time was movement. Thinking of time, she felt her nerves tightening; she was in need of time, in fact, running out of it, with a lot of work on the finishing line. Mistress of mistakes, she placed her hands upon her brows, why did you set out after them?

Shaly opened the doors of her room, which had once belonged to Kamala, and stepped into the long corridor outside it. The room, the corridor, the building, everything reeked of prehistoric aliens from another time, another space. There were bird droppings all over the floors of the corridor—must be the pigeons, she thought, for endless cooing echoed from lintel shades. The night they arrived, she had been startled by the sudden, almost unexpected, flapping of wings and the abrupt flight of a flock of birds from the windows of her room, reminding her of some old English movies

142

she had seen—was it *Agnes of God* or *Birds*? She couldn't remember, but she asked the woman who accompanied her upstairs to shut the windows immediately. While the woman was busy closing the heavy shutters, she got a glimpse of the backyard of that ancient mansion, a wilderness of branches and creepers, which at that point bore no resemblance to the forest she had always known, and seemed nothing but spooky, making her wish for the shutters to be closed at once. With each step she took, there was a flutter of wings at the windows, agitated beatings, and a heavy feeling that something unpleasant hovered overhead. Both of them had lost their peace of mind, she thought, the birds and the human being. The next uncanny thing she found in the room on that same day was the electric bulb—it had been years since she had been exposed to such a primitive source of light. Immediately, she had turned it off—she didn't want all the objects bathed in that harsh, eerie yellow light, and certainly didn't want her room to look like the ghostly viscera of dark rooms for developing negatives—but now she could look at the filament with a greater interest, and smile at the way it flickered non-stop. The light fell into a circle on the black shiny floor, like spotlights for performers, falling on some droppings—it was clear they were not expecting any guests. A big rocking chair with one arm missing was in the other end of the veranda along with some piled up, old, dilapidated furniture and a beautiful round table with the head of an elephant carved on each leg, the ivory looking unbelievably real. If real, it was a shame. She detested such showiness. What she liked on the veranda were the windowsills; she counted twelve at a stretch where two or three people could sit at ease looking outside, which was a luxury. She sat on one of them and looked outside. The beauty of the courtyard was quite exciting—she had noticed it on the night they arrived but since they were in mourning and the relatives were throwing hostile looks at them, she didn't show any special interest in it. She remembered clearly how and where they had parked the car and walked parallel to the entrance gatehouse, from which a slightly

143

winding path of brownish-red laterite flagstones ran along the length of the courtyard to the main building, which was half-hidden then by the tarpaulin awning. She also remembered the difficulty with which they had wheeled Shiva across the path, for at certain points, some laterite stones had come loose, giving the path a dishevelled, old-world look. One had to walk cautiously so as to not fall down. The frayed edges of ancient trees marked the boundaries of the courtyard and there used to be small and big piles of dead leaves all over the ground. But the courtyard seemed rather neat today; someone might have cleaned the ground for the rituals in the morning. Suddenly her gaze caught on something— something was moving in the rose apple tree, shaking its branches violently. It was dark and almost the size of a ball of yarn—she felt a shudder run down her spine. Could it be a flying rodent? The light from the solar lamp fell straight over the tree, giving the rose apples a lustre. Was it love jiggling, shaking its ass inside the darkness of the branches? She walked down the stairs, the old caracole stairs with landings in between sections of stairs, decorated with pineapple finials of carved rosewood that seemed real except for their wooden colour. She touched the pineapples, felt the contours under her skin. Suddenly a bell rang out, startling her; she realized that she was descending the stairs like a thief. She looked around in fright and to her great relief she found that it was the clock. It went without saying that that too appeared to have been dug out from the bottom of history, its gong like an asthmatic patient. 'It is time, it is time, go, get out of this place, it is not for you,' the clock told her. That was when she noticed the shadow of the long rope that hung down from the ceiling to the landing on the floor, looking enormously exaggerated, spooky.

This shadow belongs to Kamala's mother—the thought crossed her mind—and it was for her they hung the rope down, for her convenience. This is *her* rope, would Kamala need it? Shadows are not always a pleasant sight, nor the thoughts that accompany them. The shadow was swaying, the end of it was almost pirouetting. This house doesn't fit me, for I still have blood in my veins, Shaly thought, even Kamala has become a shadow now, an illusion I had in my mind in the past. The children have disappeared too, again I don't know into where. I have been trying to push bits of me—say my head, arms, half a leg—through, since I came here, but this is a rather strange network, a labyrinth that leads you to the open gates. Like Alice, I have tried to peep through the keyhole. I am neither tiny nor gigantic, just the normal size, and the keyhole, the door, the latches, they all seem just as normal as myself, but whenever I try to peep through the hole, I feel I am a patient in front of a tonometer, failing to resist the power of the puff of air blown straight into the eye, I shut my eyes, I withdraw. No time, no sense of time, no direction, no sense of direction.

Why did she drag me into this? Why couldn't I take my own decision?

She said, 'I need you because I am lonely.'

Rita Mama had said the same. 'I cannot manage it all, I need you. I will not let you go, even if you don't have a job, it doesn't matter. We have more than enough to survive. Stay with me.'

Old curmudgeon! When I absconded from there, I thought I had won a battle, the battle of Aizawl vs Kerala, and what did I gain?

The landing led to a closed room that opens on either side to the big, half-open veranda outside and to the large entrance hall inside with its huge, open courtyard in the middle. The moment she stepped on the veranda, something came flying past and slapped on her face, leaving her with the feeling that she had been attacked by a bunch of sharp, pointed edges. At first she screamed at the unexpected attack, but when she saw the beast or bird hitting itself against one of the pillars she checked her voice and observed the 'thing'. It fell down on the floor, and with it the twig of rose apples it carried in its mouth, making the fruit roll all over. Gathering courage, she came nearer and got a better view. It was a bat. So this was what was wiggling amidst the branches.

Whatever it was it was dead now, such a short life. Was it the greed for foraging that had failed the echolocation? There were no beats, no motion—but was it dead, or just pretending to be dead? She bent over to examine it, the wing membranes and bone structure resembling the human hand, the large ears; she stretched her fingers to touch it. Someone called to her just then, and she started.

'Who are you?'

She lifted her face and saw a woman looking at her; exactly in the same way she had been observing the bat. Her eyes that seemed like pickled eggs were fixed on her, her brows arched in surprise.

'Who are you?' the woman asked again.

'I'm Shaly, a friend of Kamala's.'

'Where is Kamala?'

'She is inside, I think she is sleeping.'

The woman pushed the door open and went inside with the same surprised look on her face. Shaly turned to the bat and saw that it was moving, very slightly, but definitely moving. 'Thank god,' she sighed. In no time it flew back into the thicket of the rose apple bush. Again it appeared on the veranda, this time with a twig of even bigger rose apples, and she couldn't hush her laugh. It took three turns of the veranda and instead of flying away, entered the hall, the doors of which had been left open by the surprised woman. 'Go away,' Shaly tried to shoo it away, though she was afraid of getting hit again. 'Go, go away.' Her surprise, her inflexible curiosity still not diminished, the woman came out and smiled pathetically at Shaly. Shaly furtively arched her eyebrows and smiled back.

'See you,' said the woman.

'Yes,' said Shaly.

But she heard one more whisper, or a voice so feeble it was difficult to determine if it was voice or air, and turned back and found Kamala standing at the threshold looking like a ghost.

Her face twisted in a sneer of disappointment as she asked Shaly, 'Why can't you just sit upstairs till all these horrid people leave?'

'What?'

She felt insulted, infuriated. She went out to the courtyard, walked on the laterite pavement, pushed open the wooden gates of the gatehouse and disappeared into the darkness. Suddenly she felt that she had become something that was worth nothing, like a useless rag that she needed since she woke up to scrub the bird droppings off the table near the window. She had no idea where she was headed, but she kept saying as she walked, 'I am not your slave, Kamala, not just yours, nobody's'. She took her cigarette case from her pocket and lit one. A cyclist approaching from the opposite direction looked in disbelief at the apparition of a woman smoking a cigarette in the dark, and almost landed his cycle on the hedges on the other side. She didn't seem to have noticed him. It was a steep slope and she hurriedly walked down. Unmindful of the slope and the increasing darkness and strange faces, she absently walked towards the place where she saw light—or was it a fire?

This was a large tract of open land, and there were small heaps of fire, cinders, light and smoke scattered all over. Only when she came closer did she realize that they were funeral pyres and that she was the only person around. The kingdom of the corpses lay desolate, for the relatives, she guessed, might have gone after setting fire to the pyre, and it was the fate of the corpse to get burned to ashes unattended. She heard the rupture of bones breaking apart, exploding. Suddenly, with a deafening bang, a skeleton sat up on the burning pyre with a jerk. In the light of the pyre she could clearly see the white of its bones, and the laughter on its face. She turned and ran.

Kamala didn't see her rushing in, walking up the stairs in stupor, and crying out of breath in her room. Shaly threw herself on the bed and said to herself, 'This is a haunted house, how can

I spend a night here?' Her entrance downstairs was restricted, and every other minute raccoons ran wild on the roof, scratching the wooden planks. Each manoeuvre frightened her. It frightened her more when she thought that she was the only human being upstairs. Even if she ran downstairs in an emergency, she knew, the huge entrance with its heavy doors would be closed and her cries wouldn't reach the insides of the house. She looked at the single bulb hanging above her in the air, suspended on a thin electrical wire—now, she realized, she shivered more than the filament inside the bulb. There was no supper waiting for her on the table. Hunger and thirst didn't bother her.

She turned off the light, and the white laugh of the skeleton appeared before her. She turned the light back on. 'How slender was its hip bone . . . was it a woman or a man?' The bulb dangling above her head with dust gathered on its very thin, yellowish glass surface, its filament burning furiously, was an acid bulb, which could drop at any moment.

Downstairs, in her mother's bedroom, Kamala was talking non-stop, talking and laughing, and at times crying. Still laughing, she sat on the floor and crawled towards the corner where the walls met. She sat on the cold, rough granite slabs which were used as a channel for draining water, a traditional urinal of the native houses. The coldness of the stones pleased her.

27

'Wake up, wake up, have tea.'

Shaly opened her eyes and saw Kamala. So she does know the way upstairs, thought Shaly. As the most intense experiences from the previous night had died down, she didn't feel anything against Kamala. She took the cup from the tray and sipped the tea at ease.

'When did you come back yesterday? I didn't see you come.'

How on earth does she expect to see me come, thought Shaly, when her doors are always closed and she never comes out. The doors of the spacious entrance hall—from the centre courtyard of which different pathways led to different rooms—opened to a comparatively small visitor's room, which again opened on to the long veranda. The doors of both were always closed or very rarely partially open. The staircase with the rosewood pineapple motif that led to Shaly's room was at a corner of the veranda, cut off completely from the rest of the house. Shaly herself couldn't recollect how she had come back from the cemetery, walked up the stairs and collapsed on the bed out of breath, fear burning over her head.

'Where are the children?'

'They are downstairs. There is a large bedroom that opens to the east. I have arranged their beds in there, cross ventilation is okay there.'

'Just okay, isn't it?'

'For the time being we need to adjust a little bit. Is this room okay? Do you want to come down and take one of the rooms downstairs? I thought you would love to have some privacy.'

'This is fine.'

'This used to be my room. If you sit on the windowsill, you can see the main gates.'

'Those who come and those who go, isn't it? I saw a large burial yard yesterday. I saw a corpse burning there, just nearby.'

'It is down the slope. Why the hell did you go there?'

'I was bored here and I thought I would go for a walk. Kamala, have you seen corpses being cremated?'

'No, and I have no wish to see them. Never in my life.'

'Do the dead bodies sit up while burning?'

'Shaly, talk sense, no more nonsense. Go and take a shower, then let us go down and look around.'

'That sounds like the ban is over.'

'What ban? You don't understand what I am going through.'

I understand perfectly well, thought Shaly. Kamala was woman stuck in the air like Dali's Rose Meditative, no tethers and no relations, no worries yet full of worries.

Kamala led her through the house to the dining area at the back, through the entrance hall and some small verandas. The children were already at the dining table, waiting for them. They looked tired, extremely anxious. It was obvious that they didn't like this place. The maid greeted her with noticeable pleasure, a young woman of not more than twenty-two.

'I think we must all have breakfast together every day, let us consider this our quality time,' Kamala said ceremoniously, with furtive strain visible on her face.

For breakfast there were idlis, white, soft, with red chutney and sambar. But the children were not hungry. Their expressions weighed heavily on their mother. There was not even a decent TV in that house—how could they call the heavy old box in the corner, not much bigger than an instrument box, a TV? It was not even ten inches wide and there were no channels except news channels and Doordarshan. The boys didn't even glance at it. If there had been a modern TV in the same room, they might have loved to conduct a comparative study of the two, amused by the old world, but since there was nothing like that it was better not to think of it.

'Amma, when are we leaving?' Shiva asked while eating.

Shaly felt the food get stuck in her throat, so she asked the maid for a glass of water.

'We came here just two days ago. What is the big deal? Just make yourself comfortable till we move to the new apartment. I really don't know how long it will take.'

Shiva's face fell, lines of exhaustion visible on it, but he could not cry as he was not a child. This November, they were going to be eighteen. He slapped at a fly that was walking up his tea glass, spilling the tea all over the brocaded tablecloth and on his shirt.

Kamala didn't seem to have noticed the mess he had made. Paying him no heed, she said, 'I would like to go and meet my cousin Usha.'

If she went, she knew she would go alone, but she debated whether to go at all. After a while, she spoke again.

'Actually, I am not going anywhere. If they want to see me, they can come here.'

After breakfast she took Shaly to the pond, taking her hand as they walked, delicately stroking her arm with her fingers. Soon it started drizzling, but she didn't seek shelter, nor did she ask Shaly if she wished to go back. With rapture which was not usual in her, she walked through the overgrown plants, her index finger hovering over Shaly's knuckles, as if she wanted to share something dark. A small cat came to play at her feet; a little way off, a heavy black dog was busy nuzzling the earth, secretly watching them. The strong odour of water lilies welcomed them, and Shaly couldn't contain her surprise when she saw the pond in full bloom, happiness searing into her flesh with wetness.

Shaly feared that this old property, this land, this house which was no longer a house but a place that kept vigil for the dead, would tie her down forever. She walked down the steps that led to the water. The stones were smooth, covered in a thick layer of velvety moss. As her feet brushed the rushes Kamala breathed in the ancient smell of the slimy world underneath and said, almost mildly, as if she didn't want anyone to hear what she was saying, as if there was a life enclosed within the water which was totally different from theirs, 'Watch out, the ground can be slippery.'

'All I need is a lotus, I will be careful,' said Shaly, wading in.

Kamala imagined Shaly drowning, water filling her lungs, flooding her sinuses, her body sinking after minutes of struggling for breath. She also imagined her rising from the raucous ripples in a flash, head up, torso straight, her feet touching the surface of the water, eyes eaten by fishes, sockets swollen and white—falling down, floating face down. She thought, in that case, that she would walk back home with a heavy heart. The next second she regretted her vicious thoughts. But those who did not wish for the death of their partners, even if for a matter of seconds, were rare. Those seconds remained as the time they were afraid of. Kamala knew that if Shaly ceased to exist, she would grieve the most.

28

Anticipating the honking of the vehicle from Movers and Packers, Shiva lay on his dismal bed like the most fragile thing in that room. Handle with care.

He could not image a world outside gadgets. It was not easy to wheel him around as there were no even roads inside or outside the gates; the terrain yawned in hollows and bumps. Each room had a threshold so high one could even sit on it. He could never think of crossing them on his own. He had seen long ropes hanging down from the ceiling at different places in the house. The maid told him that they were meant for his grandmother, for when she had found it difficult to walk around and cross the thresholds. But she could at least cross the thresholds, even if it took time. She had managed walking without slipping in the centre courtyard, in the entrance hall paved with rough granite. Even Aadi seemed worried when wheeling him across the hall near the depression in the centre—the wheels, sometimes, could turn and move on their own.

In their house in Bangalore, there were no thresholds except the one at the entrance, and that too was barely noticeable. The floors were even, like a flow; he remembered skating from one room to the other as a boy, and he had wheels underneath his soles then. He wondered why these old houses need such high thresholds; a word recently entered into his vocabulary. But still, both the boys loved the centre courtyard from where they could watch the moon at night. And sometimes, when the wind blew, mangoes fell down through the opening with a soft thud and Aadi rushed to collect them. They were waiting; they would love to watch it rain inside.

What are the other things that I like about this house, thought Shiva. Nobody had taken him to see the pond so far, he had heard a lot about it. In his bedroom a window opened to the backyard, but the pond was still far away, not visible. He had heard that it was his mother's secret place as a child. I would love to sit on the steps of that lotus pond the way my mother did, he thought. Noon inside the house was unbearable; especially once the sun soared high, the smell of drying grass would fill the insides of the room with the odour of damp and suffocate his olfactory senses. The bed sheets and pillowcases were fresh, but something about the smell was just not right, something he hadn't been able to adjust to so far. The maid said that was the smell of the starch on the clothes and the incense sticks they kept inside the cupboards. She said they also put anti-roach tablets inside the shelves, which had a strong, unpleasant smell; though she liked the smell of it, some people might find it repulsive. The cotton-filled bed had been dried in the sun one week before they arrived.

I will tell Amma not to put anti-roach tablets in the shelves, he thought; he was allergic to it. He also wanted to tell his mother that he didn't want starch on his clothes. But where was she? He hadn't seen her since they had come here except during breakfasts. Once, she had come to his room, but she retreated faster than she'd entered, and she didn't even bother to wish him or say something. She looked bleak and tired. Sometimes, when they had visitors, she accompanied them to his room, but she didn't speak to them or him—it was as if he were a show piece and she a tour guide—and left as soon as they did.

Nights were manageable. But how long could a person stare at the wood-panelled ceiling? Even if he kept his windows open it was not much use, there was nothing but darkness outside. He wished some lamps would be lit on the path that led to the pond. Sometimes he felt afraid of the windows that were opened to the darkness, and it was a difficult task to close the heavy wooden shutters. He made Aadi close them, though he said he needed air, that he had claustrophobia and felt he was suffocating. Both of them wished they had separate rooms again.

In the mornings, Aadi cautiously wheeled him towards the *padippura*, the entrance, which had two rooms on either side. It was an effort to climb the steps, but somehow they managed it and reached the gate with the conviction that they had scaled an important height. What they liked most was the mound of red laterite loosely cemented together outside the gate, which was not a structure or a seat or something with a definite shape. It was just a heap of stones, made with the purpose of building something or maybe just found like that, with the roots of proud ancient trees running across them, running out as letters of the earth, stretching towards the ground, the red earth. When poked or scratched with fingernails, the surface of the roots oozed water; there was probably a small pond inside the roots, or a river. That would be more correct—'river' was the right word, a milky, luminous stream. And above them, on the branches, birds chirped incessantly. Now and then Shiva said, 'What a nuisance!'

From there, sitting on the roots, they could watch smoke rising from the chimneys, enjoy the smell of smoke and fried shallots blending with the early mists. Side by side, they would sit, their fingers intertwined like roots. Every house in the neighbourhood had a chimney, like those they had read about in comic books as children, where a woman comes down through the chimneys to the living rooms with her lovely umbrella. They could also see the road sloping down to where smoke rose without chimneys and they wondered how. There were no houses, they were sure. But they could see smoke lingering on the treetops on either side of the path. Aadi said that it was a crematorium, a place where they burned dead bodies. Shiva had also heard of that, though he had but a vague memory of it. When he was a child Aadi would go and sit on the same roots, counting the vehicles, carts and people passing by, while Shiva played near the well. But, except for that large piece of land and the trees outside, he couldn't see anything from there, any activities taking place in the crematorium. The possibilities suspended over the land, the ideas formed, the knowledge gathered, were all enough to keep them company for the night anyway, for the fear children long for in their beds while they sleep. Kamala used to tell them that they were all fables people made out of sheer fancy, that the land was just a barren piece of earth which happened to be very large and desolate with no real owners. People burnt their waste there in the early morning or during the night, hence the smoke. The children didn't like her elaborate explanations; they preferred it the other way round, as a place for burning real flesh. Three paths diverged from their entrance gate: the straight one led to the junction of a small township, the left towards a vast and beautiful field bordered with fragrant screw pines and patchouli, and the right sloped down towards the river bank, near the cremation ground.

That was the place where lives that had turned cold with the touch of death were enveloped in blasting flames and burnt to cinders, where the earth was heavier, unlike under their feet. The smoke that rose from there was the smoke of burnt-out thoughts and memories.

Shiva wished he could see that place, but Aadi had no confidence in being able to wheel his chair down that slope. If Shaly agreed, the three of them could go together. When she came, Shiva said, 'I want to see the burial ground. I want to go there and see human beings getting reduced to ashes, and nothingness thereafter.'

It was a shame to hear someone declare something so awful but Shaly smiled and gave him a nod of consent.

An old woman—must be a distant relative—had come the other day and sighed at the sight of Shiva in the wheelchair. She said she remembered how sprightly he had been as a child, and said, 'Don't you worry, my child, in the next life you will be running as a sprinter.'

'The thoughts of this life are responsible for the next life, Aunty. The next life exists only in our thoughts,' said Kamala.

Looking at the smoke rising from the nearby pyres, Shiva said, 'And such thoughts are burning in grounds like this.'

29

The three acres of land near the river had been granted for the crematorium by the rulers of what used to be the medieval kingdom here long ago. Anybody who didn't own six feet of land for the burial of their near and dear ones could carry the corpse there and cremate it for free. But if they wanted to observe Hindu rituals they had to pay a small, a very nominal amount for the services of the priest. The incense sticks, ghee and the choice of wood would be an add-on. If they wanted a mortician, that would be extra. People of the neighbourhood, Shaly found, were happy to share whatever information they had, bemused to see a woman asking such questions.

Cautiously, they wheeled Shiva down the slope. It was not as steep as it had seemed from a certain height. But towards the river it became really steep and could be slippery as well. They decided not to go to the river. But Aadi said he was going to the riverbank as he was afraid of the land of the dead.

After the end of the crown's rule came the Panchayat Act and, thereafter, responsibility for the funeral ground fell to the local Panchayat-level jurisdiction, but the land remained under the autonomous authority of the state. With the development of information technology, cremation became a quick and easy process and bodies started coming from far and wide. Local people were against cremating a large number of bodies, or bodies that didn't belong to the community, but the local rulers claimed full right to the dead bodies, causing endless arguments and skirmishes.

'How much does a cremation cost?' Shiva asked.

'Three thousand rupees including wood and other materials. People bring only the corpses, the rest of the materials are provided here,' said the manager.

'The rest of the materials?' So the body was just a material? Shiva expressed his uneasiness at this.

Shaly wanted to know something else. The pyres they saw around them looked graceful, burning properly and peacefully like at the end of a peaceful death, exquisitely perfect. But what she had seen and experienced the other night was something horrible. She described the restless skeleton that had risen with the flames and sat upright on the heap of burning wood and the deafening noise it had produced, and how she had run for her life. The manager and the mortician laughed.

'Have you ever seen a wood-fired stove?'

Bemused, she looked at him.

'Everything runs on a systematic basis here, but there can be exceptions. Everyone who visits the Guruvayur temple does not make offerings, does not feed the elephants; some people go there to pray and some to visit. Likewise, some people come here and burn the corpses themselves—either they don't care to pay the mortician or they are too poor to conduct the funeral rites. But try to understand that people do not burn corpses on a daily basis. While it is not something to be practiced to achieve perfection, the task does demand a certain expertise, a certain kind of intelligence and the ability to calculate. The body is built with five senses, five essential elements, and there is a mysterious proportion, an estimation, in which the fire spreads and devours it. The body, the flesh, will struggle inside the fire, and if things do not fall in line, the skeleton or a part of it may spring up. Such incidents are not common though.'

'There was this deafening bang . . .'

He cut her off. 'No, no, good heavens! It is true: there will be some noises, of the skull or the other calcified parts breaking up, but nothing like what you described. No, it is your fear, the fear of the unknown.'

Shaly left the cremation ground feeling lighter; she whistled at Aadi who was standing near the river bank, and when he saw them coming out of the cemetery gates, he gingerly walked up the slope. On their way back, Shaly noticed the long row of beech trees which she had failed to see on her first expedition. Now, she saw vividly the trees and the smoke caught in the branches, she felt the hot air that passed by them.

Nothing remains for us to be frightened about. What was there before life? What follows after life? All the sorrows, dolorous unhappiness, fears of rejection, bitterness, abandonment lie within life. What was there to be afraid of at the grounds of the dead? But the voice had been there. She had heard it and it was real, nothing magnified, not a figment of her imagination. Inside the flames, in her brain, it felt like a sun bursting noisily.

It was getting dark. Shiva asked, 'Will Amma be angry with us?'

'No, why should she?'

It was becoming increasingly difficult to deal with Kamala, especially since they had arrived. Recently, even the children had begun noticing the change in Kamala's behaviour; her anger, withdrawal, anxiety and the way she was transforming the house into a place unsuitable for living. If they asked her something, or if the phone rang insistently, she would not answer, instead she would give them a cold, severe look or make an unearthly gesture until they would feel uneasy and retreat. Perhaps she would scold them if she learnt that they had been to the crematorium. She had been there too, not exactly to the crematorium, for she had never entered the gates—she didn't want to enter—but to the riverbank. As a child she had preferred to walk down the slope like every other child of her age, rather than see what was happening inside the land of the dead, covering her ears with both hands whenever she passed by the gates of the cremation ground. God knew they grew wings that in an instant helped them fly till they landed on the riverbank. They went to the water not to see their images reflected in it, the way the prehistoric nymphs had done, but like a snake drawn to the charmer; they were cajoled by the ribbon-like golden-yellow flowers of the fragrant screw pines that lined the banks. They made knots tied with two loops and two loose ends that looked like pieces of decoration on a fondant cake, which they cautiously put on their hair with a hair clip. How happy they had been, for they were children and once they flew back and perched on their windowsills they told the story of the dancing ghosts and the grinning ghosts and laughed aloud, savagely out of tune, and cried all night, desperately shaking in fear. But her children, she believed, were invalids. What if they got frightened, seeing something awful?

'We will not tell Kamala,' said Shaly.

'What?'

'That we have been to the crematorium.'

'What will we say then?'

'We will tell her that we went for a walk.'

As it turned out they didn't have to explain anything to Kamala. When they reached home, they saw an old man sitting in the entrance hall talking to her. Though he tried to smile at the children, he had a severe grimace on his face which was not easy to countenance. He was particularly unhappy to see Shaly, but unmindful of his uneasiness Kamala said: 'This is Madhavan's father, my uncle. He says he will buy the house and the other properties. Obviously, if he buys this it will still go to his grandchildren, but I don't understand why he is making such a fuss over all this. I can't afford to sell this property at such a low price, it'll be making a huge loss.'

'What guarantee do I have that you will be giving the properties to my grandchildren, especially when you have so many parasites around you?' said the old man.

Embarrassed, Kamala looked at Shaly.

'Is this the woman who is going to sell the house to me? Look at me and talk,' he said to Kamala. Gesturing to the children, he added, 'Go inside and do something.'

The grandness of the seventies, thought Shaly, Kamala should not have explained all this to me in front of him. She was gripped by a feeling of unease. She went outside and walked towards the caracole stairs, her fingers playing on the wooden pineapples for a while. She heard shouts from the entrance hall. They are not talking about me, she realized, it was money and land that mattered. You could not tell whether there was any family feeling in their voices, or stark business.

'I cannot dispose of it like that. Let me see if I can get another buyer.'

'Who on earth do you think will buy this property which lies so close to that crematorium?'

Kamala knew he was arguing for the sake of it, out of his greed for more. She had researched the matter, enquired about the value of the land earlier; she had connections with some land brokers in the neighbourhood. Her dreams revolved around selling this old wreck and buying a brand new apartment in town. It goes without saying that those who want to sell their land, particularly out of desperation, cannot hope for too much; money flows in only when we wear an air of nonchalance. Maps are written and rewritten every other second; the land she wanted to sell would not be the land in the broker's handbook. Last time also she had tried to sell a portion of it, but her uncle—or if not him directly, then his men—had blocked the buyers from proceeding, informed them that the place was haunted, had poor water supply and what little there was, looked yellow, that the land was not suitable for digging septic tanks etc. She wondered what he meant. How could anyone sully such pure water?

The earth was good, pure and gold; it should travel down the bloodline, through Madhavan and his children, or his sisters and their children. The tension over the deal was unbearable. It had started before her mother died. Kamala had wanted to settle in Cochin, in Kadavanthra town, a long time ago. She had said she would take her mother with her after disposing of the properties. But that didn't happen, and then her mother died. She could have handled things more easily if her uncle had not interfered. Madhavan had tried to negotiate with his father; over the phone he had said, 'It is not easy to buy a flat in Kadavanthra. She should get the full amount. Don't forget that the children belong to me as well.'

All those who sit under the bodhi tree do not become Buddha overnight. Restlessly, Madhavan wandered in his mind all day, and at night he lost his sleep thinking of her. It was the wedding chain that she didn't bother to wear any more, which set his words free. He had been acting like a mad person, a cruel person who, after throwing his invalid children away into a dark forest at the mercy of wild beasts, was trying to find solace in bars. At times, when his friends gathered around him, as he tried to contain his sadness within pubs, his sorrows multiplied. Endless talk proved to be of no use. He couldn't love the woman for whom he had abandoned his wife and children, and the woman in turn harboured a bitter hatred towards him in her mind, for all the ways he had ill-treated her in the past, for denouncing her, marrying someone else.

'Can't you just try to get some sleep, Madhavan?'

'I am thinking of buying some land.'

'What land? Why do you need land in the middle of the night?'

'Kamala is selling her land.'

'Aha! Now I get it.'

'What do you think?'

'What do you need my opinion for? Obviously, you have decided everything. You want to help your ex-wife, so go ahead with that. She probably thinks that you are very rich. No shame,

163

that woman! Do what you must, but don't expect me to be here any more.'

Kuljeet nurtured an intense dislike for Kamala, and took great pleasure in stirring up trouble. She knew Kamala had never loved Madhavan, even though they had played some sex games together, some sort of nightly exertion. Her biological weirdness she could very easily forgive, but still she hated her. Whenever he spoke of Kamala, she was overwhelmed with irritation, marked by an unwanted curiosity. She was vengeful; for it was because of Kamala that she had been forced to live a useless life, *this* life, with a husband always pining for his two sons. If only Kamala had loved him, he would not have abandoned her and her children; Kuljeet, for her part, would have married someone good, someone from her own community, someone who grew a beard and wore a turban—the gift of the Guru, and become one half of Mr and Mrs Singh.

She had sent a letter saying she was pregnant on the fourth day after her abortion, which Kamala received the day before her wedding, running short of enough time to act. It was not the loss of Madhavan but the rage one woman felt towards another which pushed her into this nothingness. She wanted no other woman in her place, no one else to share the violence of her desire. Nothing would discourage her, neither unhappy consequences nor the storms of wrath. Even after his wedding, she continued her affair with him; she started using him as a toy, a mere dildo that satisfied her physical and mental itch. She would persuade him to travel with her in secret, and on the way back she would deliberately leave an earring or hair clip in his car. But to her great disappointment the telltale signs remained unnoticed wherever she had deposited them—in his pockets, bags, and car. She prayed for the day when they would separate, but when it happened all of a sudden she regretted that there was no more game left to play. The fruit called Madhavan had lost its flavour; it no longer appealed to her appetite, in fact, it had become a burden, an obstruction in the food pipe.

She detested everything about him: smoking, drinking, his friends and whatever his habits were. She loved a life of luxury, she thought he was extremely rich, a landowner who had a handsome job, but he, on the other hand, never spent a single extra rupee on luxuries, lived the life of a simple man, devoid of gaudy cars and dreams. She loathed even his faded yellowish bath towel, for which he never wanted a replacement. He would say with the conviction of a bumpkin, 'My mother and I shared one bath towel as far back as I can remember. My sister always wanted a new one, and changed her towel every year. New towels are difficult to handle, they don't wipe your body dry, your skin takes time to get accustomed to them. And at times, at home, there would be just some buttermilk to go with rice for lunch, and my sister would go off, frowning. I would make my mother happy by eating her share too. You know, Kulji, Kamala's mother used to make five separate dishes every day.'

It was wealth that cheated Kamala, her estate that forced her into this unhappy wedding, poor woman; she was left with no choices then. He said to himself, I must give her the maximum price for her property, let that be my penalty kick.

In her sleep, around three in the morning, Kuljeet shouted, 'If you buy that estate, consider our relationship over.'

30

Desire could be palpable, like the strong sense of forfeiture she felt within, but it could never be concrete, never graphic. What did she really hope for, what was her desire? If she had achieved what she dreamed of, then what was the point in being bitchy, getting mad at things and behaving in a moody, unpredictable way? With a stern expression and severe tongue, what was she trying to prove? Was she trying to convey that she was not the polished woman they believed she was, that her language could get even darker? Last night, she had pushed her plate so hard that it had fallen down, scattering rice all over the floor. Even Aadi had been furious at this. If she did not want her uncle to interfere in her business, she should tell him to his face. There was no use in making others stand facing a loaded gun. The three of them were always supportive, willing to do whatever she wanted them to do, talk the way she talked. They carried her anger on their shoulders though it weighed heavily on them, making them stoop. But still the dyspepsia persisted—they crouched down, they wanted to throw up.

Shiva raised his voice when he heard that the movers would transfer their things directly to the flat they were going to buy in Kadavanthra. What was wrong in getting mad about this? As it was the children were already bored and going through a very bad phase of their lives in slow motion; it was hard to believe that this time would also pass. True, she had paid a token amount as advance, but that didn't guarantee them anything. The flat would be theirs only when she paid the full amount, otherwise it would wait for her for some more months, and then the advance would cease to exist. Now that her uncle wasn't helping, he was being vengeful as well, and disposing of her estate and moving on with life seemed almost impossible. At first, she took no notice of what Shiva was saying and tried to concentrate on her plate, on the dishes her maid, Janu, had made. He started shouting, and when she thought it was getting out of proportion she pretended to listen. He yelled about the huge sum Movers and Packers were going to charge her for keeping their things for so long. He demanded that she have their things brought to the house so that they could keep them there and open only what was absolutely necessary. When they got the apartment they would make arrangements for another vehicle and people for transportation. The only extra amount would be the money for the second transportation but in a sense, compared to this, that seemed profitable. In short he wanted his gadgets back; he was sick of living here. At least they'd be able to watch TV or listen to some real music. Shaly intervened and spoke for Shiva and asked Kamala to call Movers and Packers. Kamala glowered at her in great anger as if dismissing her authority with her scornful looks, and she fell silent in no time. Shiva kept protesting, undeterred, and after a while she grew tired of going through the motions; having no idea how to handle the situation, she gave a violent push to the dish in front of her, towards him, overturning everything everywhere.

'This is no place for throwing parties! I hope you are all aware that the woman who passed away was my mother.'

She thrust her hand into the other dishes, grabbing at bowls and spoons, letting them all fall on the floor in random directions with loud clatters, the sound of steel crashing to the floor. She asked the children to get out of her sight. They hadn't even begun their dinner, but she didn't care even if they were hungry, and gave them a nasty look when Aadi started wheeling Shiva out, as if it was their fault, as if this show of cruel euphoria brought her satisfaction. Shaly thought Kamala would slap her, but that didn't happen.

Without even looking at her, Kamala walked unsteadily towards her room, once her mother's, now hers.

Shaly didn't bother to pick up the dishes or clear the table or the floor. Let Janu see when she comes to clean the house in the morning, she thought, and walked towards her caracole stairs. But she couldn't sleep at night, for more than anything else she was hungry, hunger gnawed at her. She considered going down and rummaging through the leftovers, but then she decided against it, for she feared that the children might see her. The house had erased the happiness of the cremation ground from her mind. Truth be told, there was just one problem in the world—hunger, the rest was all transitory. Kamala had never known hunger and that was the reason she woke with a new problem, a new dislike every day. She hadn't seen little children sitting half-naked on the streets trying to sell half-baked rats.

There was no blindfold darker than light. Kamala, listen, turn off the lights. Try to lie down on your bed peacefully, like the woman you saw in your dreams, lying belly-up in the water, dead and floating. Open your eyes into the blackness. Open your eyes to the darkness where you and I don't exist, not even Brahma. Try to look at yourself, this thing that you call your body, try to look deep down. Remember, you touched your body as a girl, didn't you? Now, try to say aloud that you are a lesbian, a beautiful word, isn't it? Haven't you seen how beautifully girls make love to girls? Like exquisite birds of the east, like the dawn inside a river, like a feather on the rooftop. Haven't you seen girls getting high drinking moonlight? When they hug each other, and hold each other close to their bosoms their faces glow with pride, a sense of achievement. Sounds like an overrated, outdated cliché, doesn't it? Make your heart vulnerable; give a chance to romance that always ends happily, like the stuff in Mills & Boon novels. But you can never be happy, for you are pretentious; you suffer from the discreet pretentiousness of the yokel bourgeois. You let me stay in your house, but you put me upstairs, in the company of the birds, so that no one would know of my presence in your house, like a cat that shuts its eyes while drinking milk. I know you feel safe within your secrets; even if they were to striptease in front of strangers with or without your knowledge, you would feel safe with them, these secrets you consider darker. Whom do you wish to please, you dirty female? Now, come on, shout, shout the way those hip-hop singers do. Tell the world,

> I can love only one woman,
> I can kiss only her,
> I am like that,
> I have two sons and
> I am bringing them up happily . . .

Kamala was never willing to come out of the closet. Shaly raced through the veranda outside the doctor's room. The doctor had asked her for the patient's complete history. Shaly guessed Kamala might have told him about the condition of her sons, about how she and her husband had separated, about how Shaly had forcibly given her drugs, but she would not breathe a word about what was eating her soul up, leaving her looking like a pile of dust within. Shaly was decisive, and that was why she fixed another appointment with the doctor secretly.

'Repressed emotions can drive a person crazy. I am afraid I don't think she is normal. I came so that I could talk with you; maybe, I could explain things better.'

'Yes, I have recorded her details here. I know she is keeping things from me.'

'Her sexual preference is different, and that is the main reason why she suffers a lot.'

'But one thing you should understand. Lesbians and gays are not free to come out in a country like ours, where people don't really have any respect for each other.'

'But how can you say that, Doctor? We do have gay pride parades here, I have seen them myself.'

'You might have seen the parades, but have you ever wondered how many lesbians or gays actually participate in such parades? Do you get what I'm saying? I would like to make my point clear. In LGBTQ only T is the active participant here in our country. How many of the others are willing to join hands with them? Hardly any. We are all tangled in a mess of knots, our history, tradition, socio-economic conditions, laws. First, I guess, all of us need to come out, and then everything will fall in place. The people who are still in the closet believe that their orientation is straight; they are the real sick people, lesbians are forced to remain in the closet because they are afraid of those who brag about their normalcy.'

'What exactly do you mean, Doctor? Should they live like this all their lives?'

'I am not a person for a discourse, child. As long as people do not hurt each other in the process, I strongly believe they should pursue their happiness, they should find meaning in their lives— it is a responsibility one should feel towards oneself, even if the person concerned is a homosexual or a bisexual. Kamala was in the closet as you said, but she hadn't created problems for anybody, she was enduring it alone, the ultimate helplessness of the human mind. You said she is highly philosophical—this could be a veil, a kind of reaction of the mind to cover up certain other things, or maybe she is genuine in her outlook, we can't say that now. The trouble came in the form of the acid, you know. You should not feel bad when I say this—I know you are already repenting—but the truth is that Kamala did not have enough mental strength to deal with the drugs and that is the reason for her present problems, not just her preferences. She was strong enough to handle her biological troubles, but not strong enough to deal with her mind, which was vulnerable to damage, and could be broken very easily.'

Shaly bent her head and fixed her eyes on the desk calendar.

'Can I ask you something?' the doctor said after a pause. 'You said you are not a lesbian. Then why do you support her, even when you know that you are cheating her. Don't you think that your indifference might have added to her sufferings? Can you say that you don't suffer? Isn't it all a stress on you too? If whatever you say is true . . .'

Kamala is trying to hold the repelling ends of two contradictory lies at the same time. As if caught inside a whirlpool, she is swirling around in a life deprived of even the slightest concepts of non-duality. The poor woman!

Kamala, whenever you tried to kiss me in the ecstasy of love, I told you in a voice almost hushed, 'Kamala, I am not what you think.' But you didn't hear me speak. I was too cunning to say it out loud, because I wanted your friendship, because I needed your company. Your desire was so strong, so savagely happy, I could not even think of making you unhappy, for I love you more than myself. Remember the first time we played at sex on your great, wide bed? The next day when we went out for a walk in the park, I told you: 'Kamala, I am not a lesbian.' I thought you would be taken aback, but you didn't show any signs of discomfort, you just smiled. Do you remember what you told me then? You said: 'I am not a lesbian, too.'

Shaly felt pained as she walked down the stairs, cautiously, without making any noise. The boys were sleeping in their room. She went to the kitchen and took the broom and the dustpan, two things, two objects she considered powerful enough to bring peace home. She put the dishes in the kitchen sink, cleaned the floor and wiped the dining table with a rag. Has she slept already, or is she still awake in her room? Before going back, Shaly carefully pushed open Kamala's door, but the bed was empty. She turned the lights

171

on. Kamala was sitting in a corner of the room, on the floor, on the rough granite stone with the drainage pipe; she had told Shaly on the day she showed her around that it was used by the older generations as a urinal at night. She clung to the edges of the stone with a terrified look on her face.

'What the fuck!'

Shaly rummaged through her shelves and cupboards for nearly forty-five minutes, and all the while, Kamala sat motionless in the corner, on the urinal stones, unparalleled fear in her eyes. Shaly tried to drag her to the bed, but she didn't move an inch, she simply sat there clinging to the edges of the stone like a ghost, and Shaly had to give up. Leaning against the bedpost, Shaly sat on the floor, beside her. Eventually she fell asleep; in fact she slumped on the floor, and like a night owl, Kamala sat in the corner, watching her. Suddenly Kamala remembered: people fell asleep like this, on the floor, on certain funeral nights.

'Mother died, she has gone to a better place,' she consoled Shaly.

31

The human mind is both memory and the loss of memory. Unwilling to be buried in forests or to drown at sea, insatiable and uncontainable inside the flesh and the skin that wraps around the body or within the cells of the brain, it pokes its head out, shedding different layers of flesh, blood, plasma and skin. The mind! Kamala opened her doors to the temporary tombs.

Not just one. Standing outside her closed doors, Shaly had experienced the many deaths of her beloved friend. The house where the relatives had assembled during the funeral rites, like flies around a kerosene lamp, buzzing non-stop, was almost desolate. It had been more than a month. The children were upset; they wanted freedom, peace of mind. Their things had not arrived yet. Aadi spent his time leafing through the pages of the book Anuraktha had given him, reading without order, reading without comprehension. Shiva spent his time sleeping, for he was upset and angry when awake.

'Could you please take me out of this stuffy room?' Shiva said, as if he were on the verge of a panic attack.

'Where do you want to go in this rustic neighbourhood?' Shaly asked.

'Even that cremation ground is better than this place,' Shiva shouted.

It was not easy to control anger. They were, all three of them, not usually angry; Shaly had always known them as timid, submissive people who spoke softly, as if afraid to hurt something in the air with their voices. But now she saw things changing, voices hiking to insane heights, fears returning. She felt life was faster in the cremation ground, moving at a high speed where bodies became ashes in turbochargers, in zippy seconds. The smoke that rose from there could be the mortician's anger; it could even be his poverty, the situations that had led him to the life of an undertaker.

In Kamala's house the antique clock was a gastropod stuck on her walls, with a second hand that moved once in a while. The snail on the wall arched its antennae to look at Shaly; the mucus line it left on the walls disturbed her. She felt the walls were swabbing down the greenness of her body, though one couldn't easily make out the difference inside the prehistoric darkness of the room. How long was it going to be like this? The picture of her mother on the wall resembled Kamala; her uncle had brought it here two days ago, an old passport-size photograph enlarged and framed. It seemed he was no longer hostile; he just wanted to explain the situation. But Kamala was unfriendly; she said she wanted no further rituals, nor did she wish to feed any more relatives in the name of her mother. In the end both of them came to a solution by deciding to conduct the funeral banquet at an old-age home on the forty-first day of her departure. 'How many days more,' Shiva asked. Nobody answered him. His mother had been acting standoffish since she had come here, like the lotus pond in the backyard, murky with green algae. He didn't expect an answer. He knew she was becoming unapproachable, at first with her relatives, then her children—and finally Shaly.

Kamala's stubbornness had hardened like steel. The thought of yet another day reaching nowhere maddened Shaly. Just because Kamala's time had frozen at a certain point, it did not mean she could freeze others' time as well.

Shaly withdrew her hand from the wooden pineapple only when she felt its sharp edges digging into her flesh. It was painful. How long had she been standing there? She saw the impression of the pineapple on her hand and stared at it for a long time, as if she were reading her palm. Hurriedly she went inside and knocked on Kamala's door.

'Kamala, open the door. I want to talk.'

When the door opened Shaly was taken aback, for Kamala looked almost like a shadow. When she stretched her hands out and touched Shaly's cheeks as if to welcome her in Shaly felt the pallidness of her presence, deprived of the usual signs of physiology. With an angry shove, she pushed her back and stepped inside the room. She sensed a kind of nervous excitement in Kamala's look. With a tension which was not easy to conceal, Kamala asked, 'What happened?'

'How long do you expect me to remain here? I am tired of it, I want to go back. I am sorry.'

To her surprise Kamala smiled, something of her old beauty showing. Maybe some part of it would come back to her face. She said, 'You can go. I don't think I am happy here either, I also want to go. This is what we call helplessness, but I really don't want you to suffer like this. You can go back. I will call you once everything falls in place. It's strange . . . last night, Aadi came to my room, he also told me the same thing, that he wants to get out of here, he wants to leave, he who is silent all the time. I cannot decide anything unless and until I do something about the property. I am stuck—you know that, Aadi should know that. I am trying my best, I have even given an advertisement online, two or three brokers have already promised to help me, but they all demand time, the one thing we don't have. I am afraid I am going to lose the advance amount as well. Bad luck.'

'That is because you are difficult, you are not cooperating. I told you I would give you the money, what else can I do? I have money and I am happy to share it with you. Such obstinacy is not good, especially in times of crisis. The seed money for the project which is not going to happen anyway is in my locker. If you can give me one week's time I can get you that. Buy the flat immediately, you can return the money later, when you get a buyer for your property.'

'Are you sure?'

'I couldn't be surer. I want you to do this for me.'

She smiled, but her face showed no signs of relief. She was like a computer that had stopped responding, no matter how hard you pressed the buttons, how much you tried a forced shutdown. Ctrl+Alt+Del: she must be rebooted and recaptured, with immediate effect.

Love obscured by immediate problems, Kamala said: 'The washing machine has stopped working. Janu will get your clothes washed for you, I have told her to do that. Please keep your laundry outside your room.'

'Yes, I will, or, I think, I can do it on my own. It will help me kill time.'

'I know you are going through a difficult phase.'

'My problem is not your washing machine or the mixer-grinder; it is the distance you are keeping and your health. Janu is here to look after the boys. If you would come with me to Bangalore, we could consult that doctor once again, it would be helpful, and you need a good doctor.'

'No, no, I am perfectly all right. Maybe I am thinking too much of my mother these days, I can't sleep well . . . but this is all quite natural, no need for a doctor.'

'No, this is not natural. I have been observing you these past few days.'

'Why don't you understand, Shaly? I said I have no problems.'

'Leave that for the doctor to decide.'

'Can't we just talk about something else now?'

It was not easy to talk with her. Shaly sat on Kamala's bed with her head bent, looking down. Kamala probably didn't remember how she had sat on the stone urinal in the corner of her room as if sliding on an infinite surface, in the dead of the night. The doctor had clearly said that bad trips were likely to happen even without taking acid or any sort of drugs and Shaly was sure Kamala was going through one such bad trip. He had prescribed some medicines too, but they wouldn't work sitting inside their blister packs. Shaly sighed.

The Kamala she remembered was like a moonlit night filled with music and laughter, like listening to Frank Sinatra with a glass of wine. But now her gestures frightened Shaly, neutral and cold, obscuring anything that was good, and possessing a discreet beauty of its own, like the patina on the brass knobs on her chest of drawers. It must be the bad trips, her face was tired, she was tired—maybe, it was just tiredness.

How, when, what, Kamala kept asking herself. Shaly touched her hands to calm her. She noticed the dark circles around Kamala's eyes, the sharp lines that were not there before on her forehead. The blood seemed to have drained out of her eyes and her body, and her lips had become slightly disfigured since Shaly had last noticed them. Even two days ago she'd looked all right; at least, Shaly thought, I hadn't noticed such visible signs of withdrawal so far.

She's the woman who taught me to abandon my headphones, Shaly remembered, and helped me enjoy music with my ears, eyes and other senses, my body receiving it. She led me to music beyond the popular bands, to the oriental waves of Hindustani and Carnatic—both strange to my ears at first, but I loved the feel of them in no time. And I gave her my English music collection in return—something like a give and take.

My ears were Indian-born, but maybe because I lived on the borders, on the hills, guitars were much appreciated and I grew up in tune with western music. My body swayed to the rhythms of Michael Jackson. As children, we loved rock 'n' roll, pop and country, we sang Abba and Boney M, though we had no idea what the lyrics were, what the songs were all about; they were something we imitated, and something we tried to reproduce in our dialects because we loved the music. It's English, someone said, and I remember how I longed to learn that magical language at the age of four. It took me years to understand that Rasputin was a sex machine, and that we were singing in praise of his dick when we were just three or four.

Shaly also remembered how she adored the bookcases on Kamala's walls, laden with books and music CDs, and the bedroom where some instrument was always playing in the background. But these days Kamala only played Karen Dalton on an endless loop.

While she was going through one of her first trips, Kamala had hugged Shaly once and said in a jubilant voice, 'This is fun! I am listening to all my favourite audios without really playing them. The music is in my ears! With digital clarity!'

What she needed were not some commonplace psychedelic experiences. And Shaly rejoiced at the prospect of making her ride. Kamala was not one of those boors who savoured a pill for the sake of getting high, for a kick-start. She was a psychedelic with class, one who wouldn't falter even if she had to pour Prosecco when she was already high. Adorable!

There used to be a lot of friends at one time, especially from Kamala's office, who visited her just to make their evenings wonderful. Sometimes they raided her bookcases, though she didn't appreciate it much. They assembled on her terrace garden, the place she called her 'barsati'. Shaly had helped her set up the trellis for passion fruit on the terrace, and a lattice for a beautiful espalier. In no time, the passion fruit vines grew in abundance and laced the trellis with their purple and white flowers. Obscured by the leaves, the fruit that filled the sun-gaps within the foliage became visible only when they started to turn orange. Her friends, Shaly's friends, all gathered in the beautiful, fruit-filled barsati with smokes and drinks. Shaly sliced the golden-yellow passion fruit into two and scooped out the insides, packed with surrealist seeds, into the glasses of vodka. That sight itself was life: the unreal blurredness of love, the interpenetration of happiness with the sour taste of vodka. 'Cheers!' they all said aloud. Bhavana, Ashika, Arjun, Daksha, Vinobha, Lakshya, Ratik. Cheers!

'Rane, could you please lower the volume of the music? I can't hear anything.'

'Faizy, watch out, you are going to step over it.'

Sometimes her boss said that he would like to have a barsati on his rooftop at the office, for he considered it a beautiful option to relieve their heads of tension, to let a little bit of wind in.

Who hitchhiked to where was always irrelevant in the night. Weekend passions placed them up too high to bother about realities. Someone picked up someone, someone dropped off someone—it was always *someone*, never a name.

'Strap her tight to your body, or else she will fall down,' someone screeched.

Those who went back from the barsati were more charged. In they came like timid cows to a meadow, shaking their udders, and out they went like fiery fighter bulls, balls fully charged. Unconscious of the night police on vigil, of the traffic signals, they flew through the night.

The staircase to the barsati was at the back of the house; attached to the house, but outside it. There was enough space to park the bikes and Bullets, but not the cars. Those who came by car parked at the entrance of the next street and returned with either a long scratch on the door or a glass missing. This was the main reason they preferred bikes on weekends, the safer option. They were careful not to disturb the children, but still, before going up the staircase, some of them went straight to the children's room and gifted them chocolates or something else. How happy they were! Those were the days. Shaly tried to remember them in more detail. Kamala had stopped listening to music for the past six months, at least. This, she thought, was not her Kamala.

Shaly closed her eyes tight and saw that doctor. Handsome, with a sweet smile, a twinkle in his eyes and a receding hairline. A large bookshelf behind him, panelled with glass and decorated with big books; she did not think he opened it ever. He was sitting in a black revolving chair, and in a pleasing voice, he asked, 'Do you regret anything?'

Shaly looked at him with hatred. She didn't say yes or no. She had confessed many times that the idea of drugs had been her mistake. They had started it just for fun, and the same fun had turned Kamala towards eternal sadness from which she saw no recovery and a lack of remedial measures. How could a person regret more than that? The doctor knew it, but he was asking such questions on purpose, just to poke her, scatter her to irreconcilable bits.

'It was my mistake, please don't remind me again.'

In a sweet and cautious way, he asked again, 'Shaly, are you bisexual?'

Pathetically, she looked at Kamala.

Kamala was thinking of something else. 'She has been the most exceptional joy of my life, the most justified pleasure. I haven't exposed myself in front of any other woman, and I don't think I will do that ever again. With her it was art, and I was the body artist. But look at her—like one plucks a green worm out of a garden plant and tramples it under the soles of their sandals, she is plucking me out and throwing me away with a scornful smile, the bad girl.'

32

'Can I go with her too, Amma?'

'No, I cannot manage him alone. Moreover I have certain issues to sort out here.'

'I am getting bored to death here.'

'And so is Shiva.'

Aadi felt worn out.

'What does she want? Does she think she can tether me to his bedpost all my life?'

For a second, he hated Shiva. Shit! I am paying for his disobedience. He was the one who broke the rules and ran out of the hostel and I am the one who is paying the penalty. It was not the fact that Shaly was leaving that provoked him; he couldn't help thinking that one of them was escaping. The woman who was responsible for more than half their problems was sneaking out, with permission—no fair. Shaly immediately picked up on the meaning of his dark stares, not at all in keeping with his customary peaceful face.

'It is just a matter of four days,' she told him. 'I need to arrange some money, and as soon as I'm done I'll come back. The money is crucial otherwise we will be trapped here forever. We need money to get out of this fucking place, Aadi, try to understand.'

The children also wanted to get out of this fucking place, at the earliest. But the thought of her leaving made them at once sad and jealous, the disappointment particularly visible on Shiva's face. When Shaly said goodnight, to her surprise, Aadi followed her to the veranda. When they were in Bangalore, she used to come down to their rooms and spend time with them, but then as now, no one came up to her room, except Kamala, and she too very rarely. Even the birds were silent at that hour of the night. They walked cautiously, and at one point she wanted to ask him to go back, but she didn't.

There were no night tables or chairs in Shaly's room, so he sat on the bed. He surveyed the room and saw the old lampshade with its electric bulb dangling above his head; the shade almost looked like an upside down brass bowl. He ran his fingers over her bed sheets, which smelt like her, of her French perfume. For a second, he wanted to lie on his back looking at the electric bulb. Shaly had kept her bags and other stuff in the cupboard on the veranda outside her room. She brought a big bag and some of her clothes and placed them all on top of the bed beside him. She took something out of the bag and put something else into the bag. The packing, she said, was done.

She felt uneasy about the way Aadi was lying on her bed. The way he had taken this liberty, it was a kind of encroachment, coming into her room without permission and behaving in a way that was disconcertingly familiar—though she used to go to their room whenever she felt like it, whenever she felt lonely. There was nothing to give him, not even a piece of chocolate. He was her guest that night, the only person who had taken the trouble to climb the steps. But this was not her house, there was nothing, no fridge, no anything inside that bleak-looking room save the bed on which she slept and the windowsills that protruded inwards. This was her separate place in their whole mansion. She realized she was thinking nonsense; she had been a no-nonsense woman all her life. Was she afraid now because there was a guy on her bed? No, she had many male friends, and this was a child. But somehow, it seemed improper, no matter how much she loved him. She loved him so dearly, like a mother loves her son, she had seen him as a child, had shared in his suffering with him and experienced the pain of his eyes within her own bosom. At times, she used to think that she was guilty in his eyes. She wanted to say something now, but both of them didn't speak. The children had been taught not to enter other people's rooms, and they adhered to this the way people followed an unwritten constitution. Shiva couldn't, even if he wanted to, and Aadi didn't feel the need usually.

'Is it hot in here?'

'Comparatively,' he nodded.

Slowly, he closed his eyes. It was the hour of the serpent flowers in the backyard—they were blooming.

'Aadi, get up, please don't sleep in here. I need to leave early in the morning. Please.'

'Even before we wake up?'

'I am afraid I will have to, Kamala asked me to take the car, but I have booked a ticket for the morning train. I think that's the better option.'

'Aadi, what are you doing in here. Shaly, it is time you sleep. You need to wake up early in the morning.'

The harshness of Kamala's voice startled both of them. An unwanted turd of tension hovered under the dangling bulb. Aadi immediately left the room. Both of them heard him running down the staircase.

Shaly retorted in a voice harsher than Kamala's, 'It is no good for anyone to be so insecure.'

It wasn't light yet. On either side of the pocket road, black trees were shedding, not water, not leaves, but the sorrows that multiplied every other second. Kamala was heading for the main road, where she hoped to see at least some of the headlights of the vehicles that raced over the tarred roads. There was not even a lamp post on the way. What is this place, she thought. She was neither running nor walking. In the distance, she saw the shadow of a huge boulder, indicating either a dead end or another opening. Ghost or just a shadow! She tried hard to concentrate on the rock so that she would not deviate in the darkness. A single goal! How quickly the pocket roads ended and dawn rose in the distance. Light! There was a huge red flag on a metal iron pole, almost on the ground level, maybe five-and-a-half feet or so—she realized she was not good with measurements. But something kept telling her that red without signals meant danger. Did it mean something dangerous was ahead? Like a wind-up monkey, but without the golden cymbals, she walked forward, mechanically. The dark ghost she had seen was there, only, she now realized, there were three such ghosts—or rather shadows, houses at three different angles. Suddenly morning light filled the sky and she became fully aware of the vast ground on which she was standing. Those were newly built shelters painted in dark green. Dwarf-sized boards marked the boundaries. Ha! She was standing in a meadow, a clear, green meadow, with either velvet or buffalo grass, she couldn't tell which. As the light intensified around her, she tried to read what the boards had to say. It said 350 yards on the first one. She checked the other boards too, and found the number getting smaller: 300 yards, 275 yards, 250, 200, 175, 150 . . .

What the fuck was this! Where was she standing?

The heights that cupped the firing range were lined with trees that grew upwards in straight lines, it seemed they never cast their shadows. What she loved was the lawn beneath. She hadn't seen such a lively lawn since her childhood. She wanted to smell it, feel the wetness all over, the wetness of earth and grass, the wetness of a woman, the wetness people may forget the second they walk away, like the way she had forgotten the grasslands of her childhood, those of her adolescence. She lay face-down on the lawn, sniffing the grass with the intense passion with which one sniffed cocaine. A flash of remembrance rushed through the prairies of kite-runners. Kites always belonged to the boys: Madhavan and his friends. They ran wild after those exciting kites. Where was the fun in holding the end of a thread and chasing after something that hovered high in the sky? She used to wonder, but now she knew—the fun lay in the way they controlled things, especially the kites, kept them under their command. They would let them fly for a while but never out of their purview, and once the kites broke away from the threads of control, that would be their terrible fate, a doom the boys on the ground could not assuage. They would wander for a while in the sky against the winds, the beaks of birds, and later perch on some godforsaken tree, almost broken, only to get scorched and fade under the happy sun. Those were the days of earth and grass, cookie-shaped cow dung cakes and dragonflies with glassy wings. Kamala raised her head and looked up. Where are they coming from now, she thought, those most ancient of insects? She lay supine, facing the dragonflies, the flies of September. Were they still not extinct? She let the flies float like war-copters over her. Beyond the flies, in the sky, the clouds were forming patterns of animals and faces. Now the face of a girl—the longer she looked, the clearer it became, the kaleidoscope eyes letting out iridescent happiness. She lay with her back to the skies, parallel to Kamala and facing her, suspended in the air but not floating. Her face was not clear, for in between them were dragonflies, mist and a layer of sunlight. But Kamala could clearly see her T-shirt, the edges of which were within the grip of the air. She read the alphabets that ran across the tee: LSD.

My god, an open manifesto! She lifted her arms towards the sky. Either her arms were stretching a bit too much or the girl was descending, for she touched her stomach and felt her nipples, like the knobs of a joystick. To the strumming of a guitar, the girl smiled, dimpling.

Now, Kamala floated in a paper boat, in crystal clear water. You want the water blue; yes, you take blue, green. But the tangerine trees and the marmalade skies that surrounded her had the same colour, immutable. Through the cellophane flowers of yellow and green she searched for the girl with the kaleidoscope eyes.

Somebody was calling her. Unhurried, in a voice not audible to others, Kamala said, 'She looks like her.' A newspaper taxi was waiting for her outside the firing range, on the shore, an open taxi; she could ride with the clouds on her face.

She remembered there had been no trellis for passion fruit, nor espaliers on a lattice in her garden a long time ago. Her garden was not even named. It was Shaly who had named it 'barsati', the terrace garden that had then only some wild creepers, cotton plants, a variety of orchids and an old barbeque in the corner. She was the one who took care of the garden; her barsati changed its colours and contours faster than Kamala changed the curtains in the rooms. The old terrace had been just a smoking area for Madhavan, to spend his idle hours in or sometimes play cards with his friends. Once he left, it breathed with the pleasure of women, of the earth they brought in small bags to the concrete terrace, of the green plants.

Bits of moonlight fell on the indoor plants in the pots. There was a party going on there; the invitees were mainly his friends, some hers. Kids also played on the terrace, including Shiva who was making a mess out of everything. In fact he was attracting attention; making faces at the visitors, picking his nose, and jumping down from certain heights making the guests say 'Oh my god' every now and then, forcing them to remark that he was the most adventurous soul on earth. Aadi, on the other hand, played his silent games sitting in the centre of the terrace, watching the people moving around. Some of the guests wanted the kids to talk. Some of them asked, 'Hello little one, what are you doing?'

'I am practicing being a hungry, wild lion, which hasn't eaten for a month,' Shiva said.

'But it seems like you have eaten too much already. What is there for the party? What is your mother going to give us?'

'Roach-rice,' he said.

The children made a lot of noise and laughed aloud at that. The guests joined them in their laughter mechanically, mostly because they didn't want to offend the boys' mother, as she was an extremely beautiful woman. When the children started circulating the menu with the special mucus rice their mom had made for the guests, Madhavan dragged them downstairs.

Rane, Javed and Faizy along with their girlfriends were from Kamala's office. Faizy's girlfriend was German, a beautiful blonde called Astrid. Each time they met she gifted Kamala a new book, even on the day Kamala resigned. The last book Astrid had given her was *Public Library and Other Stories* by Ali Smith and on the first page she had written in violet ink, 'There should always be a book between us' in small letters. She remembered the first book, *Madame Bovary*, and what she had written: 'For Kamala, for being the fairy you are'. It was the same book she had taken years ago from the college library.

Javed always used to bring two girls along with him and he would say like a public announcement, 'I won't be marrying either of these girls, such pains in my ass,' and the girls would titter. The people from her office were Madhavan's friends too; he had worked at Purple Ocean for a short while. Kamala had invited just one girl for the party, someone she had met during her travels, who had given her her phone number and address. Kamala had offered to find her a job, and she hoped this party with lots of people would help.

'If she is smart, there is nothing wrong in giving her a shot,' she said looking at Faizy.

'This is the third time you are saying this. But where is your girl, will she ever turn up?'

Someone put on some music, and the voices of those who had gathered rose above it; someone started swaying his body and others joined, followed by torrents of drinks.

She should have at least telephoned me, thought Kamala.

Then they saw a large bunch of red roses coming up the stairs; they were really wonderful with the silver ribbon lacing around the flowers. It was Shaly. Kamala felt her heart beating uncontrollably for some time, and then she took a deep breath. Shaly was waving the bunch up in the sky and smiling with her kaleidoscope eyes. When she saw Kamala she threw the bouquet at her. Kamala had to not let it fall.

'This is Shaly, my friend.'

All eyes were on her then. In the yellow lights mingled with the moonlight they read the letters on her tee: LSD.

Someone wanted to make fun of her. It was Parvesh who ate grass the way cows ate it.

'Hey girl, I understand, I got it, you LSD chick,' he said.

'Fine,' Shaly smiled.

Kamala was upset by the way he behaved. She knew he was a man who annoyed women. A friend of Madhavan's.

'Would you like to have some wine, or Bailey's?' Kamala asked.

'Wine! Kamala!' Parvesh mocked. 'Don't try to domesticate her,' he said, blocking Shaly's way.

'Parvesh, could you please move aside? You're making her uncomfortable.'

'Okay, I will get out of the way, but just one question. Could you please give me the full form of the letters on your tee?' he asked Shaly.

'Of course, why not,' she smiled and said, 'Lucy in the Sky with Diamonds.'

That night, Kamala dreamed of the sadness in the eyes of cows. She had not experienced remoteness so intense. What did those eyes say? She listened to the language of the eyes, their lashes laden with anguish. With an implicit apprehension, they kept saying, 'If I were free, I would have talked with you more often.' Then she saw Astrid coming towards her, dragging along a humongous, worn-out hessian sack. She emptied the contents in front of her—books, Kamala realized, from her own bookcases—and ran away. When she ran, Kamala saw her white thighs through the slit of her wrap-around skirt. She looked down at her books. Oscar Wilde, Dylan

Thomas, Vincent van Gogh, each jacket reflecting the sadness of cows' eyes, the sadness of the lives they had seen—the sadness of insatiable love and that of much endured loneliness.

Kamala had swallowed three pills long before her eyes transmogrified into those of the cow. It was with the cow's eyes that she looked at the bunch of sunflowers and waited for Dylan Thomas's ball that had not reached the ground yet. In between her wakefulness and sleep, she saw a person standing in the corner of the terrace leaning against the railings as the last remnant of the boozy night faded, barefoot and shaky. He was in a white nightshirt, the long strands of his hair swaying in the night wind.

I know this man, I think I have studied something somewhere, she said to herself. Was it he who said, 'The book of life begins with a man and a woman in a garden and ends with revelations?' What did he mean by revelations? What kind of revelations? I have always wanted to know more about this, the man and woman and then some other revelations, the first part concrete and the second part intangible. I am happy to meet this guy at last; I never thought I would be able to.

'Where . . . where is your lover Lord Alfred Douglas?' she asked.

33

In the afternoon, children were practicing dance in the school compound. It was a dress rehearsal and they all seemed extremely happy.

'We will be champions this time,' Fila said, happily kicking the stones along the pavement.

He wanted Shaly to come and see the dance, but she was in no mood to do so. Fila came to her house wearing the traditional piece of cloth with black and red stripes for the bamboo dance. He plucked a frangipani flower and stuck it behind his ear and walked gingerly, calling out her name. But for the piece of cloth around his hips, he was naked. Rita Mama felt enraged at the sight.

'Hey, Shaly, aren't you coming for the dance?' he asked.

'No, I am not in the mood,' she said.

'You said the same thing on Wednesday and Thursday. Today is the final rehearsal. Are you sure you are not coming?'

She shook her head as if to say no.

'Go get dressed and come,' he insisted.

'She is not going anywhere!' Rita Mama shouted.

Fila's face turned pale but Shaly said, 'Wait just a sec.' She ran inside and came back without bothering to change her dress.

'Come,' she said, holding his hand in hers as they walked. She could sense Rita's disappointment in the background and felt a thrill of satisfaction.

The girls were also in their ethnic wear, in red and white striped shirts and long cloths. Silken strands of their hair were swaying with the movement of their bodies. Boys were squatting on the ground, holding the ends of the bamboo staves in formation on the ground. They were waiting for Fila. When the music began the boys started moving the bamboo staves in rhythmic motions, and the girls, dancing to the tune, stepped in and out of the blocks. But Shaly couldn't focus on the dance or the dancers' attire—they did the same dance every year, no change, nothing new. Fila had promised to accompany her to the hilltops with his friends after the dance. So she waited, watching them dance. It was all a kind of calculation, she thought. The boys had to be very careful, for they had to clap the bamboo staves together on a particular beat and girls had to keep the count in mind while stepping in between the staves. This was a mathematical sort of a dance that demanded brilliance, it kept them going, no matter how mechanical the counts were.

The views from the hilltops were splendid; it was not like the dance they did every year. Every day she saw something new, behaved as if she had been caught in a storm, with a euphoric sense of liberation.

'What's over there?'

'A moving panorama of wildlife.'

'You must be kidding!'

'No, I'm not. I think I see things, extra,' she said. 'Colonel, open your eyes and see.'

Children used to call Fila 'Colonel'. He partly closed his eyes and tried to concentrate, and saw the usual grassy knolls, mounds and valleys in green.

'I want to see more . . . more!' Shaly shouted. 'Colonel, can you see the sea? Can you see small vessels, ships floating over it?'

'Yes, I'm trying.'

He looked again at the knolls, this time with greater attention; it must be the end of the sky she calls sea, he thought.

Shaly was proud of her eyes, nothing like the slanted eyes of her friends, and those who have large eyes, she thought, get to see more. Then she said she wanted glasses, something to enlarge, widen her vision. Fila smiled.

'Is that something you would love too?' she asked.

'Yes, I would love to have glasses.'

'We should do something to boost ourselves, our senses, on a daily basis. You got me?'

He gave a nod of understanding.

Rita Mama was left with no choice but to take her to the doctor. When the doctor asked her to read the board of alphabets that was on display, she pretended she couldn't see the letters clearly.

'Why don't you read? Try to read,' the doctor said.

'I am afraid I can't, it is all hazy.'

The implicit sadness she faked seemed so real that the doctor tried many lenses on her eyes, and she enjoying watching the doctor's pleasant smile turn grotesque and humongous with each new lens. She wished she could look at Rita Mama through the lenses, to see what she was in reality. She felt happy and extremely satisfied with the no-power lens, 'It's all very clear now, I can read.'

Rita Mama didn't let her take off the glasses even for a single minute. At first, Shaly was happy about this; she sincerely believed that she was seeing more, but soon the glasses began to seem like a burden.

The children poked around in the undergrowth for tinder. They gathered dried bamboo leaves and twigs from the fallen branches and the scorched logs they found on the way to keep the fire burning. They lit the fire and danced around the flames which were eating the bamboo leaves trying to escape with the wind. Finally, when the fire was down to embers, they threw in raw cashews and waited for the nuts to sizzle.

Meanwhile Shaly climbed the hills with her glasses on, but when she started to brag as usual about her magnificent vision, the boys scrambled up the hilltop and grabbed her glasses off her face. There was a big row over it—and then they saw the glasses flying down, tumbling on the rocks, smashing to pieces.

'Do you think they grow on trees?' That night, Rita Mama struck her violently till she stopped crying.

The next week Shaly heard Rita Mama cursing her mother, whom she had never seen. In fact, she had never thought of her mother so far. She tried to smile at her as if to say: Rita Mama, you are all I have, I don't have any other mother. But Rita was so uncontrollably furious, she yelled, 'I will wipe your smile off your bloody face.'

Shaly pushed her from the veranda with such force that she fell and got the first bandage on her rheumatic leg two hours later.

It had been almost one hour now, waiting outside the doctor's room. Shaly heard a woman cry from inside the room. When she remembered her days with Rita Mama, it evoked good memories and she was seized by a strong desire to see her again. Poor Mama, she manages herself alone these days. Shaly sat there, devastated by thoughts. It was important that she discussed Kamala's situation with the doctor. Something had to be done, or else things would fall out of place, irreparably. She looked at the closed door, behind which the subdued weeping continued, and decided to linger. There was a large poster on the door, in black and white: *To live is the rarest thing in the world. Most people exist, that's all.* She read it, the words printed over the picture of an old man helping a boy to walk.

The woman looked at Aadi for two or three minutes. 'Aadi, how are you? What are you doing these days?'

He hesitated for a moment, then said, 'Nothing. I just finished my PUC. Now I'm waiting.'

'Is your mother home?' she asked in a cordial voice.

'Yes, I will tell her,' he said. But she shook her head and went inside.

Kamala was fiddling around in the kitchen, a packet of bread in her hand. Janu had not come for the last two days and Shiva wanted her to make something edible, not like the fried onions Aadi bought from the shop. He said they made him puke.

She thought of making French toast. She put the packet of bread on the side table and made a mental inventory: eggs, milk, sugar. She paused again, made some calculations in her mind. She took three eggs from the fridge and broke them into a pan, then added the milk and sugar. But something was just not right. She thought again and jumped up in alarm. Oh my god, the bread! One needs bread to make toast! Thank god! She was happy her memory was working. A lapse of memory makes a person suffer. She could not let that happen to herself, she was happy there were eggs, sugar, milk and a packet of bread readily available in the kitchen; she even found a packet of butter in the fridge.

'Kamala!'

She turned back and saw the woman. She couldn't remember who it was though. How dare people come to another's kitchen without notice?

'Don't you recognize me?'

Demanding recognition is something awful, thought Kamala. The woman, whoever she was, looked dismayed, as if she were displeased with either the look on Kamala's face or the way her face had altered with time.

'It's me, Maya,' she said disinterestedly.

Taken aback, Kamala said, 'My god, Maya, is that you?'

Kamala looked at the woman's double chin and the pendulous breasts, sacks like those of any other jaundiced woman of the neighbourhood. Though she accepted it resentfully, she couldn't believe it. The Maya she remembered had been a very beautiful girl. Maya too might have been looking at Kamala's hollow eyes and colourless face similarly.

Little by little, she remembered how graceful those days had been. Maya used to have a handmade notebook in which she had copied her favourite lines of poetry, which she used to read aloud in times of leisure—one beautiful thing she loved about her. She also remembered the day they all went to the cinema in town; it was like a festival. In 1984 they were children and so their parents had driven them to town in their old-fashioned cars to watch the movie. It was about a fictitious good little ghost, the first Indian movie to be filmed in 3D. The children were quite excited about wearing the black 3D glasses. Someone said they could go inside the movie, and someone else said, 'No, actually, the cinema will come to us.'

'Do you mean to our seats?'

'Yes, actually, the cinema will come to wherever you are sitting.'

'Then what will happen?'

'I don't know. Something will happen for sure, if you don't want to see it you can take off your glasses.'

Fancy 3D glasses or not, they all went. They didn't get the tickets for the morning show so they had to wait for the matinee. It was a long queue, plus everybody crowded around everybody else, scrumming for a little space. Madhavan's mother was not very happy about waiting for another three hours in the queue, but he was very adamant, and he started yelling at her. The children didn't see anything wrong with this, for half the children gathered there were either yelling or crying. Besides, they had come all the way from their neighbourhood to town just to watch this movie and, maybe, if time permitted, they would have some ice cream too. While they waited, the children took turns playing on the stairs carpeted in red velvet. This was a luxury their village theatres lacked. They leaned over the railings, stretched their arms as far as they would go to touch the cement heads of the elephants which kept spraying water through their trunks down to the artificial pool in the middle of the theatre. There were policemen too, to control the crowd. Everything about the movie was hilarious, the movie itself and the games before the movie. But afterwards, when they got out of the theatre, there was no queue or order. Where are the policemen, they wondered. Kamala started crying in the crowd, she was worried she would lose her folks.

'Where have you parked the car?' her mother asked the driver.

It was difficult to navigate the crowd with children, especially little girls. But suddenly something happened and they saw the policemen charging towards them, shouting violently. The crowd turned into a mob: people were running amok, some fell down, others moved through the crowd in a frenzied and uncontrollable way. The girls were crying, including Maya and Kamala; Maya the louder of the two. Kamala, Maya and Madhavan saw it all, the other children might have seen as well because they all started crying too. But they couldn't believe what they were seeing. In front of the people who had come out after the show, amidst the crowd, two men went berserk and killed each other. With their dying breaths they said something, their ultimate, final words, and the reports travelled through the crowd in less time than required: they said it was not murder but suicide, a planned suicide by both the parties. The men were dressed alike, in the same tight-fitting, striped T-shirts and pink pants, and they had even tied colourful bows around the knives, but the knives themselves were deadly, with long concave depressions in the metal blade meant to inflict maximum damage. They might have swirled the knives, twisted them inside the bodies in the same pattern, maybe a left turn or a right turn or a sharp move upwards and then downwards, for when both of them fell motionless, their right hands were wrapped around the handles of the knives with which they had each stabbed the other's body, a shockingly decisive suicide. It seemed that they had coordinated the deed to the last detail. No one could do anything.

The deaths shocked the town. Why had they planned this in such a public place, amidst women and children? What was their motive?

The children had forgotten everything about the movie as well as their plans to go to the ice cream parlour. As soon as they reached the safety of their cars, they let loose a barrage of questions.

'What happened—'

'Why did they stab each oth—'

'Was it a real knife—'

'Was it real blo—'

'Enough!' Madhavan's father thundered. 'Stop talking.'

Suicides pacts were not common in 1984. The next day, the children saw the men in the newspapers: the youngsters who had committed suicide by stabbing each other.

Maya said, 'Actually, the papers say they were homosexuals.'

'What does that mean? What is . . . homo . . .? What?' Madhavan asked.

'Actually, I don't know what it is. I think it means they were pilots in airplanes.'

'Oh!'

'But then why should homosexual pilots die like this?'

When had Maya left? Did she say a proper goodbye? Why did she bring back memories of those valiant samurais who performed a planned seppuku in public like two actors doing a street performance?

She remembered running through the festival grounds of the temple with Maya in search of broken pieces of glass bangles. It was fun to play with bangle pieces. In a game, the person who collected more scored more; possession was all that mattered. She thought about having fun with bangles. She had seen Kuljeet wearing green bangles. Green bangles stand for fertility; she wondered why Kuljeet hadn't conceived yet. Green or red, bangles were real fun. They say the honeymoon ends when the last bangle breaks. Why was Kuljeet still wearing them then? Was she still playing with Madhavan?

Now Kamala's French toast was inside the black cat. She tried to remember, she forgot. She focused. There were no more eggs. She remembered the tall ceramic jar with a big round belly in which her mother kept pickled mangoes, and she also remembered the circus people who practiced cycle shows. Both the memories served no purpose. Her brain heated her up. She wanted to react. Off she went, out of control. She beat her head. Calmed down. Thought the unthinkable. It sucks, she said to herself. She looked desperate and nervous. After some time, she remembered the words of the Ramana Maharshi. 'Both remembrance and forgetfulness are part of our pride. Fear comes when the mind pressurizes the brain. Fear is the manifestation, the bubbling up of pride.' She asked her mind to calm down. In response, her mind stormed through her veins against her brain.

34

'How dare you talk to me like this?' said the doctor.

'Doctor, please, I didn't mean it,' said Shaly.

'I don't understand why you said all homosexuals are drug addicts, it is rubbish,' said the doctor.

'No, I didn't mean that. I said Kamala has an inclination towards drugs because she is a lesbian.'

'Again you are talking nonsense, Shaly. There is absolutely no relationship between homosexuality, drugs and AIDS. Do you get me? These are three different things. You said it was you who gave Kamala LSD the first time. Then how come you are not a lesbian? I've never heard you admit that.'

'I am extremely sorry about all this. What I meant was, it must be her distress that led her into such uncertain situations. I couldn't be the partner she has always wanted in life. It is true, I tried earlier, but my focus was not on pleasing her, rather finding a job for myself in Bangalore and making a name and address of my own. Yes, I was selfish then. I was also suffering from certain other problems . . . It was all such claptrap, I regret it now.'

'But once you were out of that situation you should have said goodbye to her, you should have admitted your mistakes and helped her break free of disillusionment.'

'Unfortunately, I couldn't do that. Madhavan had abandoned her and she was going through a very difficult time in her life. Even her children had some problems by then . . .'

'Sympathy or empathy—what is it you suffer from?'

'No, nothing like that. It is true that I love her, sometimes more than I love myself. But not the way you people judge it.'

'Yes, I can understand your feelings. What you've said is partially true. Distress must be the main reason she gave in to drugs. But is suppressed sexuality the only villain? What do you think?'

'The one thing that worries her is that she's afraid she's never been sincere in her life. She strongly believes that she is not reliable.'

'That's it! No one is sincere in society. We should be fair to ourselves and our bodies before anything else. Otherwise we suffer. Have you ever been sincere to yourself? Is the life you are living real?'

I should have talked to the doctor more reasonably, Shaly thought later. She felt ashamed recalling the way she had spoken. Was she rude? She couldn't tell. He was a wise man, no-nonsense. Though he made it sound like LGBTQ people were the only really happy people on earth, regardless of how badly society treated them. They were happy because they were happy inside. A time would come when people would say, 'Excuse me, my sexual preference is different, I cannot imagine being in a relationship with a man.'

Like they used to say, 'Excuse me, I am married, I cannot imagine being in another relationship. I am afraid of my husband.'

Shaly looked at her watch; it was getting late. The doctor had asked her to bring Kamala for one more sitting. But Kamala was no kitten she could wrap up in a sack and bring. Anyway, she bought the medicines he had prescribed, tranquilizers probably.

She thought she would spend the night at Jithan's place. He wouldn't make a scene if she was a bit brusque. But he felt obligated to not wear anything other than his boxers at home, and he would come two or three times to her bedside during the night, showing off his thighs, which were sparsely covered with hair. In a gentlemanly way, he would ask, 'Are you sure you don't want it, baby doll?' With each peg, he would repeat the question, but he never compelled her to do anything and never admitted that he wanted anything. He wanted to check if his thing would be of any use to her, a self-proclaimed dildo. Who knows what a woman's bust might look like, and if her nipples poked out through her clothing at the slightest provocation he considered it his responsibility to offer, though the choice was always hers.

She called him, and as expected, he was exaggeratedly happy.

'You are my trophy friend, baby girl, you need not even call ahead. Just step in and the house is yours. I only have Bacardi and vodka though, hope you can adjust, baby.'

What a bore, she thought. She hated the way he called her 'baby'; she was not a baby, and she wanted him to know that. She searched for the number of Meru cabs or that of other taxi services. The call was not going through and it was really getting dark. She tried some other phone numbers, but it seemed that her phone had stopped working; her network had jammed or didn't recognize the shift that took place between states—it happened sometimes. It was then that she noticed a familiar figure moving falteringly across at the other end of the pavement. Following him in a hurry, she saw Madhavan's car drive by with Parvesh at the wheel.

Madhavan, who was sitting next to Parvesh, saw Shaly clearly. For a second, his face twisted in a grimace, and the next second it brightened with some remote hope: Have they returned?

He remembered the day Kamala had almost drowned in the lotus pond while swimming. She was a little girl then, and if his memory served him, she was just trying to swim then, in her own way. It was he who had grabbed her hair, pulled her to safety and dragged her out of the pond. She had already taken in some water and he had to give her CPR. When she came back to her senses, she said boastfully to whoever came her way, 'It was my brother who saved my life.'

Now he recognizes the tears in his eyes, his little sister.

It was Uncle Raphael, her teacher from Mizoram. He was walking leisurely like someone who wanted to be the last always. When Shaly recognized him in the moving crowd, she walked faster to reach him and hugged him from behind.

'Jeez, I can't believe you're here,' she said.

Raphael was startled and turned around nervously.

'My God, who is this?' he shouted, for he was uncontrollably happy. 'Shaly! You look so different.'

'Now tell me, what brings you here? Rebels like you in a metro like Bangalore?'

'I live here these days. There is no one to order me out of here like your father used to do. Those were the days, now that's something, tell me. How's Rita Mama, is she all right? Do you live here?'

'Uncle Raphael, I think it would be better if we could go to your place and sit and talk, don't you think that would be wonderful?'

Shaly rang Jithan once again.

'You are not lucky, you idiot trophy friend, I am roasting dragon prawns here.'

'Let me see if I can make it. Keep some in the fridge, if I don't turn up you can microwave them and have them in the morning.'

'I am making some gooseberry chutney as well, baby.'

She disconnected when she heard him call her 'baby'. She turned on airplane mode and kept the phone inside her handbag. In the auto they sat close, in a warm, comfortable way. Stroking her hands, he said in a sing-song voice, 'Long is the way and hard, that out of Hell leads up to light . . .'

Uncle Raphael's house could not be called a house in the true sense of the word, for it was merely a room on the second floor of somebody else's house. It came with an attached bathroom, but the flush was not working and the plaster was peeling off the walls. The terrace, with the garden plants neatly arranged in waste bags, was relatively larger than the single room, which contained a bed, an air conditioner, a recliner, a table and chair, some fake paintings on the wall and a mini fridge the size of a large printer where he could keep six bottles at a time.

'So, you are living in luxury. An AC and a fridge! Fit for a king. Congratulations!' she said.

'Just to make certain chicks run into my arms with the growing night chill,' he said jokingly.

'That's the spirit, Uncle,' she laughed, examining the booze bottles on the table. 'What are these empty bottles doing here? Are they for show?'

'Don't break them. I keep them because they are beautiful. Look at the slender waist, the necks, the fat bottoms, what more do you think a man needs?'

'If you want beauty in your life, why don't you set up a terrace garden? Of course, I will have to charge you for the idea, they don't just flow in, you know.'

'If only I had some visitors. This is the dump I live in, me, myself and me again, no one gives me a piece of ass, no sense of humour left. No one comes here dear, you're probably the first person to visit after I settled here.'

'Don't call it a dump. It is a den, Uncle. You are the one who is living in here, the lion of the forests.'

She touched a few things on the table and looked at the empty bottles in the dustbin.

'It seems you drink a lot these days.'

'Occasionally.'

'I see a lot of occasional bottles down there. A man must really be lucky to have so many occasions in life.'

'Solitude is a sin.'

'And is booze the redeemer?'

'Sometimes, but it has already made its impression on my liver. Anyway it's been a long while since I was so happy.'

'Now, don't get emotional.'

'For this old man your visit is like a dream—I believe, and I do not believe. It feels wonderful.'

Raphael poured vodka into Martini glasses.

'Let the eyes, liver, and heart go with it, but the right-sized cocktail will never stop finding its way into the sexiest Martini glass. Cheers to all the happy fools of the world.'

'Cheers, but I would have preferred a rock glass. I took these Martini glasses out just to please you. I know the things girls like.'

'Luckily I don't belong to the usual "chick" category, Uncle, feel at home. Cheers again.'

This was the fourth time Madhavan was trying Kamala's landline after he had left Peacock Bar. No one was answering. What did that mean? It could mean only one thing: they were all back, in Bangalore, near him. Since he had quarrelled with his father over the land sale issue he didn't feel like calling him and asking about their whereabouts. He tried her mobile number, the automated answer came in Malayalam and he understood they were still in Kerala. It was good Shaly was not with them. Was there a chance they had fallen out with each other?

'No, I haven't quarrelled with her, uncle. The thing is, Rita Mama hates to see me. I have tried my best but it seems impossible. Sometimes she doesn't recognize my presence at all, or she shouts at me or curses herself.'

She lay down tiredly in the recliner, watching him make the bed. It was not a recliner where you could stretch out your body, but it was comfortable.

'Come on, you can sleep on the bed now. I'll sleep there,' he said, pointing to the recliner. 'You should be treated like a princess. Do you want a T-shirt or something?'

'No, thanks. I guess there is enough room for both of us on the bed. As you said, you keep the air conditioner on high so some chicks can hug you tight.'

He walked over to the table, and mixed himself another drink.

'Do you want to lower the AC?' he asked.

'No, I want you to stop drinking now. The air conditioner is fine. What I can't bear is the sight of people doing harm to themselves.'

'Ah, dear Paul Mauriat, don't get too emotional.'

'Yes, I admit, I was always bad with guitars, I couldn't even hold my striker properly between my thumb and forefinger. Such a failure! But I love emotions, I love Mauriat, and I want you to stop drinking now.'

'That was orchestra and a grand piano, not for beginners to strum on their acoustic guitars, but there is nothing wrong in giving it a try, like we all do, like we are always doing.'

'Thanks for reminding me, now drink and die,' she said, moving to lie on the bed.

He poured the rest of the vodka into the basin and turned the lights off. With heavy steps, he went and lay down beside her. She hugged him tightly and wept for a while. He ran his fingers through her hair, neither of them saying anything. It seemed they were remembering how Mauriat echoed through the hills of Aizawl, wondering who introduced him there and when—not so great compared to the great masters and a bit too emotional, but lovable, adorable all the same.

After some time he said, 'Try to sleep, my darling baby.'

Shaly had the feeling that this would be her best sleep in a long time, no troubles and no worries. She heard the forest echoing the strums of guitars; she saw herself lying on the bare earth, the trees surrounding her; she felt herself becoming the darkness.

Children used to call him Raphael the Rogue with love. He was straddling his fifties, and was a rebel among the teachers, who had been expelled from the school three times and taken back out of love. He taught the children rebellion, he asked them to fight.

'How can you be at peace and eat like pigs when Irom Chanu Sharmila is leading a hunger strike in the neighbourhood?'

True, the children thought for a while, she lived in the neighbourhood. Invariably, all of them belonged to the seven sister states. Sharmila had vowed not to eat, drink, comb her hair or look in a mirror when she started her fast. She was protesting something called AFSPA, their parents said. They had heard their parents speak about her at home, though they could not understand what it was all about. What were the children supposed to do about something they did not understand, something their parents themselves were not sure of? Raphael the Rogue would shout: 'Children should do nothing, absolutely nothing, and when the kidnappers come to abduct the children, the others will do nothing. Those children who shudder in the face of the news,' Raphael continued, 'are the promises of tomorrow. The others will go on enjoying a good meal and a long and slow crap in the toilet.'

He made the children stand on their desks in a circular pattern and then taught them a poem that was not prescribed in their textbooks. He said it was by Gerard Manley Hopkins. Together they sang, and it was like a prayer,

Márgarét, áre you gríeving
Over Goldengrove unleaving?
Leáves like the things of man, you
With your fresh thoughts care for, can you?
Ah! ás the heart grows older
It will come to such sights colder
By and by, nor spare a sigh

Though worlds of wanwood leafmeal lie;
And yet you will weep and know why.
Now no matter, child, the name:
Sórrow's springs áre the same.
Nor mouth had, no nor mind, expressed
What heart heard of, ghost guessed:
It is the blight man was born for,
It is Margaret you mourn for.

When the small eyes of the children dimmed in fear, Raphael said to them, 'You should be brave, like our women who stripped in front of the soldiers and yelled, "Indian Army, rape us."'

He asked his students to ponder on the matters India was going to discuss in the coming days.

When she woke, she found him sitting on the recliner. She sensed him looking at her. It was not morning yet.

'Uncle, you haven't slept?'

'My nights are terribly long usually, sleepless and disturbed, but last night I slept very well, thanks to you.'

When she came nearer, he kissed her hands. 'Thank you,' he said, 'nothing more beautiful than this night is likely to come again in this old man's life.'

'You like it melancholic.'

'Whatever! Oh God, are you hungry? That must be the reason you got up so early.'

'I am happy you asked.'

'I can scramble some eggs or maybe make you a bull's eye if you like.'

'Yes, I would love to, but not now. I want to sleep some more. It is so comfy in here.'

'I still cannot believe this rain in a desert.'

'Just say goodnight now, conversations are boring in the early morning.'

'Would you like to say cheers to the sixth occasional glass?'

She saw the Martini twisting in between his fingers. She covered her face with the blanket.

Slut! How dare she turn off her phone! Kamala threw her mobile on the bed. What was she doing all night with her phone switched off? Was she fucking someone? Madhavan had called her many times on her mobile, but she didn't feel like calling him back. Now, a fear, distinctively insane, started gnawing at her insides; she felt the pressure in her bowels, a gastric pull in her intestines. She took the phone and started calling them both. Her phone was switched off and though his was ringing, there was no answer.

Slut! Slut! Slut!

35

'If only we had access to the Internet we could have said "Hi" to Shaly on Facebook,' said Shiva.

'Does she have a Facebook account?' asked Aadi.

'You are the only person on earth who doesn't have one, Aadi.'

'It doesn't make any difference; you are in no way better than me.'

'It makes a hell of a lot of difference to me. A netizen is never lonely, never bored. And what do we have here, except the fried eggplant Janu cooks? The Internet allows us to imagine that we are surrounded by many people—girls, women, men. Their company, especially that of girls, makes us feel rich. I can't survive here; this is like living in hell, a pandemonium of serenity. There is no use trying to talk to Amma.'

'True, it's been two days since we ate anything nice.'

'We should ask Janu to make something edible.'

'When Shaly comes back, we can ask her to cook.'

'Shiva, I miss Bangalore a lot. If I ask you something, will you get mad at me? When Shaly comes back can I go to Bangalore for a while? I would like to meet Rhea; you can't imagine how much I miss her.'

What Aadi said was a lie, for he knew Rhea was not there, but he considered her the sentimental trump card with which he could make his brother cave. Totally against what he had expected, Shiva smiled pleasingly.

'You go and come back, for you Rhea and for me Shaly.'

'I didn't mean it that way. I only meant that if Shaly comes back, there will be someone to take care of you. You know Amma can't handle everything.'

'Of course, but what the fuck is she handling these days anyway?'

'Shiva, she is sick. She is not well, and we should realize that.'

'I was just joking, I think I can manage myself. Don't you worry about me, Aadi.'

'In that case, I will send her a mail when I go to the town in the evening. Do you know her email ID?'

'Why the fuck do you want to send her a mail? Can't you just telephone her?'

'No, no way! She makes fun of me whenever I try to begin a conversation. It would be better if I sent her a mail instead. Give me the ID.'

'It's talktoshaly@gmail.com.'

Solitude was the silence buried deep within. Two teenagers going on nineteen, confined within the white walls of an old house, looked at each other in silence and savoured the taste of the poison on their tongues. It was something they could not swallow like they could finish a piece of ginger cake or tablespoons of bitter honey collected from a snakewood tree. It was real, though impalpable. In the mornings it woke with them, and they wondered at how slowly it spread, taking its sweet time. They saw it crawling over the white plaster of their bedroom, and strengthening its grip on the warmth outside. Their taste buds and food pipes suffocated under the strange smell of ash gourds cooked in water and turmeric, sometimes there would be raw mango and drumsticks, sometimes raw banana—whatever the vegetable, it was always cooked in the same way, the same recipe: water, salt and turmeric. But lately they had been hiding their distaste, for they knew their mother was seriously ill, weak or tired, though she was still young and somewhat beautiful. The sight of their mother shrinking every day, her clothes hanging off her shoulders like the coat of a lawyer, like the folds of a wild bat, deepened their insecurity. They had not seen her veins looking so prominent before, or hers eyes so hollow or her laugh lines so clearly visible. At times, the vein that began on her forehead seemed to pop onto the surface as if it were a pronouncement of her severe headache.

Though they all lived inside the same house and they all wanted to separate and go back, at times they sat around the big dining table without seeing each other. Sometimes, the landline rang, but no one cared to answer, they would let the rings echo throughout the house. Each thought inside the house was plainly suicidal. If they had had a loaded gun, they would have fired without aiming; it would have been easy for Aadi to end Shiva's solitude. Like Brecht had said all living things need help from the rest of the living. Once, in their room in Bangalore, they had watched a Hrithik Roshan movie. The hero was completely paralysed and bedridden, pleading for euthanasia. It was difficult to watch that movie sitting beside Shiva. Aadi had wanted to leave the room, but Shiva insisted he stay. When the hero asked a well-wisher for a packet of condoms, Shiva laughed aloud, and Aadi shuddered.

They remembered what Shaly had told them the day after they had arrived here. 'Breathe in as much as you want, the air is pure, not polluted like the air we have in Bangalore. No excess of vehicles, no mobile towers—life is like heaven, a paradise of trees, far away from the maddening wires and signals.' They tried to draw in a deep breath, but their lungs choked as if attacked by deadly, acidic bee stings. Shaly, maybe you don't know that solitude is the deadliest poison on earth. Pathways that don't reek of diesel smoke and green fields without mobile towers are not always free of poison.

Aadi was leaving the bedroom when he heard Janu cry out. He rushed towards the entrance hall, from where the cry had sounded.

'What is the matter?' Shiva was asking behind him. Kamala lay prone, near the threshold steps of the entrance hall.

'What happened?' Aadi asked Janu.

'I don't know! She hasn't eaten anything since yesterday,' she said. 'I will go and get a taxi, let us take her to the hospital.'

'It's vertigo, no need for a doctor,' Kamala said in a weak voice and in a dialect neither of them understood. Somehow, they picked her up, and lay her down on what used to be her father's bed in the room next to the entrance hall. Aadi sat on the edge of the old four-poster bed, unsettled. Janu rushed to summon a taxi. Aadi heard Shiva calling him from his room, but fear didn't permit him to answer or go to him.

Kamala lay on her father's majestic canopy bed like a misfit frill that has frayed a bit. The car in the temporary garage was of no use to her. Aadi remained on the edge of the bed, petrified, thinking about a time when his mother would not be around. He sat there motionless, unmindful of Shiva's calls, till the taxi honked from outside and Janu rushed in.

In the sunlight, two water droplets oscillated on a lotus leaf like two precious pearls that had no roots, no reality. The leaf, on the other hand, was mute, its mouth strapped by long cellophane ribbons of veins, it had no way to support them. Like toddlers taking their first steps, the droplets wobbled on the leaf's surface for a while, then in unison they flowed towards the centre, to the heart of the leaf, as if going back to the womb: they shone there like a priceless gem.

He waited around in what used to be her father's room even after they came back from the doctor, even after Janu had gone, even after it struck eleven. In the end, Kamala had to force him to leave her room. She said having low blood pressure was normal, and that seven in ten suffered from the same issue.

'What is there to worry about so much? Just go and sleep,' she said.

But this didn't improve the feverish condition of his brain. Fear had transformed into a deadly ghost by then, one that threatened,

'Your mother is about to die, you don't have much time left with her, watch out.' Fear, he had identified, had the smell of old mud walls getting wet in the rain. If only there were more light and wind in the room, if only she could keep one window open even if it was night, he sighed. Kamala's headphones were on the table. He took them and walked towards her. He asked her in a gentle voice, 'Would you like to listen to some music, Amma?'

'Yes, I would love to.'

Shiva had no complaints even after that long and weary day of abandonment. Aadi didn't tell him much except that their mother had had a severe headache and they had taken her to the hospital. At one point, when he was alone, Shiva's throat was parched and he had cried aloud, 'Aadi, please come here! Janu! Anybody there?' but there had been no answer. He kept calling them for some more time. Then he realized that the more he shouted the thirstier he would get and hence he decided to remain quiet. The water that remained in his body had to be preserved; no more anger, no more tears. He could not have climbed down from such a tall bed and got into the wheelchair all his own, nor could he imagine crossing the antique thresholds in his chair. Shaly used to tell him the story of a man who was the supernova of physics, who had spent a good part of his time in a wheelchair, to motivate him, though Shiva never felt inspired enough. The design of each flower and each plant in this universe is different, the needs and blueprint change with the playtime fantasy of the universe.

After Kamala heard the door close, and Aadi's footsteps recede down the corridors, she sat up on her bed and glanced around the room, taking in the anaemic white walls, the closed shutters of the window, the headphones he had given her and the huge black dog wagging its tail at her bedpost. There are people, she thought, who never get tired of the countless insipid coffees waiting for them every morning, from cradle to grave: no real sex, no mental nymphomania, no worries. The dog climbed into the bed and sat there, resting its head on her lap. She ran her fingers through the folds of its neck, the fur on its back.

There were dirty clothes piled up around the room. She wondered why Aadi hadn't felt like tidying up the place, for she knew he had been there all the time. At the very least, he could have put the clothes in the laundry basket.

She got down from the bed and with much difficulty picked up the dirty clothes, her lingerie, wondering if he had seen them lying on the floor like that, and put everything in the laundry basket. She knew it was the room, its watered-down, unreal walls that were not letting her sleep. The lack of air inside the room was always trying to smother her and she pushed open a window, her arms suffering a twisting spasm of pain. An almost unexpected gust of wind rushed inside and somehow she stepped out of the room and stood on the veranda for some time, leaning against one of the pillars of the central courtyard. Afterwards she made her way across the threshold of the entrance hall. She wondered how she had fallen down there and why, whether there would be a decent way to settle her problems. She clasped the pineapple motif and looked up the dimly lit staircase. Shamelessly, Satan, the fallen angel who had become an antique piece, incapable of even a decent cough, looked at her. His yellowing teeth and decaying bones didn't hold him back from chasing fallen angels, and so he followed her, climbed the steps after her. He knew he could no longer coil around the wilderness luring women, but he knew he had the potential to do something, though not in an elaborate way, something of his own, like old women chew betel leaves, like old men curse the young ones. He stealthily walked behind her, for his skin was no longer young and shiny, but weirdly shrivelled up and unravelled at the same time.

Kamala pushed open the doors to Shaly's room. She remembered how Sankaran and his woman and the other workers had pulled everything out of that room once. The heavy chest of drawers had knocked off some of the plaster from the wall then— the mark was still there, like a gash on the skin. She remembered the cardboard boxes, the junk that even ragpickers would not have dared to take for free, and the sadness in her mother's eyes over the burnt waste. 'Just in case of an emergency, my child, just in case,' Amma had said repeatedly.

There were no more just-in-cases there. The room looked washed out, except for the dangling bulb. She remembered how Maya and she had stood locked under that bulb once.

'Shall I turn off the light?' Satan stammered.

'Yes, please.'

On the bed, there was no scent of Shaly, nothing that reminded Kamala of her. Instead, some of the old voices came back, scampering moves, and the sound of short, quick steps. She thought she even saw the loft open, which had not been the case when she had gone to Shaly with a cup of hot coffee in her hand. Her mother would no longer come hurrying in case she gave a cry of alarm. She didn't wish to disturb her sons, Aadi was already very upset. She couldn't close her eyes; she sat down on the bed and looked around; she felt the old glances and the old fear again; she tried to concentrate on the loft that was not there. Satan was hiding behind the door, in the lingering light of the hour, she had seen his shadow on the floor. She thought it was Madhavan.

'Madhavan, why are you standing there?' she asked.

Her children were sleeping on either side of the bed.

'I want to go back tomorrow,' he said.

'Can we come with you?'

'Wait for three more months. What will you do there with the babies? Stay with your mother, that would be better.'

'Haven't I told you, Madhu, that something always bothers me here? Something crawls into my ears. I want to be back in Bangalore.'

'It's just a feeling, dear, you are worried, that's all.'

She watched him pack his things, the zipper of his travel bag opened wide, and for a second she imagined packing the babies, putting them inside the bag, without him knowing it. Satan

215

deliberately dropped something, making Madhavan bend over to retrieve it. When he came back to the room after packing his things and taking his nightly shower, he saw Kamala and the children sleeping peacefully. He sat down on the mattress stretched out for him on the floor and before slipping into a comfortable post-shower sleep he looked at the babies once more. This time, he heard something hissing very softly. Without waking her up, he lifted the edge of Kamala's mattress slightly and checked. 'Oh God!' he drew his hand back as he felt pain seeping through his veins. Clumsily, he pitched forward to the switches.

'Kamala, wake up, get up,' he said.

Still asleep, she sat up straight. 'What happened?' she asked him.

Satan lit the bulb, in the light of which she saw the marks on Madhavan's arm, two tiny red spots adjacent to each other on his left forearm.

Madhavan is dying. Who will give the obituary? Do I need to wake up his sons?

'Kamala, take the children and move aside,' he shouted, his voice fearful.

'I told you, there is something.'

When she stepped backwards with the babies cuddled in her arms, he, gathering strength, turned the mattress upside down onto the floor. There, on the wooden bed planks, they saw two little golden snakes crawling about helplessly, and which, when she came forward to take a closer look, opened their purple mouths.

The wind ruffled the curtains of the room. It couldn't lift the curtains or make them sway uncontrollably, like the curtains in ghost movies, for the curtains were reluctant to leave the wood grills of the window shutters. Tormented by disturbing thoughts and sleeplessness Aadi walked towards her room, though he was not sure of a welcome. He thought, at the least, he could check whether she was sleeping or not. If the music had helped her sleep then he could go back and try to get some sleep himself.

The silence of the furniture was audible in the dingy moonlight that was reflected on and through the courtyard. The days, nights, afternoons and mornings were chained to each other, to a tangled labyrinth of no time and no space and no concepts. Unbelievably, there was no difference between wakeful hours and sleeping hours. He hadn't even read a book since he had come here. While they were in Bangalore, Kamala used to brag about enrolling him in some coaching classes in a neighbouring town in her native place, but it seemed she had completely forgotten about that, or that her son had passed PUC and it was her duty to think of his future. What a blissful sort of forgetfulness this is, he thought. Does she think her children were some sort of furniture she bought on the way to keep inside the 'relatively big' bedroom of her house?

The doors to her room were ajar; even the window, which had been closed while he was there, which he had wanted to open so badly, was open now. She was not in the room. He saw her headphones on the bed. He searched all over, in the bathroom, in the kitchen, in the dining area; he even went back to his own room to see if she had gone there. Shaly had told him that the house measured more than eight thousand square feet. Suddenly, each room, each space, each void frightened him. Most of the rooms remained closed all the time, and he shut the doors faster than he opened them. He didn't even stop to check whether she was inside the rooms. He ran amok, breathing in the rusted smell of darkness. Somewhere in between the corroded shadows he hesitated, he thought he saw long hair, a swivel chair, a black cat and the ghostly doll his mother had abandoned a long time ago. He turned back and looked around in fright, calling aloud, 'Amma, where are you?'

There was no answer. He ventured outside the entrance hall. The old staircase with its pineapple projections was not welcoming, but the thought of pigeons sleeping upstairs strengthened him. Yet, with each step the phantom of darkness bit his ears, poked his eyes and tickled his stomach where he sensed a jerky stroke.

He tried to think of something sweet, something pleasant. He remembered the two oscar fish he had had in his tank when he was a boy. At first they used to be inside the small glass tank but later he put them in the cement pond tank Kamala had bought to grow water lilies in. He cleaned the tank thoroughly, for he knew oscars lived only in fresh water. It seemed the fish immediately liked the place Aadi had arranged for them. Whenever he went near the tank, one of the fish swam across to reach him. He started bragging about it and his friends corrected him. They said it was because of the food he was giving them, that the oscars came to the surface of the water no matter who came to them as long as they brought food. Kamala used to bring him bags of guppy fish from the market to feed the oscars. The second they smelled the rainbow fish they would come to the surface dancing. He soon realized that the oscars were not so good at catching fish. The rainbow fish would stealthily evade the open mouths of the oscars and it was he who fished the guppies out and fed the oscars at times. But it takes a certain amount of skill to feed them, and it's best not to try if you don't have it. Many of his friends had failed hopelessly; Shiva had frowned, seeing them suck their bloody fingers. Aadi, he had said, was exceptionally talented. He closed his eyes and climbed the steps. It was not just a small water tank; he saw fresh water spreading in front of him and a surprisingly clean layer of plankton over it. The lapping of the water filled him, he said, he was thankful to the Oscars who helped him climb the stairs.

Even the verandas upstairs smelled of Shaly, the slightly intoxicating perfume of a woman. He felt no fear, no trace of anxiety. But suddenly a shudder ran down his spine when his mobile beeped. The message had been sent in the morning, some kind of good morning wish, and had reached him when his phone entered the receiving zone. There were two flickering signal marks, he looked carefully, just two lines of signal that kept appearing and disappearing. He tried to dial Kamala's number, but it said her phone was busy; he hated the automated voice at once and wondered who could be calling her at this hour. The doors to Shaly's room were open and cautiously he went inside. The bed was vacant, the room heavy with the smell of perfume. He decided to sit on the bed for a while; now that his tension had eased a bit, sleep was working its way into him. Then he saw his mother sitting in the corner, next to the bed, her eyes, mouth, everything about her almost purple in colour. Though fear blocked his way, he thought he heard his mother say, 'Spare them, let them crawl over to the backyard, let them live.'

His tongue was stuck to the back of his throat, he looked at her expressionlessly.

'They have been living with me for so long now, please don't kill them,' his mother said to him again.

36

'What happened to you? You didn't even take off your shoes last night. And your phone was ringing inside your pocket all night long. If you keep up these habits, I warn you, our relationship is not going to last much longer,' Kuljeet said.

'What habits?' he asked.

'Both, drinks and phone calls.'

She was afraid she would lose him again; afraid of Kamala and her sons; afraid that any moment they would snatch him away from her. The more frightened she became, the more vicious she grew. It is not easy for a person to keep another person in a wallet or inside a closed fist. Physically, it is impossible, and mentally, it is unthinkable. Moreover he had started showing signs of boredom and depression these days. No matter what she asked, he answered with no emotions: 'I can't help it. What can I do?'

'Do you remember you threw up on the bed last night?'

'I did?' He looked at her in disbelief, and then at the bed. There was no trace of vomit, the sheet looked good as new, the carpet smelled fine. She pointed towards the laundry basket from which the crumpled edges of a bed sheet stuck out. As he glanced at it, he felt a crick in his neck.

'I am fed up, I didn't marry you so that I could clean up your puke while you chat happily with your ex-wife and children.'

He took the phone out of his pocket. As if to convince her, he said aloud, 'It's an unknown number; let me check who it is.'

He was showing off, or rather attitudinizing apathy as she looked at the missed call display; all the while his heart thudded like hoofbeats. His phone had been in silent mode since he had been at Peacock Bar with Parvesh. But the landline number from which a call came after eleven o'clock in the night was a familiar number, one he had known by heart since the day the telephone had first been installed. And the mobile number that had flashed on the screen after midnight was also dear to him.

'Now, don't cook up any bullshit stories, I am not buying any of it,' Kuljeet said.

He could see his image getting tarnished in her eyes and so he said, 'I'm hungry. Could you please get me something to eat?'

While Kuljeet was in the kitchen, he tried to call Kamala, but she returned with bread and fried eggs before he could reach her.

'Now tell me who it was,' she demanded.

'I cannot have eggs in the morning. Can you please make something palatable?'

She knew there was nothing wrong with the eggs, and that normally he preferred having them in the morning. When she left the room, he dialled the number again. She could sense his nervousness from the kitchen. She returned with a plate of poha and a bowl of sugar and placed them in front of him. 'You've been fretting over your phone for a while now. Tell me what the fuck is going on.'

'I have a lot of people to call,' he said defensively. A little later he said again, 'Okay, all right, can I tell you something?'

Her lips stretched thin, she said, 'Tell me!'

'When they were in Bangalore, I thought I had no problem with the separation. But now, I don't think I can manage this, I cannot live without them, Kuljeet.'

It made her laugh, and laughingly she spat the catarrh on his face.

Sometimes, shattered pieces of glass join back together like magic, like one of many photo shoot tricks, like they show on the music channels. He remembered how he had admired the way the petals rose from the ground and joined the flower when he saw the 'Return to Innocence' video for the first time, years ago. How easy it had seemed, he thought now, leaving no scars, no marks in between, or on the margins of the wounds. But lives were difficult, otherwise, they would have been like the one-line story by James Joyce: 'They lived and laughed and loved and left.' Madhavan found nothing laughable or adorable though he was congenial at times, and behaved in a gentle way. The package of life came with no promises, no laughter and no love included. Nor did he find anything worth mentioning in the years he had lived or in the one, he knew, were to come.

He spent the entire day in the park, in the Lal Bagh botanical gardens. In fact, he got there very early, and was able to find parking space near the big divider at the end of the zebra line. Overwhelmed by the dark silhouettes of the huge trees and the not very pleasant smell of wet grass and fallen leaves, he smiled nervously at the festive, sleepy, yogic mood of the early walkers.

He sat on a bench facing the lake, the lowermost flower boughs of a tree brushing his head with the intermittent rush of wind. He watched the red lotuses in bloom, the reflection of the pink shower of the apple blossom tree in the water, the water birds in motion and, at some point, he started counting the people, like little children count the vehicles that pass by. At first the people caused some unease—he thought too much happiness was artificial and these people were not real. He waited for his senses to get accustomed to happiness, a word he hadn't known for years. He observed their strides, each person moved with a rhythm entirely different from that of the other, but somewhere, at some point, the rhythms resonated, bridging gaps. He marvelled at his capacity to link people, make connections and conjure their stories; for example, he kept imagining the different ways they might have made love in the mornings, before they set out to walk, long before they were busy wearing their jackets and walking shoes. He looked at those who walked together and felt satisfied, as it was easier for him to imagine this when there were two concrete figures to participate in the action. He also pictured those who slept with their backs turned to each other, defeating each other with endless farts. Then he noticed two women walking together, the exhilarating harshness of their gestures, the true pleasure of existence. Next, he started taking stock of the men who walked together, particularly the sets of two, his attention focused on the intensity with which their fingers intertwined. He looked at all the lonely walkers, men and women, their weight weighing on their minds, slowing down their pace. He sensed a spasm of emotions, a shiver hardly noticeable. He took count, in between he missed the numbers again: man, woman, man and man, woman and a woman, man and a woman—to be more precise, penises and cunts on the move in different combinations. He wished he could pile them all up.

Who was he, in between, what was his position? Tonight he could imagine himself dead, blissfully he would be dead. But how long does imagination normally last? Was he just another link in the chain called humanity? If so, what was there to worry about? No great deal. No big fuck. Links have always been there for the sake of making connections. He was a link, an in-between, between Kamala and Shaly, like the one in a pair of handcuffs. If so, why the fuck was he never satisfied? Recurrently, he had been thinking of, or imagining, a large wall lined with stone coffins that looked almost like drawers with knobs. It was easy to pull the knobs, and he wished he could open them, to know what he would be like when asleep, his colour gone, the corners of his lips slightly open, some parts of his body even decaying. Inside one of those coffins he saw a man and a woman sleeping in the puddle of rotten breaths and body fluids, but the outer shell was visibly beautiful. He had to close the door as the stench was getting on his nerves, reminding him of the dirty odour of mechanical sex. He was just bending his body to open one of the lower coffins when someone said, 'Don't open it, for you don't know what awaits, don't do that, just don't do it, some of the bodies might be pretending to be asleep, pretending to be making love.'

He tried to touch the knob once again and someone whistled up ahead. 'Stop! Stop!' said the voice. He gave up.

Like Hitler's arguments on the defilement of blood, people argued about the defilement of sex—they wanted it pure, they shouted, pure blood, pure sex, for they were incapable of capacities. To join the bandwagon, he too had to blow the oxygen out, sacrifice two darling boys, boys who laughed and loved and ran after the butterflies in Lal Bagh gardens. People were crazy. They banned relationships, but only those with particular combinations, god knows why. People, he was convinced, were the vilest worms roaming the earth, ruled by conceit and ignorance, for they could not enjoy even a good night's sleep.

He wished passers-by a good morning, people he didn't know. He doffed an invisible hat and bowed and smiled. Love is a sea where people floated like guppies; one's fin touches the mouth of the other, no man and no woman but gills and fins in motion. Good sense, good water, clean thoughts. Inside the water, there were stars and rivers in their eyes. If there happened to be a rainbow in the skies, above the gardens, he would have bowed down, touched the ground and cried for forgiveness.

Love was no sin to be hidden, to be kept away, nothing sinful, but somewhere, somehow, it had got stoned to death, burnt and hanged. It was the same love that was dragged in history from the church of Santa Croce to the Rialto Bridge by a horse's tail and had its hands cut off at the scene of its crime, and was then dragged off again to be beheaded. Since then, the moral police had known no rest, here, there, far across the world, they were happy to be proclaimed as bedroom peepers, sometimes in the dark, near the outer walls of those bedrooms, they peed and shat, for they believed that their furtive pleasure demanded free bowels, clean and empty, to be on vigil, to be stronger than the victims. Surreptitiously, they took their turns to look through the windows through their cheap sunglasses, to observe horrible, unsafe things, and to poke questions of the utmost relevance. Who should a person love? How should they make love? When was the perfect time for making love? How long should lovemaking last? When to stop making loving? Was love some sort of soup to make? They were happy the windows were not closed tight, that they lacked latches. Hey you, moral police, how many people can be killed at a time to execute the rights of your manifesto? Any specific numbers?

37

'I'm home!'

Her perfume filled the dining area much before she stepped in. They were having breakfast when she came, loaded with and weighed down by bags. She was wearing military green baggy trousers, a black shirt with blue stripes and a scarf of mixed colours, all quite out of tune. She didn't look tired; it seemed she had had a good time on the train. Excitedly, she crossed the room and dumped her bags on the floor in her silly, childish way. The boys were electrified to see her, but Kamala's face darkened and she helped herself to another dosa, her hands trembling. She smiled as if to convince the boys not to make a scene. After a few moments she said, 'Take a seat, have . . .' and pointed to the dishes.

The same stale dosas and sambar, Shaly thought it was disgusting, they were eating like cows, chewing hay. The dosas didn't even have a proper shape, not just that, they were thick at the edges. She had brought a variety of breads from Hot Breads but she didn't feel like taking them out. Kamala was behaving as if she were a stranger, which made matters worse. Not that this was something new, but the children's faces fell. They wanted to talk, ask her about Bangalore. They chewed on the edges of the dosas in silence.

When Kamala finished her breakfast and went back to her room, Shaly got up from her seat and followed her as if to wheedle her way into their lives again, pulling away in the face of the boys' pleading looks. The boys heard the door shut, they knew something was wrong. Aadi wheeled Shiva back to his room and took a few steps towards his mother's room like a thief. It was amazing to know how badly he wanted to know what was going on inside. They sort of missed the women's fights. Here, in this house, this was their first experience of it, the first fight like the first rain. As usual, he heard things flying, up, and breaking, down.

From the broken bits he heard of the spat, he understood Shaly had been irresponsible, that she hadn't taken his mother's call or made any effort to call back. Poor Amma, he thought, she must have gone through hell last night. He felt sorry for her, for he knew this had happened with him as well whenever he came back late from college. It was not easy to calm her nerves. Suddenly he heard the sound of a slap. And it was true that he had already heard such similar sounds when they were in Bangalore. Had Shaly slapped Amma? How dare she! How could she do this? He wanted to kill her.

Abruptly, the door was pulled open and Shaly rushed out, covering her face with her scarf. She ran upstairs to her room, her sobs audible all the way. He didn't feel like going after her, but he wanted to console her, apologize.

Much later, Shaly heard Kamala approaching and noiselessly taking her slippers off. She didn't raise her eyes, but saw the faint light of the moon falling upon Kamala's silk nightdress. She knew it was her turn to abandon herself to a strange form of humility and hence, she waited. She knew Kamala was as devastated as she, as disoriented as she. 'Forgive me, Kams,' she said, not raising her head from the pillow, not moving an inch. How often, Shaly thought, had I lain thus in her embrace, docile and happy.

How long had Kamala been stroking Shaly's cheeks, the still fresh finger marks? The more she stroked, the wetter her cheeks became, drenched by Kamala's tears and kisses. 'My little one,' Kamala murmured as she kissed her mouth. Her kisses were as indisposed as herself, sick, sick, always sick. Shaly didn't say any of this, she felt relieved on Kamala's lap. They could hear the boys talking downstairs. They were purposely making a lot of noise, they wanted to know what was happening upstairs; they couldn't bear the silence and separation any longer, they too were sick of nothingness. Kamala, numbed, sat on the bed, unmindful of the noise, mechanically stroking Shaly's cheeks and crying. But Shaly thought it was all a little disturbing; she wanted to get up and go downstairs. It was already two in the afternoon. Janu must have finished cooking and was probably sleeping somewhere on the kitchen veranda. The mustard-seasoned smell of yam cooked in curd waffled in the air. Shaly knew she was hungry for she hadn't eaten anything since the night before. But what she wanted was chicken wings, seasoned with delicate spices and fried until golden and crisp.

'Can we go down now?' she asked Kamala.

But crying harder, Kamala fell down on the bed.

'Please don't cry like this, you will exhaust yourself, trust me, tears are of no use, ever.'

As she cried, Kamala felt a tightness in her chest and she thought she was going to die. In between the soreness of breathlessness, she wanted to say: Why don't you understand that I am in deep love? Why do you pretend as if you don't understand?

But she didn't say any of it.

38

Kamala felt tired by the sight of the crowd in front of the office of land registration. The land broker, a middle-aged woman in a faded green sari, approached when she saw them coming.

'How long do we have to wait?' Kamala asked.

'There is nothing to worry about, our token number is three,' she said.

There were a couple of empty chairs on the narrow veranda of that dilapidated building. Lots of chairs, tables and other pieces of furniture in bad shape lay piled up in the shed attached to the veranda—broken, legless or bottomless. Kamala examined the condition of the furniture through the window grille. She was about to sit on one of the empty chairs when she noticed that it too was in a terrible condition and coated with dust. She coughed and said she wanted to go outside. She went with Shaly to the ground covered in white sand; the sea must be somewhere nearby, she thought. There was an old mango tree in the centre of the ground. With each gust of wind, mangoes fell down at random and Shaly excitedly started collecting them. They were very small, but extremely juicy, their fragrance filling her nostrils. She squeezed the mangoes with her fingers till they began to soften, then rolled them on her thighs till they became soft and squishy, and made a hole in the top using her teeth. She sucked on the fruit as if she were having juice from a bottle or tetrapack using a straw. They saw Raghavettan's car coming in. The broker walked towards the car and Kamala followed her with timid, slow steps. There was an old man with him in the car. Raghavettan smiled with unease when he saw Kamala.

'You have changed a lot. What happened? Are you not well?' he asked her.

She didn't answer but smiled pleasantly.

'Haven't I told you about her mother? That was the reason why our registration got so delayed. It will take time for her to recover from the shock,' the broker said.

'Oh, I am extremely sorry to hear that,' said Raghavettan. 'How old was your mother?'

Kamala looked at him uncertainly, as a child faced with a particularly challenging problem looks at her maths teacher. She knew she didn't know the answer.

'Where is the toilet?' Shaly asked the broker in a loud voice from under the mango tree. The broker cringed with embarrassment: women usually asked such questions in hushed tones, yet this one had come like a gust of wind, slapping them straight on the face. Shaly, however, was not bothered at all, rather she was bored and tired of drinking mangoes. She walked down the way the woman had pointed with her hands tucked inside her pockets, the way men did.

'Is that your daughter?' Raghavettan asked Kamala, looking at Shaly.

Before she could answer Raghavettan introduced the old man who had come with him.

'This is Mr Ramachandran. He is buying the flat above the one you are buying. But I don't think he will be your neighbour. I am afraid he is buying to sell, the way intelligent people do.'

Ramachandran smiled. 'I have no plans to sell. He is just joking; I think he likes to make fun of me. We have been friends since childhood. Both my children are in the USA. I am buying

230

the property using their money, and it will go to them when the time comes.'

'Now, now, Ramachandran, this is the teacher who tricked me out of this property. She could have become a businesswoman if she had tried.'

Teacher? Kamala looked at the broker in disbelief. How on earth could she change her vocation? How stupid. The broker was all pleasing smiles and Kamala didn't venture to correct her. Be it teacher or doctor, she really didn't like these tricks. It made her so upset that she wanted to shout; for a second, she even wished she could drop the project. Both of them had talked for hours before negotiations. He had said okay because he was okay, who had cheated him?

Shaly smelled of cigarettes when she came back from the toilet. Raghavettan's face darkened and he stared down at her in incredulity. Kamala was also looking at her; she was examining her to see whether she truly looked like her daughter. Was she that young? Or am I just too old to be her friend? Shaly was wearing distressed jeans and a white blouse. Her hair looked fresh and gorgeous. Maybe my appearance has altered a lot, Kamala thought. She glanced at her reflection in the glass window of the car that was parked outside. Yes, she had dark circles under her eyes and fine lines on her face. But she knew that the mirrors of the car projected objects in a magnifying way. She remembered the letters on the mirror: something to the tune of 'Objects may appear closer than they actually are'. Her fine lines were now more projected, more exaggerated, more unreal. They didn't show up quite as much in the mirror in the house; there she still looked beautiful, at least not as bad as this. Now that she thought about it, the mirrors in the house were not very good either. They were old with mercury coming off them in random places. They are mirrors in name only, she thought, I should break them all up and replace them with new ones. She imagined smashing the old ones and buying the new ones. On the way here, she had examined herself in the hotel mirror when they had stopped to have tea. She had felt confident; the mirror in the hotel was a comparatively better choice, for she clearly remembered admiring her sari in the mirror a few hours back. But now the sari weighed heavily on her body and she felt sick and exhausted. She wanted to reach home at the earliest, no time for mirrors on the way.

But Shaly wanted to try some of the shopping malls in the city. She wanted to buy a satsuma body lotion that she had forgotten while shopping in Bangalore. There was no chance of getting it once they reached Kamala's house. But seeing Kamala's condition, she decided it would be best to take her back to that godforsaken place quickly, back to the valley of boredom, where the four of them could sit, walk, sleep without looking at each other—they hadn't started hating yet . . . good.

Shaly was behind the wheel, Kamala sat next to her, a disquieting look on her face.

'Some more work needs to be done, I don't think we can move into the flat that easily.'

'What about the rest of the work, then?' Shaly asked.

'Raghavettan has promised to help us. He said something about pointing or something on the tiles, or maybe pointing the tiles, yes it could be about pointing the tiles. We will have to supervise.'

'What do you mean?'

'What do I mean? I am thinking. Don't shout!'

At the traffic signal, she had to press down hard on the brakes.

'Can't you just concentrate on the road? Do you want me to drive?'

Shaly thought only a stray shout from outside could bring Kamala back to herself. She wished she could turn off the engine. Look at her, look at the rotten condition she has drawn herself into, but still look at the way she talks . . . what is this show of arrogance? Is she really mad? Sick in the head? She'll never leave that house.

'Can I play music?' Shaly asked.

'Yes.'

The moment it started, Kamala shouted again. 'Will you please turn down the volume? Or do you want me to take a bus back?'

Shaly turned off the system. When she saw the roads diverting to the airport, her heart skipped a beat. There was a big junction with lots of intricate crossroads, a labyrinth of imaginations. If only I could turn that way, I could fly to Bangalore or to Mizoram, she thought.

She couldn't guess what Kamala was thinking or where she was looking. She was sitting like a frozen rag doll, the one she had told her she used to have a long time ago.

When she saw an advertisement for Michelin, Shaly said, 'Kamala, it is time to buy new tyres.'

Kamala didn't answer. They didn't talk for quite a while. Kamala lowered the sun visor and examined herself in the small mirror. She looked at herself for a long time. The tiredness was mainly around the eyes, she double-checked the sunken areas of her face. After some time she asked Shaly: 'Shaly, do I look like an old hag?'

'Never.'

Once again, this time without seeking her permission, Shaly played the music, softly. In a low voice, someone sang the legend of Bharat ki ek sannari.

'Tell me, Shaly, do I really look like an old hag now? Please be honest,' she said again.

39

'How come you are not even on WhatsApp these days?'

'You won't believe me—there is no signal here. The phone says "poor", I guess that's what we are. Poor!'

'Ah, thank goodness! I thought you were avoiding me on purpose.'

'No, why should I? If I wanted to avoid you, I would have just blocked your number.'

'Now that I know your landline number I don't think blocking me will do any good.'

'Please, for God's sake! Don't make a call to this number. I called you from this number because it's an emergency. Otherwise I would not have called.'

'Agreed, but do you remember you had promised me one night?'

'Are we fuck buddies or what? I was drunk when I made that promise, you idiot!'

'Okay, okay, but next time when you get high please don't say that my thing is small, it is six plus and I am quite happy.'

'Ha ha, you stay brave. Your secret is safe with me.'

'Now get to the point, give me a deadline. I would appreciate it.'

'ASAP.'

'Nothing doing! You have to specify the date.'

'Give me one more month; you know what a sloth I am and you don't know the situation I am in.'

'In that case, do you mind if I transfer it to Meera?'

'That would be better, I guess.'

'Anything for you, baby girl, you know we miss you terribly in those Feminist-Lesbian-Profound coffee shops.'

'Who is on the phone? Why aren't you saying anything?' Janu asked.

Kamala hung up the phone in shock, for she hadn't seen Janu there, and the receiver landed in its cradle with a crash. She was devastated, like a woman caught red-handed in public. Maybe she knew that eavesdropping was a breach of decency.

'I am afraid someone has picked up the phone downstairs. I will call you later, bye for now.' Shaly disconnected the phone.

Kamala knew most of Shaly's friends, at least half of them. She knew it was Jithan on the other end of the phone, and that he was a blabbermouth. He spoke the same way to almost all the girls in his circle. Kamala didn't like Shaly toying with him, but all the same, she was dying to know more about these secret phone calls. She wanted to make sure that nothing could be forcibly inflicted upon Shaly, be it Jithan or something else.

Though she had set the receiver back in the cradle she was still clutching it. She looked at Janu in aversion. The poor woman was cleaning the floor. In that moment, she hated her overwhelmingly, hated the innocence on her face, the inquisitiveness in her eyes, her distasteful gestures to please her, and above all her large, half-exposed breasts visible through the nightgown she was still wearing. She was never dressed properly; the women in her neighbourhood considered it their privilege to wear a nightgown throughout the day. What a shame, how disgusting! They went to local shops wearing the same nightgowns, occasionally they would drape a towel over it, something only a little better than the rags one used in the kitchen to clean the service table. They called these nightgowns 'nighties', and they came in hideous designs that were displayed in clusters from the ceilings of local clothes shops. Wearing a nightie was license enough to go from door to door, to repeat everything they heard or said. The smell of the cheap fabric excited them, no matter how rich or poor they were, it was just an absence of aesthetics in them. It was also a license to show off their enormous breasts as they bent forward, the only way they could expose themselves to the world.

I can't let her dress up like this in my house, thought Kamala. 'If you make molushyam one more time, you will be out of this house,' she said.

'But you haven't told me what to do! Can I make sambar today?' Janu asked.

'Make whatever you feel like. Serve us poison if that will make you happy!' Leaving Janu unnerved and squatting on the floor with the mop in her hand, Kamala marched towards her room. Aadi was waiting inside, but when he realized that his mother was not in a good mood, he got up to leave.

'Why are you here?'

'Amma, I would like to go to Bangalore. I want to see my friends, and now that Shaly is here I don't think it would be a problem if I go.'

'Go wherever you like, what the hell do you need permission for?'

Terrified, he left the room in dismay. Back in the boys' room, Shiva consoled him, 'Don't worry, I will convince her.'

Frustrated, he sat on Shiva's wheelchair and started wheeling himself across the room, using his hands. It was indeed a small room; it took mere seconds to start from one wall and reach the other. It was an all-enclosed cycle. You start from walls, you reach walls, and in between you don't even know how time travels. He thought he wanted to be a missile to break down these walls. He wanted to be radioactive dynamite to cause the maximum destruction possible. Aadi, the suicide bomber! But the walls were thickening every minute, closing in on them. They were going to crush them.

When they initially arrived, the walls had not been so thick, not so heavy. Though he remembered Shaly asking about their width and thickness on the first day she came down to dine with them. 'It is an old mud house,' his mother had said, 'and mud walls are supposed to be thicker and stronger.' Shaly examined the walls for some time, laid her cheek against them and said, smiling, 'And cooler.'

It would take real strength to make a tunnel through the mud, he thought. He had read *The Count of Monte Cristo*, about Abbé Faria's escape tunnel that ended up in Dantès's cell. If he started digging he was sure he would find himself in his mother's room, but if he could make his escape, his mother might not even notice. Once in a while, she might look sympathetically at the empty dining chair and continue eating. Maybe she would sigh, hardly noticeable. He grew so angry at the thought that he pushed the chair hard and it crashed against the walls with a loud noise.

Bang! Bang! Bang!

'My chair!' Shiva cried.

'This is a mousetrap! We are nothing better than rats caught in it.'

'Get out of my chair! If I lose it I will end up in this bed forever. I am afraid I am getting bedsores. Please! Get out of my chair—and don't ever touch it.'

From the outside, their house seemed calm and peaceful. It was an old mansion, its exquisite beauty defined by its architectural dimensions, surrounded by trees, vines, birds, squirrels, the occasional display of sun, a large courtyard covered with fallen leaves—yellowish and brittle—and the laterite walking path on which two or three stones had come out of the pointing: all of it lay deceptively deep inside the countryside. It is said that doves live in a peaceful atmosphere, and it was ironic that on the roof of their house lived hundreds of doves, to hamper the peace of the inmates. After Kamala and her children had moved in, there was an irrefutable grief in the cooing of the birds. A miserable feather flew down each time they fluttered their wings. But they were not ready to vacate the house. Inside the house, marked by a heavy sadness, human beings moved around, breathed in and out, talked softly.

'They are our guests, we should not let them down,' the birds said to each other.

From the rooftop of that ancient house that afforded you a bird's-eye view, you got to see laughing skulls 300 feet down in the earth, cracking jokes and telling stories. It was good to listen to them, for they had crossed the miserable spell called 'life on earth', they said it was really cool underneath. They didn't care for anything any more; they really didn't care about the divergent roads or what was past. That which was burning in the pyre was me, myself, ghee and cakes of cow dung. It was easy for the fat bodies to get incinerated. All your life you strive to stay slim, but on the pyre it was a different matter. What a wonderful world!

'Where is your pride now?' asked one.

'The fire devours it all,' the other answered.

Breath stops where hopes, desires and despair stop. In the remaining, left over, one-tenth of desperation, in the unconditioned air, each human being on earth says: 'I cannot take this any longer, I am tired.'

When at last Aadi got up from the chair, examined it and said it was all right, Shiva smiled in relief. It seemed it was all he had that was reliable on earth. There was a kind of horror in his smile that was reflected in the tears that filled Aadi's eyes.

Kamala got up from her bed and walked towards the door. She closed and latched it on the inside.

In the kitchen, Janu seasoned the sambar.

40

This is my silent dark immensity,
This is the home of everlasting Night,
This is the secrecy of Nothingness.

—*Savitri*, Sri Aurobindo

Aadi shut the book. He closed his eyes to think of Anuraktha, and saw the massive stone walls of the building leading to the orchard and from there to the library adorned with hibiscus flowers and red fairy lights. Leaving this place was like plummeting hundreds of feet down from where he always loved to belong. He couldn't concentrate on the book; he read three or four lines a day, or once in three days. What was his connection to the book? Was Anuraktha keen on his reading this particular book? Or was it just a book for the sake of a book? He liked the expression 'the home of everlasting Night'. That was something, something resonated with him, but it would have looked better if it had been the home of everlasting days. There was nothing worth cherishing about his past, but his past was better than his present.

Once again he went to see his mother in her room. She was lying on her left side on the bed. He sat down beside her. He waited for hours but there was no response from her. She was not sleeping but lying down with her eyes closed, her lips tightly shut. For a moment he imagined the house without her, and though he wanted a breather from her presence, sadness choked his throat, and he wanted to cry. He loved her but a feather of freedom kept showing him the sky, he knew he wanted to leave.

All the same, he was filled with remorse, he touched her feet. She drew her feet away with a shudder and looked at him in disbelief. He wanted to tell her something, but instead he said, 'I thought I would massage your feet for a while, to help the blood circulation.' He was not sure if the words he had used were correct, but he had said something and he waited for her to respond. She didn't say anything but she inched her feet towards him so he could sit comfortably. He took her feet in his hands and placed them on his lap. How soft. He kissed her feet. Shaly saw him kissing them from the veranda—she too felt sad and lonely.

She was also engrossed in thoughts. She didn't understand why Kamala was mad at her again, why she hit her head in front of the boys, why she shouted like crazy. Poor woman, she must have hurt herself a lot. Her condition had got worse; Shaly had had to take her to the Be Well hospital two or three months before her mother had passed away. It was in the dead of night, and Shaly had no idea what else to do.

Shaly was happy she was recovering, though slowly. She had had some traces of humour left in her, at least one week before her mother had died. It was Kamala who had ordered food from Hot Pops on the day Hari Narayanan and Hafis Afsal came to her office. Shaly was also there as they had planned some shopping together after office hours. She ordered beef dipped in orange sauce and honey-glazed pork with phulka. They all knew the ban on beef was about to come, that people had problems with both beef and pork. She wondered whether it was the paprika preparation that made the zealots so crazy and hot over meat. They all laughed, there were no vegetarians in the office. But they all agreed on one point: that if they were not supposed to have beef, they ought not to eat spinach either. You cut the spinach before its time comes, you wanted it all fresh—again you were hurting a life. They said great Indian swamis waited for kernels to drop down from the heads of the stalks after completing their life cycles, yet they didn't cook the grains, for they believed the grains contained a life that would sprout sooner or later. They asked for forgiveness and swallowed the grains raw, one life to support the other. The cow and the lion sat together in mythology, on the hills of Lord Shiva, but there was no mention of what the lion ate. Would there be fallen grains enough to support the lives on earth? Hari gave a piece of pork to Afsal, and Afsal in turn gave him a piece of steak. They all had their laugh for the day, and raised a toast to all the lonely, happy-go-lucky bastards of the world.

She longed for Bangalore, memories suffocated her; she knew Kamala had no such troubles, for she was born in the house in which they all lived. She found it hard to believe that Kamala's sinking was mainly because of the acid-induced stress of the past. Her symptoms indicated nothing. They could be anything, maybe even old age. It is said that one cannot remain forever *young and easy under the apple boughs*. Rane used to say, 'Acid is cool, if you are cool; otherwise, it is suicidal. If you love yourself, it is better you avoid drugs.' What he said was true. Those who love their lives should not run after an external stimulus. Everything exists within you, hell and heaven. If you tasted a drop of acid with an equal amount of fear in your mind, the fear would intensify to humongous proportions and charge at the ceilings of the brain with unbearable noise.

If so, if that definitely is the case, I am the one who is frightening her, thought Shaly, not just her, but her kids too.

Kamala was always worried about the unfinished building on the sandy shore. She wondered why people stared into the single room that was on the ground level. The building, she said, was not even plastered, not even in good shape, but there was something inside that room, and people watched it day and night. She said she would like to go there, to see what was happening inside, but the only thing that worried her was the heavy rheumatic feeling that weighed her legs down, making her unable to walk or crawl. How many times had Shaly warned her that it was just an illusion, a hallucinogenic effect caused by the acid, that there was no sand inside the room, no dilapidated building on the sand, no room, no windows, no people? It was just her room, the room in which her mother had died. One need not fret over a nightmare as if it were real. But Kamala said it was not just a nightmare. Shaly said it must be the acid, then.

'When was the last time I took acid?'

'How do I know?'

'It must be the brain. It is working all the time.'

'What you need is rest.'

'But one thing I am sure of. There is somebody inside that room—it might be someone close to my heart, or someone I happen to know somehow.'

At times Shaly also felt like believing her, talking bullshit for the sake of it, hoping that would bring a bit of relief. Sometimes, there would be someone who committed suicide in that room a long time ago, like the ghosts in movies. There would be a skeleton prostrated inside the room, with a priceless diamond shining on its ring finger. It was the rays from the diamond that constantly beckoned her during the night. One night, Kamala dreamed of a bunch of wild roses hanging down from the loosened pointing of that old, unfinished building.

That same night Shaly too had a dream. She saw Kamala laughing, like the brook, like in storybooks. She heard jingles of laughter filling up the wind. But in the morning when she woke up she felt as if she had been jabbed deep down. How could a smile, even laughter, hurt someone so deeply? Soon, it became a recurrent dream, offering wonders at night and gashes in the morning.

'Kamala . . .' Shaly tried to call her, her voice no louder than a whisper.

But Kamala didn't hear her call. Aadi was still stroking her feet.

There was an empty bottle of Black Dog on the table. Shaly took the bottle, surveyed it for a while and walked out of the house carrying it. The dog with the saddest eyes was lying down beside Kamala. Sometimes it growled and tried to slink away, but Kamala grabbed it and tightened her hold on its leash. She caressed it in her sleep and unease swept through Aadi as she involuntarily moved in bed. As he stroked her feet, she stroked the fold of its neck. Even with her eyes closed, she was aware of the weight of its body weighing her down.

'The dog you are always carrying along with you is called depression,' her doctor had said once. 'We don't need that dog.'

She caressed it with all her strength, all her hope.

Shaly had taken a pair of scissors from the kitchen. Now with the bottle and scissors in her hands, she walked beneath the cannonball tree and, stepping over the dead pink flowers, she walked towards the lotus pond. Near the lake, the money plant ran across like mad and crept all over the ageing ashoka tree and on the tiled roof of the lotus pond entrance. She cut a portion of the money plant vine and held it against the sun; the leaves shone, indicating luck and prosperity. She walked back to the kitchen veranda, where she opened the tap and let the water run into the bottle of Black Dog. It took approximately ten minutes to remove the plastic cork from the bottle using a tool and to fill it up.

She walked towards Kamala's room with the bottle and the beautiful ivy. Kamala looked like an obstinate child on that bed. Shaly placed the water-filled bottle on the window where Kamala's eyes fell. She put the vine inside the bottle with care. She went outside and came back with some pebbles which she put inside the bottle with some sand. It looked perfect; the vine looked as beautiful as a little green grass snake. Carefully she intertwined the vine with the window grille. Sunshine kissed the heart-shaped green leaves that bloomed on the window. Kamala looked at the leaves with gratitude and smiled.

'I think it is pure,' she said.

Clumsily, the big fat dog jumped out of her bed. Restless and agitated, it walked out, marking the boundaries of the backyard. It stopped and barked powerfully when it reached the devil's ivy. Lifting its hind leg it peed on the ashoka tree as if this was a warning.

41

He called to Night but she fell shuddering back,
He called to Hell but sullenly it retired.
. . . . . .
He called to his strength, but it refused his call.
His body was eaten by light, his spirit devoured.

—*Savitri*, Sri Aurobindo

Aadi had kept the money his mother had given him inside the different pockets of the big rucksack for safekeeping, and some change in his wallet. This was his first time travelling alone and the umpteenth time he was opening and closing the zipper. The book was there, safe, and the money was there, safe. For a while, he tried to remain calm but he felt extremely nervous and insecure. He mentally chided himself for behaving like a girl. But the fact was that, when it came to your first solo trip, there was no girl and no boy, only a lonely child called fear who kept playing with a zipper. He thought he was lost in the endless honking and buzzing. There were all sorts of people and hawkers gathered under the lights, and buses ready to take off in different directions. Aadi had been there before, but it was in the morning, when things seemed clear and easy.

He went to a nearby shop. 'Can I have a lemon soda?'

'Sorry, we don't have lemon soda. Would you like Cola, Pepsi, Mirinda or Sprite?' the shopkeeper asked.

'Haven't I told you not to buy poison?' Kamala seemed angry, she hated aerated drinks.

'Mother, please, just once . . .'

'These are all bad habits, Aadi. Get a glass of fresh juice.'

'Pass that bottle of poison to me, I would love to have one,' Shaly said.

The boy who had been raised by two women stood confused in front of the shop, in the agonies of indecision.

'Do you have mineral water?' he gestured as he asked.

'Yes, twenty rupees,' the shopkeeper gave him a bottle.

He took a fifty-rupee note out of his purse, feeling proud of himself, of his independent money transactions. His mother and Shaly went on fighting.

'You should have carried a bottle of fresh water with you, mineral water is not always trustworthy,' his mother said.

'If you are going to believe each and every article you read you are definitely going to die of hunger and thirst. Magazines are a collection of printed pages, not life,' Shaly said.

When he spotted the signboard for Parveen Travels, he felt his heart beating faster. He stuffed the water bottle into his side pocket, the folded fabric of the pocket stretching to accommodate it. In his first transaction, he had forgotten to take his thirty rupees change. He walked down the aisle of the bus looking for 16F. It took a while to find it, but when he saw that it was a window seat he felt grateful. The AC inside the bus was on high but he didn't feel like covering himself with the blanket that had been provided. His mother had warned him of blister beetles. She had told him to shake the blanket thoroughly before using it, but unfortunately there was not enough space to stand up and shake it off. Instead, he took Kamala's Kashmiri shawl out of the bag, draped it around himself and snuggled inside his mother's perfume.

'Squirrel, squirrel, are you not coming to my son's wedding?' his mother asked, looking at the treetops. She was extremely beautiful and unbelievably young, her face glowing, her nose stud glistening in the sunlight.

'Whose wedding is it, his or mine?' Shiva asked.

'My son Aadi's wedding,' she said as she walked on the dead, sun-dried leaves, feeling the ground beneath her bare feet, her anklets jingling all the way.

'In that case, I am not coming.' Shiva turned away, his face down. Was he a boy of three or four?

'Squirrel, squirrel, are you not coming to my son Shiva's wedding? Do you want to see how beautiful his bride is?' his mother asked again.

Squirrels ran from pepper vines to the purple mangosteen trees and from there to the coconut trees. Pointing those terrific climbers out to Shiva, she said, 'Look at the way they are all running to buy clothes for the bridegroom.'

Aadi began to remember similar things, things forgotten. Does the rhythm of travel invite memories? He didn't know, yet he stretched his neck to look outside, where darkness sped through time, where stillness hung from the railings of bus windows. He imagined the branches of the trees that were no longer there. Her smile lingered in his mind with the chirring of squirrels, like the green scum on the surface of the lotus pond, like a spreading layer of grief, hurting him. He turned his head to look at the people around him: most of them were sleeping—some snoring with their mouths open—and the rest were straining to fix their eyes on the small TV screen on the wall of the bus. Eyes wide open, some of those with sad thoughts looked outside the windows into the darkness. He wondered how the bus would carry them all in its heavy metallic stomach, how it dragged their individual lonelinesses through the night.

He wanted to see Anuraktha and with that thought he went to sleep.

'Aadi, I would also like to come with you one day,' Shiva said.

'Yes, next time I will take you with me, and together we will go to Anuraktha's library.'

'No, I don't want to go to a library. You should take me to a pub where you get plenty of stuff to eat and drink.'

Someone must have watered the plants, for the water that had spread on the brown earth was still fresh. Marigolds and large gladioli lined both sides of the paths to the ashram, the wet earth in between. He walked with confidence, like a warrior, his steps unfalteringly strong and elegant. This earth was familiar; this was where he had grown up. Someone smiled at him and he returned the smile with gratitude. He wanted to detach himself completely from the dead land of his mother and start everything anew, a new life, new thoughts, nothing to turn him inward again. He remembered the balustrade on the staircase, the red hibiscus flowers on the photographs. Where was Anuraktha this morning? He did not answer when he knocked on the door, no one did; it was ajar and he went inside. On the staircase he realized he was panicking.

Perhaps Anuraktha was in the library, for he was not in the ashram or in the service centre. The light on the staircase was vibrant; he could see everything clearly, but he thought he missed a lot of things, mainly details, minor ones that he had noticed in the semi-darkness on his first visit. He stepped back and sat on the wooden plank, he knew he wanted to be calm before starting a conversation with him. But what was he supposed to say?

—I am sorry, I couldn't read the book, but I don't wish to return the book, I would like to keep it with me forever?

No, although that was true, it lacked something.

—I am reading it, I think I am a slow reader, but the book offers me a sense of relief?

No, that sounded silly.

It was important because he wanted to say it. Finally he got up and climbed the stairs only to find the doors of the library closed.

Gently, he tried to push them open and, amazingly, they parted, a shaft of morning descended from the glass tiles on to the wooden floor. He thought he was seeing darkness. When he looked up from the wooden planks, someone was there, standing beside him. He said, 'Swami is in Delhi. He will return after two months.'

The puppeteer's house was on the left side of the road. From across the road he saw the battered shack where he remembered the old man was happy with his wife and the six white mice inside an ordinary cage. He crossed the road; he would love to see the puppeteer and his white mice. Each mouse had a different name, and responded when the old man called them by it. He used to visit them with his friends, for the old man was friendly with children. Sometimes, the children helped the old man paint his leather puppets. He would give the children the responsibility of painting the base coats, and only if he was confident of their skills and considered them highly qualified would he hand over the brush, and give them the chance to try a stroke or two. The boys sat around him supplying colours and keeping him company and feeding his mice. But now, he too was not home, neither was his wife nor were his mice. His neighbour informed him that he was bedridden and had been taken to his village by his relatives.

Someone had told Aadi about Rhea's return from Dubai and her joining VIT for further studies, maybe Rhea herself, he didn't remember. But he did remember how she had come on her dented bicycle and cried. But two weeks after she had left, his friend Rohit showed him her Instagram updates where she had posted several happy pictures of herself, posing in front of the magnificent malls of Dubai. It seemed she had forgotten him, Bangalore and the rest. He read her comments in detail, he didn't recognize her in her words, so when he went to Kamala's old house in Kerala, he didn't wrap up her memories and store them. It was as simple as that. She lived more vividly in Shiva's mind, like a future relative, a future solace.

But still, the thought that it would take just three or four hours to reach her university tempted him—just to see how she was, perhaps to say hi over a cup of coffee or her favourite, hot chocolate. He was uncertain, even when the train started, even when he got down from the rickshaw at the huge gates of the university, even when he entered his name in the register. It was a labyrinth of lawns, ancient trees, different building blocks and sections. The students scattered as a car or a pick-up cab approached and then joined up in groups again when it had passed, making patterns. He bought an iced tea from the tea stall near the auditorium. It came in a big paper cup with pictures of lemons printed on it. As he walked, he sipped the tea, overhearing snatches of conversation. He understood that the students had classes at different times and in different blocks, and the pick-up cabs were for those who couldn't walk to reach the classes in time. Shuttle cabs that charged just ten rupees for moving around the campus were also available. It would be impossible to find her in this entangled network of buildings and paths. He threw the paper cup in the trash bin and as he walked towards a shuttle cab, he dialled her number.

'My God, I can't believe it's you!' Her voice was full of excitement when she answered the call, but when he said he was waiting for her outside the hostel, some of her enthusiasm died down. Suddenly she seemed indifferent, her voice grew restless. Maybe it was just what he felt.

'Really?' she asked in a weak voice. 'Could you please wait another half an hour? I will come down. Right now I am in the middle of something.'

The walls around the hostel complex were really high, he could not make out which building she stayed in, for there were many buildings inside the walls. There was a McDonalds, Café Coffee Day and a beauty parlour, all within the complex, all meant for the girls alone. The lady attendant and the watchman gave him a severe look; they thought he was eyeing the scantily clothed African girls sitting in the lobby.

Another twenty-five minutes passed before Rhea arrived. Aadi didn't recognize her at first, for she had undergone a major transformation; she looked like an artificial doll you couldn't feel any attachment for. She had straightened her hair and coloured portions of it, and her lips were slightly plumper than before. The other changes he couldn't quite make out, but something about her was not natural, not even the way she smiled and the delicate way in which she waved her hands. She looked cinematic, he thought. How beautiful her curly black hair had been! Now it looked like the scene of a crime. He felt terribly disappointed at this drastic sight.

She smiled at him with exaggerated surprise which he found feigned, again.

'Hi, how is your college?' he asked, realizing his voice was becoming affected, too.

'This is not a college, it's a university,' she corrected him.

She couldn't believe that he had wasted a year of his life. But later she said she had known some foreign students who were doing the same thing. After all, relaxing one year was no big deal. She showed him around the campus: It was almost like a miniature township with restaurants, ice cream parlours, salons, eye clinics, a mobile centre and whatnot. Above all there was a rail track running through the campus area, perhaps the only university in India with a railway line attached to it.

He looked at the splash of bougainvillea over the tunnel covering a small area of the track. No matter what higher degree you were enrolled in, and which university you studied at, trains were always a marvel. Trains were the long stories or novels of man's success over nature.

They sat on the steps leading to the railway tracks for a while. He counted the number of steps, she chewed on a blade of grass she had broken from God knows where.

When does the next train come?

When does the last train leave?

There were kisses left unfinished, they didn't feel like reminding each other of the debts they owed. She tossed the grass towards the tracks, it fell down somewhere on the steps. He wondered who had turned off the flames, when and how. He knew she wished he wouldn't speak of their past relationship, that he would pretend ignorance, the way she did; it would be a great help, to both of them. Yet he couldn't resist, he tried to touch her fingers, the fingers he used to smother with kisses somewhere in the past, but she abruptly drew her hand back when she realized how indecisive she could get at times. She knew it was ending already, and maybe because of this, she started talking non-stop as if she were some sort of talking muzak.

'It's been days since I have had a proper shower and sleep,' she said accusingly. 'We were busy with Gravitas for the past several days, the technical festival and workshops. I was in desperate need of an oil bath. In fact I was applying oil when you called me over the phone. At first I thought I would come down after my bath but I didn't want to make you wait, but I am afraid I have to wash this off as soon as possible.'

She held some strands of hair between her fingers as if to show him. He looked at the coloured strands of hair and wondered whether they were actually oiled. But she added, for emphasis, 'I really need to wash this off before I catch a cold. I had wanted to take a bath in the morning itself but then the seniors called and said it was time I attended the audition for international chapters. Once you become a member of the core committee you get credits plus you get to organize events and other things yourself. I never knew that I was this ambitious, but I think I am happy.'

It was all very simple to understand, he thought—she was tired and sleepy and wanted to take a shower before she went to bed at night, and washing one's hair after sunset was not ideal. They walked towards Woodstock, the garden of the provisional lovers. She seemed more upset with each step she took, but she chattered all the same. She talked about her parents in Dubai and her decision to study abroad once she finished her BTech. After a terribly upsetting and boring walk through the woods, they arrived at Darling Restaurant where they found themselves a nice table near the window.

Some of the senior boys who sat at the centre table were celebrating a birthday. They were shouting, laughing and smearing the icing on each other, in a jovial mood. Aadi and Rhea watched them, sitting in identical postures, silent and still. One more cake arrived at their table, set on a tray with a lit candle in the middle. Upon a second look, they realized it was golden fried chicken legs wrapped up artistically in aluminium foil and arranged to look like a cake. There was a lengthy pause in their celebration while they went crunch, munch, crunch. In no time the cake was reduced to a heap of half-crushed bones. A chair by a window was a blessing at times.

In the semi-darkness of the railway station, Aadi sat cross-legged on a concrete bench. Though he was tired to the core, his hold on the bag's strap was still strong. He wasn't sure just how safe railway stations were at night.

A station in the night was extremely sorrowful, he thought. He didn't want to sleep, but he fell asleep all the same. He woke up with a start after some time to find a man sitting next to him; the man's fingers were gently caressing the insides of Aadi's thigh. Before he could resist the thought slapping against his brain, he had shouted, 'Fuck off, you bastard!'

He sensed the entire Katpadi station shudder. He couldn't believe he could shout so loud. The man ran away. No more baloney, this was the exercise of travel, he lectured himself. He seemed happy with his own voice, the strength of his gestures. The length of time and the darkness didn't bother him; he sat there on the same bench, engrossed in his thoughts. The darkness was making things transparent, more vivid, with a see-through sort of clarity. Filth is a difference in thought. Shrug it off.

For a second he wanted to go back home. Shaly had told him that each trip was like opening a bottle of champagne, each time a new experience. It would be better if people made their own society, be it democratic, totalitarian, fascist, or whatever, but it should definitely be a one man society.

Initially his plan had been to stay with Anuraktha; to be frank, he had not thought of any other course of action so far. Back in Bangalore, inside the paid retiring room, he started taking stock of friends with whom he could stay for a while. He remembered Whitefield, where he had spent a good amount of time with his friends; he thought of the iced tea with the scattered pulp of orange in it served at a restaurant by the lake called Fat Chef for one hundred and forty rupees. He asked himself how many times he'd gone there, to the restaurant, to the lake. He pictured the beautiful lake. Outside the station, he waited for a long time in the queue in front of the ticket booth for the prepaid taxi, and since a cab was rather expensive he booked a rickshaw.

'Whitefield hogubeikku,' he said. Will you go to Whitefield?

In the back seat, he sat thinking of the length of the drive, ten kilometres or twenty. Cherish the good memories, he told himself, and remembered how he had stayed at his classmate Jaswant's flat the night before the school science exhibition with some other classmates. From the balcony of the flat, he had looked down at the long white wall of the Jagriti theatre, the letter R in a bright orange so that it looked like a single brushstroke on the whiteness of the wall. It was not just a wall or a barrier but a piece of art, an installation planned with great thought. It was at Whitefield that he had had his first California roll and New York cheesecake. How small is the world.

'Elli hogubeikku?' the driver asked. Where do you want to go?

'Nimage Jagriti Theatre gotha?' Do you know where Jagriti Theatre is?

The driver stepped out of the rickshaw and went to a nearby shop to ask for directions. But Aadi was thinking of something else: he was pretty sure that Jaswant would be at college now, not at home. He contemplated spending his morning near the lake and when the driver came back asked him to take him to Varthur Lake. He thought he was abandoning his boyhood in order to be there, at the lake, showing the early signs of maturity. He glanced in the side mirror of the vehicle and saw the delicate features of a young man. He ran his fingers over his lips.

At the lake, he opened his mouth in surprise. Could it be snow? He couldn't believe his eyes, the lake and its surroundings were covered in sparkling white snow, still and sunlit. He had seen such a vision only in cinemas and in his mother's early collection of Soviet Union storybooks. Was he feeling cold? He checked the temperature with the back of his hand—it was all right. Yet, he opened his bag and took out his mother's Kashmiri shawl to cover his neck and chest. He imagined himself on the back of a yak, revolver in hand, riding through the snow, and he couldn't help laughing. It was Rahul who used to say that he wanted to travel to the Himalayas just to have a glass of vodka on the rocks sitting on top of the mighty white mountains. He had said he would fill the glass with the snow he would collect and someone had retorted that the snow was deadly; it could not be ingested, for it contained millions of dangerous bacteria.

They had driven only a short way along the road when there was a commotion, and an unbearable stench pierced their nostrils. They saw people fighting over something, a parked car or some bikes. Aadi covered his face with the Kashmiri shawl, for the stench was getting stronger; for a moment he thought he would throw up. The driver pulled his rickshaw to the side, saying that the roads were blocked ahead. He wanted to argue over the two hundred and fifty rupees the driver demanded but he didn't because it was awful standing there inhaling the rottenness of the snowy wind. He walked towards the other end of the lake which looked almost like a surrealistic painting, flakes of snow, sheets of it, floating all over. Like the violent waves of the sea, the snow was moving forward and the riders on the bikes were super careful not to get hit. He stopped for a while to take a closer look at the snow, and then he realized with a shudder that it was not real snow but tufts of foam, with black spots and dips. The swirling, spilling foam was fast approaching and he virtually had to run, with the load of his bags. He must have run a decent two kilometres before he found another rickshaw, panting and short of breath. The rickshaw was almost crawling, side by side with the frozen lake shrouded in its poisonous foam.

The driver told him about how the lake had overflowed last night, causing a traffic jam and spreading panic in the neighbourhood. It's been days, he said, since the neighbourhood had opened their windows. Only then did he notice the posters on either side of the road protesting against the policies of the Bangalore Water Supply and Sewerage Board. The foam that was bubbling up over the once fresh water was toxic.

Travel helps you learn a lot of things, you discover your own way and that makes a big difference from what you have been hearing for so long. Mr Hemingway, have you seen this, this is how we travel now across the river and into the trees.

He stood in front of the theatre and surveyed the other buildings. It was not easy to find Jaswant's flat in this jungle of concrete blocks and skyscrapers. He had neither his number nor his address. All he knew was a name: Jaswant. How many Jaswants were there in this part of the city? The thing was, he did not really expect to see him; it had never occurred to him that he would feel free in the company of an old classmate. He could stay in a place he could rent, a very cheap place.

He walked slowly to the theatre. He went to the washroom there and came out and drank half a bottle of water while he sat on a chair near the staircase. He wanted to call his mother and brother and tell them everything he had seen so far and experienced, but he was too tired to speak. He texted Kamala explaining the situation he was in. Suddenly he noticed the poster announcing the evening's program. He stood up, placed his bag on the chair and walked slowly towards the notice.

Adishakti Presents
The Tenth Head
Written by Vinay Kumar K.J.
Directed by Veenapani Chawla

The Tenth Head! He looked at the poster for a long time.

'Could you please hold this teddy bear?'

He turned around upon hearing the foreign accent of a child. It was a chubby little girl, no more than three years old, with light blonde hair and blue eyes. She was barefoot, wearing a loose asymmetric cotton dress that was falling off her plump shoulders, and she was holding a big blue teddy bear in her hands.

'Could you please hold this? Please hold, please, I will be back soon.'

He took the bear from her. But without paying any attention to him, she started talking to the bear; it seemed she was giving him certain instructions. It seemed she was a little princess of gestures for she kept showing her hands and making her eyes move this way and that way while she spoke. Then, holding three of her fingers close to her lips, she said 'Shh . . .' to the teddy and turned away. After taking two or three steps, she paused, turned again, and in a slightly loud voice said: 'Mama will come soon. Don't cry.'

He saw her going up the stairs, he had no idea what was there. On the steps, again, she stopped, pretending she was talking with someone, something important. He looked at the teddy bear: it was very big, not something he could keep in his bag which was already full. When he looked up from the stuffed toy, he saw that she had disappeared, and he sat there with the teddy bear on his lap, hoping she would come soon. After some time, he set the teddy on the chair next to him, it was embarrassing for a boy of eighteen to be seen with it. Travels were always not that easy.

His phone rang. It was Shiva, he realized happily.

'Where are you now?'

'I am in Whitefield. Varthur Road.'

'At your friend Jaswant's place? Have you seen Rhea? Why didn't you call last night?'

'I had called Amma, didn't she tell you?'

'She might have forgotten it. How is Rhea?'

'She is not here. I think she is in Dubai these days.'

'Oh!'

Aadi didn't want to talk about her. So he asked, 'Are you calling from outside? Your voice is very clear now.'

'We came for an evening walk.'

'I'm happy you are having an outing. Say hello to Shaly, I will call her some time later.'

They chatted over the phone for twenty minutes and he spent another twenty minutes near the poster waiting for the girl, then he came back to his seat near the staircase and sat down with the teddy bear on his lap. It seemed its mother had abandoned it, the way rich women dispose of illegitimate children. The ticket was for four hundred rupees. He had never thought of money before, had never had to. Four hundred rupees for a ticket was not cheap, but he bought it, for he couldn't understand what fascinated him like the book of verses he kept in his bag. He had a mini lunch in between from the cafeteria and, having nothing else to do and with the additional burden of the teddy, he came back to the chair again. The girl didn't come back demanding her teddy. He observed the people who came to watch the show. There was a commonality in the way people dressed, talked and walked. They were rather a careless lot, happy and somewhat showy. He was the single man who came to watch the show with a big blue teddy in his hand. The girls, he noticed, were looking at him, their eyes twinkling with the merrymaking of a lustrous night. A boy was coming towards the staircase holding his mother's hand. His mother was charming and petite; if he had not kept calling her Ma, people would have mistaken her for his elder sister. They were walking when he noticed Aadi caressing the teddy bear, an involuntary action on Aadi's part, but the boy had noticed it.

'Amma, look, what is that big boy doing with the teddy bear,' he said.

Aadi's face fell.

'Sakthi, come here.' His mother pulled him towards her.

Aadi followed them with the bear in his hand. It was a beautiful auditorium with comfortable blue chairs arranged in a semicircle, and built around a full stage. The audience was coming in and the seats were filling up. He sat on his chair, looking eagerly at the people, looking for the little blonde mother among them. Since he could not make the bear occupy a four hundred rupee seat, he placed it carefully in his lap, just above his rucksack, the bear covering half of his face. Sakthi and his mother and father had seats next to him. Now the boy was wearing two plastic red horns on his head. He smiled at Aadi, showing his dimples, his eyes had stars in them when he smiled.

'Bro, why are you playing with a teddy like a baby?' he asked Aadi point-blank.

His mother immediately covered his mouth, 'Will you please keep quiet, Sakthi?'

He put his forefinger in front of his lips and became suddenly silent as if he were a robot. Aadi remembered Teddy's mother making a similar gesture a few hours earlier. When the lights dimmed, the very character of the theatre changed, the cacophony of the voices died down, the auditorium became quiet, and countless eyes focused on the spotlights that fell on the stage. When the play was announced, the theatre became one big space of silence. Aadi forgot the teddy, he forgot its blonde mother. There were several rectangular screens on the stage on display. Light fell behind one of the screens and an arm stretched out from behind it. The next second it pulled back. The arm moved intermittently in and out, slowly, from behind the screen, under the rhythm of lights—hand, arm, shoulder, half of the body, the full body, finally Ravana. In a sing-song manner he said, 'Call me Head, more precisely, Tenth Head.'

42

The actors came forward, onto the stage; the audience couldn't stop applauding. Laughing and bowing, they waited for the applause to abate; they wanted to introduce themselves. Aadi wished he could go near them and shake hands with them. He saw some of the audience climbing up and hugging the artists. There was a racket of laughter and shouting. The audience continued with their acclamation even after the performers had left the stage. He saw two girls getting onto the stage, to collect the portrait they had kept in the corner of the stage adorned with hibiscus flowers and incense sticks. He immediately recognized the person in the portrait, Sri Aurobindo, the author of the book Anuraktha had given him, the one still in his bag. He walked down the aisle unmindful of the dense crowd of people with the mingled images of light, pictures, music and voices playing in his mind.

The first artist said to him: 'He doesn't fit in.'

The second artist also said to him: 'No, he doesn't.'

Now it was his turn. He thought of his mother, Shaly, Shiva and himself. He looked at the audience and, bowing his head, said aloud: 'We don't fit in.'

Some of them clapped at the sudden and witty improv performance taking place in the middle of the aisle. Aadi realized that the boy who had come in had nothing to do with the man who was walking out. The blue teddy bear was no longer a problem, he could even wear a butterfly clip on his hair and walk through the crowded city centres if the need arose, there was nothing to feel ashamed of, there was nothing that really mattered. But one should always be sympathetic to those who were inferior; there was nothing to be gained by shocking them. You can dress like a cowboy and walk with a doll's wig, but do it only if you really feel like doing it.

He saw a woman carrying the teddy's mother on her hip. They were waiting near the chair he had been sitting on before the play, near the staircase. The girl seemed unquestionably unnerved, tears running down her cheeks. He recognized the woman carrying the girl. It was the young woman who had gone on the stage after the play to collect the portrait and the lamps. The girl was forcefully pointing to the seat—perhaps she had seen him sitting there before she decided to hand over her son. He tried to carry the teddy on his hip the way the young woman was carrying its blonde mummy. The moment the girl saw her teddy she began kicking the thigh of the woman who was carrying her hard and hollering so loudly that people turned back to see what was happening.

'Don't kick, it hurts,' admonished the young woman.

'That's my Blue,' the girl cried aloud.

Aadi held out the teddy to her to make her stop crying. She wriggled and worked herself free of the woman's grip and ran towards him. She snatched the bear from his hand and started kissing it through tears.

'Where did you get this from?' the young woman asked.

'She appointed me its babysitter a few hours ago,' he said.

'Thank goodness, we were going through hell.'

'Is she your daughter?' he asked.

'No, she is the one,' she indicated a woman coming towards them. A gorgeous white woman with luscious black hair—he couldn't look away from her. She had the largest eyes he had ever

261

seen. Bending down, he touched the little girl's cheek. She blushed and smiled, her cheek was still wet.

'What's your name?' he asked.

'Amy Ammu,' she said.

What kind of a name was that, half-foreign, half-native? As he left the theatre he realized he had forgotten to ask the name of the girl who was carrying Amy Ammu on the hip. That girl, he remembered, was beautiful, too. The artists were staying in the apartments attached to the theatre. He looked in the direction of the apartments for some time and walked off the premises. He needed to find a place for the night, it was important.

Somehow he found very cheap lodgings near the railway station. The room was small and so was the toilet, but while the room was bearable, the toilet was not. It was neat but the walls on either side were so close he thought he would die of claustrophobia. But he could not spend money lavishly on good hotels. That was not the purpose of his trip. Sitting inside the room, on the chequered bed sheet that was super cheap too, he listened to people talking on the veranda, the unnerved laughter of prostitutes, the clatter and din from downstairs and the traffic on the road. There was a phone in the room, but no facility for room service. He went downstairs and bought three bottles of water and returned to his room, taking the stairs both times since he couldn't bear being in another confined space. Back in his room, he drank water and brushed his teeth using the water he had bought, he didn't feel like using tap water, and then he turned off the lights and tried to sleep. Aadi had seen exquisite Russian gymnastics shows and dances that filled the senses with the pure pleasure of beauty. But theatre, he felt, was a different experience, a space where light, music, voice, body movements and texts became one, and the oneness elevated the mind.

From the background of the black and white curtains, looking at him, the Tenth Head sang a lullaby,

Once a fool wanted to fly
He wanted to leave the common ways
So he used waxed wings
And climbed to where no one had been.

43

The chair started rolling to and fro; she was using her muscles to push it hard, stopping and changing directions, it seemed it had become a game to her. Once it began rolling, it was not easy to hold it back, to stop the motion; it crashed into the wall. This was no racing chair to turn fast or stop when you wanted; it was just a wheelchair, without which he believed it was impossible for him to live. So he shouted: 'Get out of here—scram!'

She was shocked; she was playing half out of boredom and half out of her desire to amuse him. When the wheelchair collided with the walls this time, her fingers were caught in between, and blood clotted immediately above her knuckles. Her fingers were long and soft; she wore a turquoise ring on her forefinger, now it seemed the colour from the stone was spreading to the rest of her fingers. Sucking on her injury, she walked out of the room. He saw her fingers and realized how badly they were hurt. He called her back, and she returned and sat beside him on the bed.

Since Aadi's departure, it felt different, being there. His mother never came this way, it seemed she had forgotten her son, or had begun to see him as a strange monolith occupying one of the bedrooms. Some time in the future, maybe she would think of dusting it. These days, it was Shaly who helped him to the toilet, to his platter of food. The little bits of poop on the edge of the toilet disgusted her, and only then did she realize what Aadi had been going through all these years; she felt sorry for the poor child. Sometimes she asked Janu for help, though Shiva didn't like Janu much.

He took her hand in his; his hand began to tremble as he kissed her bruised fingers. They maintained a silence that was strangely pleasant and after some time he said he was sorry. She said it was all right and tried to sustain her composure, but after a gap of five or ten minutes she asked, though she wanted him not to be troubled by her question: 'May I know why you got so angry then? Nothing happened, right?'

He answered her point-blank: 'My chair isn't a plaything. I hate when Aadi sits on it; I don't want anybody to sit on it except me. This is the goddamn countryside. I don't know if anyone here will be able to help if something happens to my chair. I am afraid I would not be able to handle it. Every day I try a little to get out of this bed and sit on that chair by myself, it is not always easy for me though. Even when I do manage to sit on it, the thresholds and the antique furniture don't let me move around freely, the way I used to in Bangalore. To be honest, that wheelchair belongs to me. I've told Aadi this as well.'

She wanted to run out of that room and cry.

44

He thought he was a lone figure, walking around, up and down the streets. He was one among the many city walkers, the one against the many—the one untouched by the many. He thought he could go to Japan, if he really wanted to, if he had enough money to travel, it was easy to plan a trip—suddenly the world seemed small and the day longer than the world. But however long his day was, he didn't wish to think of his mother's native place and her mud mansion. He called his brother as if he were performing a ritual, something like the bell before the commencement of classes at school. It was necessary. Both of them behaved like perfect strangers, searching for the correct words and using the right expressions to explain things. Though the indifference in the voice of his brother alarmed Aadi, he didn't ask why he was talking like that. Maybe he was bored, maybe it was because of the signal. Aadi spent his day in the different malls in the city, which seemed an easy solution. He spent a long time in Café Coffee Day, watching people come and go, and those who, like him, stayed to while away their time.

Shiva had noticed the tears in her eyes but he pretended he hadn't seen them. He stretched his arm towards the wheelchair and touched it.

'You and me now, let us rock!' he said to the chair and laughed. He heard the chair laughing too.

Aadi dialled Shiva's number once again, as if he wanted to make sure that everything was in order. The automated voice informed him that the phone was out of range. One second you are within range, and the next second you are out of it. Instantly, hatred for that house welled up in him. Just then he was called to fetch his third cappuccino of the day. Slowly, he got up to collect it.

What is the difference between me and him, Shiva wondered. We were born on the same day, to the same mother. He has everything; he even got to travel to meet his girlfriend, Mother might have given him enough money to last a month, maybe longer, who knew. The only thing I am doing is lying in my bed! The twin thoughts, the twin troubles—he sighed and tried to kick his helpless foot on the bed. When was the last time I watched television?

One realized how large this building was only when one looked out from the top. He was kneeling against the steel railing of the top floor of the mall. If he fell now, he would be flying. He looked at the girl who was announcing something standing on the raised platform near the landing of the escalator. Her voice through the microphone echoed and scattered all over, making it impossible to understand. What was there to understand anyway? She was a babe, a beautiful one, dressed sexily like the air hostesses on board some cheap flight. Whenever she took a break between announcing the winners or before asking the next question, they played the music. *Shakira . . . Shakira . . .* Where was the song in the din?

The next time she came to his room, he was unmanageable, he refused to talk to her, and she wondered what had happened to him all of a sudden. Life was becoming rather stiff-necked these days. This was the first time the twins were living separately. Could that be the reason? She couldn't be sure. She wanted to be a nice person, a reliable one, for that was the duty she thought was assigned to her. He said he wanted to go out, he was obstinate; she said it was impossible at this time of the day, no use being pig-headed. But later on she changed her mind and went to his mother's room to ask for her permission; he smiled and she thought his look was villainous.

The girl had stopped announcing. She sat with one leg crossed over the other on the chair on the corner of the stage. She had beautiful thighs. They started the music again, people walked through the aisles with trolleys, shaking their asses to the music.

She helped him get out of his bed. He placed his arm around her shoulders, stretched it down and, occasionally, touched her breasts. He had the right to seek pleasure, he was not incapable of happiness. He probed it slowly, he wanted to excite her long nipple.

What did you do, he asked himself, where did you touch? He smiled.

Poor child, she sighed.

He tried again to reach him. He heard the phone ringing at the other end, thank God.

Janu helped Shaly take Shiva's wheelchair out of the entrance house and then she went back.

'Where do you want to go?' she asked him.

'To the riverbank,' he said.

The phone in his hand was vibrating. He checked the display: it was Aadi. He rejected the call.

It was Shaly who had discovered the short cut to the riverbank, the way Columbus discovered America. Aadi was glad she had discovered it; Shiva said he missed the cremation grounds. Carefully, she wheeled him over the uneven surfaces. She was afraid she wouldn't be able to manage him all on her own. She regretted not asking Janu to accompany them.

'Can we please move faster?' he asked her.

Once or twice, his head brushed against her hand. She pretended not to notice. She was not happy or resentful, just sad. Painfully, she smiled.

The wind was blowing non-stop near the riverbank.

'I feel like running over the bank,' he said, and watched closely for the pain in her eyes. She knew it had become his habit these days, to talk about things that evoked sympathy, that might hurt others. He had changed a lot since his brother had gone. Though Aadi was a silent presence in the house, everything was so different when he was there. There was order and a beauty to things. The nerves of the house used to calm down watching the slowness of his pace. She missed that darling boy. Now, there was pain in her eyes.

Shiva seemed satisfied and sighed in an affected way. He said, 'I couldn't do anything even if I wanted to, I am tired of life.'

She didn't answer.

'I want to commit suicide. Could you please help me?' he said.

Again she didn't respond. When he saw her eyes bore no expression, his eyes welled up. Like a child who had failed miserably at a match, he sat in his chair, his head bowed.

She had nothing to say. In a sense, she was tired too, tired of emotions, half of which were unwanted, uninvited. The sky began to change colour. He saw it changing hues rapidly. Very soon, darkness would cover everything; he was frightened, he wanted to go back. He raised his head and looked at her—she was seething watching the river. He felt her eyes were the same colour as the river.

'Shaly, come, let us go back,' he said to her.

On the way back home, she gave him considerable thought. Words, formed in the mind, stammered under the weight of boredom. She didn't want to talk to anyone. But she was determined to talk to Kamala about him: he needed a mother, he needed attention, he was no longer a child or even a teenager. In a way she was responsible for everything, in a way Kamala was responsible for everything. It was imperative that they move house as soon as possible; Shiva ought to have the biggest room, with his big screens and gadgets. These rooms with the black pathways that connected them, with their unnaturally beautiful projections on the walls and the unexpected dents and hollows on the floors were nothing better than torture chambers. They all needed fresh air.

Amy Ammu was playing inside the theatre. She had braided her hair like Princess Elsa and was wearing a loose pink frock. There were some butterfly clips in her hair, red and blue. Her mother was sitting in the front row on the second seat, chatting merrily with her friends. The pretty young woman he had seen joined them in a short while, wearing a salwar kameez with dangling jhumkas and a red bindi and a beautiful multicoloured dupatta decorated with matte-finish golden and copper sequins. Now Amy Ammu wanted that dupatta. The little princess didn't look too happy at what the young woman told her. She made an upset face and put her hand over her head as though to ruin her Elsa braids, then pouted and threw herself on the floor, on the red carpet of the aisle, and started crying. The young woman quickly removed her dupatta, draped it around Amy Ammu's shoulders and knotted the two loose ends on the front strap of her pink frock just below her neck. Now she looked extremely happy, with the train trailing after her as she walked up and down the red carpet. She walked like Elsa on the ramp and paused casually, closing her eyes and blowing a kiss to some imaginary prince.

Blue was sitting on a chair next to her mother and was watching her. When she saw Aadi, she strode towards him and asked, 'Can you babysit my Blue?'

Before he could say yes or no, she turned and started her princess glide. He smiled, and everyone else, looking at her, was smiling too. She took Blue, who was sitting on the chair idly, and came back. Carefully, she made him sit on Aadi's lap and blew some kisses at him. She talked to him in a language he didn't understand. Looking at Blue, she blinked her eyes several times and bent her head forward and sideways, all code words, maybe. The lights dimmed, the din died down and she ran back to her mother holding the loose end of the dupatta in her hands. On the chair Aadi sat with both feet on the floor, the teddy on his lap, to watch the play. The sing-song began:

Call me head,
More precise the Tenth Head . . .

Ravana's tenth head continued its sing-song, looking at Sita,

Unlike you, I've never been an independent head
A head that can think on its own
A head that can breathe on its own
A head that can fornicate on its own
The simple pleasures of an independent head
Never there for me . . .

Now he looks back and sees the nine heads,

I've always been with those nine rascals, Madame . . .

Suddenly Aadi's cell phone rang inside the theatre. He shuddered. It was his mother. The man sitting in the front row turned around to give him a severe look. Immediately he pressed his finger on the reject button. The organizers had made several announcements before the play began requesting everyone to silence their mobile phones and not use flash photography during the performance. How had he forgotten to turn it off? He remembered he had been busy with Amy Ammu and her Blue. He punched Blue on its head. It felt good. He turned off the phone and kept it back in his pocket. He decided to call his mother after the performance. He felt proud at his capacity not to panic. I don't want to be associated with those three rascals, he said to himself, but the next second

271

he panicked. He missed them badly and on the stage, the Tenth Head sang,

Once a fool wanted to fly,
He wanted to leave the common ways.

The second day, he thought it was a saddening experience altogether. Somehow he felt depressed and wanted to cry. Each word the actor uttered jabbed him straight in the middle of his heart. The moment he stepped out of the theatre, he called his mother. Her tired voice at the other end of the phone depressed him all the more. Amy Ammu was beside him, pulling at his shirtsleeve.

'Excuse me. That's my teddy bear. Give him back,' she said.

He didn't pause to wish her or admire her. He just thrust him into her hands while talking with his mother.

'Shaly, are you there?'

Shaly . . . Shaly . . .

Kamala heard him calling Shaly, his voice louder than before. She had noticed that he didn't call anyone else as frequently as he did Shaly these days. I must ask Aadi to come back soon, she thought. He could go wherever he wanted once they shifted to the new flat. There would be light, air and security at the new flat. She could even arrange a full-time tutor for Shiva. There were three new leaves on the money plant ivy at the window. Each leaf was a hope, life. She was only in her early forties; half of her life remained, still. It was time she stopped playing with it.

His voice was getting piercing. Slowly, carefully, she walked towards his room. His face turned pale when he saw her.

'Do you want something? Why did you call?' she asked.

He didn't say anything; she saw his eyes welling up. She walked towards him and sat beside him.

'What is it, my dear?'

She stroked his hair and kissed him on his forehead. The smell of sweat and dirt from his hair was sickening. She turned her face away. He didn't want to tell her that he'd not had a bath since his brother had gone. But all the same she asked, 'When was the last time you had a bath?'

He pretended not to remember, but he was deeply hurt and ashamed. He saw tears at the corner of her eyes.

'I will help you bathe today,' she said.

He thought he wanted to cry but he was too excited at the thought of a tub of lukewarm water to cry.

Ah, sweet little darling! Apple of my eye! He remembered his mother's childish, once-upon-a-time utterances, dialects of the heart; the way she had bathed him when he was a child, the way she used to massage oil on his partially disabled body after the subaqueous silencing of that misfortunate winter.

45

Aadi went to the same show on the third day as well. The same play was being performed at Jagriti continuously for eleven days; this was the seventh day of the show. When Amy Ammu, all dressed up for the theatre, came to hand over her teddy as usual, he asked her, 'How is he?'

'Oh!' Amy Ammu pouted her lips at his ignorance and smacked her hands on her head in disgust. She said, 'Look at it. Today it is not a he, it's a she.'

He looked at Blue. Yes, what she said was true. She should forgive him; he had not noticed the red bindi on Blue's forehead, like the one the young pretty woman had been wearing the day before. It even had Amy's butterfly clip on its ear.

'Hello, Blue,' he tried to talk to it the way she did. Again, the little girl pouted in fake anger and said.

'You don't know anything. She is not Blue; her name is White.'

How easily she could call the blue teddy White. He didn't like her changing its sex so smartly. To his surprise Sakthi and his mother had come for the show too and both of them smiled at him. Sakthi looked at the teddy in his hand at first, then looked at Aadi with a frown.

'This teddy belongs to her,' Aadi pointed at Amy Ammu, who was busy with something else. 'I am just a caretaker.'

'Appadiya?' said Sakthi. Is that so?

Aadi felt happy to be able to explain. Sakthi's mother smiled in acknowledgement.

'Hi, I am Vinita,' she said.

They shook hands and Sakthi asked him, 'Why do you come for the same show every day?'

'Where are your horns?' Aadi asked him in turn, speaking in Malayalam as he hadn't since leaving his family.

Vinita became excited upon learning he was from her native place. They spoke mixing Malayalam, Tamil and English. She said she was living in an apartment near the theatre and that there was a scene in the play where the Tenth Head was feeling his underarm with his fingers and licking it. Sakthi had come again that day to check whether he was really licking it or faking.

When Sakthi noticed that the conversation was mixing different languages and that it was about him, he announced, 'I know three languages: Tamil, Kannada, and English.' Then he thought for a while and corrected himself, 'No, I know four languages. I know Malayalam, too.'

Later, he said he liked the way the actor licked his fingers, and the woman shouted on stage and the percussion that followed with a hullabaloo of confusions.

Before the play began, when it was announced, 'Adishakti presenting *The Tenth Head*,' Sakthi looked at Aadi in surprise.

'It's you and me,' he said. Aadi didn't understand what he meant at first.

Vinita explained that he was referring to their names.

Outside the theatre, Amy Ammu and her mother were waiting for Blue, now White. When Vinita wished her as Baby Amy, her mother corrected her, 'She is three and a half, not a baby.' Sakthi looked at his mother triumphantly, for he had asked her several times not to call him Sakthi Baby in front of his friends.

'Would you like to join us for dinner?' Vinita asked Aadi.

He immediately accepted her invitation with thanks. It was a modest and elegant apartment nearby, with a number of water colours on the wall to the left of the entrance hall, a sort of memory wall. Vinita showed him Sakthi's room. A huge cardboard ship in the centre, with an eye-patch wearing captain at the wheel, a donkey hanging from the mast and a cobwebbed niche on the east wall—the webs, she said he was growing on purpose. There was a figure of a Minion in the niche half obscured by the web. It would be fun to see once it was completely covered over.

He was happy with the chapatti and korma as he was already bored of the food they served at the hotel, the repetitious and poor breakfast spread.

'Won't you get bored here once he goes to school?' he asked.

Suddenly the twinkle in her eyes faded. She looked down at the table and nodded indistinctly; it was neither yes nor no.

Who else knew better than him that some lives, some specimens got caught in the tragic spaces of the webs of boredom, like the Minion on Sakthi's wall.

'That's a big TV you have here, this looks almost like a theatre,' he complimented her.

'I love to watch movies. That's how I spend my time, and I go to plays whenever I find time, I like the atmosphere there and the people. If you don't have any other appointments in the morning, come over; maybe we can watch a movie together. There is a good video shop near Jagriti. What do you say?'

'But bro, this TV is mine,' said Sakthi. He added, 'I have a PlayStation, do you want to play a game with me?'

'Yes, but some other time, it's already late,' he said.

'I am a pure vegetarian, Aadi. I shall prepare rice tomorrow, I hope you don't mind a vegetarian menu.'

Shiva's call came while he was on his way back to the hotel. At one point, Aadi thought he was crying, his voice sounded so feeble and heartbroken.

'What's the matter with you? Is everything all right?' he asked.

'Aadi, Amma helped me bathe today,' his voice choked as he said it.

Now Aadi was the one who was crying. He couldn't hold back his tears. He walked fast, ignoring the boy at the desk, shielding his face with his cell phone. Back in his room he searched for his mother's Kashmiri shawl. He missed her scent, the scent of the woman wrapped in a tragic dream. He too wanted to find the way that led to her. 'Have I ever been a baby in my life?' he wondered.

On the shores of the lake, under the cover of darkness, a little face looked at him, all shrivelled up and sad.

46

The next day he went to Vinita's apartment with a packet of chocolates for Sakthi. She said he would be back from school by two o'clock in the afternoon. Together, they had strong filter coffee and then went to the DVD shop.

'Are you going to the play again today?' she asked him.

'Yes, I am planning to,' he said.

She thought it was a little strange, going to the same play again and again, though she herself did the same thing at times.

'If you don't mind, could you please take Sakthi along with you? I will prepare dinner by the time you come back. Anyway, you have to babysit the teddy bear.'

In Cinema Paradiso people were reading at leisure, sitting in the corners of the coffee bar. He looked at those who were browsing while sipping every now and then from coffee mugs. He also noticed a wonderful set of drums and a keyboard near the manager's desk. Aadi instantly liked the place.

'What kind of movies would you like to watch?' she asked.

He was not sure, he was not really into films. He shrugged as if he had no idea and looked through the racks.

'Hosa CD yen banthithe?' she asked the shopkeeper. Do you have any new CDs?

He was showing her some of the new movies when Aadi spotted an old film.

'Which language do you want?' she asked Aadi, but he was not listening to her. He had taken the disc in his hand and was looking at it intently. On the cover was written: *Molière*. Starring: Romain Duris, Laura Morante, Fabrice Luchini, Edouard Baer, Ludivine Sagnier. He flipped the cover over in his hands. 'Speak to me in the language of Molière.'

She took the disc from his hand. While she was examining it, he found one more: *Molière*, starring Philippe Caubère. They decided to take both. When they passed the white walls of the theatre, he glanced inside with an eagerness that surprised him. What would Amy Ammu with her blue-white teddy be doing now? From the window of the seventeenth room, Amy Ammu saw him walking down the lane with Vinita. She got excited and called Nimmy by her side, 'Nimmy, Nimmy, look at him.'

Nimmy was busy preparing for the eighth day of the show. She looked out of the window and saw the whole city walking. She couldn't see who Amy was pointing at.

'Look at this, 260 minutes. How much does that come to, four hours or four and half?' Aadi and Vinita calculated the length of the movies. It would take at least two days to finish watching these. They felt happy, they laughed.

Back at the house, Vinita scooped the vanilla ice cream into vintage cocktail glasses like a professional.

'Ferpect,' he said.

Then she poured the extra strong filter coffee over the ice cream scoops. What was she doing? She was ruining it! She didn't even ask him whether he would like to have his ice cream plain or coffee flavoured. This, he thought, is not even flavoured; this is dipped or immersed in coffee. She put an ice cream spoon in it and gave it to him.

'My god, this is fantabulous!' he shouted.

The coffee, with its frozen sweetness, was hitting him straight in the brain. Some jabs are ecstasy. They sat on the sofa and began to watch the movie. A little later, he got up from the sofa and sat on the floor with his legs stretched out. He was afraid his coffee ice cream would not last long.

Abruptly he felt afraid of being abandoned, being alone; the same idea he had embraced so passionately on the first day of his journey. Family means a hell of a lot of happiness too. O God!

When Sakthi came back from the school they all had lunch together. After the lunch Aadi thought they could resume the movie for a while, but Sakthi didn't let them. He made him play with him instead. He watched the language of his brother filling the big screen in low spirits. Bang bang bang bang.

Vinita told him she had a family pass to the theatre, that he didn't need to buy a ticket anymore.

He was thinking of Molière's exile on his way back from the theatre, of the thirteen years of abandoned wandering through the streets of France, of travel, money, passion. Poor guy, how the audience marvelled, how he survived fights and storms, how earnestly he fell in love with the mother and daughter alike, how honestly he couldn't separate the strands of life and theatre. When the boy behind the desk wished him, he smiled, still preoccupied. He saw two carpet moths dead on the stairway.

Kamala was trying to make a comeback, each minute, each second. It was not a matter of remaining in the closet or coming out of it, like what the doctor had told Shaly. It was all about coming back, to life. She was observing how quickly life sprouted on the money plant, each second there was a new leaf. No wonder people called it the devil's ivy, for her window was now rich with precious green, the newness of life, the absolute bliss of living, making life succulent. Each day she woke up to the beauty of this sight, life stemming from the glass bottle that had contained whisky once. She wanted to be Behrman's last leaf that never fluttered or moved when the wind blew. When new life sprouted outside, buds, blossoms, tender green leaves, swayed in the breeze under the happy sun, in the lightness of living, while this one leaf was caught inside the room, struggling against the cyclone confined within the four walls.

Aadi!

Now she was really worried about him, the boy who had gone out to learn life—like her mother who had worried about her. This was the cycle. She too had gone through the same situations, she too wanted to challenge, and she too had sought the cover of darkness. She was afraid of the world outside, yet she had said: 'I want to see the world. I would like to know myself better.' Her mother must have lost her sleep on occasion on the same bed. She too must have looked out of the same window. All afternoon, all evening, all night, she must have kept herself busy opening and closing the door. She must have lit the lamp with her insides boiling over. Return was a bitter word at times—it is bitter when it never happens.

What does the word 'mother' mean?

Worry.

Trauma.

Tragedy.

Noun, verb or adjective—she wished she knew whatever the fucking draining out meaning was. Today, she was worried, worried because her son was far away, because she thought her son was still young, at least he had been young on the day she last saw him. He had a blue haversack on his back and a smile on his face; this was how she remembered he had gone to kindergarten on his first day. But he had started crying towards the afternoon, a lot of other boys were crying too. Shiva complained that his cry was mute and went on for so long he felt ashamed of him. Would he be crying now? Had she ever cried as a young girl? How her mother might have suffered. Her mother was always her problem, she was always on her way to her, like so many other mothers the universe bore. She had thought she would be free once her mother died. But after her death, her mother had taught her this was wrong. No child could be free with the death of its mother. Kamala's mother now slipped into Kamala's body, and killed Kamala who was once her child. The one who died was not the mother but the child. Mothers never die; they keep rolling like money in black markets. They kill the children, they continue, they multiply. The mother Kamala thought was hers was the first woman, from whose womb it all began. It would be difficult to track down the first woman who was single and devastatingly docile in her ways. She should have taught her children the *Story of O* instead of keeping them chained within the dark rooms of submissiveness. Kamala's mother also had no idea what she was doing, what she was supposed to do. She entered the living flesh of her daughter and destroyed her daughter thinking that she was doing justice to her mother who had in fact killed her a long time ago. Now Kamala's mother, after entering her daughter's body made her believe that it was she, the daughter, that was living.

Kamala remembered she had slept on her mother's bed—her own bed—the night she arrived for the funeral. Someone told her that they had burnt the mattress her mother had slept on; the one she had now was new. New or old, wakeful or not, she was sleeping and while she slept she remembered she was talking to her mother. They were planning, plotting and fooling the rest. People thought it was the sickly old mattresses and pillows, the smell of the rotten dampness of death that spread sorrows, but it was the loss of the child, the baby girl, the love of her mother's life, her pleasure, her happiness, her relief, the loss of everything she had longed for, the loss of Kamala that made her mother weep, made her shut herself away from her grandchildren, from the woman her daughter had loved so dearly. Everything, the mother thought, was sickening.

They talked the whole night. Kamala lay on the bed in the foetal position. Her mother said that was the perfect position for the beginning and the end.

At first, her mother thought Kamala wouldn't come. She was worried. She wanted to run away when they were about to set fire to her body. She cried, 'Wait! Let my daughter come,' with her lips shut tight. Nevertheless her face was covered with flattened cakes of cow dung. They would not be able to see her even if she opened her mouth and yawned. She remembered how she used to train Kamala as a child; she fretted about etiquette and ethics.

'Ammukkutty, remember to cover your mouth when you yawn. Little imps and gruesome ogres are waiting to get inside your mouth and slide down through the food pipe.'

She laughed remembering little Kamala covering her mouth with her little hands. Ha ha! Oh God. Cow dung tasted awful. A little bit of it entered her mouth and got mixed up with the remaining saliva. She wanted to get out before they set fire to the pyre. She thought she would wait outside and watch her body getting incinerated. She had been stubborn throughout her life, she wanted to see Kamala married to Madhavan, and she wanted to see Kamala follow her rules—now she wanted Kamala to come before she was completely burnt. It took enormous effort to escape from the closely packed wood and cow dung cakes. Never in her life had she struggled so much. Once out of the blazing pyre, she ran to her bedroom and waited. She saw the women taking out her old mattress, on which she had breathed her last, on which she had peed many times. Wondering where they were taking all her stuff, she followed them and she saw them burning her belongings, everything that had been hers once. She had seen her body reduced to ashes and was calm—what did the form of these materials mean, after all? But when they didn't bring a new mattress in she started to worry, again one of her traumatic, tragic worries. Kamala would need bedding to sleep on when she came. When the women returned and started washing the furniture in the room she went out and waited under the tree that bloomed glow worms in the night. In the light of the glow worms she saw some parts of her skin, a teenager's skin—she couldn't believe it! Now that she had freedom in the night, she came back late, very late, to her room that looked sullen and desolate, with a sheet on her bed that she had not seen all her life. She was feeling sleepy but then she heard her daughter ask: 'Mother, how are you?'

The daughter sat on the new bed sheets looking at her mother. Both of them maintained the etiquette around silence for a long time. But she wanted to talk. Kamala wanted to talk too. They waited for the lights to dim, the buzzing of the funeral flies to stop.

When did her daughter yawn, forgetting the social niceties her mother had taught her as a young girl? When did her mother slip into her mouth, slide down her food pipe, play around her windpipe?

'These traumatic, tragic worries are all for nothing,' Shaly said. 'Just drama, I would call this only drama. Where has your son gone? To the place where he was born and . . . fine, not born, but where he grew up. M.G. Road, Richmond Road, Indiranagar, Lingarajapuram, Whitefield, Chamrajpet—all these places are fucking familiar to him, he has friends there. He is a young gentleman, not a child any more. That is his place, do you understand that? Just the way you say this place belongs to you. At least he will think of his future, I don't see any point otherwise. Let him decide if he wants to join fine arts or engineering or whether he wants to become a poet or start a business. Let him come to a decision, he is not a babysitter. I hope you understand.'

All this had only troubled Kamala, though she knew everything that Shaly had said was true. Bangalore was not an unfamiliar place; he knew the nooks and corners of the terrain. But when had he learnt all that? How? She had never seen him learning. If only he were a little older, she sighed. Shaly said the young gentleman had friends there, many friends. Friends help you find ways to move forward. But many friends, as a matter of fact, find many ways, some of which could be treacherously boggy. A joint of smoke would be enough to . . . She shuddered at the thought. She was wondering if thinking helped.

'You think so because you don't know your son; you don't know how pure he is.'

The world is not just a tragic place always, there is light scattered all over, the most flexible thing on earth. Why do you want the climax to be in darkness always? Why are you so obstinate about seeking escape routes? Face it, face life, face light, do not be afraid.

Laboriously, Kamala looked at the window bars. She saw life burgeoning out of the green shoots. Morning was calling.

Shaly came in with a cup of hot tea in her hands, and the two of them talked for a long time. It was Shaly who dialled Aadi's number and gave it to her. Unbelievably, the signal strength was strong and she heard him clearly, as if he was talking from the foot of her bed. In the energy of his voice, in the happiness he breathed out through the phone, she kept saying: 'Life starts from here.'

The next day Kamala prepared to leave for the flat she had bought in town, she said she would go alone in her car with a hired driver, she said she could manage on her own and asked Shaly to take care of Shiva. As they drove, she concluded that life was the only thing that would never fail you in life. Each minute you could have it back, all the same, it didn't matter how badly you had dumped it. It remained yours. Be glad, she told herself, no more bitter jokes. Though she was tired physically, she was delighted by this new rhythm of speeding up. The vehicle was racing ahead, and she felt like kissing the driver, for the speed he offered.

There were domesticated rabbits and ducks in the garden that didn't seem scared of strangers. They walked towards her and she had to shoo them away, for *she* was scared of them. Initially, she had trouble locating her apartment, though she had been there before. At last when she managed to find her door and opened it, the smell of newly whitewashed walls and the freshness of distemper that still lingered inside the room sickened her. She hurriedly rushed to the windows to open them. She glanced at the backwaters through the living room windows and through the glass wall that opened to the balcony. When she turned back, she saw the rooms were bleak without furniture and a little scary in their nudity. That was all right, she thought, she could fill it with furniture and people. She would buy some new curtains and bring all her stuff here when it was ready. But when she opened her bedroom windows and saw the water again, she shuddered. Could water be so still always? She remembered what Shaly had said: 'Money was no massive dump to be disposed of easily and flushed out.'

Now she couldn't remember why she had wanted the sight of water so badly, why she had paid so heavily for it. She couldn't understand what there was to hope for in the sight of water that looked still and dead and windswept. She had paid for this lack of colour, with money that was not hers. She was afraid she would miss her native home, even the smoke that rose from the pyres. The more she looked out, the more restless she grew.

She would buy green curtains, she would cover the bleakness, and she would get as many indoor plants as possible. She would need some paintings too.

Shopping malls, she thought, were tiring. But she went all the same. She artlessly gave herself the burden of buying things: curtains, paintings and little works of art. In a coffee shop, on her chair, she dozed for nearly half an hour. When she woke, she found to her relief that nothing was missing, her purse and mobile were on the table, her bag on the chair next to her, her money safe in it. 'Thank God,' she said as she walked out.

In the end, when she got home, she looked extremely tired but happy. She was happy she could move, lift a pinky and break through the monotonous grove. Though she said the day had been exhausting her pride was visible in each syllable she uttered, about how she had selected some curtains and bought some paintings for the rooms. She wished Shaly had been there but she was glad she could manage everything without much effort. When she walked to her room, she said: 'Shaly, there are some chicken rolls and pastries inside the brown handmade bag in the back seat of the car. Shiva would love them. Could you please go and get them?'

Kamala had forgotten some small things while executing big tasks. For example, she had forgotten to take the brown handmade bag from the shop and keep it in the back seat of her car. Maybe she had done this in her mind. She had forgotten to pay the hired driver and send him back. When Shaly came out to get the brown handmade bag, she saw the driver waiting on the doorstep.

47

Once upon a time there was the Internet, a decent Wi-Fi connection.

A little bit of sadness dissolved in each cup of morning tea, sadness without benefits. But the tea tasted better these days, and it lasted longer. Now Janu knew tea was to be served to Shiva in the biggest cup available at home. She helped him sit up. He leaned on the two pillows she set against the headrest.

'Don't bother, I can manage,' he said.

All the same, he didn't try to move an arm or a leg. Managing all the parts of his body was tiresome and boring. His mother was busy overseeing the work on their new house. He was happy as there was hope. But it had been days since he had brushed his teeth. When Janu or Shaly came into his room he felt awkward and he pressed his lips together tightly. What was shame? He was afraid, he still remembered.

What made him think the world was his? It belonged to him only because Aadi had left. He couldn't look at Shaly the way he wanted to when Aadi was there, nor could he talk to her the way he wanted to when his twin was there beside him. He wanted to tell her something, but what he wanted to say hung halfway in the air like Dylan Thomas's ball.

He looked outside his window; he saw the cannonball flowers in bloom. They said the tree attracted snakes, he hadn't seen a single snake so far. What could be sadder than the sight of a tree in full bloom? He thought he wanted a pack of condoms like the paralysed hero in the movie. Condoms were the awakening calls of souls. He was ashamed he couldn't own a single one.

'Hi! 'Morning. Have you had your tea?'

He looked up from his cup and saw Shaly smiling beside him. She gestured to ask whether he had brushed his teeth or not, to see if he wanted any help. He was half sitting, half lying, all crumpled up in his sheets. Shaly was making his bed, quite a task with him still in it, but he didn't try to move. He was ashamed of his manhood rising, poking its head out pleadingly, something organic, something helplessly zoological about it, something out of proportion.

Looking at him, she was also thinking of an animal, of the dog that used to lie all shrivelled up in a corner of the school building in Aizawl. 'Look, how I trust you,' he would say, wagging his tail tirelessly, giving her the most pathetic expression in the world whenever she squatted down beside him to stroke his neck. Sometimes, when he saw her walking down the hillside, he would run towards her with a sandal or a ball in his mouth to present to her: useless things, of great value. A happy gesture or a touch of recognition was more than enough to make him feel good. He would go back to his corner and lie down again. She saw tears in Shiva's eyes. She sighed.

When she left the room, he realized that he had no love towards her, no lust. What he had felt was pain. He hadn't heard such an expression before. People were known to say 'I love you' or 'There is pain and pleasure in love', but never did they say 'I have pain for you'.

He knew he was boiling in pain.

Shiva surveyed his half-paralysed body. Aadi had broken his pupae. It was easy for him, for his legs were strong. He remembered the first cake Aadi had baked. It had come out still yellow, with soft dips in the centre. He had covered the uneven surfaces artistically with butter and chocolate sauce, and even put some sugar rings and wafer rolls on top of it. His cake looked yummy. The children clapped their hands; they waited for Kamala and Shaly to join them, and when they all came he cut the cake and the half-baked chocolate dough oozed out of the centre along with the raisins and nuts he had soaked overnight in rum.

Three more flowers of the cannonball tree fell down in the wind. They looked soft, fleshy and pink.

Tonight, I need a slut!

48

Kamala had not eaten anything the previous night. When Shaly had gone to her room she was not in the mood to talk, she said she had a headache and dismissed her just like that. In the morning, Shaly was not sure of a welcome, but all the same, she went to Kamala's room. She peeped inside through the opening of the door. All she could see was a new red sari sprawling luxuriously on the bed near a brown paper bag that had been cut open. Was she going out again today? She didn't remember her saying anything. She heard the doorbell ringing. It must be the hired driver. She went to answer the door. There was an old man waiting outside.

'I have come to cut the weeds and grass.'

'What?'

'To clean the backyard.'

'Oh!'

She thought he had rung the bell in the morning to give her the words she feared most, about the most deadly weed. To cut: It could mean to chop down. It could also mean to chop up and give.

Janu came from the kitchen and said, 'He is my father, he has come to clear the overgrown weeds.'

Shaly gestured for him to go to the backyard with Janu. True, Kamala had warned her about the poisonous plants growing in the yard, and on the path that led down to the river. She had asked her not to pluck or touch the flowers. But when Janu and her father were out of sight, she sat on the doorstep thinking over the different possibilities. Does a person need to go every day to Cochin to buy curtains and bathroom fittings? How much can she fit into eighteen hundred square feet? What is she hiding from me? Shaly tried to recall the faces of the peddlers of Bangalore, who spread like air, like cancer across the universe. There was no use asking Kamala anything, she would be better off talking to the stones on the pavement. Stones did answer at times, in this house, particularly. She told herself to calm down.

Cautiously, she walked into Kamala's room. Breakfast was ready in the dining room. When Kamala saw her coming, she said, 'There is too much starch in the sari, I cannot manage it.'

'You look good only in silk saris, this doesn't suit you,' Shaly said. She wanted to see her get angry and pulled the border of her sari to annoy her on purpose.

'Oh dear, I will change it. I don't want anything that you don't want,' Kamala said. 'Yes, my old saris are a lot better than these new ones. Maybe you could try a sari too for a change; it's good to change things up once in a while.' She laughed, and took off the sari in a hurry.

She was thinner than Shaly remembered. Shaly's thoughts adamantly circled around the same words: weed, grass, peddlers. Kamala ought to tell her where she was going—she believed she had a right to know. She was the one who had introduced the first blood-fucking peddler to her, and she recalled how mercilessly Kamala had slapped her when she didn't hear from him, the whirring noise of his fucking Bullet. She had heard a vroom last evening and when she went running outside, she saw a Fat Boy roaring down the lane. Was it going to the graveyard? A Fat Boy in this godforsaken part of the country! Kamala selected a dark violet silk sari with a yellow border from the cupboard.

'I need a blouse to go with this sari.'

She squatted on the floor and rummaged through the bottom shelves of the cupboard. This was the portion of the cupboard where Madhavan had secretly kept his sports magazines when they had all been young and things were good between them. Kamala's mother had given him permission to keep his things in there. He was not confident of keeping or hiding his books in his own house. Memories became so loud she smiled. An issue of *Sportstar* cost six rupees or something during those days. Madhavan was the only boy who owned those magazines in their village. He would sell tapioca and coconuts and collect money for the magazines without anyone's knowledge. This, he thought at the time, was the riskiest game of his life—maybe it was just one of those first links in the long chain of cheating. Those magazines were his hard-earned, ill-gotten property and Kamala was their temporary custodian, watching over them then the way she looked after her other charges these days—the children he had given her. Sometimes he rented out the magazines for a rupee or two to the local boys, sometimes in exchange for some *Playboy* stuff. Sometimes he would remind her, 'If I find out that a page is missing, I'll show you.'

She was not afraid of him anyway.

The magazine was a biweekly. Soon, the space granted to him became packed with books. One day, when his father came home, Kamala's mother said: 'When the carpenter comes, I am planning to make a bookshelf for Madhavan; the bookworms have started eating my clothes as well.'

His father didn't understand what she was saying, nor did he see the connection between her clothes, Madhavan's bookshelf and the bookworms, for he had always been a slow learner, the man who got information second-hand. He was not aware of the things stolen from his own house.

Where there were books, there would be bookworms.

'My dear father-in-law, there are things called bookworms on earth,' Kamala said, taking some blouses out of the cupboard. 'Have you ever heard of termites and roaches?' She smiled, unable to contain the strapping happiness of nostalgia. Shaly couldn't understand why she was smiling.

Kamala started trying her blouses one by one. Her body had shrunk, becoming unbelievably small in them. 'Someone has come to remove the weeds today,' Shaly said.

'What weeds?'

'The weeds in your backyard, you said there are some poisonous plants growing there.'

'Yes, I remember.'

There was no change of expression on her face and Shaly grew all the more upset.

White trumpets had been flowering at night in the backyard, for the last two weeks. In the morning, over the green expanse of plants and grass they remained furled, along with the thorn apples hanging down from their stems. Kamala said they were poisonous, that they could be harmful to them, to her children. She told her about the woman in her neighbourhood who had committed suicide by eating its seeds. The woman, she said, was heartbroken, a failure in love or something like that. Madhavan had gone to see the dead body with cousins and friends, but she was not allowed. She had wanted to see it so badly.

Shaly admitted that she was incredibly ignorant of botanical facts. 'Poisonous or deadly, they are beautiful,' she said, stressing the last word. But all beautiful things need not be entertained.

They heard Janu's father raking the soil in the background. Kamala scrutinized the stranger in the mirror, inside the loose blouse. She said she needed to put on more weight, she seemed cheerful. There were no signs of weed or smoke on her face. At one point, Shaly thought she was regaining a little bit of her old charm. But still, she couldn't believe it. She wanted to know what was happening, where she was going, all alone.

'You seem in a good mood today,' Kamala said, looking at Shaly.

'No, I am not. I think Shiva has not been to the toilet today,' she said, mockingly. She wanted to irritate her, make her bad again.

Kamala's face darkened. She put away the sari she was trying on and pulled her nightdress over her blouse and hurried to Shiva's room.

If a single drop of water could contain a sea, Shaly knew Kamala had it in her eyes then.

She followed her and said, 'You go, dear, I can take care of it.'

'It's all right, Shaly. Ask Janu to get me a strong tea.'

After speaking to Janu, Shaly walked out to the backyard. She saw the white trumpets, now lying dead on the brown earth as if they had been drawn on it with a piece of chalk. There were ants hurrying around and over the thorn apples. Would he set fire to them once he finished uprooting them? Would breath be choked under the poisonous smoke?

Shaly was frustrated when she learnt that Kamala had left without a word of goodbye. When had the driver come? When had she gone? What exactly was happening in this house? 'Can someone tell me something, anything, everything?' Everything was the better word. Good for you if you know everything.

'Ridiculous! She treats me like a slave these days.'

She saw Shiva sitting on his bed, looking out of the window. He knows almost nothing, she thought. Maybe he was watching the man clearing the land. He looked surprisingly sad even after a nice bath and a dusting of talcum powder. It seemed he was afraid of the light outside, nonetheless he was looking at it. It seemed he was tired of the already long day, the maid who cleaned the dishes and prepared food in the kitchen, or maybe he was simply afraid of the afternoon sleep he knew would never come to him. 'You didn't have to be sad to get weak, my dear,' she said as she climbed her stairs. Obviously she was thinking of him. She had even waited for some time on the landing before climbing the stairs, thinking he would call her.

There were white trumpets in Aizawl too. They called them 'hell's bells' and 'devil's trumpets'. The children of the forest who loved fruit, sweet or sour, stretched their arms towards the thorn apples. The elders warned: 'Don't touch, don't go anywhere near them.'

Aadi had not seen Vinita look so down and shabby before. Today was the eleventh performance of *The Tenth Head*. How long had it been since he had come to Bangalore? He had forgotten to keep track. Anything was better than living trapped in maddening silence. He was no pearl to suffer like that.

The day after next, the actors would depart. It was like a festival, Vinita said, when they were there. Aadi was happy, for the actors had promised to take him along with them. The promise was made by the Tenth Head, the lead actor; Aadi liked to call him Molière, regardless of what his name was. On their way back from the theatre, he told Vinita: 'Did you hear—it was Molière who invited me to join his group, to be a part of the theatre?'

'Yes, I did. I was there too, but I didn't hear him say anything about becoming a part of the theatre. I heard him inviting you, he has invited me too.'

'But I am going with them, in their car.'

'They have space in their car; you need not hitchhike, thank God.'

'I don't care, just two more days to go.'

He was making gestures, using his arms liberally and she had to remind him that this was no theatre but a busy road in Whitefield.

Sakthi was sadder than his mother to see Aadi go; he didn't let him return to his lodgings that night. He wanted him to play with him, or watch him play. On the TV screen, the cricket lawn stretched out to its full length, waiting for the players. When Sakthi gave him the joystick Aadi realized he was not happy, after all.

The next day they went out for a short drive.

'Somehow I could never fit into a driver's seat,' Vinita said.

Aadi also thought the same. She looked nervous and tense at the wheel. They ought to have hired a cab. She kept craning her neck awkwardly to look at the road, and honked even when there was no vehicle in front of them. He remembered the elegance with which his mother used to drive. He noticed to his surprise that the red Maruti Swift was moving in second gear. It seemed she didn't wish to try the third or the fourth at all. His mother used to shout at Shaly, 'You are not selling ice candy on the streets that you need to honk like this.'

He thought he would repeat the same words to tease Vinita. Maintain class, the aesthetics of a beautiful road. Sakthi started singing already, 'Pompom vroom vroom . . . Pompom vroom vroom . . .'

She parked in the middle of a large parking lot. Aadi looked at the banners and posters around them. Dogathon. It was no dog show, Vinita told him. The dogs, she said, were going to run. He had seen elephants running in his mother's native place, at the temple they used for such shows. But he hated to see the elephants chained and struggling under the sun, especially in the midst of the deafening roar of percussion instruments. People, especially those who were drunk, were crazy for the booming drumbeats. As a child, Shiva used to ask, 'Amma, tell me, what if the elephants don't like music?'

He would say he didn't like the sound, Kamala would say she loved it; he would say he knew some of the elephants in the row who didn't like it, for he saw water running down from their eyes.

All the dogs were barking. Sakthi said aloud, 'Ma, barking dogs seldom bite.'

They walked towards the dogs; they were on leashes. There were advertisements for choosing the right leash and collar for the dogs. Different breeds of puppies were on sale too. It seemed Vinita knew almost all the names: Siberian Husky, Dalmatians, Golden

Retriever, Labrador Retriever, bulldog, German Shepherd, so on and so forth. Aadi wondered how she knew all this. Sakthi said he wanted one, a tiny one, maybe the tiniest. Aadi asked him to buy a Tibetan dog, a Lhasa Apso. The dogs used to be sentinels in the Buddhist monasteries. Vinita said no one was going to buy a dog there; they were there to watch the show.

'Ma, I want him,' Sakthi's voice ricocheted around the ground.

They went near the Buddhist sentinel and examined it closely.

'Some sentinel,' Vinita said, 'look at him, can't even see anything. If you let it loose it will run into something for sure.'

What she said was true. The sentinel had long white hair on his body, covering his face and falling over his eyes. Could he possibly see through it? His eyes were hardly visible, but what if that didn't matter? Aadi whistled to him, and he went the other way and stumbled when he bumped into the wall, just as she had warned them. They didn't miss the smile on her face, all of them laughed except Sakthi, who was wailing by then. They had to go back to their car without waiting for the dog show. But inside the car it was a disaster: Vinita's honks plus Sakthi's screams. In the end she had to pull over near Vittal Mallya Road in search of a pet shop.

Together, they bought two hamster pups. They were not even half the size of Vinita's hand. They bought two pink balls too for the hamsters to lie in.

'Ma, do I like pink?' Sakthi asked.

When the pups started moving happily inside the balls, he laughed and clapped his hands. He had not seen such small pups in his life, and neither had Aadi. Vinita bought a cage and a packet of food for them. The shopkeeper helped her load it in the boot of the car.

'They will die if they are exposed to sunlight,' the shopkeeper said.

Aadi imagined Shiva sitting in his room, with no light, no wind and no air. If he does not get any more sunlight, he thought, he will die. He could not let the one who was a part of his body, the one with whom he had shared amniotic fluid and the dreams and happiness of being before birth, die. He dialled Kamala's number. It was out of range. He hated the automated voice. He called Shaly.

His concern for his brother touched her; she was also thinking about Shiva when Aadi called her. In fact, she was thinking of Kamala, Shiva and the concept of love. What was love? Kamala had once told her that love was the only way for miserable human beings to cross the threshold of *adwaita*, non-duality. It was a gift nature had bestowed upon humanity, a temporary space to forget the tree of maya, illusions. Once at the zenith of consummation, human beings became part of nature, they abandoned duality. At the pinnacle of making love, they embraced the blissful state of forgetfulness, the state of being thoughtless. They became simple and pure creatures, like snakes, crows, fish, cats and the like. Thoughts were the curse of humanity. Once they start thinking, forgetting the euphoric heights of no abstraction zones, men and woman started blabbering again, praising the act of love. They forgot the universe in which they had dissolved, temporarily; they forgot the air, fire, earth, sun and stars. But the memory of the short-term reality filled them with the energy to move forward, ballast, so they could keep their balance.

Sex was just one of the many ways to reach the short-term destination—call it love, call it whatever you want to. There were a lot of other ways too. Overgrown with luscious undergrowth, they yawned, waiting to be discovered.

Kamala was the most beautiful concept of love on earth. A touch or a glance would be enough for her to wake up, shaking off the scales of duality. Yet, who was it that kept devastating the happiness that was allowed, happiness per person? She pondered over the rights and wrongs of personal pleasures and temporary pleasures.

She opened the bottle of eau de cologne and poured some drops from it into the big bathtub. She inhaled the perfume diffused in the coolness of the water. Thanks to the well attached to the kitchen in the backyard, she could have a herbal bath with water that was blessed by the fragrance of lemon clover and wood sorrel. In their bathroom in Bangalore there had been large, full-length mirrors that almost covered the walls. She remembered the reflection of her nudity, her splendid hips and slim waist. This bathroom, in which she was imagining herself, waking herself with the help of what she had seen or experienced, had the smell of wetness. She realized she was wet. It smelled of wet wooden frames and old red-oxide walls; she had the smell of wet flesh. She noticed a lizard watching her as she anointed herself with lavender oil, the insides of her thighs, the incredible softness of her supple breasts. There were lots of things to look at, the way the lizards did. For example, one could see in this bathroom that had a faint whiff of eau de cologne, lavender and the oldness of the wooden frames, the Indian version of the Venus of Titian. She leaned against the big bathtub and looked at her reflection in the water. Feeling happy, she mumbled, *'I sing the body electric . . .'*

This was a no-movement zone. The spades fell continuously on the roots of the poisonous weeds; the flowers of the cannonball flew down in each breeze, and in the cremation ground skeletons happily exploded in the pyres. Still, the place remained deadly silent. The rhythms of the spade and the bones were not distinguishable from the rhythms of stillness.

'Aadi, you know what? I could experience a sparkling city in this silence. You won't believe me if I tell you about the things I see every day. Till now, there was a beautiful Czech girl in this room; you couldn't take your eyes off her behind. Her name was Georgiana, she looked almost like a Brazilian pole dancer. Her skin is the colour of yellow sunlight. And inside, she is the same colour of the flowers that bloomed on the cannonball; I guess it was the same scent. I used to warn all the boring bitches not to come anywhere near me wearing ordinary white bras. Such a turn-off, I hate to see white ordinary stuff. But Aadi, Georgiana is an amazing bitch. She was wearing a blood-red PrimaDonna with lace work, brocaded around her nipples. The bitch, she killed me. I can imagine the wearisome wandering you are undertaking. But if you think it is good for you, you should carry on. Sometimes, I imagine you in a gypsy wagon. I have visualized you shouting slogans, of whose meanings you have no clue. You said you were part of the bandwagon. You were wearing clothes double your size. I felt like laughing. But sometimes I feel jealous of you, thinking of the wonderful things you are eating every day. I am sure you are having soup and starters before you try a variety of other cuisines. You are lucky! What Janu makes here sucks, her sambar looks like a bog. The same taste every day, the same feel, and the same smell. But recently she has been trying some new recipes. I loved it when she fried slices of bitter gourd last night. I must tell you, those were the sexiest chips I have ever tasted. I still have some in my pocket. I am sad you could not be a part of all this fun.'

Inside her bedroom, Shaly opened the little bottles of perfume. She couldn't decide what she wanted. She sat naked on her bed, musing for a while before dabbing herself with the scent of her choice.

Like lightning that was struggling to escape the grip of the night, the scent of lotus flowers floated down the stairs, touched the pineapple carving on the handrail and jabbed him in his heart. The pigeons were cooing like never before. It seemed they were happy for no reason, or they were warning of something unknown. He was not aware of the cooing, on an afternoon that was frothing like mad. He touched himself but he couldn't remember Georgiana's face or her pert nipples no matter how hard he tried. He heard someone knocking on the door, the door which was open. He began to break out in a sweat and closed the windows against the flowers of the cannonballs.

The police were having a tough time at the junction, controlling, giving instructions and redirecting the drivers. The jam was getting longer and uncontrollable. Amidst the chaos, the hawkers were coming with car screens and plastic toys, shouting the names of their products and knocking at windows, making helpless gestures. Kamala looked at the impoverished little girls, their eyes, faded clothes, cheap ornaments, sun-darkened faces, weak smiles, white teeth—everything about them was poverty-stricken and unpleasant. She yawned, for she was extremely tired and bored of the long jam. She had been thinking of Aadi and occasionally of Madhavan all the way from Cochin. She even feared that Madhavan would get mad at her for letting Aadi waste a year. She thought literature or economics would be the best options for him. She also wondered if she had ever been a good wife or not. When she was good and obedient, when Shaly had not become a part of her life, Madhavan was lenient and generous, though at times kinship poked its ugly head into nocturnal fumbling and vice versa. Then he had to drink (a habit he developed quickly) to banish the thoughts of blood ties and familiarity from his mind, before the desired–undesired nightly fumbling. A custom, he said, which youngsters could not agree with these days. A strange custom, she sighed. By the time the doors were opened they were all gone. And the wealth they wanted to amass so badly, that their parents longed for, the family fortune—swindled out of two young lives, trapping two new lives—turned out to be of no use to anyone. Most women her mother's age were dead and his father would be dying soon. They realized they didn't need money, money couldn't buy them peace. Some not so distant day, they might be bedridden too. Invariably, all of us are born sick and die sick and live sickened by thoughts.

She remembered their little expedition, how like warriors they had charged through grassy knolls and scattered hillocks towards the mountains. Madhavan used to be the hero of the pack—they were a super-excited group of eight boys and six girls, obedient and happy. They called him Comrade Madhavan. While they were still climbing Madhavan said, 'No one is supposed to turn back until I say so. Watch out. Don't step on each and every stone you see on the way, some could be shaky, you will end up in trouble.'

He carried a long stick in his hand to keep the stray dogs at bay. No one else was allowed to use the stick. It was like the extension of his body, the symbol of his sovereign power. He whipped the air with it as if he had the right to do anything he wanted, and the children admired it all for god knows what reason. Sometimes he walked in front, sometimes in the back, threatening them with shouts.

Kamala was tired by the time they had reached the top of the mountain. She squatted on the ground; her yellow skirt expanded in a balloon-like swell around her. Immediately he wanted to deflate it, he struck her with his stick; she jumped to her feet. Forgetting his instructions not to look back, she turned around to give him a bitter look of anger. He seemed frightened, the blow was harder than he had expected.

But my dear Madhavan . . .

Her eyes sparkled with fireworks of wonder. In the gleam of her eyes he saw his fear vanishing. She saw the green earth, down, much further down from where she was standing. It was her first bird's-eye view. She was thankful to Madhavan for giving her such a splendid vision, for forcing them not to turn back, for the vast expanse of the green earth, the blue sky, the bridge across the river that extended like a child's toy train, small, smaller than they could ever imagine. The children were not aware of what had happened behind them. Madhavan came closer to Kamala and whispered in her ear, his lips almost brushing her cheek, 'There is another spot on the mountains I would like to take you to. Come, the view from there is unbelievable.'

Sadly she turned back and saw the maddening queue of the vehicles. The people were tired of being jammed in, sandwiched in-between metal bodies. They honked mercilessly. Under the cruel sun, the policemen were also mentally cursing the beacon-lit vehicle of some minister they were all waiting for, for whom they were holding up the traffic. Something told her that Madhavan was also there somewhere in the long queue. He might be on his way to see his children, the woman he had left behind.

The words of the prophet were true. Once, a woman sat down between two men, half of her face blushed with happiness and the other half pallid with bitterness. If Kamala were to climb that mountain once again and turn back, she would realize that Madhavan was walking on both sides of her, simultaneously. And that would frighten her.

They went into the restaurant carrying the pink balls in which the hamster pups were running amok. They were not sure about leaving the pups in the car. They were afraid the little things would die. At first Aadi thought the restaurant had no lights inside, but slowly his eyes adjusted and he realized it was the heat and light outside that dimmed his vision inside. They were tired, they collapsed on the swivel chairs in the corner. Though the hamsters were small, they were a big nuisance. He immediately wanted to get rid of the scratching noise they made; it pissed him off.

Sakthi started reading the words on the menu card aloud.

'Oh my!' Suddenly Aadi took a hamster ball and held it in front of his face.

'What happened?'

'Nothing.'

He passed the ball to her hands and bent down as if to tie his shoelace. Even the hair on his head reflected the fear he felt within. From under the table, through the legs of the long line of tables, he could see his father walking in with Kuljeet. In the dim light he clearly saw his father's unpolished shoes, and the brow marked by sorrow.

He became lighter than milkweed, he started floating. He couldn't differentiate his face from hers. Now his face her finger, his groin her skin. The abandoned love he harboured in his mind so far, grazed on her skin like a lamb in an enemy's farmyard. He craved and feared all the same. She thought, he has the face of a newborn. With his eyes shut, hands fisted, head leaning against her body, he sought her and felt her nipples with his lips. His mother was banging her head against the door. She had to pluck him out of her body and run to help his mother. She thought she was helpless, he was helpless, and the mother was helpless.

When he lifted his face from under the table, his eyes bore his father's life and depressions. All the sorrows were fragile, like buds, like the bubbles over clean water.

49

I remember walking with you a long time ago, through the aisle, with ten thousand paintings that carried no signature on either wall. Maybe it was in a dream. But I know I have walked with you. I remember the aisle ended in a garden. You looked vivacious, like the effervescent soft drink we had had while walking, giving off your bubbles; I wondered whether you were the spirit of some of the flowers in the garden. The garden, you said, had no rules, it crossed out the narrow boundaries of rights and wrongs, dos and don'ts, where any nymph could easily turn herself into a tree, I felt happy. I had heard Bob Dylan speak on YouTube the other day. He said he didn't understand what John Donne meant by 'the Sestos and Abydos of her breasts. Not of two lovers, but two loves, the nests.' But he said it sounded good. And you want your songs to sound good. The garden you showed me looked attractive, attractive enough not to seek out meaning. You said, we would make a nest on the topmost branch on the tree in the centre. You said, for the four of us. And the four of us, you said, would live happily. I loved all of you, the two born in my body and the one in my mind. I cannot abandon you now, but how could I ever think of taking you back? When I find myself deeply in love with love, what difference between man, woman, bird and hippopotamus? I know this much.

You know this much too. I should've thanked you for the hope you gave his paralysed mind. Yet, you are busy packing your things in the room upstairs, you are getting ready to leave. I can see you folding and rolling up your clothes, putting them in your bag, the stuff that will obey only you. I am not crying, but I can see you crying, like a rain that is not likely to end. We haven't eaten anything, the three of us. You didn't say we would have to starve in your garden. You said the word 'plenty' and I remember, I loved the word as soon as you said it. But my child is starving now.

I know one more thing: If you turn your back on this place, the memory of your perfume will kill me. So don't ever think of abandoning us. I have never been a good wife in my life, nor a good mother. Madhavan would say it was my fault. I should have kept my mouth sealed with the happiness of my son. No, I won't let him be happy, and I won't be happy either. I am a suckerfish at the bottom of the bottom, foraging for misfortune among the aquatic invertebrates. I won't let you live, but I don't want to stop living.

Shaly was crying in her room. She looked at the clothes she had gathered on the bed; she forgot how to fold them into her travelling bag. She tried not think of Kamala or Aadi. She thought only of the kiss, the kiss that had burnt her lips a few hours ago. She had never had a first love in her life. She had had her first sex in Aizawl, but that was sex for the sake of it, the way people do it because they are supposed to do it. She had felt ridiculous when she found herself in the midst of an orgy, on a night of joints; she had yearned to get out of there, for that was not her idea of making love. Now, she realized what suffering was, the suffering of the most innocent soul on earth.

Kamala was silent. She didn't say anything, instead she lay prostrate on the ground, crying. Janu helped Shaly carry Kamala to her bed. Janu wanted to know what had happened; the dishes she had prepared remained untouched on the table. Shaly wanted to get away before dawn, before Janu returned. Kamala might be sleeping. She wanted to look at Shiva one last time, but she didn't dare.

Her hands slipped over the pineapple carving when she saw Kamala standing on the landing like a rotten log, looking at her. She dropped her bag on the floor.

Touch wood, touch wood. A perfect journey begins like this, he said in his mind. The Toyota Qualis PY 1 waited for them near the white wall of the theatre. It must have been a very old car. The presence of the actors and the steaming cups of coffee in their hands enlivened the morning mist. It was Vinita who brought them coffee in a large picnic thermos. There were some other friends from Bangalore who came to say goodbye to the team. They all hugged and kissed each other. It was a happy sight to see human beings hugging each other, there was warmth and pleasure.

Vinita was holding a bowl of sugar in her hands; all of them ate a pinch of sugar when she said it was considered auspicious to do so before starting a journey. Her eyes welled up when they waved to her. They had been living the carnival of Molière for the past few days, she couldn't resist sobbing.

Aadi wiped her tears with his handkerchief. Rane sang from the back seat of the Qualis, 'No woman, no cry . . .'

The rest of them sang in unison. 'No woman, no cry . . .'

Now there was a bashful smile on her face.

'Vini, you should come to Adishakti, we'll have a nice time there,' Nimmy said.

When the engine started, Molière played a song in praise of Lord Ayyappa:

Saranam saranam ninpadha kamalam . . . Pulivahananaam . . .
Ayyappa . . .
Panthala Rajakumara . . . Njangade sankadamellam theerthidane . . .

Each trip was an invitation to the mountains. She wished she could hide somewhere inside the folds or heights of the forests of Aizawl. The pastures of human beings were more terrifying than the forests where rats bloomed. Uncle Raphael had left Aizawl when the rats had finished eating Andrews Papa. Shaly did not wish to go back to a place where Andrews Papa was no more.

How far am I supposed to walk, she asked herself. How long?

She looked at the path leading to the burial ground and sighed. The ground she felt under her feet was paper-thin. Tread softly on me, the ground said. Her night slippers tried not to touch it. She ran. She ran till there was light, till there was not a single silhouette left of horrifying yesterday. Then she sat on a big stone along the way and cried for a while. She noticed the passers-by looking at her; she looked back at the milk bottles dangling in their hands and sobbed. A radio snapped on in a nearby tea stall. It was morning, she realized. Then she got up from there and wandered for a while, dragging her bags behind her. She had forgotten where the bus stop was, she remembered she had nowhere to go.

When they travelled, after the unfortunate rat attack, back to their motherland—the Judakkunnu, the hill of the Jews, which the Jews had colonized once upon a time in history—no one recognized the good old maskiamma, the wife of the priest Andrews. Rita Mama had left when she was young and beautiful; she came back fat and saggy. She was sad to see that the place had changed a lot, that many of the people who lived there now were new. But the people, new or old, looked at beautiful Shaly in surprise, talked behind her back in hushed voices. 'They behave as if they haven't ever seen young women,' Rita Mama said.

It was a street loaded with histories and beliefs, laid out in the shape of a cross, packed with houses; and the houses in turn were crammed with people. Most of them were business people, doing small-scale home-based stuff. Whether they were gossipmongers or not, gossip was happiness, as it was in other parts of the world. They still believed that the spring of fresh water they were blessed with on the top of the hill resulted from the whiplash of St Thomas. They loved miracles; they loved miracles on a daily basis. They loved watching the young woman, new to their town, her gestures and way of dressing, extremely modern to their sensibilities—but her face and the shape of her body they would swear they all knew, or they all wished to know. She looked exactly like the beautiful girl in their parish, the girl they all loved alike who was the daughter of the one-time altar server Joseph, the rich merchant of their town. Her name was Miriam and she was irresistible. Joseph too had been fucking handsome when he was young, everyone knew. Now with the arrival of this new young woman in the neighbourhood who looked almost like Miriam's twin, they had a lot to bitch about. There were lots of doors open into other people's lives.

Andrews had always wanted to tell Shaly and Rita; in fact he had tried many times, but he couldn't confess, the foolish days of his youth, for he was the one who used to sit inside the wooden confessional listening to penitents. He sat, freezing at the thought of opening up. Damn it, he said to himself.

He remembered the insides of the holy confessional, faith unfaithful, strange moments of deathly darkness. He liked it especially when the women came to confess, their woes and sins softer than their dreams. He became excessively sentimental when the women from his own parish knelt in front of the latticed opening. He answered them with broken words. In his mind he was a young Lothario, a gentle priest in the flesh, the kindest soul on earth, who at times returned from the confessional with grief in his heart. He was sad for the saddest woman, the abandoned, the hopeless and the ugliest of them, who scratched their groins and farted while Mass was in session. He knew what they needed was an angel in their lives, an angel to guide them.

Some women spoke of bitter things with the unbearable pain of opening up; he listened to them with the pleasure of deceiving little children. Sometimes, very rarely, he invited some of them to an occasional dalliance within the sickeningly yellowish walls of his bedroom. The women who accepted his invitations were mostly hysterical, they said they were thankful there were no latticed openings between them; they opened themselves with an air of triumph. Like stinking air they covered him, made him confess that both the priest and the woman were starving in the parish, and smiled at him, showing the yellowness of their white teeth, the age spots on their lower chin and the newly formed wrinkles on their neck. Sin was a faraway concept, abstract in itself, but flesh—flesh on the other hand was tangible: the supple, moist cunts, the religion of carnal pleasure. He was thankful people lived in ant holes, he was thankful for their limitations.

But on the day Emily came to confess, he understood how pathetic his life had been. He remembered for no reason his beautiful wife Rita and the ugly or the not-so-beautiful women with whom he had been to bed. Emily had the voice of real angels, and she resembled one of those wild white rose briars on the altar. She was no easy piece of cake he could nibble on, but nonetheless, he saw her in his dreams as a bride wearing nothing but a very thin veil and holding an exquisite bouquet of white flowers. He knew he wanted to fuck her.

She was a woman of the past, of old tastes and fashions, who called herself an artist and who was the rich wife of Joseph, the most handsome man in the parish. One day she came to see Andrews after Mass (of course she was in her finery) and asked his permission to supply candles to the church. He gave her his consent immediately, he didn't even wait to see whether her candles were good or bad. But soon, he realized that she was an expert in chandlery—the term she used to describe herself was true to the core, she was Emily the Artist. On every market day, Emily brought home blocks of wax and chopped them into smaller chunks using her sharp kitchen knife. She could have very well controlled a man with that knife. Under her artistry, scented wax melted to form roses, lilies and grape bunches at the feet of the tall candles. The entwined vines of the forest, the birthday roses, the white lilies that reminded one of the little breasts of the maidens of Jerusalem, everything was ready. What she needed was a connoisseur. And this is where Andrews came in.

One day, after Mass, Andrews went to her house. She said her husband was not home, he had gone to deliver some candles to his aunt. But she was extremely happy with his visit; she wanted to show him her workshop, which was her private bedroom, the one she kept for her art and craft. He marvelled at the paper flowers and candles, at the wonderful crochet work on the tabletops, the adorable bedspreads. He praised her elegant fingers, such as could belong only to an artist, and pitied those who didn't know the art of spinning yarn. He couldn't help admiring the painted flowers on her bedspread, the fragrance of her room.

Aunt Cèlina had asked for some of the candles for All Souls Day. It was on his way there that Joseph remembered he had forgotten to take the parcel Emily had kept on the mantelpiece. So he went back. At an odd time of the day, totally unexpectedly, he was met with the perfume of agar wood chips burning in coal from his house girdled by ancient trees. His steps faltered. With his heart thudding against his throat, he sneaked into the house. He peeped into her private bedroom through the crack in the window. He saw Andrews melting down on the bedspread delicately painted with roses. He didn't want to wake them. Stealthily he went out of the house and walked away. He bought a packet of ordinary candles from the grocery shop. He thought he was spreading on the road like molten wax.

'Aunt Cèlina, where is your house?'

50

'Thou hast also taken thy fair jewels of my gold and of my silver, which I had given thee, and madest to thyself images of men, and didst commit whoredom with them.' As he walked he continued, 'Therefore a lion from the forest will slay them, a wolf of the deserts will destroy them, a leopard is watching their cities, and everyone who goes out of them will be torn in pieces.'

People were saddened by the sight of the good old altar server, the handsome and rich Joseph walking about like a mad, sad man. Those who tried to calm him down came back with their heads bowed and their minds shaken. Blasphemous! They shook their heads in disbelief, for Joseph was the finest of the finest altar servers, had been right from his days of childhood. Wounded by the rain of gospel he had called down, he walked crazily, all over the town with a packet of candles in his hand.

'She lusted after their genitals as large as those of donkeys, and their seminal emission was as strong as that of stallions.'

When he was a child, his mother used to tell him stories at bedtime. There was a picture of St George slaying the dragon with his long spear. The spear, a symbol of peace, troubled him all the same; he was afraid of the weapon, he was afraid of violence. She told him the stories of Satan, the power of his verses. Satan was there in the same room, listening to the same stories with a frown. When Joseph was a child, his Satan was also a child, who was incapable of doing anything to the picture of the saint on the wall. Thus he lay supine on the floor next to Joseph listening to his mother's stories, playing with the sharp end of his tail, poking Joseph occasionally, especially when he or his mother fell asleep without completing the story of the saint. Thus he grew up hearing the stories of his defeat, waiting for the perfect chance to take revenge. Joseph grew up too, fearing the temptations of Satan. He sat down on the pavement in the rain.

'You are the game of Satan now,' his mother whispered. 'Don't forget: Hell is for sinners. You should grow up to overcome this phase, for what you experience now is not real. The sorrow you think is weighing down on your heart is no real sorrow, but the pranks of Satan.'

His mother was dead, and a dead person had no cause to lie, but still he thought she was lying on purpose. He didn't want to listen to her. He wanted revenge, revenge for the good, like St George on the wall had exacted. The concept of Heaven was a trap, the trap that would deny justice while alive, for one knows what would happen after death.

His faith was stronger than a mountain and hence he sat on the pavement expecting a flood through the night. On the next day, shortly after evening Mass, Joseph went to talk to Andrews in the church. Andrews's face was defiled by another memory, but all the same, he couldn't hide the glow of adulterated pleasure. When Joseph saw him, he declared, 'No one whose testicles are crushed or whose male organ is cut off shall enter the assembly of the Lord.' And so saying, he showed him the knife in his hands. Andrews shuddered at the new sheen of the metal. He turned pale like the flowers of henna. There was no one to be seen on the premises. The hands of the altar server rose across the altar, his weapon tight in his hands. Who would get through, who would break free, O Lord, if you remember our sins?

But Joseph didn't wish to kill him. He had three commandments, which he said Andrews should obey.

'I will let you go. If you really want you could kill yourself tonight, but I am not particular about that. You need not be afraid. I will not come to your house to disturb your woman. Let me tell you in the presence of the God of this altar, I want you to do three things. First, leave this place. But I want you to help me keep track of you, because at the end of the day, at the end of temptation, if I feel like killing you, I don't want to have to wander about crazily in search of you. Second, never continue as a priest in your life. Our Lord does not deserve to get blemished. Third, donate your wealth to the orphans of this parish before you leave.'

Joseph left the church without waiting for a reply.

Paradise was a piece of cake religion gambled with, for they wanted people to gather around like rats around a block of cheese. Joseph said he was not afraid; he would rather lose his reward than live the life of a coward. He knew the moment you touch the truth, the idea of Heaven would dissolve. Last week, he remembered he was in Heaven. If you stopped being lecherous, and found satisfaction in what you had, there would be Heaven on earth. Who knew who would be who after death?

But what did Joseph win in the end, after his innumerable revelations and justifications? Why did he send a wireless message to Mizoram asking Andrews to come back with immediate effect? The moment Joseph thought he had triumphed, the moment he stepped out of the church after threatening Andrews, Satan jumped on to his shoulder and settled there—Joseph's shoulders began to hurt under the weight. Back home he didn't say anything to Emily; he didn't even look at her. He heard her cry in the night, but he pretended not to hear. Satan was happy to be in control; he didn't let Joseph sleep a wink.

Satan jumped off his shoulder the day Joseph learnt that his wife was pregnant. Joseph said he was tired of never-ending examinations, he was humiliated. He believed Emily was hatching

Satan's offspring. He ran off, Satan trampled over him as if he were dirt on the pathway. He couldn't bear the cry of the newborn baby girl, the daughter of Sin. Drawing the sign of the cross, he sent a wireless message to Andrews: Come back immediately.

At last, when Andrews came, Joseph handed over his own flesh and blood, four months old. Satan couldn't help laughing, 'Joseph, you are impossible! How could you be such a fool? The girl is your blood.'

In front of the candles that bent and bowed over, the soot that formed on the surface of the mantelpiece because of the unusually thick wicks, candle wax encased in the glass liquefied to oil, in front of all the vigil lights that burnt and burnt out, Emily cried. She wanted her child back. In her house, Rita yelled: 'I don't want it.'

Another girl resembling Miriam! Stealthily, Emily came to Rita's house to see the child Joseph had entrusted the priest with. The changing roses had the colour purple on them when she arrived. She looked like a stained candle, with its wick withdrawn. When she saw Shaly, she gave a loud cry of horror. She could not get enough of what her eyes had seen—she felt her life was closing down. Rita came running downstairs when she heard her cry. The woman was reluctant to speak; she went on crying as if she had seen her dead mother walking towards her. A stranger crying in her house, Rita was alarmed, and when Shaly asked her what the matter was, she said she couldn't understand a fucking thing. She pulled open the door with such force that it rattled on its hinges and asked the woman to get out. Shaly felt sad, she took the woman by her hand and helped her walk out. And finally, when they came to the road she thought she would follow her to wherever she was going. Rita was calling her name, but she didn't look back. She followed her as if she were in a trance; she knew there was something behind her tears.

It was a princely house girdled by ancient trees. The woman was still crying. When they stepped inside Shaly looked at

Miriam, not in discomfort, not in surprise, rather as if she had been expecting something like this. Normally, twins had such a resemblance, like Aadi and Shiva. The girls looked at each other; Miriam was younger, maybe two or three years younger than her. The girls sat down at the table, had tea and listened to Emily's story. She saw Miriam crying too. She didn't feel like crying, didn't feel like waiting for Joseph, her biological father. She said she had a terrible headache and set out in the darkness. Her head actually was aching, painfully dizzy. As she walked under the ancient trees, Andrews Papa called out: 'Where is your butterfly?'

Now she knew she wanted to cry. She didn't need anyone but him. When she reached home, she saw Rita prostrate on the floor, crying. It was a message from Mizoram, announcing his death. There was a ban on the transport of infected bodies, so he would be buried there soon. The next day Shaly set out for Bangalore. She didn't want to face anyone any more.

51

Their embraces were not over yet; Aadi knew how happy he was, and he also knew this would be the most wonderful trip he would ever take. Inside the Qualis, they were busy cracking jokes, eating and singing songs. Occasionally, one of them would bump into the person sitting next to them to amuse themselves and to evoke laughter: such happiness, such joy. Sometimes they let loose loud farts and described how inspiring they were. Aadi thought about the loneliness he shared with his brother in their room at home, the isolation they sliced up while they all travelled together.

'Would you like to have a milkshake or a banana split?'

Amy Ammu was busy taking orders. She had a plastic juicer and frying pan ready by her side on her mama's lap.

'I am afraid I don't have choco chips in my restaurant now. Sir, would you like something else?'

Yes, sincerely, they all wanted her to sleep. Nonetheless, the game continued. From time to time they took turns amusing her, acting as her clients, telling her stories. Aadi must have dozed off in between for he woke up with a start to loud shouts of joy. He saw a long mud path stretching out in front of him, lined by tall mango trees on either side. Geography changed at the speed of light. It was highways and tarred roads minutes ago, now the redness of earth and greenness of nature welcomed them. The vehicle stopped in front of an enormous gate, on which was a piece of artistically dilapidated wood with the word 'Adishakti' written on it in small letters so as to not upset the exposed bark and the tree rings. Aadi couldn't help the smile on his face when he saw Nimmy swinging on the gate, opening it, making a funny, exaggerated gesture of welcome.

It was a happy site set against the background of khus-khus grass. There was a cowshed near the entrance on the left side of the gate, with eight or nine cows, perhaps more, in it. They drove slowly over the mud path and arrived at what seemed like some kind of a parking lot surrounded by trees, and parked under a lovely lemon tree that bore hundreds of lemons, splashes of yellow amidst green. Aadi imagined the picture he wanted to draw.

When they were about to get out, dogs came barking from almost all sides. Aadi was frightened, he thought they were attacking. They were jumping all over; some of them were trying to place their paws on Molière's shoulders.

'Faristha, Itchimba, my darlings!'

Aadi saw the actors hugging the dogs.

'Won't the dogs go away?' he asked Nimmy.

'Don't call them dogs, they are his sons,' she corrected him.

'Oh!'

Once the cuddling was over, the noise died down and they all dispersed in different directions, dogs and actors. He saw Amy Ammu and her mother walking straight to the back of the property, taking a path decorated with the fallen petals of pink bougainvillea. There were long stone benches along the way under the splash of colour.

'So, do you like the place?' Nimmy asked with tenderness.

He said yes, very much.

'Muthu, take him to the guest house, room number 7,' she instructed someone who was there.

As he walked he marvelled at the fullness of the brown sapodilla fruits on the trees and the vision of the orange tangerines and the pale yellow star fruit. There were many cars in the parking lot. Pointing to a red Mercedes, Muthu said, 'Some film star from your place, a big actress.'

Aadi nodded as they continued. It was a place for research in theatre. Lots of people came from different parts of India, from different parts of the world, some of them became a part of the place and decided to stay. Be it real life or theatre, Aadi felt the place had a special energy of its own. The walls of the guest house were the same red colour as the earth they walked on. It was no colour; it was the earth itself, the mud house. He thought about the whitewashed walls of Kamala's mud house, the low ceilings, the rooms with no ventilation—the contrast brought about by the years of architectural experimentations, the same medium and the different form. He inhaled the aroma of essential oil and noticed the pot of the reed oil diffuser in a corner and the beautiful paper lanterns hanging from the ceiling. There were black-and-white photographs of the Mother and Sri Aurobindo decorated with deep red hibiscus flowers on the walls. Anuraktha had also had the same pictures on the calendar in his library. But he stopped, short of breath, in front of another black-and-white picture: a woman in her early twenties—his mother, Kamala. Carefully, he walked closer to the picture and touched it as if to feel it: it was his mother in a sleeveless blouse and sari, sitting in a posture befitting royalty. She had the same nose pin, the single diamond on her right nostril. Right or left, he pondered for a while till water filled his eyes. He felt the shine from her nose pin was filling up the room. When Muthu noticed him looking at the photograph with intense care, he said: 'This is Veenapani amma, our mother.'

Veenapani smiled at him with her whole heart and soul, she said in a whisper: 'You are family. Now go and rest.'

She must have been a feather or a dream when alive, for he hadn't heard a voice more delicate than this. The moment he reached his room he dialled his mother's number. It rang, but no one answered. He walked to the window from where he could see the blue-green swimming pool with floats and balls netting the edges. The walls of the pool were also of mud, with an ancient clock hanging in the middle of it. He tried her number again, but the recorded voice reported that the person he was calling was not responding. The night tightened its fearful grip when the crickets went suddenly silent. He saw the lights shining on the surface of the water. He kept dialling her.

It was difficult for her to continue living in the same place with her sister Miriam living just two streets away. Nor was it easy for her to convince Rita Mama to stay, or to go and settle down in a faraway place with her. The memory of the rats running amok on land that didn't belong to them made Rita reluctant to leave this place she was so fond of, the serene atmosphere, the undisturbed roof over her head bordered by beautiful changing roses. Her wedding, she remembered, was happy, because of the fortune and the wonderful house Andrews had inherited. She was overjoyed with the new title of maskiamma, the wife of the priest. But Andrews had tossed out the fortune and the title in no time for whatever blasted reason, as easily as disposing of a cat or a piece of unwanted furniture, and then gone to live in the folds of the forests like a primitive person, cheating her, cheating her family. She still remembered how the people of the parish had called her Madame, with great admiration.

Shaly was not sure of a welcome. It had been years since she had deserted the place. Let her say what she wants, thought Shaly, what Rita Mama needs in her old age is company, the company of a person who is sincere towards her. When the wind ruffled her hair, she said, 'Rita Mama, I haven't talked enough to your changing roses, tell them, please tell them I am coming home.' The changing roses were wild, and if left unattended would form a wilderness.

With the passage of time, pain would become a memory. She wondered whether the wind that rushed and roared with the speed of a bus was leading to her past or future. She closed her eyes and turned the music on.

Shiva hadn't washed himself or brushed his teeth. He was hungry and he knew he couldn't stand it any longer. When Janu came to clean his room, he asked her in a feeble voice as if he was asking her a favour: 'Could you please get me something to eat?'

Kamala was holed up in her room. When Janu asked, she said she didn't want to eat anything. She remembered the bleak, dull white walls of the flat that the dealer said were in vogue. But she was not after fashion; she wanted colours, as bright as they could be, colours that would emanate happiness. She remembered how long she had spent at the paint store holding the catalogue of colours the shopkeeper had given her. The catalogue was too long to concentrate on, but when she noticed the shades of pink she remembered how Shaly hated pink.

'Pink again? I told you I hate it,' she would say. She would say no to anything that was pink. No pink shoes—she had never seen her wearing ladies' shoes or fancy slippers—and no pink hair bands, even if her hair was blowing in the wind like mad. No pink tops, for she said they would make it seem as if she was trying to look like some pretty princess. What was more, she said no even to pink margaritas.

Kamala sat down on the sofa with the catalogue of shades for more than forty-five minutes. She pondered over John Cheever's yellow room. The way he stepped into the yellow room, the way he felt the peace of mind that he had coveted when he first saw the walls in a walk-up near Penn Station. He believed we would feel unexpectedly at peace with the world when we stepped into a tack room, a carpenter's shop or a country post office. She too wanted to sit in a chair by the window feeling the calm of the walls restore her.

Her fingers tapped over the shade called 'hidden spring'. There was a spring which was hidden, a faded shade of blue. She thought of choosing that colour for Shaly's room; Shaly could sleep in a blue room and dream about the hidden spring of pink daisies. Once one colour was fixed it was easy to decide upon the others. The shopkeeper, who had acted like a charlatan so far, proved very helpful. He said Prussian blue would go well with the faded blue. She agreed immediately. Next he suggested ocean blue for the children's room, turquoise blue for the bathrooms, 'maiden voyage' for the balcony, 'rainstorm' for the reading room, 'serene sky' for the entrance hall and 'wipe-out' for the kitchen: in effect, a blue house.

It occurred to her only when she was caught up in the too long, too slow traffic that blue could signify melancholy, it was an essential colour of sadness. It was difficult to comprehend colours, though. The sameness of the colours could be boring; the same sea, the same sky. She was convinced she wanted to cancel her order. She opened her handbag and searched for the shopkeeper's number. Had she thrown away the bill? She was certain she didn't want blue. At a certain point, she even thought about turning back. It would have been better if she had. Instead, she turned the music on and tried to concentrate on forgetting the din the drivers were making outside. The song announced: 'When she came back, she was nobody's wife.'

For a second, Shaly halted. She looked closely at the purple yam she was about to cut into pieces. It resembled the paws of a dog or the paws of a tiger; it could be both. The finger-like extensions, she decided she didn't want to cut them away. It was her idea to prepare food for Rita Mama before she came back from church. There had been a change in their relationship since she had returned after a gap of years. Rita Mama had become more severe with her tongue and gestures, and with her famous goddamned speeches. The lightness was missing. Had it been there before? Whatever it was, a sort of bond that was stronger than before was forming between them. Rita Mama wanted Shaly; it was clear she was not willing to give her back to Emily.

Leaving the tiger paws on the kitchen table, Shaly came outside and sat down on the doorstep, waiting for the whistle of the fishmonger. Rita Mama had asked her to buy mackerel. While waiting, she searched on the Internet for good mackerel recipes. She remembered Rita Mama had been neither good nor bad to her on the day she arrived. What she had expected was a ramshackle house with a dilapidated gate drenched in bird shit and a garden overgrown with grass and wild plants forming a wilderness around it, blocking the way, and Rita Mama inside, bedridden, just like you saw in the movies. She was extremely surprised when she saw both Rita Mama and the house in robust health. Rita Mama, on the other hand, did not even seem surprised; she behaved as if she had been expecting her. She prepared tea for her and gave her boiled tapioca to eat. She had displayed no signs of vexation and hence, Shaly could look only at Rita Mama's changing roses with anger. But from the second day onwards, Rita Mama started behaving as if she were Cinderella's stepmother. Back to her normal self, but a little bit harsher, a tad more sour and dour. And Shaly knew she was home at once, and happy.

Shaly heated oil in a wok, and fried the ginger-garlic paste. Then she added the paste of spices she had prepared along with gamboge and salt water. Once it was golden-brown in colour, she added the fish pieces one by one.

When his hunger subsided, he remembered Shaly, the hunger of his flesh, his mother's friend. Would she never come back? He knew his mother was angry with him. She had stopped coming to his room—like the hands of a clock that had suddenly come to a stop, whose rotations had ceased, and a stillness had taken hold. He remembered her lying prone on the bare floor. He had heard her cry, a din of voices from the three women present at the time. His memories served him right.

Now with pain, he remembered the woman who had abandoned him as he was crawling up to her breasts, his eyes closed and his mouth open. He sensed her nipples erect, hard as they brushed against his lips. What he had lost, he knew, was a continent of love. He wanted to lie down beside her, inhale the feminine, seductive smell of desire from between her thighs.

Janu came in with a glass of buttermilk and placed it on the table. She said she was busy helping her father in the backyard. It had been four days; they had been cleaning, destroying the poisonous weeds in the backyard. Poison grew in the backyard in abundance, she said, it was so deadly it could even cause the death of a person. When she left the room, he thought of his brother, Aadi. Later he started thinking of his own death.

52

All port towns have the same secrets to reveal—stories of weed, money and prostitution. Business always flourished no matter how many died while trafficking, or how hard the crackdown from the police and vigilance. Invariably, the peddlers had the same face; the same expressions. Surprisingly, their eyes were the same colour as that of the eye of a dead chameleon. Children were their targets, the ones who loved to sit patiently for hours in some parlour or salon to get their hair fixed, make dreadlocks by twisting and ripping their very soft Indian hair. They screamed in the name of what was not theirs and loved the tangles and mats of abundance, the wooden beads of Jamaican colours, and considered themselves descendants of the beloved black singer. Sad, they admired him not for what he had done but in the name of a joint. People were to blame; they were the ones who marketed the Rastafarian. They pushed his songs to the background, for they found more business in his uncut matted hair and the smoke that got tangled in it.

'No, no, not this, this is not what I intended,' he would have told us if he were alive. He died young. His voice carried the pain and the dreams and the freedom of his people. The peddlers gave you neither the dreams nor the freedom, but they did give you the hurt, distress, anguish, and trauma compressed and wrapped up in a small packet. They would let you scrape the goodness off your soul, jeopardize you, your generation and existence. It is heard that the trafficking was strong on the borders; countries yearned for the devastation of their neighbour's country, the way you craved the annihilation of your neighbour's paradise.

Cochin is a port town. Kamala had bought a flat somewhere in the heart of Cochin.

The rest of the story was a figment of Shaly's doubtful imagination. Kamala had not seen a Fat Boy dashing down the lane or conceptualized the possibilities of the Cochin town. What she had in her mind was the beautiful home she was going to make for her children, for Shaly, for herself, the beautiful frills of the layered green-and-white curtains with which she was going to adorn the windows, the smiling faces of her boys, and an evening walk with Shaly by the shores of the black waters.

But now Kamala knew she was tired, her hands shaky.

The first time, it was the fingers. They grew out of proportion and got dissolved in the air. But that was the first experience, like a first kiss, or first sex. It wouldn't be repeated. People would not have to stop on the way in the storm or in the rain to look back and ponder. By the time one would realize this, one would be immersed in the poisonous dungeon, all wrecks.

All peddlers shared the same face, the same expression and the same eyes, so the one she was going to meet in Cochin would be the same one she had met in Bangalore, with the same name. Last week he had been in the Port of Spain, doing the same business, the business of death, the peddling of marijuana and acid. They were happy, they were proud; they had the same manifesto irrespective of nation, creed and sex.

What the fuck, you live or die!

If Cochin was a port town, Kamala was just an infinitesimal particle in a handful of sand. Her hands still shaky, she dialled the number.

He wanted to go and tap on her door and peer inside, or walk in, just like that; he wanted to get out of his bed, first. He wanted her so badly he had been trying to call her since morning. For the last two days, shortly after that most unfortunate of incidents, he had been experiencing a strange kind of spasm on the left side of his body—it was becoming uncontrollable, like a tic. Above all, he was tired of isolation, he wanted his brother back. He wanted someone to help him with the phone. He had woes; like ants gather grains, he gathered his woes one by one, and the more he gathered the more they swarmed around.

The tea Janu made wasn't strong enough.

His bed sheets stank.

He needed some books to read.

Could she bring the old TV set to his room and ask the electrician to set up a connection there?

Could she at least tell him the date she had in mind for the move?

Was Aadi ever going to come back?

Where had Shaly gone?

He talked about freedom, worried about the dreadlock Rasta driven from the mainland to the heart of the Caribbean. He said smoke was his personal freedom: We should have the right in this country to do what we want, if we don't hurt anybody. But he died of something like a cancer when he was thirty-six. His voice continued to enliven the hearts of many that lived a miserable life.

The wrong signal: Kamala bargained with the go-between. The unfriendly face of the Cochin port frightened her. In Bangalore, business happened within friendly circles. A busy port should be somewhat like this. But why the hell had he asked her about her children? He must have asked the same question two or three times. Her children were her private sorrow, her happiness, her pain. She didn't want outsiders poking their noses into her private affairs. She didn't wish to share her personal data. She looked out at the sea, her fingers tapping on the menu card on the table. The restaurant, she noticed, was not busy. The man in front of her stared at her.

'We guessed you wouldn't want to share your details when we learnt that you're not into socializing.'

She felt uneasy, listening to him address himself as 'we'. She knew there was more than one person involved, that she was only a microscopic link in this. He might have noticed the painful contraction of her facial muscles, for he stopped talking immediately. Those who came to buy weed were weeds; things would always go badly for them, no matter whether they believed in adwaita, had a different sexual orientation or had the additional burden of a paralysed teenager on their shoulders. As they went bankrupt, they became the difficult weeds, the ones which were plucked and thrown out. Shamelessly, they would come begging for alms.

'Shame on you, you are no longer any good, a piece of shit, a heap of crap . . .'

She noticed the man who was sitting opposite her in the restaurant. Was he a peddler too? He must be a petty officer on leave, for he had the ways of a seafarer. His T-shirt said: 'Don't ever worry about things that don't worry about you'.

Kamala tried to recall who it was that was worrying about her: her children, her friend or Madhavan?

Not Madhavan.

Not her children.

Not her friend.

Pussy, money and weed, the peddlers could not cross the boundaries of thought. Weed and whores are money, thought Kamala; they partake in rotating the economic wheel of the country. Peddlers on the other hand, were just the go-betweens, they did not have any special rights or position, and they were not powerful like whores. The country wouldn't allow them to climb up the ladder the way ministers and businessmen did, to raise their own GDP.

The peddler was getting visibly irritated by the long silences of this strange client. He tried to convince her and they argued, and in the end they came to an agreement. She left with the small packet clasped tight in her hands.

She was not happy about what she had earned through the long hours of bargaining. At the back of her mind, she knew her son had not had a bath in days. What she wanted now was a home nurse, someone who could attend to his needs day and night. A male nurse would be the best option for a boy straddling his twenties. She wondered why Aadi was not worried about her. She was the one who kept thinking about him. She regretted that she never thought much about Shiva.

When she was a girl, she had seen a cow giving birth to its calf. She remembered how long the children had sat in the veranda, their eyes unblinking and necks craned to see the calf pop out through the mighty hole. A woman gives birth in a similar way, except no one sits around to admire the child popping its head out of her hole except for nurses and doctors. Sadly, human babies are born into the weary hands of some strangers, the mother's face white and bloodless, the doctor's pale.

53

The actors buzzed around the permanent tables under the fig tree, beneath dangling, lit-up lanterns. The group of aspiring actors—jolly people from different parts of the world—had come together for a theatre workshop. Pondicherry was the land of booze, you got alcohol really cheap here, but Molière didn't let them drink while the workshop was in session. The merry youngsters campaigned for it and the happy adults jeered at them. It took a while for Aadi to realize that they didn't mean anything when they spoke, that they were too happy in this company to be serious. Most of them spoke for the sake of keeping their thoughts warm, keeping the merry-go-round on the move, keeping the serious reflections of the morning at bay. When they clamoured for booze it didn't mean that they wanted it desperately, it meant they were happy with the mere mention of it. What a wonderful world of words, thought Aadi. They talked and laughed and talked till two o'clock in the night. They knew the sessions would start at five in the morning, yet they were reluctant to leave the table.

Aadi was not part of the workshop but he joined the actors in the morning batch of Kalari. They said its practice awakened the hundred and seven energy centres in the body. His body, smeared with oil, sweated out on the red earth.

Stretching down . . .

Walking towards the right . . .

Paying homage to Kalari . . .

Touching the sole of the left foot . . .

Stretching out the hands to touch the ground—the red earth . . .

Folding the hands and touching the forehead . . .

Walking towards the left then right then touching the sole of the left foot . . .

It was amazing to see the rag man with his matted jute hair sitting on a chair near the gate. His boots were worn-out and so was his attire. He had two large eyes and a nose made of newspaper, but he was no scarecrow, he looked very real. Girls chirped like birds around him. Aadi had not heard about Thanthrotsav. It was only then that he noticed the colourful strips of paper ribbons swaying in the wind along with newly made cylindrical paper lanterns. The morning looked happier than ever with all that colour hanging from the treetops. There was an air of festivity around them. The paper cylinder lanterns had eyes, noses and mouths and long tails like paradise flycatchers, cut out of thin Chinese paper. With their funny looks and bright colours, they seemed happy in the wind.

'Wanna join?' someone asked and Aadi turned around to see who it was. There were three of them. They were sitting on the veranda of the picture gallery, making paper planes and flowers. There was a basket beside them; it was full of paper flowers. Aadi looked into the basket: blue, green, yellow, orange, red, violet. There were paper boats and rockets too. But why so many?

'Why don't you help us make some rockets?' they asked.

Aadi looked in disbelief at the face of the man who said this. He had long hair that curled all round his face and down his neck and back. He had lined his eyes with kajal like dancers. He also had a small red ball stuck to his nose like the clowns you saw at the circus. Before Aadi's surprise could die down, another man came to the veranda wearing a broad, coloured band on his hair and carrying a guitar in his hand. He sat down a little away from the group and started playing his guitar.

'Hello!' The man with the apple nose reached out his hand to Aadi. They shook hands and exchanged smiles. 'I'm Martin; I am a wanderer, a singer, a kind of gypsy if you will.'

'I'm Saji,' the guitarist said, strumming his instrument without lifting his head.

'I'm Sudhi,' another man said, blowing a paper plane towards Aadi.

Happily, Aadi caught the plane and joined the others in making them. It was something he knew very well. He had made many paper planes out of textbook pages with Shiva during their vacations. It was fun to blow what you had learnt during the school year into the wind. Anything hard-earned is easy to blow out at a certain point of time.

In the evening it seemed like a festival of lights: together, the hanging paper lanterns and the mud lamps filled with oil and cotton wicks and kept on the ground marked out the walking paths. Nimmy was busy lighting the lamps, she was all dressed up for the occasion and looked stunning. Suddenly, in his mind, he saw his beautiful mother walking down the pathways lit by lamps.

Amy Ammu came running with a garland of chrysanthemums around her neck. She hid behind him and peered through the holes of her knitted stole at the evening guests. In the open kitchen, unattached to any of the main buildings, people were drinking black coffee and eating beaten rice flakes mixed with shredded coconut and jaggery. Taking Amy by the hand, Aadi walked towards the performance area.

She got excited seeing the shaft of light from the projector right above her head and frightened when she saw the *Theechamundi Theyyam*, wearing tender coconut leaves and plunging into the bonfire with a roar.*

---

* A ritual dance performance presented during the night as an offering to the incarnation of Lord Vishnu.

By the time dinner was over, people were in a jovial mood, their faces excited and relaxed at the same time. There were people from the neighbourhood and Auroville and Kalarigram along with actors from Adishakti. Aadi walked as if he were in a dream, tangled up in the breeze from the banyan tree and in the flags and paper ribbons hanging down from the branches. Suddenly, he heard a whistle blowing, a bell ringing, people shouting. All heads automatically turned in the direction of the cries of laughter. A black bus was approaching.

'A bus, look Aadi, a bus inside our place!' Amy Ammu jumped to her feet.

People hurried towards the bus. He saw Amy Ammu already dancing around it. His eyes sparkled when he saw Martin sitting on the driver's seat wearing the clown nose. In an instant, the side of the bus sprang open, revealing a brightly lit stage with drums and guitars and singers on it. Martin, in a sing-song tone, told the story of how the bus had taken a detour and fallen into a ditch. People gathered around the bus like flies and started dancing as the songs progressed. Instantly the many-coloured planes started raining down from the sky. There must have been someone hiding on top of the bus. The children started shouting and gathering the paper toys in ecstasy. Aadi was amazed to see the copters he had helped with in the morning. Even he wanted to run and collect them; Amy Ammu already had a collection of five or six copters in different colours. He looked at the other children, the village boys and girls running like mad after the paper toys. The singer, in the meantime, was singing of the trees people felled and the concrete jungles they were building in the name of development, the thudding pulse of modernity.

People came together, entwined their fingers and embraced each other. They looked at each other through the rain of flying paper planes. Holding the paper flowers in their hands, they began dancing. It was refreshing to see men with birds, flies and flowers. He had been like that a long time ago. As he danced for the first time in his life, Aadi felt he was floating, becoming lighter than one of those paper toys. He started singing, shouting and whistling. He wanted more. They all did. People cried for an encore. At the borders of Auroville, it didn't matter if people spoke Tamil, Malayalam, Hindi, English, Spanish, German or Latin, they all repeated the one line the singers sang:

We want more . . . injimvenam . . . we want more . . . injimvenam . . .

54

The love which is always turning over in one's mind is not real love. The coupledom that gives no relief even in the flower of consummation is imagined.

'As I cannot continue with my marriage this way, my dear friends . . .'

Inside the bar people looked at Madhavan, who was not drunk, but seemed to be making an announcement in public, a personal announcement. His eyes, voice and ears seemed more inebriated than those of the usual drunkard, for he kept repeating, asking and blinking. His clothes, though seemingly new, were torn in places; the keys of his car were hanging out of his jeans, looking as if they were about to fall out. He looked like all his life he had eaten nothing but shit. He was not an unfamiliar figure at the Peacocks bar. People knew him. His soulmate Parvesh was with him, his face bearing signs of tension. After a spat with Kuljeet, it was Madhavan who had driven all the way to Peacocks, steady behind the wheel.

'Cheers!' Madhavan shouted. 'Are there any bitches in this room?'

'This style is no longer fashionable, people will laugh at you. This is the reason I call you outdated,' Kamala whispered in his ear.

He raised his hands and slapped his own face.

'Don't raise your voice here,' he said.

Kamala became silent at once.

'Friends . . .' he continued. Parvesh, his only friend, sat down on a chair next to him, his head bowed.

'I don't know how to love . . . I know nothing about the psychology of women. I tried to love my own sister once, my family supported me. I ask you: Have you ever heard of such a thing? Don't go deaf, you, modern society, listen to what I have to say! I cannot love this new woman either. The woman who could give you a wonderful blow job need not be a companion, a soulmate or something of the sort. You get me . . . don't you? I know I am getting all dramatic here, but life, my friends, is nothing if not a drama. Let me say a final cheer to mark the end of my relationship with women. I thank all the whores of the universe for what they have given me and what they have not. Please don't count Kamala in this group of women, for she is my little sister who used to trail after me when we were children.'

Parvesh tried to make him sit down, probably to make him stop, but he continued, 'I am a dead person, and love is terrifying to those who are dead.'

He wanted to see his children. He wanted to see Kamala. He knew that lust and base cravings had deprived him of the three souls dearest to his heart, those he loved most on earth. Society was always busy issuing bans; it would neither let him live nor love. He knew he was not the only soul on earth in pain, and that was the reason he toasted all those who were present there, all those lonely people. The wedding photo he had set fire to—his second—was lying on the floor of his bedroom, half-burnt, and his wife—his second—was looking at it with hatred in her eyes.

After a few more quick shots, he got out of there somehow, leaning heavily against his friend's shoulder. His friend was unaware of the burden that was weighing him down. He had no idea that with each step, his friend was moving towards his old age. When Madhavan said he was upset that he couldn't give his sons a chance to dump him in some old-age home, Parvesh's steps faltered. Madhavan was not worried about what life had taught him. He knew the next day when he woke up he would see an old man in the mirror, that he would walk around the streets feeling old, that he would sit on the steps of a mall and smoke like a stranger in grey.

There was an open-air restaurant on the lawn outside the bar. The place seemed surreal in the evening display of light and shadows. Madhavan surveyed the people scattered there. His eyes rested for a while on a couple dining at a nearby table. All of a sudden the woman accidently spilled rich hot chocolate over the white linen of the tablecloth and the man hastened to place a tissue over the spreading stain. They smiled at each other in understanding, but the stain continued to seep through the edges of the damp paper. A lit candle stood on the table between them amidst a basket of select fruit and flowers and a heap of chicken bones. He looked at the bones, the better part of which that beauty had eaten. They looked crushed and defeated on the chequered tablecloth beside the burning candle. The woman, he thought, was a witch, there was blood on the corner of her lips—or was it lipstick? Asking Parvesh to wait for a second, he joined them at their table without permission. He said he knew he was a stranger, but there were things he wanted to tell them. The man looked at him with surprise, she with hatred. She was a woman in her early forties, wearing heavy make-up and an outfit that seemed to belong to a teenager. Her gestures, especially her eyes, reminded him of the picture of a bored toad he had seen in a children's cartoon strip. She yawned looking straight at his face and he realized that that was one of the ugliest sights on earth. There was a bit of meat and parsley caught between her molars. He didn't say anything to them. Leaving them to their uncertainties, he got up and left. Just then he received a message from Kuljeet. He read it as he walked. He handed over the car keys to Parvesh and sat down in the bucket seat, trying to concentrate on the keyboard

338

of his phone, trying to text back. With his ten fingers moving in twenty different directions, dropping down and flying back, he typed, no spelling out of place:

Please don't call me again. It is my helplessness. If you haven't deleted the messages we had sent before, please go through them and see who spoke badly and why. I hope you understand.

He switched off his phone.

Who said the happiness of an expedition receded once you reached the top of the mountain? He had seen the face of a teenager glowing, once, atop a mountain, when she brushed the clouds aside and peered into the skies, when she looked down and to her amazement saw the valley. That moment, he considered, was his secret truth. After that day, he had seen himself falling from mountaintops many times in his dreams; later he called it his frightening recurring dream. He worked his fingers to the bone in his dreams, pushing hard, trying not to hurt himself. Sometimes he started falling in his wakeful hours. Each mountaintop was a lesson. People were happy in the valleys, but he wanted to know the secrets of the heights, for he was never satisfied. He wanted to reach the top, nothing else mattered to him. All the same, he knew he would be falling down.

Aadi woke up dreaming about Shiva. It had become a habit of late. These days he got his mother on the phone very rarely. Sometimes he felt it was his grandmother who was on the other end of the line, for her voice had become feeble and shaky, the words jumbled and mispronounced. He couldn't understand why Shiva kept his phone switched off nowadays. The only person who called him on a daily basis was Shaly. He was thankful for her routine calls. She said she had gone to live with her mama who had fallen ill. He wanted to tell her that he was incapable of happiness of any kind.

He found himself lonely, though his present situation helped him to cling to his delusions. But in the TV room, on the tennis court, in the pizza corner, he contemplated one thing only: whether he should go back or not. Once, he asked Nimmy, 'Nimmy, I think I want to go back. What do you say?'

'If you feel like going back, you should go at once.' Nimmy's tone was abrupt. 'You can come back whenever you feel like it.'

What she said was true, but he didn't pack his things. His brother was crying in his bed. Janu had applied ointments to the sores that had formed on his back recently, she had told him. His mother, who had stubbornly shut herself in her room, had not eaten anything for the past three days. Sometimes her voice could be heard like the flutter of a fly from within the room. In the veranda attached to her room she was growing mint in mud pots. It would take barely a month for the mint leaves to grow and fill up the pots. She was planning to make pulavu on the day Aadi returned. She hadn't watered the plants for the past three days. There was no way Janu could reach the veranda, unless she opened the door.

He walked out into the morning redolent with the fragrance of fallen frangipani flowers, onto the red earth. He took off his sandals, for he wanted to feel the petals on his soles. His feet tickled when he stepped over the carpet grass covered with drops of dew. He wanted to lie down on the bed of grass and kiss the dew; like kissing the secrets of a beloved woman. But the thought that had been disturbing him since the night before poked its head up again: You have to decide something, it said.

He made a video call to Shaly. She marvelled at him walking under fruit trees, amidst flowering shrubs. Each day he showed her each new scene: the swimming pool, the Kalari, the pizza corner, the guest house . . . Today it was the shrubs loaded with flowers. He wondered why she didn't come running.

'Is it possible that a person could live their whole life there? Are you paying money?' she wondered. 'What interest do you have in theatre? I have never seen you act in a play. Or are you planning to become a devotee?' She was full of questions.

'Hey Shaly, is that your Rita Mama?' he asked, without hiding his surprise.

Shaly turned and saw Rita Mama standing close, behind her.

'Rita Mama, this is Aadi. Could you please say something to him?' she asked.

She made a gesture that communicated quite clearly.

'Some new fads,' said Aadi.

'That said fuck off,' said Shaly.

After disconnecting the video call, he walked again, pondering over what she had said. This was a place where people came and went; indeed they did pay money, and money was important. Amy Ammu and her family had been living here for the past few months. It was her father who had come first and decided not to go back—he brought his family over instead. Amy Ammu, he said, would be enrolled in the ashram school here once she was old enough to attend.

The blue teddy was very heavy these days. Amy Ammu had made him bathe under the garden pipe in the running water. It was not easy to carry a wet teddy around. Aadi didn't go anywhere near her teddy these days, be it blue or white. For him, it was a load of damp, wet cotton. These days, it was Red. It was Rane who came up with 'Red'. One day as she was fighting with Anu over the name of her teddy, Rane said aloud, 'Amy . . . call him Red.'

She was happy with the name, but she didn't stop crying.

'It is not a him, it is a her.'

The man who lived opposite his room in the guest house was a north Indian poet. He was working on his new book. He said it was called 'Serendipity'. Aadi wondered what he himself was doing here, besides walking around watching people. Wasting time?

When he went to the ashram perfumery, the old woman at the desk asked him, 'Are you a resident? You look very familiar.'

When he said no she said again, 'You look so familiar, like family.'

Aadi was amazed to hear this. He remembered Veenapani had told him the same thing on the day he had arrived.

He walked to the theatre, pushed open the heavy doors and walked through the corridor inside. It was dark inside, except for the light that seeped in through the perforated brick facade. Since it was a free day for the workshop participants, they had all gone to the beach. Aadi didn't feel like going, so he had stayed back. There was a party the following night; he had said he would participate. He stepped into the performance area paved with wood. It felt good standing over there, watching the empty galleries. He imagined they were full of people, that he was facing them. He walked towards the centre of the stage and stood on the spot where he assumed the beam from the spotlight would fall. He decided he would tell them a story—what story if not his?

He started telling them, his imaginary audience, his tale, the real play of his life, the women, the boys, the pond, the father, the brother in the bed, the mother on drugs. He had not analysed his life so far, he felt it was threateningly terrifying, pathetically withdrawn. He worried about what the world, the audience, would think of him, an ordinary bloke with such a long-drawn story to tell. He realized he was crying. But when he finished telling them his story, he gracefully bent forward, showing gratitude for the time his imaginary audience had given him. When he stood upright again, iridescent light fell over him from the glass symbol of the Mother fixed on the wall. He thought he was imagining this and the other things. The symbol, he remembered, was called divine consciousness.

Kamala happened to peep in through the door that was open.

Who is he? She was aware of fear slithering down the length of her spine. She saw a stranger on her son's bed with the growth of nights and days covering his face like a beehive. The home nurse who had promised to come was late. Was it stinking? She sniffed around as if she were a dog. The air inside the room was heavy with a pungent smell. Lying on his bed, he looked like a fat, overgrown boy with mental health problems. She was afraid he would bite her hands or shoulders if she went anywhere near him. She knew she wanted to run away from there. She loved him dearly, yet she went on asking herself who he was. He had entered her mind like he was the boy next door, who had been there right from the beginning but whose name she had forgotten. At times, his face seemed sadly strange to her, she couldn't make him out.

Exhausted, she went back to her room and sat on the bed. She had received calls from Movers and Packers, who were literally shouting to be heard over the phone. Nothing on earth mattered now. Cochin was an island beyond countries. As a child she had thought that people lived safe and secure inside the earth, outside of which was a terrifying void. There was safety inside the big blue-green ball. But once, years ago, when she learnt for the first time that she was on the surface, and that terrifying lava and unfathomable depths bubbled inside, she was petrified. She felt abandoned and homeless but from that day onwards she knew that she could face anything on earth, anything on the surface.

That night she dreamed about helping Shiva shave his beard. Even in her dream she puked when she saw the hair floating on the surface of the water over the foam. Her hands shook and she made a gash on his chin. Suddenly, Shaly sprang in, God knew from where—it was a dream and dreams could be as they liked. Shaly was trembling too, but she was shaking with anger.

'If you can't do that properly, give the razor to me. I will do it for him,' she shouted.

'Is he your son or mine?'

Shaly had to get out of this dream. She had no right to be in it. The moistness of the cunt was different from that of blood; she didn't belong in this dream, it was time she stepped out of it. But Shaly was reluctant and stubborn as always. She tried to seize the razor from Kamala's hand. The blood from the gash on his chin mixed with the shaving cream. He wanted to wipe it off and drink some water.

'I know how to take care of my son!' Kamala continued protesting in her sleep.

Shaly woke, hearing Kamala's feeble voice. It was not morning yet. She wanted to call Kamala. She told herself that that was the first thing she would do once the day dawned. She cried thinking how mutable things were. In the next room, Rita Mama was sick. She had fallen down two days ago and badly hurt her leg; above all, she had experienced severe vertigo and had thrown up everything she had eaten, some three or four times during the day. It was all a combination of bad luck and bad timing, and now this dream, which she didn't remember, but she had heard Kamala cry in her dreams—she was afraid Kamala needed help.

Rita Mama had been scolding her for a minute before she fell down: 'Why don't you get married?'

'How on earth could you ask me such a substandard fucking question?' Shaly asked, and Rita fell down and broke her leg.

The communal dining area was an open space for actors and visitors. Outside the thatched dining room, under the breezy branches of the trees, round tables, stone benches and dogs waited for the diners to come. Like the flowers that grew out of the void around and above the bus, people filled up the places, benches and seats with laughter. As usual, they started singing:

One young tiger we are told
Got tired of being yellow gold
He concentrated all day long
And sang the tiger witch's song

He practiced till he learned the knack
Of changing yellow fur to black . . .

As the drumbeats grew louder, people squeezed into each and every available gap. One of them became the tiger and jumped on top of one of the round tables. The others became the cheerleaders.

'I will get you a beer!' someone said.

'Do you want a whisky on the rocks? My turn.'

The tiger was happy, the cheerleaders were prompt. The tiger began the drama. Looking at Itchimba, the dog who was lying on the ground, he asked, 'Dog-etta, will I meet man? Will it stand on its hind legs?'

The game continued into the night. For the first time since Aadi's arrival they opened the beer bottles. Making toasts to each other, they started singing louder and talking non-stop. Nimmy looked terrific in her black spaghetti and green skirt. She had stuck big white frangipani flowers in her hair; she seemed to have come straight from the beach.

'Nimmy, you look so sexy!' someone shouted.

'Thank you! Thank you!' she hollered back.

She was carrying a glass bottle containing orange juice in her hand. It looked beautiful: the orange against the green of her skirt and the sheen of the glass in between. Someone said they would mix orange juice with vodka and drink. But there was no vodka. Nimmy said it was from the tangerine tree in their yard. Aadi remembered having seen the worker pluck the tangerines in the morning. He was happy he could drink something. She proudly offered him the bottle, but the juice, to his disappointment, was sour.

The smell of basmati rice, chicken and Chettinad masala spread around the tables as she unsealed the lid of the biryani pot. In no time, the round tables and stone benches were empty as they all rushed to the thatched hut, tiger and dog-ettan in the lead.

55

'Amma . . . Amma . . .' Shiva yelled at the top of his voice.

Half asleep, she could hear him calling her. Lying still, she waited for his summons to stop. Slowly it did. But even after that, she concentrated in the dark for so long that she thought her ears would melt. She wondered what was wrong with him in the middle of the night, she clearly remembered Janu going with a platter of food to his room after eight. She had even asked Janu to keep a bowl of warm water by him, with a piece of lemon in it—the way they did in hotels, near the food—so that once he finished eating he could wash his hands and mouth. But after some time, right when her eyelids became heavy again, he started calling again. This time she sat up in her bed. He must be saying something in his sleep. She had no idea what the boy was up to. As she stepped out into the corridor, the shadow of the massive pillars in the courtyard frightened her. Leaning against the wall, she walked towards his room slowly, as slowly as slowness could be. She didn't venture across the threshold into his room. The door was open. She told herself she would close it when she went back so that his voice wouldn't trouble her again.

'What is it?' she asked, standing outside the door.

'Amma, could you please take me to a restaurant? I would like to have a milkshake and some chicken legs. Or get me a family pack of ice cream, a big one.'

It was repulsive to see a man with a visibly unattractive growth of moustache and beard asking for ice cream in the dead of night. She couldn't believe it.

'Do you know what time it is now?'

'I am hungry.'

She looked at the plate of food on the table. In the moonlight it appeared untouched.

'Could you please ask Aadi to come back?'

How many more questions? She looked at him with growing unease. Good that it was dark; they couldn't see each other, only their silhouettes. Her arms were growing heavy and weak, and so did her legs, she wanted to lie down at once. She couldn't bear so many questions at this time of the night. What was he asking her? She turned away, closing the door behind her. She could hear him ask her, 'Give me my father's number. I will call him.'

It seemed a hopeful, frightening, taunting, derailed group of words.

It had been days since Shiva's mobile had stopped working, or he would have called his father sooner. He wanted to ask Janu to help him use the landline. He was afraid he was developing problems with his bowel movements these days. It was important that his father know how they were living, what they ate, and what conditions they were trapped in. Janu said the doors of his mother's room never opened. When Shaly had been there, everything had been in place. Janu was not confident taking him out. She said he might fall down. Doesn't matter, he told her. It would not make a big difference whether he lay prostrated on the ground or in bed. In fact he thought he might be better off on the floor—who doesn't welcome a change once in a while?

'Janu, could you please ask your father to chop down the thresholds of this house?'

Janu looked at him as if she didn't understand.

'I would like to shorten the length of the legs of this bed too.'

347

She said her father was no carpenter and he said anyone with a saw or an axe was enough to do the job. He said he hated beauty, anything beautiful. He didn't say he was missing a certain scent, one that his mother got high on, the scent of a dear woman.

Janu thought Shiva was becoming unreasonably irritable of late. He fought with whomever he saw, and unfortunately, the person he saw was always Janu. She was not afraid of him, for she knew he couldn't move from where he was. But she was afraid of the woman who remained like a dumb ghost, shut inside the room.

'If you are going to make the same dish, I am going to flay you alive,' he said.

When Kamala closed her eyes again, she saw colours, a number of colours coalesced into strange contour lines, like when you look down through the microscope to see the divisions of cells. A splash of chlorophyll, she thought, was missing. She closed her eyes against the artistic abundance of light, the display of designs and patterns, and the movement of the contours as if across a graph. Then, she heard music. Someone sang, Goodbye blue sky. Goodbye to the sky and the milky river. Now, she could hear it all, loud and digital. She heard bombs falling. She saw faces down below, faces with no names, but with voices. She didn't hear the feeble voices of children; all the other voices were loud, loud enough to explode. She listened to people going mad, guitar, cymbals, drums, vocals. A minor? No, D. She could hear the bass, the height and fall, each note separate and steady. She walked through the acid bulbs that were exploding like bombs on the pavement.

Shaly was a terrific cook; Janu came nowhere near. The best dish she had ever made or tasted was sambar, the luxury she had at her house once or twice in a month, and the curry Shiva said he was tired of having. Janu loved pickled mangoes so much she would eat even the stones. But Shiva said he could not eat any more of her sambar, curd and pickled mangoes. That day when she came to the kitchen with a new recipe a distant relative had taught her, her face revealed both hope and stress. She didn't put rice in the cooker; instead she put it in a mud pot and kept it over the firewood stove. She sliced the tender ash gourd thinly and cooked it over a low flame with a pinch of salt, turmeric and some green chillies. She mixed ground coconut and curd in it and tempered it with sesame seeds and curry leaves. When the rice cooked, the greed of hunger escalated through the viscera of the house. Her eyes watered when she saw Shiva chewing noisily, greedily. She thought this would settle her worries for some time. She had seen three ash gourds on the rooftop, ready to pluck.

She took a deep breath before knocking on Kamala's door.

'Kamaledathi . . . Kamaledathi . . .'

There was no response. She tried to push the door open, but it was latched on the inside. Janu felt disappointed, she wanted Kamala to try her new curry. She went outside to peep into Kamala's room from the window. The one she knew would be kept open for the sake of the money plant in the whisky bottle. She needed a leg-up over the wall to see inside the room. Somehow, she balanced on the projections of the sill and managed a sneaky look from behind the fading leaves. The bed was empty. She craned her neck some more and saw Kamala sitting on the floor in a corner. She was mumbling something Janu couldn't catch; she saw her lips move and that was it. Kamala was not looking at the window, she was not looking anywhere, her eyes, Janu could see, were blank, expressionless or, rather, motionless.

Now Janu was worried, she couldn't understand what was happening inside the room. She didn't have numbers for Aadi or Shaly. She was not sure whether to send for a doctor or not. She thought Kamala's face looked distorted, but again she was unsure. She tapped hard on the window. At that Kamala looked at her and shooed her away, as if she were shooing the pigeons on the sill. Janu was relieved: there was no problem.

Kamala was shooing the eagle away. She had not seen Janu; she thought it was a huge eagle tapping its wings on her window. When the bird flew away, she saw a squabble of seagulls hovering above the dry dust bowl inside her room. She knew they were powerful, those seagulls, so she prayed to them to ensure an easy death for her. The white seagulls, she remembered, were different from the eagles of the wasteland. It must be at the point where the blue sky merged with the blue sea that the seagull abandoned duality and soared to the heights. His feathers, smooth and white, shone in the rays from the sun. She had read the story of the magnificent bird, the story of its flight. The bird asked her to break the chains of her thought, and break the chains of her body. His name, she remembered, was Jonathan. But she had no strength to fly over the dust bowl. She kept crawling; the building was a long way off from where she was. There were people, scattered all over, straining to look through the window. She wondered what was inside that building that the people were so mad about, what was wrong with the people? She was sad that people could never return to their innocence, because the faces of those who came away from the window looked vicious, alarmingly disturbed. But whatever it was, she wanted to see it. She tried with all her might to crawl, scratching her ankle on the rough surface of the granite. It had been days since she had eaten properly. If someone tore open her stomach right now, they would only get a handful of tablets.

Janu was upset because Kamala was ruthless with her.

'Don't you worry, she will eat when she feels hungry,' Shiva said. He was grateful for the food and he wanted to console her. He said he wanted new bed sheets as that one stank of dirt, sweat and food. But he had other woes as well, which he couldn't tell her. For example, he wanted to change his underwear. The sore below his hip was itching, itching like mad at times. He was ashamed of that. He worried that one day he would have to suffocate in his own shit.

Janu heard the phone ringing when she was about to open the entrance gate. She ran back, feeling grateful it didn't stop before she reached. 'Hello, hello,' she said even before she had picked up the receiver. It was Aadi. In an instant she forgot everything she wanted to tell him. He kept asking, 'Is it Janu? I've been trying since morning. Why isn't Amma answering my calls? Her mobile is ringing.'

After a gap of what seemed like hours to her, but was in reality a matter of seconds, Janu replied, 'Amma has not eaten anything. She is not well. She didn't touch the new curry I made today.'

Immediately, she understood that mentioning the new curry was out of place there. So she said again, 'She says she has a headache.'

'Is it a migraine?'

Janu had no idea what a migraine was. So she asked, 'When are you coming back? Shiva is also not well these days.'

'I'm planning to come back. Could you please give Amma's mobile to Shiva? I want to talk to him.'

'I don't think I can get it, I'm sorry, but Kamaledathi has locked her door from the inside.'

'Janu, listen to me. There is a cordless phone somewhere upstairs. Could you please go and get that? Give that to him. Tell him I will call him after half an hour.'

It had been days since he had talked to his mother or brother. Sometimes he spoke even when he doubted that there was someone at the other end, or thought the receiver might have slipped out of the cradle. He sat down on the beach and watched people recording videos of the sunset. Everything seemed heavy and dark, even the water that lapped against the shore. He had been visiting the Samadhi for the past two days, but the stone, the flowers, the serene calmness, everything reminded him of the anguish of the brother who was waiting for him in his bed.

351

He stood at the tail end of the long queue to get into the golden globe, Matri Mandir. People in the queue were silent, there was silence everywhere. It was not enough to calm his nerves, for silence, at times, could become unbelievably rude. In the quiet he remembered the library, the endless rows of books, the ancient fans and chairs that bore the imprints of souls. It was good to remember things, good to know that you were not alone; there was another man, a woman standing in the avenue. People were waiting patiently for their turn to step into the meditation chamber.

Light purer than water called him inside. He knelt, closed his eyes and kissed the floor. He dreamt of warm breath and cleanliness, he didn't understand why. Later, he dreamed of the single glass tile on the roof of Anuraktha's library. He saw the doves cooing and light from the morning filling up the vacuum and a raindrop falling on top of the glass tile and exploding into seven colours.

'What should I think?' he asked the light.

'Think of me.'

He shuddered. That voice was familiar, he knew it, it was his own voice. The rainbow colours disappeared from the glass tile, making it look desolate. Erasing and drawing, drawing and erasing, the glass started shining again. It said, 'Think of me, Aadi, think of the poor life you abandoned.'

Aadi opened his eyes. Now he could hear Shiva knocking against the tile. It grew louder, frighteningly so. Suddenly, the whirlpool that was hiding behind the gold-plated doors of the globe covered him from tip to toe, and in the room of silence, he heard someone crying aloud, someone crying from within.

'Amma . . . Amma . . . I'm hungry. Janu . . . where are you? Is anybody there?'

Janu wanted to answer his call, but she was busy. Kamala had said there were two little snakes in her room; she said she had seen them. She wanted Janu to clean her room. This was the thirteenth time Janu was cleaning her room; there were no snakes. She ran from the kitchen to Kamala's room like a tennis player. She knew no rest. Sometimes the phone rang in between, but it would stop by the time she got to it and then she would hear Shiva and Kamala calling her from two different directions, from two separate rooms.

'Light the torch if you can't see well. I'm sure there is something crawling in there.'

'I need a cup of coffee, Janu. Janu . . . are you there?'

Janu, too, was getting tired of it, sick of mother and son. Sometimes she went to the lotus pond, sat down on the steps and watched the flowers in full bloom.

'Will I never die?' Shiva sighed in his room.

56

Shaly wanted to go back and proclaim that she belonged to Kamala. She was willing to admit her mistake, if Kamala still considered it a mistake. It was torture being separated from her and her sons. If love was entrapped in a moment, she wanted to have that moment back. Had they shifted already? Aadi had not mentioned anything about it. She was sure Shiva would be happy in the flat with his gadgets, light and air. She imagined white curtains swaying in the wind. Beautiful people inside a beautiful house—she remembered them in her prayers. Recently, she had joined Rita in her evening prayers.

She drew a window on the wall with a piece of charcoal. From the window she wanted to look at the sun. So she drew a charcoal sun, round and plump. Four or six strokes more and her sun had rays. Then she drew two eyes and a laughing mouth, and called it her smiley sun. Then she proceeded to draw a staircase and an open terrace at the end with a barsati, charcoal fruit and leaves, and two women in a deep embrace.

In the evening when Rita Mama emerged from her room, she let out a horrified cry looking at the wall, her exquisitely pink walls. Shaly heard her mutter as she pissed in the toilet. In his will, Andrews had left everything to Shaly. He had done this with Rita's consent, but she was determined not to breathe a word of it until she died. Look at the walls now.

Shaly wanted to forget about Kamala and her children. But her memories entwined around her as if they were afraid of being blown out, like the flame of a lamp in the wind. They grabbed more memories from the past, as if making a trade union. The family was *hers*; the children belonged to her and she belonged to Kamala. Was she a friend, a lover, a slave or a concubine? She didn't know. Sometimes she broke down, crying. Kamala would ask, 'Am I a mother? Can my children call me mother?' She was the one who played with her own life. She did that foolishly. Of course, some people do that. But they end up asking questions the way she does.

'Tell me Shaly, how can a woman become a mother? I want to be like you.'

What Aadi said was true, thought Shaly. If you have a window that opens to the city, a nice cup of frothing coffee and a book of verse by your side, your life will be okay and somewhat happy, even if not hilarious and exciting. You can choose your poems. Since you are living in a city you can amuse yourself with tales of the countryside, but remember to be in the city, that's important, if possible, in a metro. You can read poems written about valleys and hilltops, grandfather clocks that tick endlessly and age-old mansions where ghosts take rounds every now and then. Once you master reading, try to compose a poem of your own. Write on the mud lamp in the spooky snake garden, the wick of which is lit every evening by prayer time without anyone having lit it, even when there is no oil in it.

These dreams are not likely to leave me . . . Kamala twisted and turned in pain on the bed. She had thrown up many times that day. The cramping of her muscles made her want to vomit more. As there was nothing left inside her stomach, she spat up yellow water that looked like bile.

'Can we go to a doctor?' Janu asked. She knew Kamala would get angry if she insisted.

'Could you please go and clean the room, Janu? How many times have I told you I saw something crawling in there?'

Janu scratched her head at this, for she knew that if she went there with a bucket of water and a mop one more time, the room would get erased.

At night, Kamala was disturbed by the noises again. The loud chirping of the insects was so clear that anyone could hear it. Even if it were the nocturnal concert of nature, or the disease called tinnitus, she realized she wanted to consult a doctor, for she feared, sometimes, that she would not hear her son calling above the night-long soprano of crickets even though she ignored him when he did. She remembered Madhavan. He had said that it was tinnitus, a disease that affected the ear. He said he would take her to the doctor. But where was he? Was he dead already? When Madhavan came home, she would go to consult a doctor. But where was he? Where was Madhavan? Was he the one who had passed away? They said it was her mother who passed away, but she could not remember. She remembered the golden snakes she had seen under her mattress once. Yes, she had come back home with her children when Madhavan got bit by the snakes. Madhavan wasn't there any more, to take her to the doctor. But the boys were babies then. She remembered how loudly he had cried when the snakes bit him. Everything seemed so clear now, even the stuffed cardboard boxes that had belonged to her mother burning to cinders in the backyard. She remembered the mouths, the purple colour, the smell of the wetness, and how they had crawled over her breasts. Someone should set fire to this place. She knew there had been a snake garden in the backyard once, but she didn't know what had happened to it as they grew up. In her village, almost every house had a snake garden of their own where they lit lamps and prayed for the prosperity of the family. Madhavan said it was the best example of a sound eco-system. Good for him. She was the one who suffered. She closed her eyes and tried to concentrate on the darkness.

She saw a woman lying on her mattress, nude. Two teenagers who were also naked were trying to feed on her breasts. They moved like snakes over her body. She could only see the boys' exposed thighs and their backs and the rest of her body. Her hair covered their faces. When they lifted their heads, she saw her sons; the woman was Shaly.

Shaly! Like a woman possessed she threw herself on the floor and cried. Let Kadru come down to my womb and eat my children. Kamala had fever. She was sick. She wanted to sleep.

Shiva stretched his hand towards the table for food. But unfortunately he knocked the plate down. He looked at the rice scattered all over the floor. Now to clean this mess up he would have to wait till Janu returned the next day. Sad, he drank the sambar in the small bowl. He remembered Mary, their maid in Bangalore. How easily she used to make roti and sabzi, in no time. His mouth watered.

'The more she saw Kadru's children the more Vinata burnt in jealousy . . . Are you listening?' Amma asked as she combed Kamala's hair. She had a high fever. She was lying in her mother's lap.

'Yes, I'm listening' she replied in a very feeble, fragile voice. Amma continued with her story: 'Vinata was heartbroken. She battered on her womb in frustration and it opened. A body, half-formed, came out of her womb and began to blow in the wind around her. The child cursed his mother, "Woman, you could have waited a little longer," and flew away to the Sun to become his charioteer.'

Kamala didn't want to listen to the story of Vinata and her sons born with deformed bodies. She wanted to know about Kadru's thousand baby snakes that crawled all over her big breasts. She didn't want to get frightened by the stories of unformed bodies when she was running a temperature. She wanted to hear something pleasant.

'Mother, talk to me about the crawling snakes, the beauty of their black bodies.'

Patting her on her forehead, her mother continued: 'Anilan, Vasuki, Nilan, Sankan, Pinkalan, Vamanan, Karkkaran, Mani Nagan, Akarkkaran, Mahodaran, Karkkodakan, Dhananjayan, Purnanagan, Thakshakan, Sumanasu, Kumudhan, Ugrakan, Kaliyan, Iravatan, Tithiri, Kadran, Halkkan, Seshan, Subahu, Padman . . .'

'Kamaledathi . . . Kamaledathi . . . Please get up and have something. You haven't eaten anything since last night.'

57

Aadi couldn't recognize Amy Ammu's mother when he saw her from a distance. She had cut her blonde hair really short, so short it resembled that of a boy. Not just that, now it was coffee-brown in colour, a sad change. She laughed, though. She looked extremely pleased with her new hairdo. She had pierced her nose too. There was something different about the way she dressed as well. Aadi looked at her and then at Amy Ammu, who was on the verge of tears.

'We got separated . . .' her mother said, maintaining a sad smile on her lips.

Amy was pouting her lips and crying now. He looked at her and realized that her face resembled his in that moment, the face of Aadi and Shiva, the face that was petrified with fear, the face that drowned in the pond.

At last, Aadi received a phone call from Shiva. It was Janu who found the cordless phone lying under Shaly's bed in her room upstairs. He couldn't be angry with Shiva for not calling him so far; in fact, he couldn't even control his tears. He had set out on his journey to experience life, but he found himself weeping at the other end of the phone. He felt ashamed.

Shiva said a great many things; Aadi heard a great many things. But then Shiva asked something that made Aadi shudder, all over.

'What—? What did you say?' he asked.

'I said do you think Father will take me with him to Bangalore if I ask him to.'

'No,' Aadi retorted immediately and after a pause he added, 'Father has another wife. I don't know whether they have children as well, but I don't think that woman would accept us. We would be a burden.'

'Mother also considers me a burden these days.'

He had no idea his mother was dying in the next room. Janu, being a fool, also hadn't considered the possibility. 'She stopped throwing up when I gave her porridge mixed with medicine,' she said with pride the last time she came out of her room, as if she were a doctor.

'Aadi, could you please do me a favour?'

'Please, tell me.'

'Ask Shaly to come back, or you come back, or bring her back when you come. That would be wonderful. Nothing else, just come back home.'

'I'm coming and I promise you I will bring her too.'

The moment the call ended, he dialled Nimmy's extension number and waited, listening to the muzak. When she came on the line he told her that he was planning to leave and wanted her to settle the accounts.

'Are you sure you are going tomorrow itself?' she asked.

'Yes, I think so,' he said.

'In that case, could you please come over? He wants to see you.'

'Sure.'

He ended the call and after a quick shower, walked towards their home. Nimmy and Anu were on the portico practicing the flute. Pascal was there too. Aadi had heard him playing the saxophone the other day. He looked at him with admiration now; Pascal smiled back. Nimmy shook hands with him and turned to Pascal.

'Pascal, our young friend is leaving tomorrow.'

Molière spent his evenings in front of his TV set—cricket, cinema, news and debates, whatever. There was no other furniture inside that room except the big TV and the speakers and some cushions. Molière had a big bowl of chips and a small bowl of ice cream in front of him. He was eating with both his hands. Dudu and Faristha were lying on either side watching him sitting there. When they saw Aadi enter, they lifted one of their eyebrows in greeting and continued as before. Nimmy brought a bowl of ice cream for Aadi. As usual, she started cracking jokes, but Aadi couldn't join their laughter, he could scarcely breathe. He looked at the open curtains for a while and when he was about to leave, saying goodbye, Molière asked him: 'Do you mind if I tell you a story— my story? Though I don't know if it is relevant here?'

Aadi nodded eagerly and sat down on the floor.

'I was born in a house near an old school building, a school for the primary classes. During the holidays, a theatre group used to come there for rehearsals. It was a kind of festival for us children. We loved to sit around the actors and watch them practice, rehearse their dialogues. Sometimes the rehearsals lasted till the morning. The school didn't have electricity at all at that time, and so, they extended the line from our house for the electric bulb. Not just electricity, my grandmother used to make black tea and snacks for them. Thus, we kids became popular among the actors. My sisters and I were the only children of the village allowed inside the rehearsals. Sometimes when there was a shortage of actors, they made my elder sister join in the sing-song of the chorus. Sometimes they allowed me to touch their musical instruments. Once, they even took me with them to draw the curtains before the play. I thought I was a real king, in control of the reins of a real stage. That was the happiest day of my childhood. Slowly I started doing minor roles in school dramas. Once I played Hitler, and Gandhi, who was the real hero of the play, came and converted me to non-violence—as easy as that. But that was not the real beginning of my life in theatre. That was a period when communism flourished in our area and my house was almost like a Communist Party office. We children used to wait till late night for the party meetings to end so that we could have our house back. During that time, the theatre came up with a new theme. They wanted to tell the history of the Communist Party in Kerala. It was a comparatively long play that went on for almost three and a half hours. There was a role for a boy in the play. Perhaps it was my luck, but the boy who had promised to do the part fell ill and couldn't come for the rehearsals. They waited for him for days on end. In the end the director was forced to take a decision. He was depressed and he desperately wanted another boy for the role. It was when he asked his crew to gather around in a circle so that they could discuss the situation that he caught sight of me sitting in a corner. It seemed he hadn't thought of such a possibility so far. In a flash, I saw his eyes glittering. He asked me straight away: 'Why can't you do this?'

I had but one answer. 'I will do it.'

It was a sentimental or rather a complicated scene. The other actors were not sure of my competence. Every one of them was confused, except thirteen-year-old me. But the role was not as simple as I had thought.

The boy had to hand over a very secret, confidential letter to the leader of the comrades. If discovered, he would be beheaded in no time. On the way, he got bitten by a snake, but his passion made him hand over the letter to the leader before he died. His name was Kalanthar. At the end of the play he returns to the stage once again, carrying a red flag. It was a feeling equivalent to nothing else. E.M.S. Namboodiripad and Jyoti Basu were among those sitting in the front row for the premier show. The play had seen some three hundred other stages and Kalanthar, undoubtedly, was well accepted. That's when I decided to be an actor. I knew theatre would be my life.'

Aadi smiled in admiration.

'Have you any idea why I told you all this?' he asked.

Aadi had no idea what to say.

'I want you to remember my story when you travel. Now, I will tell you a secret. Do you remember the day you told your story standing on the performance floor of the theatre?'

Aadi drew in a shuddering breath and looked at him in disbelief. 'Yes, I was sitting in the top gallery. You bowed at the end of your speech, didn't you?'

Aadi smiled in embarrassment, his face blushing. The gallery was dark and the pillars inside the theatre were black and there was no light inside except for what filtered in through the slits on the walls. He had thought there was no one inside, he had not seen anybody.

'It was touching. Beautiful,' Molière said.

Aadi knew his eyes were welling up, he thought he would break down.

'You can come back here whenever you want, you are family. The doors will be open for you, Aadi.'

Molière hugged him and waved him off.

'Love you.' Nimmy kissed him goodbye.

They laughed aloud. They were happy about the newness of the heavily brocaded layers of costumes, crowns, stars and decorations they were wearing. Golden cornrows glistened in the hue of the evening sun. Laughing, they looked at each other as they ran and tumbled down the slope to the soft meadow, which was slightly overgrown. They got up. They got up as fast as they could because they were on the run. They ran after the stage that revved and moved across the meadow on heavy wheels. They were clumsy, lovable, and laughable, like termite flies, hoping against hope. The air was filled with the flapping of their rainbow wings. Some of them crawled on the meadow, chasing after the running, rolling, thudding, jumping stage. They called themselves actors. A hilarious group of people—at times sorrow-stricken like the rest of humanity. Their costumes proclaimed their manifesto. They had stories to tell. Invariably, they all wanted to mount that running stage and perform. And they wanted you to watch them, to shout for an encore and applaud. Their steps steadfast, their voice candid, they would announce themselves:

> The bell tolls for you. Come, join us. Ask your children to join in the race. We are sure your kids have not been exposed to the kind of stories we have in store. We are afraid we can't stop and wait for you. But we must talk to you. Carry your old people on your back and run. Don't shy away. Remember, only your babysitter complained about how much you weighed. Who is he? Your grandpa, your Spiritus Mundi of story-store house! Let the old man clamber up on your shoulders. Let the land and house and lords be abandoned. What is there to safeguard now?
>
> What did you say, your 52" TV set?
>
> What, refrigerator?
>
> Folks, please go easy. Bring them all. We may need them on the way. Grab that brand new recliner too. Let the lambs stay back and free birds fly. Sometimes we do need materials, don't we?

They kept calling.

Come.

58

'I want to talk to you,' Madhavan said as calmly as he could.

There was no change of expression on her face even when she heard his voice over the phone. She didn't answer either.

'I'm planning to come home next week. If I come there can I see you and the children?'

There was no answer. She was still thinking.

Anybody else would have stopped talking, but he continued.

'Could you please give me an answer?'

Madhavan was literally begging. Kamala thought she was pleased about this. She tried to smile. How should we move our lips when we smile?

'Hello! Hello? Are you there?' His voice was louder now. She wondered what was wrong with him. Somehow, she said yes. Her yes was nothing better than a puff of air.

'Are you ill? Hello . . . are you okay?'

She said, 'Fever,' and disconnected. She kept the receiver near the cradle, sat down on the chair and leaned her head on the table near the telephone stand. Now she could hear the endless humming of the receiver out of the cradle. It felt good, the humming, buzzing, and roaring—it felt good inside the brain. Good for her. She imagined him as a burglar, breaking a pane of glass in one of the windows in her bedroom and letting himself in. She was glad there were no glass panes; they had solid wood windows, not easy for a burglar, not easy for anyone, least of all Madhavan.

He must be missing them a lot. Good for him. She looked at the few small objects on the table and sighed.

'The children won't be any trouble for you, don't worry, but spare me,' she whispered. 'I'm too tired to look after the kids, to take care of my things.'

She looked like a crushed woman drawn with charcoal on a cheap, torn, yellowing piece of paper. She was in pain when she crossed the threshold of her room, in deep pain when she heard his voice over the phone, but it was a sort of numb pain. She had sent Janu's father to the flat in the morning to help the Movers and Packers men unload their stuff and to give them direction. If they dumped all their stuff in the front hall it was okay, she had her own dreams for arranging it. The interior design could wait, let her fever break first.

Shiva had stopped calling for his mother. He hadn't even asked for Janu in the past two days. He was happy after the phone call with Aadi. He was sure his brother would come back, perhaps even bring Shaly with him. Shiva wanted to get out of the house, at the very least go to the burial ground—anything more than that would be a surplus of pleasures.

He turned back when he heard footsteps near the door. He was frightened. He saw a dark silhouette. Was that his mother?

His mother, who was standing by his door, was also taken aback to see her son, now a total stranger. They looked at each other with the threat of pain in their eyes, their eyes screaming in terror. The next second, they withdrew their eyes, their voices didn't come out: only the shock remained.

This was not the mother.

This was not the son.

Kamala looked at his wheelchair. The look in her eyes frightened him again.

That wheelchair was his.

The black hole, the darkest, and the blackest! As she looked, the blackness of it flowered in front of her. There was nothing but darkness inside. Outside she had seen the sun blazing on the top of trees and on the fallen trunks and leaves. In the yellow light of wrath, the sands on the shore pretended to be asleep, remembering something. In the blindingly incandescent light she saw the darkness of the circle widening in front of her eyes, engulfing her. Which was the star that was perishing itself to swallow me in the middle of the day? She felt weaker than a leaf, and believed her death would be weaker still. But the hole remained where it was, the mouth of it started working like the suction hose of a vacuum cleaner, sucking up the spiders in the corners, ants on the floor, moths on the wall and small lizards on the roof, cleaning by consuming everything that was living. She waited for her turn. But in the whirlpool of the wind the hole was sucking in, faster than the fastest speed she could ever imagine, she saw two boys swirling in, uncontrollably, helpless in the constant suction. Her heart thudding, she realized what this was.

This is a supernova explosion, Kamala; there is no escape for anyone. Inside the black hole, you, your children, the Brahma, will all be one.

'But isn't it the mind that devastates Brahma?' she asked.

'Who said that? The mind is just a game of Brahma, a toy, you might call it. Using the toy one may get to know Brahma, but the access to Brahma is very limited my friend, you could never create Brahma, or recreate him.'

White dwarfs and black holes started dancing around her. She was scared out of her wits, she grew submissive, and she saw her power dissolving. She couldn't lift her feet, for they were glued to the ground. Meanwhile, her children were slipping into the hole faster and faster.

'You are the one who wanted to know the Brahma. But when you see the ways open in front of you, why do you hesitate? Why do you cling on to the ground as if you have no other recourse?

Look at you; you are shivering like the leaf of a banyan. But the desire to know the Brahma is killing you, all the same. You are a joke, my dear, you look like one of those tiny paradise flycatchers with long white tails.'

She drew her wings, her feathers closer to her body, she knew that the sun that was about to die was pulling everything towards its centre.

It is insane to stare at oneself.

59

Shaly sat down on the chair in the kitchen, shelling beans and watching Rita Mama staggering through the house with heavy steps, the weight of her body troubling her as she moved around. She knew Rita Mama could not manage on her own for long. This she had discovered on the first day itself, when she was trying to get a foothold in the house after her exhausting journey. She had seen Rita Mama injecting insulin into her swollen thighs and sighing with a display of pride and achievement.

As usual her cache of memories started hovering around and above the forbidden old house where her soulmate lived. One by one, she analysed the changes that had slowly taken over her, the way she doubted, the way she feared, the way she had lost her confidence and health, the way she had started isolating herself, begun exploding for no reason. There were times Shaly had forgotten to make a phone call; there were times Kamala had walked through the night like a madwoman with the cell phone in her hand calling her a thousand and one times, if time had permitted her. There were times her spirits were running low, and there was a time they simply stopped running.

No joint on earth can give man the pleasure of the first experience a second time.

Shaly lit a cigarette. Instantly she hated herself. She wanted to quit smoking. She had seen Rita Mama crossing herself before the crucifix. The smell of the smoke might have disturbed her prayers for she heard her curse. She threw the cigarette away. Rita Mama was a special lady, she thought, beautiful in a way, but her beauty was masked by a veil of hatred, which was not real. Had she ever known the loving presence of anybody in her life?

It was all her carelessness. Janu felt terribly sorry, she went about barefoot and running to where her father was pointing. The temporary shed-like structure in which Kamala had parked her SUV was covered in overgrown stems and leaves of trailing creepers that formed a wilderness. A small portion of the steering wheel was visible through the tender stems poking their heads up. The last three or four times she had to go to the city, she had hired cabs as she thought the tyres were in bad shape and it would be dangerous to use the car. It was fortunate that they had seen it, otherwise it would have been completely overgrown with weeds in just two or three days. Janu went inside the house and returned with a wooden stool with a saddle seat, and a large and heavy knife from the kitchen. How fast these creepers grew, with white and red flowers hanging down in bunches from the stems. It was sad to cut down flowering vines in bloom.

The paint on the gate was not yet dry. The pink paint was clogged in several places, making simple patterns on the railings. The house, with its flowers and balconies overlooking the mud path, had such a clean and inviting look in the evening that he felt like simply walking in. Cautiously he opened the gates and entered; he was careful not to step on the wet cement on the landing. But still, the gate marked him with a pink line on the back of his Inlander rucksack. He could hear his heartbeat from outside, as if a dog were panting nearby. Like the gate, the house was also newly painted in pink. There were white strips on the lintel that ran like a carousel along the length of the walls and a European-style wreath of roses hanging on the door. He searched for the calling bell. It was not easy to find it as the bell was fixed on the centre of a bronze dragonfly which again was hidden in a riotous profusion of colourful jingles. Altogether, it seemed like Christmas and the house looked like a huge Christmas cake, like one of those old-fashioned plum cakes with hard icing. Before he could ring the bell, Shaly was there in front of him, crying loudly and hugging and kissing him. Hearing the noise, Rita Mama came outside, dragging her feet.

'Who is this boy?' she asked.

'This is my son, Aadi,' Shaly said.

Rita Mama smiled at him.

'Haven't I told you that I have two sons and a husband and a wife?'

Rita Mama's smile faded at her poor joke.

'Ask him to come in, don't make him stand outside.' Rita Mama walked in and they followed her into the house. Shaly wanted to hear each and every detail of his travels, his experiences, the lessons he had learnt, his happiness. Aadi had brought her candles from Pondicherry, for he knew she loved candles. He remembered she always had candles in her room, back in Bangalore. These candles, he said as he opened the pack, are special, scented and beautiful.

She had already declared a holiday for boiled tapioca and yam in advance and had made mutton stew and palappam for dinner. But she had prepared fish for Rita Mama as usual. Rita Mama loved the mutton stew.

Aadi said he had started missing her cooking a long time ago. It was such a grand and lovely dinner, in the light of the candle he had brought, its perfume washing over them, they felt like crying. After dinner they went to the veranda and sat there for a while. It was windy there, cool and pleasing. The breeze brought them the scent of the nocturnal flowers. Aadi talked to her about Kamala. Somehow both of them had avoided the topic so far, in the presence of Rita Mama. But he couldn't contain it any longer. 'I think Amma is not very well these days.'

Shaly didn't show her sadness, and tried to console him instead.

'It must be the migraine; you know it hurts badly. You must take her to a good doctor as soon as you get back. It won't be easy to convince her, she will not be ready to consult a doctor, but Aadi, you have to do this for me.'

'Yes, I will do that.'

'Promise me, because it is very important. I don't want her to suffer.'

Shaly knew how difficult it was to take Kamala to a doctor. If there was a way to avoid going to a physician, Kamala would find it. Shaly wanted to go there herself and drag her to the doctor. She wanted to knock on her door until she opened it. She remembered the drifting smoke from the burning grounds and she also remembered how important it was not to remember that. She knew she wanted her. Aadi held out his hand to offer his promise, and she pressed his hand with hers as if she were giving him a living imprint of her heart.

Who said that when music hits you feel no pain? She remembered all those wonderful singers who had to leave the stage in pain. All of them were young when they said goodbye to the stage. We haven't seen their wrinkles, the crinkled skin, the turkey neck, spotted hands, crow's feet and fine lines, all the wonderful signs marked by age, and those singers, in turn, haven't seen the happiness of the setting sun; it hurts to leave like that, halfway, on the way, a sudden full stop.

It was nothing like Ariwara no Narihira's celebratory poem where cherry blossoms scattered in the wind so that old age couldn't tell which path to follow. It hurts, like when one of those dear young trees gets burnt by lightning, the green of its sap still flowing, its rings in the process of forming. It hurts, all the way.

There was Elvis Presley.

There was Michael Jackson.

And so many more people—preceding them, following them and in between them. They didn't cross their fifties. Jim Morrison and Kurt Cobain were twenty-seven when they died. Whitney Houston, who sang, 'I will always love you', accidentally drowned in her bathtub in a cocaine-induced haze. Sad, sad, sad, nothing could be sadder. In Aizawl moments were counted by the strums of a guitar. Music was the heart of the forest.

They didn't say anything for a long time. But their eyes welled up all the same. Once your heart overflows, it becomes the sea itself, beware. They went into her bedroom when Rita Mama went to sleep.

'I promised Shiva that I would bring you back.'

Suddenly, she became silent. It seemed she even stopped breathing. She looked at him. She wanted to tell him something.

Love was living with them. She remembered the games of hide-and-seek she had played as a child, her heart thudding against her throat in fear as she hid, feeling the pressure of her ribcage under the skin, as if she was going to get flayed soon in the open. But this house that looked like a huge strawberry cake was no hiding place for her. Rita Mama was no ploy to buy time, to wait for the perfect opportunity to come out. Rita Mama had gone to the paint shop on Sunday, on her way back from Mass, and selected the paint that would go with the flowers of her garden. She arranged for the workers too. It was the first time the house was being repainted. The much-faded green colour of the walls gave way to the pink fantasy in the name of Shaly, just to make her stay more comfortable, to please the owner of the house, so that she would not run away again. She dumped her old clothes, anything that was smelly and unbecoming, and stopped farting loudly in public. Minor tip-offs, maybe, but they could not be neglected.

But how on earth could she tell him that she was trapped like an ant within the honey cake, that she couldn't pull her legs out of the hard icing? Sometimes, spiders flew away using their webs as parachutes, carrying everything that was in it with them. Recently, the dreams of the spiders had frightened the shit out of the people in Goulburn. People panicked seeing hundreds of ethereal white threads floating in mid-air and settling down on their ground. There was nothing unnatural about the dreams of others devastating our sleep. And it is purely our choice whether to live for the dreams of others or not, a matter of choice: *votum* in Latin.

There was hope in his eyes. He wanted her to go with him. He was young and he thought everything was possible, he didn't wish to go back without her. But when he went to get a bottle of water from the fridge, he saw Rita Mama's swollen legs and thighs naked on the bed. It was a sickeningly painful sight, her legs separated like the legs of a compass, her nightgown lifted up above her thighs, her snoring uncontrollable and frightening.

60

Kamala knew she would die if she swallowed one more drop of acid. She knew she wanted to live for her son, Shiva.

Janu said she would not leave Kamala's room as long as Kamala refused to eat. She stood there, stubborn as she had never been before, going above and beyond her duties as a maid until Kamala had to give in.

Mother and son had rice porridge with fried ivy gourd and pickles and papad sitting in his room. Kamala knew no taste. At times, she looked at him with an expression of disbelief, as if she were searching for her son in the forests of his overgrowth. 'I will help you shave tomorrow,' she said, somehow.

He knew her fingers didn't have the strength even to hold the razor.

'Aadi will come tomorrow,' he said. He saw her quiver.

'Good, now let us not send him anywhere,' she said. Like a kid she repeated, 'We will not send him away again.'

Kamala's mother was laughing, listening to her blabber.

'Why don't you send him away, Kamala? Let him see the world and be exposed to its cruel ways, let him have a taste of the real life outside, eat the food of his choice, the chips and other munchies, help him fill up his backpack and let him go.' Her mother pretended to be surprised. Kamala refused to look in her direction. She didn't wish to push this further. She was tired of arguing with her. She knew they didn't have an audience.

'Amma, we should go and see a doctor when Aadi comes back, I had no idea you were so tired, you look unbelievably pale and weak.'

'Yes, my dear.' She bent forward to kiss him on his forehead. The smells of man, porridge and fried gourds mingled: she felt nauseated. She couldn't hold on to anything any more. She heard her mother shout.

'Kamala, stand straight. Don't frighten the child with your silly drama, you shameless drama queen.'

She wanted to fuss over him, show him that she really cared for him, but she stepped away from him. At the threshold, she stopped. How could she go without kissing him? Again, she walked towards him. How long, it seemed like she would never cross the miles, hours, eras from the threshold to his bed. She embraced him like never before and smothered him with kisses till she thought she would collapse.

'Sleep well, my darling. Tomorrow I will help you take a bath.'

In the night, looking into the open drawer of her night table, she said: 'I must live for my son.'

When did her fingers scrabble around the insides of her tongue? When did the sand bowl stretch out in the room again? When did the seagulls start hovering above?

The singers walked away leaving the orphaned, dying figure in the desert. As usual, Kamala saw the building rising up from the desert. People came in to peek through the open window. Kamala dragged herself through the desert with an unbelievable energy. She was determined to see it, whatever it was. She sensed the distance getting shorter and her heart pounding faster—thud, thud, thud, each beat she could hear separately. She thought it was pygmies beating on their drums. Drawing the people aside, she looked in.

She saw an old woman lying supine on a bed in ruins. She was wearing a battered piece of cloth which could not be called a dress or a gown or anything meaningful. Loosened bags of skin remained where her once robust breasts had been. What was wrong with people? Why the hell were they staring? Kamala felt scared of the ogling humanity. Were they looking at the fleshless skeleton covered in naked wrinkles to make their swelling pricks calm down? She turned to look at the people with hatred. The people had the same look, the same smell and the same colour. Their eyes reflected the gestures of the old woman. Kamala couldn't believe that woman was capable of making any gestures. She looked at her, lying on the bed. Her left arm, which seemed almost like a piece of rotting log, moved up and down, with the speed of a poor motor engine in dilapidated condition; shaking and vibrating excessively in between abrupt stops, engine stiff, disconnected, battery sulfated, contact weak. Her fingers were moving towards her grey triangle.

'Oh God, what is this old hag doing?'

Kamala pressed her hand over her forehead; she wanted to cover her face. Her youth, that had known no ecstasies of making love, mocked her as she moved closer towards the window of shame. She tapped on the panes of the open window. She wanted the woman to stop whatever she was doing. She tapped louder, she wanted to call her, but a woman performing such an act in public could not be addressed as mother, or grandmother. Smelly crone! What a shame, she had no idea what was happening outside her window. Why the hell couldn't she close the doors?

Standing under the yellow sun, in the desert, some of them talked about the flood. Kamala remembered Janu had not turned off the old black-and-white TV that was in the entrance hall. Kamala had seen the city of Chennai immersed in water before she stepped into her dry desert. She craned her neck to listen to the news. They were talking aloud, still standing under the scorching sun. They said that the flood had devoured the temples and mosques, human-built, and they saw a Brahmin crying aloud and lifting his hand from the topmost level of a skyscraper to the piece of bread a Dalit was throwing him from the sky. Imagine; imagine all the spaces made equal in flood. She couldn't so she turned back to the old hag, to the ruined window choked with breath.

There were two boys at the window. Kamala shooed them away. The old woman turned her head at last, towards the window. Now Kamala could see her face. She shuddered.

Eyes

Nose

Eyebrows

Lips

Wrinkled forehead

Each of them was a grenade in a nutshell.

Grenades were blooming inside her brain.

Covering her face, waving her arms, making her voice louder than explosions, she frightened the people away. She stoned them and threw whatever else she could find at the running people. She didn't want anyone to know that it was her. Yes, no one could know that the old woman was Kamala, she was particular about it.

Wearing Armani perfumes, clad in the purest silk clothes available and adorned with red glass bangles and a red bindi, Kamala looked at Shaly and smiled. 'Class, that's what we have to maintain while living.'

61

Suddenly, Shaly burst out laughing. She went on. As if she couldn't stop; it seemed she was deeply hurt in her soul. It was hard for him to watch her laugh. Then, out of nowhere, she said, 'I have this feeling that we have been taxing her too much, all of us, without exception, you don't understand as you are still a child.'

'I'm not a child any more, Shaly.'

Shaly laughed again. How long would the memories be silent? She remembered his face on the first day she saw him hiding behind the curtain of their dining room, looking at her with wonder and excitement, happy for her because she was happy, happy for his mother's sparkling eyes, happy for the happiness of the moment. Memories came and went, every now and then like an old-fashioned bulb that dangled under a loose contact, flickering: on and off, off and on. She remembered the woman who lived like a fleeting dream, tender and fragile like the truth, who could not withstand even the simple woes of life. Like a lotus leaf she lived, and her children and all those who came close to her heart were like those unsteady water beads you may find on leaves: she didn't take them in, instead she let them wander abandoned over her surface. And not finding a foothold they rambled, unsettled, in the constant fear of falling down into the water that was everything, the same water she was not afraid of. Kamala, the flower in the water.

'So, tell me, did you miss Shiva?' she asked.

'Very badly.'

'Yes, I know. I can imagine how excited he will be on your return. Poor thing, his brain must have transmogrified into a big clock right now, counting splits of seconds. Ha, ha.'

They laughed; all the same, they knew it was not that funny. After that, they were silent for a while. Then she asked without ceremony, 'Would you like to have a mug of cold beer with me?'

He looked at her in surprise and said, 'No.'

'You are no longer a child now; you are a traveller, aren't you? You have seen the world . . . Don't you want to share a drink with me?' she arched her brows mockingly.

'No, I don't think I want to do that. I don't think I am going to touch booze in my life. The world I had seen even before my travels had taught me this.'

'You have grown smart enough to answer back, it's an improvement. I appreciate that, and I understand what you mean by the life you had seen. I'm sorry I asked you.'

'You needn't be sorry.'

'Aadi, it's very important, this real education—what you learn as you grow, what you read, what you see and what you experience. I grew up admiring the travels and happiness of gypsies, but I must tell you I have never seen a gypsy in my life, for they were never a part of our terrain and culture. It was the Bohemian dream I had as a girl—roaming around the world in groups, having no responsibility, indulging in everything, always in excess: music, dance, graffiti, love, sex, and it felt good. It felt good to think of wandering around with people with the same thoughts and interests, with— What do you call them? Like-minded people. Yes, that was the catchphrase at the time. Maybe, the gypsies won't forgive me for the wrong notions I have had for so long, but baby, it really felt so good. There was no one to guide me to Stendhal, Balzac, Flaubert, and Proust, or to the great Indian philosophy your mother has studied so well, or to ancient Chinese or Japanese literature and philosophy. It took me years to discover that Casanova was not just a seducer, but one of the greatest minds of the European Enlightenment. You learn all this if you decide to grow up and as you travel, and remember, you can travel a lot sitting inside your room, on your chair next to the table you love so much, with your favourite cup of coffee by your side. The body has limitations, it rots, but you have something wonderful within you and that's what makes you truly remarkable. I hope you understand.'

She spoke with the grace of someone he had always wanted to see. But then she asked again, in a silly, villainous way, 'Do you mind if I ask you one more time? Well, I hope you really don't mind . . . can we have a glass of cold beer by the light of the candle you bought for me?'

'No!'

'With chèvre, talking about John Cheever.'

'Hah! I said no, never, and I always mean what I say.'

'Good,' she tapped him on his shoulder. 'I'm glad you are a man now, no longer just that good boy I used to know. My boy, I tell you, it's not easy to withstand temptation.'

The next morning, as he was saying goodbye to Shaly and Rita Mama his eyes filled with tears.

'Oh, so this is the man I was talking to last night.' Shaly winked.

At that he started crying harder, holding her hands tighter, sobbing uncontrollably like a toddler, until Rita Mama asked him to stop. She went inside and returned with a small figurine of Mother Mary and asked him to keep it with him to ward off troubles on the way. He embraced Shaly one last time, and she said, though it was clear it was hard for her to do so: 'No one is going anywhere, Aadi, all of us are here, Shiva, Kamala, Madhavan, me . . . And you won't believe how small the world is, even if I tell you. It is true we are not living under the same roof, but what difference does that make? You take care, and take your mother to a doctor. That's what matters now. Consider it your priority. If you need my help, don't hesitate to give a ring. I'll always be here for you. Give your phone to her and ask her to speak to me, force her in case she is not willing. Will you do that for me, Aadi?'

Aadi knew something was twisting into a rope inside him, but he managed to smile and nod. The gate still looked slightly wet and unbelievably pink. He opened it with the same cautious effort with which he had opened it the previous day. It was dry except for the clogged paint beads. He turned back to wave and listened to her call out from the entrance: 'Don't forget, it is always $E = mc^2$.'

It was a simple equation, it said everything was there in the universe, he and his family, nothing but infinitesimal fractions of particles. People, being simple and miserable, could not contain things as simple as them; otherwise, everything would have been much easier.

The memory of white hills didn't trouble him these days. What he wanted was fresh air and cleanliness, something to match the purity he felt within. He awoke feeling peaceful, composed and glad his mother was going to give him a bath and his brother was returning. He was badly in need of a haircut and shave; he knew he looked like a girl with a long beard these days. There was a time he had fancied that he would look like a rock star if he could tie his hair into a ponytail with a piece of jute ribbon or hairband. But he was afraid he was getting lice, and was tired of scratching his scalp, neck and the backs of his ears, tired of living with parasites. He wanted a haircut and wanted it to be as short as possible. He waited, listening to the footsteps outside. He heard Janu's father complain to her that he would need one more worker to help him clean the pond, as it was in full bloom. Her father talked about flowers as if he was talking about weeds or a heap of waste or fallen leaves he set fire to. Shiva thought he would like to have a large bouquet of lotus flowers in his room, just for the sake of looking at it.

The scent of familiarity must have startled him, for he awoke from his daydreams quivering and palpitating. He must have crossed the entrance gate without realizing it, and was now walking on the laterite footpath. He had panicked like this before, a long time ago, when he had played hide-and-seek with his brother, but that was a different sort of excitement altogether, naive, gullible.

Aadi looked into her room through the opening of the door. He saw her sleeping, but he couldn't see her face as she was facing the window. He didn't wish to disturb her, but stood there at her doorstep for a while, feeling sorry for her, and then went to Shiva's room. Tears sprang to his eyes when he saw his brother, he couldn't believe what he was seeing. He realized the extent of his anger towards his mother for the first time. He wanted to ask her why, but all the same, he wanted to overcome his emotions. Janu came in with a cup of coffee in her hands. She saw him crying. As she didn't know how to console him, she simply said, 'Amma is still sleeping. Do you want me to wake her up?'

'No, please don't. Let her sleep, she must be very tired.'

He was at a loss, for he had no idea where to begin. He looked at the scissors and nail cutter he had taken out of his bag in dismay. He closed his eyes for a while, as if he were praying, before he started cutting his brother's womanish hair: the long, black abundance. Then he cut his nails short and flat. As he wheeled him to the bathroom he asked Janu for a change of bed sheets and pillowcases, insisting that they be really clean. It was only inside the bathroom, while he was helping him change his clothes, that he noticed the pink-brown patches of sores on his brother's back. He let out a furious cry and thought he was about to break down, horrified by this sight he had never wanted to even imagine. He stood there rubbing his brother's shoulder between his thumb and forefinger, pressing his hands against his palms, listening to the running water. They had grown up inside the same water in her womb, the flesh of his flesh of her flesh. Aadi sobbed as he cleaned Shiva's wounds, the backs of his ears, his buttocks. He couldn't understand what had gone wrong in the house during his absence. He had been happy with Shaly's updates about his mother going to supervise the finishing touches in their flat in Kadavanthra. But after that—what?

Becoming aware of Kamala's unblinking gaze on Shiva then, Aadi wanted to smile, but fresh tears choked him in horror at seeing his mother. This was not his mother; she looked paler and more bloodless than a fleeting spectre that hovers in dreams at times. It seemed she had not recognized Aadi's presence, for she was staring at Shiva with gratitude and amazement, deep down from the bottom of her heart. She knew Shiva was safe in the hands of his brother.

Janu was in no way better off, she too was crying inside the kitchen. She felt she had never been so happy in this house before, that she was filled with a sense of obligation even towards the vegetables on the tray, the bitter gourds, ash gourds, pumpkins and the drumsticks. She started slicing the ash gourds with the avidity of someone reading a new chapter in a novel. For the first time, she knew exactly what to make. Aadi realized there was no need to ask his mother's permission to fix an appointment with the doctor. He came to the kitchen when Janu was still busy attending to something on the stove, and asked her to arrange for a taxi by five in the afternoon.

'Let me finish this and I'll go and get the taxi man.'

'Ask him to come by five.'

'How was your trip? It's a silly world we are living in, isn't it?' Kamala asked him as she walked towards the dining table, leaning against his shoulder.

'It was exciting,' he said, in between shuddering breaths.

'I'm glad you didn't find it insane,' she said.

'I'm glad it's all over and I'm back,' he said.

She sat down, clutching the side of her chair while they ate. It was a picturesque sight, the mother at the head of the table and her sons on either side, except for the lack of vigour.

'I wish Shaly were here, I miss her,' Aadi said.

Kamala listened to him as if she was listening to something remote and faraway, and Shiva dropped a spoon on the floor as if by mistake. It was essential they remain happy, preserve the beauty of the moment, and capture whatever they found beautiful, even if it was a smile or a kind word. It could even be a thought. And hence, uncovering the dishes one by one, he laughed, 'Look at Janu, she has gone nuts. Look at all this food. From where did she get time today?'

They saw Janu blushing in the corner of the room. They all laughed.

But Kamala didn't feel like eating anything, even though she had a strong acidic burning inside her stomach. She watched her children eating with a sense of well-being.

Janu was very quick at changing the sheets and cleaning the room. She wanted to finish before Kamala returned from the dining room. But her eyes welled up when she noticed the dampness of pee on the sheets. She saw the scorched and wilted leaves of the money plant with yellowing veins inside the whisky bottle on the windowsill. The little water that remained in it had a very unpleasant and unhealthy stench. She removed the diseased plant from the bottle and threw it outside through the open window. Then she flushed the water and the rest of the contents of the bottle down the toilet and cleaned it with a bottle cleaner. She filled the bottle again with fresh water and placed a bouquet of lotus flowers inside it and kept it back on the windowsill where it belonged. She burnt camphor in a small mud pot and kept it in a corner of the room, right on top of the granite structure Kamala would sit on during her trips. When Kamala and her children had finished eating, she cleaned the table and took a tray of food for herself and her father and walked towards the kitchen veranda.

Kamala walked back to her room, leaning against Aadi's shoulder. She was surprised to see her room looking neat and tidy, with pleasant scents. She wanted to show how happy she was. She asked him to bring Shiva; in a way, bring everything that was hers.

Aadi wheeled Shiva in.

'Sit here by my side,' she said.

It was a small bed compared to theirs; there was hardly any room for the three of them. She was tired and so she had to lie down, but she didn't let her children leave. She asked them to lie down beside her. Aadi helped Shiva stretch out beside her, and somehow he too squeezed in.

'I love you,' she said.

She wrapped her arms around them and pressed her hands tightly over them. They offered no resistance. Aadi remembered lying in the same way a long time ago, in the same old house. She never let them go out and play in the afternoons; instead, she would make them lie down on either side of her and hold them so tight that they could not run away. Shiva would be grumpy, but she paid no attention. Aadi on the other hand, would lie calmly, holding onto her body and looking at the khus-khus curtains they had had on the windows, the curtains that emitted the scent of coolness, the breeze. He wondered where those curtains were now.

The mother started growing cold long after her children were fast asleep. But even in their sleep, the heat of their tender bodies embraced her tightly, not allowing her to grow cold.

Acknowledgements

My thanks most of all to my friend Sachu Thomas for his assistance, his correspondence, his patience—for everything.

My heartfelt thanks to Rajni George for showing great interest in this novel since first seeing it in manuscript form a year ago and being an invaluable supporter at every stage.

I want to give robust thanks to my inspired editor Ambar Sahil Chatterjee for his sensitive suggestions to do with the making of this book.

In preparing this English translation I have had the benefit of a patient and perceptive editor in Shatarupa Ghoshal. I can't thank her enough for her support.

And, as always, my endless thanks (and eternal admiration) to Veenapani Chawla, my guiding spirit.

I would like to acknowledge material and inspiration drawn from a variety of sources: *Savitri: A Legend and a Symbol* by Sri Aurobindo; *The Tenth Head* written by Vinay Kumar K.J. and directed by Veenapani Chawla; *On Love* by Stendhal, translated by Philip Sidney Woolf and Cecil N. Sidney Woolf; *Molière* by Ariane Mnouchkine (1978); 'L'invitation au voyage' by Charles Baudelaire, translated by Arthur Symons; 'Fern Hill' by Dylan Thomas; 'Spring and Fall' by Gerard Manley Hopkins; 'The Soul of Man under Socialism' by Oscar Wilde; 'Latent

Homosexuality in Malayalam Literature and Kerala Society' by P.A. Shan; and lines from Frère Jacques, Swathi Thirunal Rama Varma and Oorali.

Also, I would like to extend my gratitude to Adishakti Laboratory for Theatre Arts and Research, and Kalarigram, Puducherry.